PROMISE ME SPRING . . .

is a stirring account of the early ranchers who
settled the valleys east of the Sawtooth Mountains, and the courageous women who loved
them . . .

Gavin—The loner who put his heart into building his ranch, until the right woman taught him
to love.

Patrick—The warm-hearted Irishman who
would give anything to win the girl of his dreams.

Drucilla—the pioneer wife who gained her
strength from the rugged beauty of the land.

Rachel—The pampered beauty who was willing
to sacrifice everything for the man she loved.

Other Leisure books by Robin Lee Hatcher:

"WHAT DO YOU WANT FROM ME, RACHEL?"

What did she want from him? To love him. To spend her life with him. To be a mother to his children. To be at his side through good times and bad. To grow old together.

But she couldn't say those things, and so she did the only thing she could. She stood on tiptoe, placed her arms around his neck, and kissed him.

What she'd meant to be only a tender gesture, a means of telling him how much she loved him, became a fire in her veins, spreading violently through her, leaving her skin tingling and her limbs weak. When he clutched her tightly to him, she could only moan in acquiescence. His mouth moved hungrily over hers and she responded with equal greed.

"No more, Rachel," he whispered huskily as he swept her feet up from the floor. "God help me, I can't resist you anymore."

ROBIN LEE HATCHER

PROMISE ME SPRING

LEISURE BOOKS NEW YORK CITY

A LEISURE BOOK®

July 1991

Published by

Dorchester Publishing Co., Inc.
276 Fifth Avenue
New York, NY 10001

Prologue

Idaho Territory
March 1883

Rachel Harris wasn't sure exactly when she'd become aware that she was destined to make a difference in the world. She'd simply awakened one morning, filled with a kind of expectancy, and known life held something special, something significant, in store for her. She didn't know what that something would be, but she would know it when it came. She was certain of that. She'd been waiting and watching for it for years now.

But as the stagecoach rocked and creaked its way across the Idaho desert, the biscuit-colored landscape dotted with silver-green sagebrush, Rachel began to doubt her intuition. She'd been certain she would discover her destiny back East. There had been so many opportunities for

7

something special to happen to her. Yet nothing had.

Now she was returning to Boise City, back home to live with her sister, Maggie, and her family. She'd missed them all terribly while she was away, but she couldn't help wondering if she'd made a mistake in returning. If she'd stayed in Washington just a little longer, might she not have found what she'd been waiting for?

What on earth could she accomplish in Idaho that would make a difference to anyone?

Chapter One

Boise City
September 1883

One thing never seemed to change, whether a person lived in the capital of a great nation or the capital of a distant western territory. Young, unmarried women always discussed the same thing when they got together—eligible men and the prospect of marriage.

Rachel allowed her gaze to move among the members of the little social group, three young women who were quickly proving the truth of her silent observation. She had arrived at Mr. and Mrs. Walker's autumn cotillion only a half hour ago and already she'd heard detailed information about several of the men in attendance.

"But he's so very wealthy and quite distinguished," Margaret continued in a stage whisper. "Perhaps he's not everything I personally would like a husband to be, but he's a good catch for Dorothy. He isn't objectionable to look at, but Dorothy isn't exactly a beauty, and at her age she can't hope to make a better match."

"She's nearly twenty-four," Pamela added with great emphasis, making Dorothy sound ancient.

"Have you met Mr. Stephens' new junior law partner?" Susannah asked, changing the subject to one of more interest to her. She peeked over Margaret's shoulder toward a tall, fair-haired man standing near the punch bowl. "Mr. Newcomb. Isn't he positively the most handsome man here tonight? He's already claimed two dances on my card. And everyone knows he's going to be a successful lawyer someday. Papa says he's an up-and-coming young man with a bright future."

"Look!" Pamela interrupted. "There's Rodney Parkinson. Do you think he'll notice me? Oh, if he doesn't ask me to dance, I'll simply die."

Although Rachel tried to concentrate on what the three young women were saying, she was having a difficult time. The topic of conversation bored her almost to tears. She realized that her point of view would be considered radical. She was, after all, rather advanced in age herself, having turned twenty-two last May and still no husband in sight.

But surely, she thought as her attention drifted off in another direction, there were more important things in life than being married— not just married, but well-married, preferably to a wealthy man or at least one with prospects of being wealthy.

"Excuse me," she whispered absently, then moved away from the three friends who, she supposed, began gossiping about her the moment she left their midst.

She looked fleetingly for Maggie or Tucker but found neither of them in sight. She caught a glimpse of Matthew Foreman on the dance floor, an attractive brunette in his arms. Matthew had been the most persistent of her callers at the Branigan ranch since her return to Idaho, but she felt no more desire to encourage his interest in her than she had had for any of the other gentlemen.

Hoping Matthew hadn't noticed her, she turned away.

The tall doors leading onto the terrace were open, and she slipped through them. The music and conversations dimmed as she was enveloped by the night. A quarter moon rocked on its back against a sky dotted with stars. The air was crisp but not unpleasant. She walked down a path leading to Mrs. Walker's gardens, feeling the need for solitude.

Is something wrong with me? she wondered as she settled onto a stone bench.

Over-educated. That was what most people no doubt had to say about Judge Branigan's unmarried sister-in-law. And perhaps they were right. She'd had a fine education, but what was she to do with it now? What use was it if the only important thing was for her to snare a husband before she got any older?

How do I make a difference in this world if marriage is my only choice in life?

Gavin Blake drove the wagon down the center of Main Street. It had been years since he'd last come to the capital of the territory. The town was growing. There had to be some fine physicians living here. One of them would be able to help Drucilla. If he didn't think so, he never would have let her undertake this trip.

He turned to look at his wife. She looked tired and wan after a week on the trail. He could read the exhaustion behind the flecks of gold in her hazel eyes. She looked as if she'd lost more weight, though there wasn't an ounce of fat— hardly any meat either—on her gaunt, five-foot, seven-inch frame.

I never should have let her come, he thought.

But it had been hard for him to deny Dru anything lately. At least the weather had been warm for their trip to the capital, and he'd made her a comfortable bed in the back of the wagon. They'd lain beneath their blankets at night and stared up at the stars and talked about Sabrina's and Petula's futures and what Dru wanted for them.

Gavin stopped the wagon in front of the Overland Hotel. He set the brake, then looped the ends of the reins around the brake handle before hopping to the ground. He turned, raising his arms and holding them apart.

"Come on. Let's get you into a nice soft bed for a change."

"Shouldn't we go to the newspaper office first?" she asked softly.

"I'll take care of that later."

"Gavin, I . . ."

"You heard me. Come on."

Dru forced a weary smile, acknowledging her defeat. "I suppose you're right, but we came all this way to . . ."

"I know why we came," he interrupted in a gruff tone. He couldn't help himself. He felt suddenly angry. It never failed to alarm him when he lifted her down from the wagon and his fingers overlapped around her waist.

He remembered her when she was pregnant with Quentin, her body swelling up like a ripe pumpkin, her face round and rosy, her eyes shining with happiness. Lord, it seemed a lifetime ago. Look at all that had happened in the few years since then. First Quentin was stillborn, then Charlie died, and now this. If only he could take her back east to one of those fine hospitals. There must be something someone could do. . . .

"Gavin?" Cool fingers touched his cheek.

He knew she could read his mind, see what he was thinking.

"Let's go inside."

With a nod, he placed a solicitous arm around her back and guided her into the lobby of the hotel.

Wanted: Governess and teacher for two young girls on remote mountain ranch. Sep-

13

arate living quarters. Apply Mrs. Blake, Over-land Hotel, after 2:00 PM Friday.

Rachel set down the paper and stared out the window at the tall poplars, cottonwoods, and willows growing alongside the river. A warm breeze lifted wisps of blond hair across her forehead and caressed her skin with the last breath of summer. A large blow fly buzzed noisily beneath the porch awning, occasionally bumping into the clear glass window, then flying away before returning to try again.

Perhaps the fly seemed unusually noisy because the house was so silent. Kevin, Colleen, Tara Maureen, and Colin, Maggie's four oldest children, were all in school. Sheridan, at four the baby of the family, had gone into town with his mother for some shopping and would no doubt return with a peppermint stick from the mercantile.

Rachel left the dining room and wandered into the parlor. Her fingers idly caressed the photographs and knickknacks that filled the room. Memories. Lots of memories. Happy memories too.

Why wasn't she content with the notion of making the same sort of memories for herself, the way everyone seemed to think she should?

She paused in front of the oval mirror with its ornate, gold-flecked frame. She stared hard at her reflection. She supposed she was pretty. She'd been told so since she was little. She wasn't particularly fond of her baby-fine hair— it was as pale as a field of drying wheat and impossible to keep trapped in a chignon—and she wished she had Maggie's wide gray eyes instead of her ordinary blue ones. But all in all, it wasn't a bad face staring back at her.

She certainly had never lacked for suitors. She'd turned down several proposals, both here and in Washington. Even James Whittier, her best friend's husband, had offered for her several years ago. Now James and Fiona—deliriously in love with each other—were the parents of a beautiful baby girl. Myrna Whittier was only a few weeks old, and already she promised to be an auburn-haired, green-eyed beauty like her mother.

If Rachel had accepted James's offer, would she be happy now? Would she have found what she'd been waiting for? Had it been there, staring her in the face all the time and she too blind to see it?

No.

Had she missed her chance by leaving Washington? Was that where she was to have found it?

No.

She was surprised by the sudden certainty that filled her. It made no sense to feel that way. What could possibly happen to her, stuck away out here on her brother-in-law's ranch? If she didn't want to marry one of her gentlemen callers, what else lay in store for her than to stay here, caring for Maggie and Tucker's children, attending the theater, supporting the charities?

She shook her head and walked back toward the dining room, pausing by the window and staring across the yard toward the river. Bed sheets fluttered in the golden September sunlight. Tucker's old hound dog lay in the shade of a tall poplar, his tail intermittently slapping the dried grass.

Life is passing me by, she thought desolately, *and there's nothing I can do about it.*

She sighed again, the sound seeming to fill the empty house with its loneliness and futility. Was this *it*? Had she been wrong in thinking there was more in store for her? Was she resigned to let things continue this way forever?

No, she wasn't. Perhaps she'd been wrong to wait for something to happen to her. Perhaps she had to get out and make it happen.

Her heart began to race as she turned away from the window. Her gaze fell upon the folded newspaper lying on the shiny oak table.

That was it! Teaching. How better to make a difference in the world than to share all the wonderful things she'd learned, first in school and then under Professor Abraham Fielding's tutelage? And who better to share it with than children who lived far from a school?

Rachel crossed the dining room with several quick steps and picked up the paper. Her eyes returned quickly to the brief notice in a lower corner of the page.

Wanted: Governess and teacher for two young girls on remote mountain ranch. Separate living quarters. Apply Mrs. Blake, Overland Hotel, after 2:00 PM Friday.

She was good with children. She'd helped
Maggie with all her nieces and nephews. She
certainly knew about living on a ranch. She'd
lived on this one since coming to Idaho when
she was six. She was qualified to teach, having
completed her education in the best finishing
school back East, not to mention the years she'd
lived with the professor and his family.

It would definitely be a complete and total
change from the vacuous life she was living
now. Did she dare even consider it?

Rachel tossed the paper back onto the table as
she spun around and swept resolutely out of the
dining room.

Drucilla Blake awakened slowly from her nap.
On days like this, when she wasn't feeling any
pain, it was hard to believe she was dying. She
felt tired was all. Very, very tired.

She pushed herself up on the pillows, then
swept her graying brown hair back from her
face as she looked at the watch pinned to the
bodice of her dress. One-fifteen. She would have
to get freshened up if she was to be ready to
meet people at two.

A cold feeling suddenly engulfed her chest.
She closed her eyes, her fingers still clutching
the watch. What if no one came? What if they
came and no one was right? It was so important
to find the right person. Not just for Sabrina and
Petula, but for Gavin too. He had given so much
already, and when she was gone, he would still
be giving.

Dru relaxed her fingers and allowed her hand to fall to her side. It wasn't right what she'd done. When that old sawbones first told her she was sick and dying, she should have left. She should have taken the children and gone. But where? Where was it she *could* have gone? Her heart and home were both in Idaho's mountain country. There wasn't anywhere else she could go—or anywhere else she wanted to spend what time was left to her.

She filled her lungs with a deep breath, then straightened and dropped her legs over the side of the bed. She had no time for feeling sorry for herself. She had come to terms with her illness long ago. She knew Gavin would love and care for the children. She had only this one last detail to take care of, and then she would be able to go in peace.

Dru rose from the bed and walked toward the bureau. She glanced into the mirror as she picked up the hair brush. She tried not to look at her reflection. Doing so depressed her. She looked far older than her thirty-five years. She ran a hasty brush over her hair, then tucked the graying tresses into a bun at the nape before turning away. She looked presentable, she supposed. That was the best she could hope for.

She opened the door to the small sitting room adjoining the bedroom. Gavin was standing at the window, gazing down at the busy street below. She paused a moment to look at him. His black hair was shaggy around his shirt collar, badly in need of a trimming. She should have seen to that before they left the basin.

18

He turned at the sound of her entrance. "Did you sleep?" he asked.

She nodded.

"Are you hungry?"

"No," she responded softly. "I don't think I could eat anything yet."

"You barely touched your breakfast." It was a tender admonishment.

Dru simply shook her head and turned toward a nearby chair. She hated to see that look in his gray eyes. It made her feel guilty for all she had put him through, all she had yet to put him through. It wasn't right that she'd saddled him with her troubles.

"I wonder what the girls are doing this afternoon," she said, her tone light and cheerful.

Gavin knew her well enough not to press the subject of food any longer. Instead, he moved away from the window, walking with that loose-limbed stride of his, and sat on the small divan across from her.

"Probably out riding with Stubs. They ought to have the cows rounded up by the time we get back."

"I wish we didn't have to leave the basin so soon." Dru imagined the majestic peaks of the rugged Sawtooth Mountains and the log house that lay in their shadows. A strong longing returned to her breast. She didn't need a doctor to know she wouldn't see another spring there.

Gavin leaned forward, bracing his forearms on his knees. "Dru, I want you to see the doctor before we leave Boise."

She offered a faint smile. "Don't, Gavin. We

19

both know it won't make any difference."

Before he could say anything more, they were interrupted by a knock. Dru's eyes snapped toward the door. Her pulse quickened.

"They're early," she whispered, then silently added, *Dear God, please bring the right woman.*

Chapter Two

Standing beside the buggy, Rachel ran the palms of her hands over her blue-and-white striped skirt. She looked across the street at the Overland Hotel, nervously imagining an interview with Mrs. Blake. The woman would no doubt send her away after just a few questions. It was probably a foolish thing to have done, coming into town in response to that advertisement.

It was tempting to climb back into the buggy and turn the horse toward home, but she didn't allow herself to succumb to the temptation. She'd come to apply for the job of governess, and apply she would.

Maggie would most surely proclaim Rachel mad for wanting to go off to tend somebody else's children. If she wanted to do that, Maggie would say, she could stay at home and watch after Maggie's five rapscallions. Which probably would make better sense than this.

But Rachel wanted to do this. And the more she'd thought about it, the more she wanted it. She would be doing this on her own. She would be charting her own destiny. She wouldn't be wasting her time any longer going to boring cotillions or listening to gossip or shopping for new clothes. She would be accomplishing something worthwhile.

And she would be independent. As much as she loved Tucker and Maggie, she longed for her independence. Maggie, of all people, should understand that.

Quickly, Rachel wrapped the reins around the hitching rail, absently patted the gelding's neck, then, with head held high, walked across the street and into the hotel lobby.

The clerk behind the desk raised his head as she approached. "Good day, Miss Harris," he said, quickly smiling. "I haven't seen you in town for a while. Is the Judge with you today? Will you be dining with us?" He looked at her with openly appreciative eyes, then craned his neck to see if Judge Branigan was somewhere in sight.

"No, Mr. Samuels. I'm afraid Tucker isn't with me." She returned his look with a half-hearted smile of her own. Mark Samuels had been pestering for permission to call upon her since she was barely out of short skirts. She thought him a terrible busybody and had no intention of encouraging him to snoop into her affairs. Her voice was unusually crisp. "I've come to see Mrs. Blake. Can you tell me what room she's in, please?"

His hopeful expression faded. "Mrs. Blake?" He glanced down at the registry before him. "Oh, yes. Mrs. Blake." His head came up again. "She's in room two-ten, but I'm afraid now isn't a good time to come visiting. She's busy interviewing for a woman to care for her children. There's already been three ladies come and gone."

"Three? But it's not even two thirty." What if she'd already hired someone? Rachel hadn't even had a chance. She at least wanted a chance.

"First one come more'n a half hour ago. Mrs. Blake's a good friend of yours, I take it?"

Rachel was scarcely aware of what Mark Samuels was saying. "Did you say room two-ten?"

"Yes, but . . ."

"Thank you, Mr. Samuels."

Squaring her shoulders, she headed for the stairs.

Gavin left his chair near the window to answer the knock on the door. He swore this would be the last one. For whatever reasons, Dru had found the first three women unacceptable and had dismissed them after very brief exchanges. He couldn't get her to say why, other than, "They just weren't right."

He pulled open the door, expecting to find another woman in her late thirties or early forties with a dour face and reading glasses perched on her nose. That was a rather fair description of the first three applicants, but it was a far cry from the beautiful young woman standing in the hallway.

From beneath a bonnet made of plush blue felt and trimmed with a white ostrich feather, a fringe of pale blond hair kissed her forehead and curled in faint wisps around her temples and ears. Her blue eyes, wide and frankly curious as they stared up at him, were the color of a robin's egg, the same shade as a clear sky on a warm summer day. Her nose was pert and slightly flared. Her mouth was bow-shaped and a delightful shade of pink.

He felt a bolt of awareness shoot through him. For a moment, all else was forgotten except the sheer pleasure of looking at her.

"I'm here to see Mrs. Blake?" she said, her voice uncertain as she met his gaze. "About the position of governess?"

It was a little like being doused with a bucket of mountain stream water. Her words brought him back to reality. "I'm Mr. Blake." He waved her into the room.

As she moved past him, he caught the faint scent of her cologne. It reminded him of a field of wild honeysuckle.

Dru lifted a hand and motioned to the chair across from her. "Come in, Miss . . . ?"

"Harris," the young woman supplied as she crossed the sitting room. "Rachel Harris."

"Please sit down, Miss Harris. I'm Drucilla Blake."

24

Gavin watched as Rachel settled onto the edge of the chair. Her back was ramrod stiff, her gloved hands clasped in the folds of her blue-and-white skirt. Her outfit was simple but obviously well-made and costly. This was no penniless spinster in search of much-needed employment. He wondered why she was applying for the position.

He closed the door and returned silently to his place by the window.

"I won't beat around the bush, Miss Harris," Dru began. "Gavin—my husband—and I have a small ranch near Challis up along the Salmon River, where we spend most of the year. For the past two summers, we've trailed our cows into a remote area known as the Stanley Basin. That's where you'd be for a few more weeks, then up the Salmon. It's beautiful country, but you won't find a lot of fancy parties and such, like you have here in the capital. We live a quiet, simple life, and sometimes it's a hard one."

When Dru paused, Rachel nodded her head but didn't speak.

"I've got two girls, Miss Harris. Sabrina, she's nine. Petula's five. They're bright and in need of schooling. Have you ever done any teaching?"

"No." Her chin lifted minutely. "But I've been all the way through school in Boise City, and I went to finishing school back East. And I love children. I know I could teach. I live with my sister, and she has five children of her own. I was a kind of second mother to them."

Dru leaned slightly forward. Her hazel eyes narrowed. "Why would someone as pretty as

25

you want to go off to the mountains? Are you hiding from something, Miss Harris?"

Gavin's gaze fastened on the petite blonde. He'd been wondering the same thing himself and was curious to hear her reply.

"No, Mrs. Blake, I'm not." Her voice was strong and firm. "But I am twenty-two years old and still living with my sister and her family. It's time that I made my own way. This seemed like something I could do. Something I would enjoy doing."

"The wages wouldn't be much. Only a few dollars a month. We're just getting by as it is. You'd have your own small cabin at the main ranch, and you could take your meals with us. If we hire you, we'd want your pledge that you would stay through spring. At least until the cattle return to the summer range in June. Could you do that?"

Again Rachel nodded.

Dru's eyes took on a faraway look. Gavin recognized it. He'd seen her drift off like this before. It was when she was thinking about her girls and leaving them and what would happen to them when she was gone. He'd seen it that first night she'd come to him and told him she was dying.

Dru's voice was soft, almost inaudible. "Miss Harris, you must know one thing more. I'm not a well woman. I need someone who won't mind caring for me as well as the children."

Rachel's eyes widened. As if searching for a proper reply, she turned her head toward the window and looked directly into Gavin's eyes.

Their gazes held for the breadth of a heartbeat, then she turned away once more.

"I'm not afraid, if that's what you're asking, Mrs. Blake. I've helped nurse my nieces and nephews through the usual childhood illnesses. I'm sure I could learn to do whatever is needed."

She was saying all the right things, Gavin thought. *Too* right. A man only had to look at her to know she'd been spoiled and pampered, used to having her own way, her every whim satisfied. He knew the truth about her type. She would promise what they wanted to hear now, but do what she wanted when the time came. Heaven only knew why she wanted to leave Boise and live on a ranch miles from nowhere. There had to be some reason she wanted to get away from Boise, perhaps even to hide, and he'd wager it had to do with a man. It always did when a beautiful woman was involved.

The tension left Dru's face as she smiled at Rachel. "Tell me about you and your family, Miss Harris."

With a sinking feeling, Gavin knew Dru had made up her mind about Rachel Harris.

Gavin Blake escorted Rachel to her buggy across from the Overland Hotel. As she lifted the hem of her skirts to climb into the buggy, his fingers cupped her elbow and helped her up.

"We'll want to get an early start, Miss Harris," he said. "Can you be here by eight?"

She turned to look at him as she picked up the reins. Steel-gray eyes were studying her in a disconcerting fashion. She got the distinct feeling he wasn't happy about his wife's decision to hire her. She wondered why he hadn't stopped Drucilla if that was how he felt.

"I'll be here," she replied firmly.

With another piercing look, Gavin stepped away from the buggy. Rachel slapped the reins against the gelding's rump, and the horse jumped forward, settling quickly into a comfortable trot as they traversed Main Street.

What have I done?

It had been a strange interview. Not at all what she had expected. After the few preliminary questions, Drucilla Blake had simply encouraged Rachel to talk about herself, about Maggie and the children, about her experiences back East and what had drawn her again to Idaho. She'd thought perhaps the woman was just being friendly and had no intention of hiring her as a governess. She'd been stunned when Dru brought the interview to an abrupt halt, saying she was tired and wanted to rest and could Rachel be at the Overland in the morning with whatever things she wanted to bring with her.

How was she going to explain this to Maggie? She didn't even know this woman or her husband. Her husband . . .

Gavin. He had a handsome face with bold, craggy features. A comfortable, lived-in sort of face. Tiny lines around his steely gray eyes. Deep furrows in his sun-bronzed forehead. Dark shadows of a beard just beneath the skin of his cheeks and jaw. Blue-black hair, the color of raven's wings. Tall and broad of shoulder and radiating good health and vitality. What had ever made him marry a woman like Drucilla Blake? She was plain and skinny and . . .

Rachel's eyes widened, appalled by her own callousness. She was beginning to think like Margaret and Susannah and the others. Drucilla Blake couldn't help it that she was sick, and there was much more to loving a person than their looks. In fact, Rachel thought she was going to like Dru very much.

She'd better. She was going to be living with her and her husband and their children for almost a year.

Before she could wonder again if she was doing the right thing, before she could even consider changing her mind, she had to get home and tell Maggie what she'd done.

She clicked her tongue in her cheek and slapped the reins against the gelding's back. In quick response, the horse broke into a brisk canter.

"I'm afraid your wife is right, Mr. Blake." The doctor closed the door to the bedroom. "We can try to minimize the pain with laudanum and morphine, but there's little else we can do for her."

"But she's seemed better for so long. Except for her lack of appetite, I thought . . ."

"A cancer will often go into a period of remission. The tumor, for some reason we don't understand, will simply stop growing. A patient often thinks it has gone entirely away."

Gavin rubbed his eyes with the fingers of one hand. "Maybe it will last a few more years? When the girls are older . . ." His words stopped as he met the physician's grim gaze.

"It could," the doctor said with a sad shake of his head, "but I wouldn't pin my hopes on it." He picked up his hat from a nearby chair, then turned the knob and opened the door. "I'm sorry, Mr. Blake."

The snap of the closing door echoed in Gavin's head. It had a final, deadly sound to it. He couldn't argue with the facts any longer. Dru wasn't going to get better. No matter what he did for her, she was going to die. She'd known it for a long time and had accepted it, but he'd continued to hold out some hope.

Sinking into the chair by the door, he thought of Sabrina and Petula. What kind of father would he be to them without Dru's wisdom and guidance? He didn't know the first thing about it. His own father had been lost in a drunken stupor since Gavin was ten, perhaps even before.

As for his mother . . . Well, he'd quit thinking of her long ago. Whenever he did, he was left with a sour taste in his mouth.

Gavin had been on his own since he was fourteen, and he'd liked it that way. He'd never thought he wanted anything different. It had been his friend, Charlie Porter, and Dru, Sabrina, and little Pet who'd shown him what love and home and a family could mean. He'd almost begun to believe in those things.

But now it was all gone—or just about. Charlie had died over two years ago, gored by an angry bull, just after Dru lost the baby—the son they'd all been waiting for. And now she was dying and leaving Gavin to raise her daughters. She didn't know how incapable he was. She didn't realize that he would most surely fail.

"Gavin?"

He looked up to find Dru standing in the doorway to the bedroom. Loose strands of hair streamed limply over her shoulders, and the billowy white nightgown engulfed her bony frame. He supposed she'd never been much to look at, but she'd always been warm and kind and giving, and that had more than made up for whatever beauty Mother Nature hadn't seen fit to bestow on her.

"I want to stay in the basin as long as we can this year. Let Stubs and Jess take the cows to the Lucky Strike. A few more weeks won't matter much."

"It might, Dru. The weather . . ."

"Please, Gavin. I won't ask for more than a few weeks."

He rose from the chair and strode across the sitting room, stopping within arm's reach of her. She was a tall woman, but she seemed small and shrunken to him now.

I'm scared, Dru, he thought as he looked into her eyes. *I don't know how to be a father to the girls.*

As if she understood his thoughts, Dru reached up and touched his cheek. "You're going to do just fine by them. They're going to be prettier than I ever was. And they'll be smarter

31

too. Miss Harris will see to that. I have a lot of faith in that young woman."

"You just met her. How can you know anything about her?"

"I have a feeling, Gavin. Please give her a chance."

"All right, Dru. If it's what you want." He took her in his arms and pressed her cheek against his chest.

They stood that way for a long time.

"You can't really mean to do this." Maggie's voice was incredulous.

Rachel turned from her packing. Her sister was standing just inside the bedroom door. Maggie's gray eyes seemed even wider than usual as they stared at her.

"Yes, I do mean to do it," she replied.

"But you have no idea what you might be getting into. You don't know these people. And just where is this ranch? What if you were to get sick? Is there a town? Is there a doctor?"

"Maggie, I'm not six anymore. I don't need you to mother me." She sighed, recognizing how harsh her words must have sounded. "I'm sorry. I don't mean to be ungrateful. I know you're only thinking of what's best for me. But I want to do this. I *have* to do this. It's time I was out on my own."

"That's fine, but why like this? Why not move into Boise? I'm sure Tucker could help you find something to do. Maybe you could help Harry in his law office. You'd be close to Fiona and the baby if you moved to town, and you could come out here whenever you wanted."

That wouldn't help, she thought as she turned to resume her packing. *It's not here. Whatever I need isn't here.*

"It's too dangerous," Maggie insisted, her voice taking on a stern tone. "I just can't let you do it."

Rachel dropped the gown she was folding and whirled around. "You can't stop me, Maggie. I'm all grown up. I appreciate everything you and Tucker have done for me. I really do. But it's time for me to do something on my own. You weren't even eighteen yet when we joined the wagon train to come out west. You didn't know anyone either. You had to trust Mrs. Foster when she said we could travel with them in their wagon. You didn't know where we were going. Not really. There wasn't any doctor when we all got sick with the measles. You almost died, but it didn't stop you from doing what you had to do."

Maggie's beautiful face registered defeat. "But I don't *want* you to go," she said, her voice filled with sadness.

In unison, they moved forward to embrace each other tightly.

"I know," Rachel agreed in a whisper. "I'll miss you too. Honest, I will. And Tucker and the children. I'll miss them all. But it's only until spring. That isn't so very long. And I'll write. Mrs. Blake told me the post goes up to Challis every week."

Maggie sniffed as she pulled back. "I just don't understand why you need to do this. You have so many gentlemen coming to call and . . ."

"I have to, Maggie. I can't explain why. It's just something I have to do."

Her sister studied her for a long time, staring hard into her eyes, searching for answers and understanding. Finally, she leaned forward and kissed Rachel's forehead. "Then God go with you, kitten."

Tears sprang to her eyes. It had been a long time since Maggie had called her by her pet name. It brought back a kaleidoscope of memories from her childhood, all of them filled with Maggie's image.

"We'll take you into town in the morning." With that, Maggie turned and tearfully left the room.

Chapter Three

Unshed tears burned the back of Rachel's throat as she looked at the gathering of family and friends waiting outside the Overland. With such short notice, she hadn't expected anyone to even know she was leaving, and considering the early hour, she would never have guessed they would all be there, hugging and kissing her.

Tucker's mother, Maureen Foster, and her husband, David, had come in from Green Willows, their ranch west of the city. They were accompanied by Neal Branigan, Maureen's youngest son, and his new bride, Patricia. Neal was the closest thing to a brother that Rachel had ever known, and she wished she'd had more time to get to know Patricia. She was certain they would have become close friends.

Fiona Whittier, Tucker's sister and Rachel's best and dearest friend since childhood, was there with her baby daughter. Fiona's cheeks had been streaked with tears from the moment she arrived. "You've only been back six months," she said with a whimper, making it difficult for Rachel to control her own tears.

Maggie and Tucker were there, of course, along with all five of their children, from four-year-old Sheridan to fourteen-year-old Kevin. Maggie had resigned herself to Rachel's leaving and had promised not to cry, but the strain still showed in the paleness of her cheeks and the set of her mouth. Even Tucker had been inordinately silent all morning. She was going to miss her brother-in-law's sensitive guidance and quiet wisdom.

Standing beside Tucker was Harry Jessup, Tucker's old law partner. The two men had been friends back in Georgia before the war and had started a law practice together in Boise when they first arrived. With Harry were his twin sons, Beau and Boone, thirteen years old and full of mischief and energy.

So many of them. All hugging and kissing her and saying how much they would miss her. She'd been through this years before when she and Tucker left Boise for her trip back east to attend finishing school, but somehow this time seemed different, the good-byes harder to say.

It was still a few minutes before eight when Gavin Blake pulled his wagon up in front of the hotel. Rachel felt a strange quiver in her stomach as he hopped down from the wagon seat, landing with catlike grace in the dusty road. He turned his head and their eyes collided. His brows drew together in a frown. Then his gaze swept the large gathering of people surrounding her on the sidewalk.

She swallowed the lump in her throat as she lifted a hand in an abbreviated wave. "Good morning, Mr. Blake."

He stepped up onto the sidewalk and touched the brim of his battered hat. "Morning, Miss Harris." His eyes flicked once more over the crowd as silence settled over them. "You got your things together?"

Stepping forward, Tucker said, "I've got her trunk in my carriage." He was wearing his most official expression as he held out his hand toward Gavin. "I'm Judge Branigan, Rachel's brother-in-law."

"Gavin Blake." His hand clasped with Tucker's.

Rachel had the distinct feeling there was some sort of testing going on between the two men as they stared into each other's eyes. She held her breath until Tucker released Gavin's hand and his expression relaxed.

"We can't say we're glad to have Rachel leaving us this way," Tucker said.

"She won't come to any harm while stayin' with us."

"We're counting on that. Kevin . . ." He turned his head toward his oldest son. "Get one of the twins to help you bring Rachel's trunk over here."

Beau and Boone both jumped forward, racing

with Kevin across the street, all of them arguing about who was the strongest, each of them bragging that he could carry the trunk without anyone's help.

"I'll get my wife." Gavin spun on his boot heel and disappeared through the hotel doors.

Maggie's fingers touched Rachel's shoulder. "You can still change your mind and come home with us."

It was tempting after seeing the look on Gavin's face, seeing the cold reception in his eyes. Lord, it was tempting. Her bedroom back at Maggie's was familiar and safe. Her friends and family were always close by whenever she needed them.

"No," she replied firmly. "I'm going with the Blakes."

Her comment was followed by a flurry of hugs and good wishes as everyone bade her one more farewell. Fiona had just released her when Gavin and Drucilla Blake came out of the hotel.

Dru's smile was warm and friendly. "Good morning, Miss Harris. My! Is this your family?" Hazel eyes swept over the crowd.

"Most of them."

Gavin tugged gently on his wife's arm. "We've got a long trip ahead of us. We'd best go." He escorted her to the wagon and lifted her up onto the wagon seat.

Rachel turned quickly toward Maggie. Her heart was suddenly thundering in her chest. She felt terribly afraid and incapable of doing what she'd set out to do.

Maggie's arms went around her. She pressed

her cheek against Rachel's and whispered into her ear. "I was scared too, when we went after the wagon train, but we made it. So will you."

"Miss Harris . . ." Gavin's deep voice was tinged with impatience.

Rachel blinked away her tears and turned toward the wagon. "I'm coming." Chin held high, she walked away from her sister.

Gavin was waiting for her at the rear of his flatbed wagon. As soon as she paused in front of him, he put his hands around her waist and lifted her effortlessly into it. For a moment, she just stared at the wagon bed, the back of it taken up by her trunk, the front portion covered with a tick mattress and blankets.

"Sit down and make yourself comfortable, Miss Harris. It'll be a while before we stop."

She sat quickly, twisting so she could look over the side of the wagon at Maggie and Tucker. Her fingers clenched the rough lumber that held her in.

Gavin sprang up onto the wagon seat beside his wife. He looked at Dru. "Ready? You need anything 'fore we go?"

"I'm fine, Gavin. Let's go home."

With the rattle of harness and braces, the wagon jerked forward, pulling away from the Overland Hotel. Rachel stared back at her family and friends until she couldn't see them any longer through the blur of tears.

When they stopped to rest and eat their midday meal, Gavin announced that he was going to walk about and stretch his legs. That left the women with time alone to get better acquainted. Rachel was eager to ask Dru about the children, but she wasn't given the chance.

"You stayed back East for several years, Miss Harris," Dru said as she handed Rachel a sandwich. "Why was that?"

"An accident mostly. After completing my schooling, I went home with my friend Georgia to visit her parents in Washington. Professor Abraham—that's what everyone calls Mr. Fielding—is such a remarkable man, and I was always pestering him with questions. Finally, he asked if I would stay and assist him with some historical research he was doing. I was thrilled to be a part of it."

She took a bite of her sandwich, then continued, unaware of the excitement in her voice. "Professor Abraham doesn't have those silly notions about education being wasted on a woman. He would talk to me about anything. He treated all my questions as if they had merit, even the ones that didn't. I had access to any of the books in his library and could read to my heart's content."

"Was it all study and work?" Dru asked.

"Oh, no. Professor Abraham and his wife are invited *everywhere*, and Georgia and I were forever tagging along to parties and balls. And the Fielding home always had interesting guests coming and going. The professor is the confidante of statesmen and successful businessmen from all over the country. I met so many leaders of industry and politicians in the years I was with them, I couldn't begin to name them all. It

40

was always interesting, always so stimulating."

"Then why did you come back to Idaho?"

Rachel wasn't certain how to answer. It was a question she'd asked herself many times in the past six months. Why *did* she come back?

"I don't know," she finally said, her voice soft and thoughtful, the excitement gone as she considered the question once again.

"Is there a special man waiting for you in Boise? Someone you plan to marry?"

"No," Rachel answered firmly.

Dru lifted an eyebrow. "Are you saying you don't want to ever get married and have a family?"

"Not at all," Rachel was quick to respond. "I *do* want it . . . when the time is right."

"You've never been in love, have you, Rachel?" The expression on Dru's face was strangely wistful.

She shook her head. "No, but I've seen what it's like, living with Tucker and Maggie. That's what I want it to be like for me. I don't mean to marry someone just because he's important or wealthy. I mean to be in love with the man I marry." She felt a bit silly for the emphatic tone of her voice. "But," she continued, "the time isn't right for that yet, so there's no point worrying about it. I still have things to do." She laughed at herself. "I just don't know what."

Dru grinned back at her. "I'm sure you'll figure it out."

"I hope so. It sounds absurd, I suppose, but I've always had the feeling that something special was going to happen in my life. When I decided to come home, it was because I had a feeling I would find it waiting for me here." She shrugged. "If it was, I didn't find it."

Dru tilted her head slightly to one side as she observed Rachel. "Perhaps you found it and don't know it yet."

Rachel smiled and gave a little shake of her head. How could she have found it and not know it? She'd been waiting for that "something" to happen for years. Which was exactly why she was here with Dru now. Because she was tired of waiting and had chosen to go out and *make* something happen.

"Perhaps," she said, not wanting to argue a futile point, but certain the woman was wrong.

Later that night, Gavin sat beside the dying embers of the campfire and ran his fingers over a worn piece of harness. He would have to do some repairs on it before long. Perhaps, come spring, he'd be able to afford a whole new harness. If he could get the right price for his cows after round-up and if the rest of his herd wintered well, he should be able to . . .

"Mr. Blake?"

He glanced up, surprised that he hadn't heard her approach.

"May I talk to you a moment?"

Gavin waved at the log opposite him.

She sat down. He noticed the graceful movements of her hands as she smoothed the skirt of her dress over her knees. She lifted a loose strand of pale blond hair and looped it behind her ear. The tip of her tongue moistened her lips as she stared into the red, glowing coals. She looked lovely, despite the long, dusty, tiring day.

"Is there some reason you disapprove of me to teach your daughters, Mr. Blake?" she asked, her eyes suddenly lifting to meet his.

"Is there any reason I should?"

"No . . . but you do all the same."

"Dru chose you, Miss Harris. That's good enough for me."

Her blue eyes widened a fraction, and her head tilted slightly to one side. The slight pucker of her lips told him she thought he was lying. He supposed he was.

His fingers tightened on the harness. "I just don't think you're cut out for the place we're going."

"Why is that, Mr. Blake?"

Irritation caused his voice to deepen. "Listen, Miss Harris, we don't have a lot of fancy things. I built the log cabin at our summer range with my own two hands. And the main ranch doesn't have much more to it. We got a couple of hired hands who help out, and the nearest neighbors in the basin are more than likely a small band of Sheepeater Indians or some of their kin. There won't be any nice teas to be shared with the womenfolk or dances to go to. Winters can be plenty long, and if you get bored easily, they'll seem even longer."

"I can do this job, Mr. Blake," she insisted.

He leaned suddenly forward and grabbed her hand, turning it palm up. "Look at that lily-white hand. You haven't done a day's work in your life. You might've been raised on a ranch, but it was

43

a gentleman's ranch or I miss my guess. That brother-in-law of yours hires on all his help to run the ranch while he plays the judge in town and you sit drinking tea on the front porch. You're just another spoiled, rich—"

She jerked her hand away from him. Her blue eyes were rounded, and she sounded breathless when she spoke. "That's not so. We've worked hard for everything we've got. Tucker built our first house himself, cutting down the trees along the river. I remember just what it was like. We all worked and worked hard. In some ways, it was even harder than the trip west on the wagon train when we were moving every day for months and slept in the rain and walked in the mud and baked in the sun." She stood up. "Maybe Tucker does have others running his ranch now, but he's earned it. And maybe I have been spoiled by his success. Maybe my life the last ten years has been easier than most, but I'm not afraid of hard work. I can teach your children and I can help take care of your wife."

"You don't belong up at the basin," he growled.

"Well, I'm going to be there, aren't I, so you and I may as well learn to get along." With a toss of her head, she turned and hurried toward her bed beneath the wagon.

Gavin's frown deepened as he returned his attention to the harness in his hand. She could say what she wanted. Rachel Harris didn't belong in the hard life of the Blakes. She would wilt there like a rose without water. He'd be sending her back to Boise before the first snows.

He'd be willing to bet on it.

He caught a faint whiff of honeysuckle and felt a strange emptiness in his chest.

Despite Dru's frail appearance and admission of ill health, Rachel began to wonder if she'd been wrong about the woman. Every morning Dru was ready to break camp before the crack of dawn. She could scarcely be convinced to rest and have lunch in the middle of the day. And at night, she always insisted they go just one more mile before making camp. Gavin seemed concerned, but he often gave in to her pleas.

Rachel, on the other hand, was exhausted and always ready to call it a day long before they actually did. She was hungry for a real meal rather than those hastily prepared over a campfire. She felt wilted and dirty and longed for a bath. A hot bath in the privacy of an upstairs bathroom, like the one at home.

Gavin remained taciturn, speaking to her as little as possible. Dru, however, was invariably chatty and friendly. She told Rachel about the Stanley Basin and the beauty of the surrounding mountain ranges. Mostly, though, she talked about her daughters. Her voice was always filled with pride when the topic was Sabrina and Petula.

The days seemed both to drag by and to pass all too quickly as the familiarity of Rachel's home was left farther and farther behind. Still, she couldn't deny a growing sense of adventure as Dru shared more about their summer range in the Stanley Basin, a valley surrounded by mountains with names like Sawtooth and White Cloud. But despite Dru's glowing reports of the basin she loved, Rachel wasn't prepared for the breathtaking panorama that met her gaze late in the afternoon a week after they had left Boise.

The valley was tucked, snug and serene, between rugged mountain ranges. A carpet of green grasses waved like the sea beneath a gentle breeze. Late summer wildflowers bobbed their colorful heads. Sage and pine scented the air. Winding its way across the valley floor was a ribbon of water. A thick blanket of pine trees climbed the mountainsides as far as possible, then admitted defeat amidst the jagged crags and towering peaks of the Sawtooth Mountains.

"Is that snow?" she asked as she spied the splotches of white nesting in the shadowed sides of rocky spires.

"Glaciers," Gavin replied. "They're there year-round."

"Can we see your ranch from here?"

"Not yet," Dru replied. "The basin's north-west of here. We'll be there tomorrow."

Gavin hopped down from the wagon seat and walked across the narrow dirt road. His thick brows were drawn together as his eyes swept the wooded area. Moments later, he strode quickly back, stopping at the back of the wagon. He pulled a heavy chain from a box in the rear corner, then marched back into the trees.

Rachel watched as he rolled up his shirt sleeves before bending over a fallen tree, slipping the heavy links beneath it. His muscles bulged as he leaned forward, pulling on the chain. The tree didn't budge.

She wondered if his shoulders were as muscular as his arms—and knew instinctively that they were. She felt herself blushing as she imagined him without his shirt on.

She glanced down at her hands, finding them clenched tightly in her lap. She wasn't aware of his return until she felt the wagon jerk as he regained his seat.

What on earth was that all about? she wondered as he picked up the reins.

But instead of starting forward and making their way down the steep descent into the valley, Gavin turned the wagon around and guided the team off the trail toward the chained log.

Curiosity finally got the better of her. "What are you doing?" she asked as Gavin jumped down from the wagon and walked toward the tree.

"It's to help check our speed going down." He picked up the chain and fastened the loose end to the undercarriage. "It's a steep grade." His tone clearly stated he found her question a foolish one, that she should have known the reason, that if she wasn't a spoiled city girl she wouldn't have had to ask.

He made her mad enough to spit. He was without a doubt the most unreasonable, unfriendly man she'd ever had the displeasure to meet. And she wasn't going to let him scare her off. She'd prove to him she could measure up to whatever he dished out. After all, she wasn't

entirely ignorant of men. She'd been squired
around Washington by some of the most powerful and influential men in the country. She'd sat
at supper tables and chatted with brilliant men
of science and government. Surely this back-
woods cowboy could be properly handled. She
would make him like her. She would force him
to admit he was wrong about her. If it was the
last thing she did, she was going to hear him
admit he was wrong.

The wagon started forward with a lurch.
Rachel's head snapped back, hitting the front of
the wagon. Her right hand flew up, and she
grasped the side to steady herself. Behind them,
the tree carved a groove in the earth as it was
dragged through the needles and grass, finally
falling onto the dirt trail.

Minutes later, Rachel understood why Gavin
had taken the time to weight the wagon. The
brake scraped noisily against the wheels. The
horses leaned back over their hind legs, strain-
ing against the weight of the wagon pushing
against them. The narrow track—too primitive
to be called a road—wound back and forth
across the side of the mountain, dropping swiftly toward the valley floor below.

"Easy, Checker. Whoa now, Patch." Gavin's
voice was smooth, gentle, calming not only the
team of horses but Rachel as well.

She twisted to look up at him, seated so close
to her back. He was leaning forward, his boots
braced against the footboard. The reins were
woven through his fingers. Sweat stained the

back of his shirt along his spine, and the muscles flexed across his shoulders.

"That's it, girl. Slow down, Patch."

Watching him, Rachel felt the last of her tension leave her body. Gavin would get them safely to the bottom.

Chapter Four

Patches of brown and white dotted the landscape across a wide sweep of meadowland where cattle grazed along the banks of the river, the lush grasses reaching up to tickle their bellies.

"We're home," Dru whispered.

Rachel rose to her knees and leaned to one side to see what was ahead. Just as she did so, she saw a horse break away from the cattle and come cantering toward them. The rider waved his arm.

Gavin drew back on the reins, stopping the team, and waited for the cowboy to arrive.

"Lord a'mighty, it's good to see you folks back agin. Them gals o' yours ain't stopped askin' when you'd be back since the day after you left."

Dru's voice was anxious. "There's nothing wrong, is there, Stubs?"

The cowboy's grizzled face broke into a grin as he looked at Dru. "Nothin' that their ma bein' home won't take care of."

"Where are they now?" she asked.

"Back at the house. Jess and Brina are whippin' us up some grub for supper. Imagine Pet's tryin' to help out. Better git up there so they can throw in a bit more." Stubs removed his hat and drew his arm across his forehead, glancing toward Rachel as he did so. "Got your teacher, did ya?"

Gavin looked over his shoulder. "Miss Harris, this is Stubs Martin. He's the foreman for the Lucky Strike Ranch."

"How do you do, Mr. Martin." Rachel stood, her hand on the back of the wagon seat for balance. "It's a pleasure to meet you."

"Well, doggies. If you ain't a pretty little thing. You just call me Stubs and we'll git on fine." He winked at her. "Yes, sir. Ain't she a pretty little thing, Gavin?"

Rachel felt the warm blush spreading up from her neck. She fought the urge to turn and look at Gavin, as if it mattered to her if Gavin Blake found her pretty—which, of course, it most certainly did not.

"I see you've got the cattle rounded up," Gavin said, ignoring his foreman's question. Without pausing, he added, "You'd better sit down, Miss Harris." He slapped the reins against the horses' rumps, and the wagon jerked forward, nearly toppling her.

He really was the most ill-mannered man. Begrudgingly, she gave him silent credit for the tenderness and concern he showed toward Dru. Beyond that, she found Gavin Blake an insufferable bore and only hoped she would see as little of him as possible once they reached their destination.

Stubs fell in beside the wagon, quickly filling Gavin in on what had transpired while the boss and his wife were away. The final count showed they'd lost only a few cattle during the summer, a couple to wolves, the rest more than likely to some of the Indians in the area. The herd had fattened up nicely on the abundant feed available. They would bring a fine price when butchered and delivered to the miners in the area.

"When do we mean to start the drive?" Stubs asked. "It's gettin' a bit late in the year."

"Dru's asked to stay in the basin for a few more weeks, but I think you'd better drive the cattle out in the next day or two. The buyers will be expecting us."

"You think you oughta—" Stubs began.

Two shrill voices interrupted his question. "Ma! Ma!"

Once again, Rachel got to her knees and leaned over for a better view. Even as Dru reached out to grab hold of Gavin's arm, he was drawing the wagon to a halt.

"Ma!"

Dark brown hair streamed out behind them as they ran. The older girl was tall and slender. The younger was plump and rosy. Each of them was smiling broadly and waving.

Gavin hopped down from the wagon seat, then lifted his wife to the ground. She turned just in time to receive the two girls into her arms.

"Ma, you're back! You were gone so long."

"I know, Brina. It seemed like forever to me, too."

Sabrina had her mother's hazel eyes as well as the same long, narrow face. Her complexion was fair except for the spattering of freckles across her nose and cheeks. Her dress barely covered her knees. She would soon be grown clear out of it.

"Ma . . ." Petula tugged on her mother's sleeve. "Look." She opened her mouth.

The younger girl's eyes were a dark chocolate brown and were capped by thick chestnut brows. Her skin was dark, her mouth wide and full. Rachel could see little resemblance to either Gavin or Dru in the child.

"My goodness, Pet. Where did your tooth go?" her mother asked, acting as if she'd never known a child could lose a tooth.

"It came loose when I was ridin'." Her eyes widened. "I swallowed it," she announced gravely.

"Well then, you probably won't be hungry for supper, will you?" Gavin asked as he swooped the younger child into his arms.

Petula promptly threw her arms around his neck and gave him a kiss on the cheek. "Will too. Mr. Chamberlain's fixin' pie for dessert, and I helped."

With his other arm, Gavin lifted Sabrina against his side. "What about you? Stubs tells me you're doing the cooking."

She mimicked her sister's actions by hugging his neck and kissing his cheek. As she pulled back, she nodded solemnly. "I made the stew."

Rachel couldn't help noticing the way he grinned at the children. It wasn't just his mouth. The smile went right to his eyes, making their gray depths sparkle with silent laughter. It was a much nicer look than the one he normally turned on her.

He must be a wonderful father.

Dru touched Rachel's hand on the side of the wagon. "Get down, Miss Harris, and meet the children."

"Yes, of course," she mumbled, remembering abruptly why she was there. Without waiting for help, she scrambled over the tailgate of the wagon and dropped the remaining few feet to the ground. She turned nervously to face her pupils, feeling as if she was stepping before a firing squad.

"Brina . . . Pet . . ." Dru waited as Gavin set the girls on their feet. "Come meet Miss Harris."

Holding hands, they came forward to stand next to their mother. Two sets of eyes stared up at her, curious and skeptical at the same time.

Her throat felt dry. "Hello, Sabrina. Hello, Petula."

They didn't say a word.

"I'm glad to meet both of you at last. Your

mother's told me so much about you."

Still no response.

Rachel swallowed hard. Her stomach was churning nervously. If the children took a dislike to her as quickly as their father had, she wouldn't have a prayer of staying on.

Petula turned and reached for her mother's skirt, tugging until Dru leaned down. "She's real pretty, isn't she, Ma?" she whispered.

"Yes, Pet, she is," Dru answered softly, her gaze lifting to meet Rachel's. "Very pretty."

Rachel was still trying to think of something to say when the peace of the valley was shattered by the baying of dogs. She turned to see three brown-and-gray blurs barreling toward them. The first two slid to a halt at Gavin's feet. The third didn't stop until he'd jumped up to thrust his muddy paws against Rachel's shoulders.

Thrown off balance, her arms flailed the air in large circles. As if knowing she was trying her best to stay upright, the mangy brute gave her a little push. With a squeal, she fell onto her backside, hitting the hard ground with a *thump*. Before she could close her mouth, the dog's long tongue smacked her across the face several times. She spluttered, raising her arm to ward off the beast, and closed her eyes, hoping all the while that it wouldn't decide she was tasty enough for a bite in place of the lick.

She heard their laughter. Particularly *his* laughter. It was deep and rich and—and insulting!

"Get back, Joker, you idiot. Don't you know that's no way to greet a lady?"

Rachel opened her eyes as Gavin dragged the overzealous wolfhound away by the scruff of its neck. Although he'd managed to muffle his guffaws, his eyes were still twinkling with undisguised merriment as he stepped forward again and offered her a hand up.

"He's *your* dog, no doubt," she grumbled as she took hold of his hand.

Gavin chuckled. "No doubt." He pulled her to her feet in one easy motion. "I hope you'll forgive him. Joker's just a pup."

"A *pup*?" She turned to stare at the enormous animal with its large square head and thick, wiry coat. "He's nearly a horse!" She brushed at the muddy prints on her bodice, biting back a few choice words about what should be done with the dog.

"Duke. Duchess. Come."

In response to Gavin's quiet command, the other two dogs sprang to their feet and trotted over.

"Sit down." Gavin waved his hand at Rachel, as if the dogs could understand what he was saying. "This is Miss Harris. She's come to live with us. I expect you to treat her with respect." He glanced at Rachel again, the sparkle remaining in his steel-gray eyes. "Miss Harris, meet Joker's parents, Duke and Duchess."

The larger of the two adult dogs lifted his right paw and cocked his head to one side. Large black eyes perused her. She almost believed the dog *did* understand what was going on.

"He's pleased to meet you, Miss Harris,"

Gavin said solemnly. "Go on. Shake his hand."

Rachel glanced over at Gavin, about to refuse, but from the corner of her eye, she could see Sabrina and Petula. They, too, were watching to see how Miss Harris would react. Tugging on her bodice, she straightened her dress, then bent forward and took hold of Duke's paw.

"How do you do, your grace." She moved the dog's paw up and down three times, then let go as her gaze moved to the female wolfhound. She held her skirts and executed a perfect curtsey. "It's a pleasure to meet you, Duchess." Her voice dropped to a stage whisper. "But, my lady, that son of yours is a disgrace. You must take him in hand quickly, or there'll be no redeeming him. He'll prove himself a fool at court."

The girls burst into laughter as they hurried forward to throw their arms around the giant dogs. Joker pushed his way into the happy group, his tongue lapping wildly in all directions. A warm thrill surged through Rachel as she watched them. They were going to like her. The children were going to like her.

Straightening, her eyes met Gavin's. One eyebrow was slightly arched as he offered a lopsided grin and a brief nod of his head. Her heart skipped a beat as she realized he was acknowledging her success. She felt a new heat spreading through her chest.

He has a wonderful smile.

"Come along, girls," Dru said. "Let's show Miss Harris to her room."

Rachel blushed and looked away from him,

feeling slightly confused and disoriented by her unexpected thoughts.

Petula stepped away from the dogs and came to stand beside Rachel. Her head cocked backward, she stared up at her new governess with solemn brown eyes. Then, without a word, she slipped her small, sweaty hand into Rachel's and pulled her toward the house.

Gavin climbed onto the wagon seat and took the harness into his hands, but he didn't start the horses forward. He sat thoughtfully, watching the gentle sway of Rachel's hips as she walked toward the log cabin, one hand holding Petula's, the other resting on Duke's shaggy head as he walked beside her.

A smile lifted the corners of his mouth as he remembered the way she'd looked just before Joker knocked her off her feet. Her blue eyes had rounded in surprise. Her mouth had formed a perfect O. He could still hear her tiny grunt as her bottom met earth. He could just imagine what she would have said if Joker hadn't stopped her with a lap of his tongue.

His grin widened. She had spunk. He'd give her that. She could have burst into tears or railed at the dog for ruining her dress. Instead, she'd proved herself a good sport and actually played along with his introductions to Duke and Duchess.

He clucked absently to the horses and followed after the others. He drove the team directly to the tall barn, stopping in the shade cast by the evening sun. He hopped down and quickly freed the animals from the wagon and harness, leading them into the corral on the north side of the barn. He tossed the horses some hay, then leaned on the fence and watched them eat.

"What's botherin' you, Gavin?"

He didn't look over as Stubs stepped up beside him.

"Is it Dru? Is she feelin' bad agin?"

He stared off in the direction of the mountains. "No. You wouldn't even have known she was sick except she doesn't eat enough to keep a bird alive."

"Must be the new teacher. Seems bright enough, and she's sure takin' to the girls. That's what Dru was wantin'."

Gavin didn't reply.

"Don't think I've seen anythin' as pretty as Miss Harris since we left home. Matter of fact, she kinda reminds me a bit of—" Stubs stopped abruptly, then whispered, "So that's it."

Gavin turned his head and glared at his foreman. They'd been together a long time. Stubs Martin had been working as a hired hand on the Blake place back in Ohio when Gavin was still just a boy. When they'd run into each other again ten years ago on the cattle trail up from Texas, they'd formed a friendship that had lasted ever since.

But Stubs had pushed the bonds of that friendship to the limit with his last comment.

"Don't say it," Gavin ground out through clenched jaws.

Stubs held up his hands. "I wasn't sayin' nothin'. Just don't take somethin' out on the girl that ain't her fault."

With another angry glare, Gavin pushed off from the corral fence and strode toward the house.

Chapter Five

In that moment before consciousness becomes reality, Rachel pressed her face against the pillow and tried to recapture the beauty of her dream. She was at a ball, a marvelous masked ball. Couples in dazzling costumes twirled around a crystal-and-glass ballroom, the women's gowns sweeping out in wide arcs in time to the music.

Rachel was dancing in the arms of a tall stranger, his face hidden behind a black mask. Eyes like steel stared at her through narrow slits. Through his fine lawn shirt, she could feel the contracting muscles of his shoulder. He wore an impudent smile on his mouth, as if he was laughing at some private joke. He was holding her closely against his chest, so closely she could feel the warmth of his hard, lean body. So closely, his warmth was becoming hers.

Her fingers tightened around his shoulder. Suddenly, he whimpered and . . .

Whimpered?

Rachel's eyes flew open to stare into Joker's fuzzy face, his shiny black nose mere inches from hers. The dog was lying in her bed and had crowded her over to the very edge of the tick mattress.

Before she could move, the wolfhound smacked her with another of his affectionate licks. She lifted her hand to ward him off—and promptly fell onto the floor.

"We're going to come to terms, dog," she muttered as she scrambled to her feet. "Now get off my bed."

He looked as if he was grinning at her as he sat up, his tail slapping the heavy patchwork quilt.

"I said, get down." She pointed at the floor.

Joker immediately leapt from the bed and flopped at her feet, rolling onto his back to expose his belly.

"Oh, no. You'll get no reward from me, you mangy beast. How'd you get in here anyway? Don't you belong outside, protecting us from wolves or something?"

He whimpered again.

Rachel moved quietly toward the door of her small bedroom and eased it open. The main room was still empty.

"Get out," she whispered, shooting a pointed look at the dog.

Tail between his legs and his head slung low, Joker slinked out of her bedroom. She closed the door behind him, but not before she'd heard the sounds of stirring from the bedroom across from hers.

She gazed longingly at the bed. She knew there was no point in trying to get back to sleep if others were up. Besides, she didn't want them to think her a lazybones, even though it seemed unreasonably early to be up and about. She'd forgotten during her years back East what sort of ungodly hours ranchers and farmers kept.

Rachel stepped over to the high, narrow window perched near the ceiling of her room and drew aside the curtain. Dawn hinted at its arrival with a soft, gray light, splashing it against the inside wall of her room.

She went to her trunk and pulled out some clean undergarments. She'd hung her dresses the night before on wooden pegs pounded into the log walls of her room. Now she chose one of her favorite day dresses. The fabric was covered with tiny sky-blue flowers against a white background. It had a simple bodice, pointed front and back, and the overskirt was draped back to form short side panniers, with long slender fullness behind.

Quickly, she poured water into the chipped porcelain basin of the corner washstand. She splashed her face, then patted it dry with the towel draped across the side of the stand. Stripping out of her long-sleeved white nightgown, she completed her morning ablutions with haste.

By the time she was finished, her skin was puckered with gooseflesh from the chill morning air. She pulled on her clothes, remembering wistfully the warmth of her bed—particularly when Joker had been snuggled up beside her.

"Mangy hound," she muttered, but she was unable to resist the pull of a smile on her lips.

As she finished closing the last button of her bodice, she settled onto the edge of the bed and reached for the hairbrush lying on the bedside table. Feeling suddenly sentimental, she ran her fingertips over the silver back of the brush. It had belonged to her mother years ago. Maggie had kept it hidden when their uncle was frantically selling off everything of value from their Philadelphia home, and she had brought it with them when she and Rachel came west. It had been Maggie's gift to Rachel on her eighteenth birthday.

Fingering the intricate design on the silver brush, Rachel wondered what her parents would have thought of her had they lived to see her grow up. Would her mother have understood the restlessness inside her? Would her father have approved of her coming to this mountain ranch to do something on her own?

She shook her head, shrugging off the strange musings. It served no more purpose to wonder about what couldn't be than to wonder about what might have been.

With brisk movements, she removed any nighttime snarls while bringing out a soft golden shine in the pale tresses. Then she caught the hair back from her face with a matched pair of ivory combs. A quick glance in the small hand mirror she'd brought from home satisfied her that she looked presentable.

Holding herself erect, she opened the bedroom door.

Dru was standing over the black iron stove. She twisted her head to glance over her shoulder as Rachel entered the main room of the log cabin.

"Morning. Would you like some coffee? It's hot."

"Yes. Thank you."

Dru plucked a tin cup from a shelf above the stove and filled it with the dark brew. She carried it to the rough-hewn table, then settled onto the bench opposite Rachel. As Rachel lifted the cup to her lips, blowing gently to cool the beverage, Dru swept her straggly hair away from her face and smiled.

"It's good to be home," she said, satisfaction lacing every syllable. "It's not much, but at least it's got wood floors and it's sound. Keeps out the wind and the rain. Charlie said I was to have just as good of a house here as at the main ranch."

"Charlie?"

Dru's smile faded as she stared at her hands, folded atop the table. "Charlie was my husband. He died the first year we summered the cattle here. Two years ago now. It doesn't seem so long. Just like yesterday." A sigh escaped her. "Pet looks a lot like him."

"Pet? But I thought . . ."

"Gavin adopted them when he married me."

She wasn't sure why, but for some reason, Rachel felt different. But before she had a chance to analyze her feelings, there was a noise from above. Moments later, the girls scrambled down the ladder from their room in the loft.

"Where's Pa?" Sabrina asked as her feet touched the floor.

"He's gone out with Stubs already."

Sabrina's face fell. "I wanted to show him the calf I found. I helped Jess rope him."

"Well, you can show him later. He'll be back for breakfast."

Dru rose from the table as her daughters approached. She gave them each a hug, kissed both their cheeks, then reached for a bucket hanging on a hook. "Say good morning to Miss Harris," she reminded them.

"Mornin'," the girls mimicked with quick glances in Rachel's direction.

"We'll work on your manners later," Dru said with an indulgent smile. "Now you two gather the eggs and I'll start frying up some bacon. Go on. Git."

"Is there anything I can do to help?" Rachel asked as the door closed behind Petula.

"Just talk with me. It's been a long time since I've had any real company, especially any womenfolk. Course, there's not many who want to come into this valley, man or woman, 'cept for the miners down in Sawtooth City. The Bannock Indians caused an uprisin' back in seventy-eight. Kept folks out of the area for a time. But when the gold strikes were made south of here, there was a regular stampede. Don't know how they manage in the winters. They're brutal. That's why we don't stay in the basin year round. Too hard on the cattle. They'd never survive."

"Why come at all, then? Why not just stay at the Lucky Strike all the time? From what you've told me, you've got a fine place there with lots of good grassland."

Dru tossed a few pieces of wood inside the black iron stove, then pulled a heavy frying pan from its hook on the wall. "Well, the feed's plentiful and unusually good up here." She glanced behind her at Rachel, offering a sheep- ish smile. "But I suppose the real reason is 'cause I fell in love with the basin first time I saw it. I had a real yearnin' to live here. So Charlie and Gavin and Stubs come in that first spring and built this house, and then we trailed in our herd. Luckily, it proved out. We took them out of here fatter than we could ever have hoped for. They brought a good price from the miners up in Bonanza and Custer."

Dru's hands never stopped moving as she talked. Rachel was listening with only half an ear as she watched the woman put fresh- churned butter into the skillet, then add sliced potatoes and onions. The room was quickly filled with delicious odors, causing Rachel's stomach to growl with hunger.

The door opened suddenly, and the children spilled inside, followed by Gavin, Stubs, and Jess Chamberlain. Sabrina carried the bucket over to her mother as the two ranch hands sat down at the table.

Gavin crossed to the stove and placed his hand

on Dru's shoulder. "How are you feeling?" he asked softly.

"Much better," she replied, turning to look up at him. She smiled. "I always feel better when we're here."

Gavin's fingers gently squeezed her shoulder, then he turned and reached for the dishes on the shelf to the right of the stove. Before he could ask for help, Sabrina and Petula were standing behind him. He handed the plates to the two girls.

Rachel felt conspicuous, sitting idle while Dru cracked the eggs over another hot skillet and scrambled them, and her daughters set the table. She knew what Gavin must be thinking of her. She wanted desperately to explain to him that she'd *asked* if she could help and had been turned down. But she hadn't the courage even to look at him.

Minutes later, everyone was seated around the big table, their heads bowed as Dru whispered a blessing over the food. "And thank you, Father, for bringin' Miss Harris to the basin. We ask you to bless her work here and make my girls smart as well as good. Amen."

Rachel's heart beat rapidly as her stomach jumped. Her appetite had suddenly disappeared. What was she doing in this house full of strangers? Dru was counting on her, but what made her think she could teach those two children anything?

As if reading her mind, Dru addressed her from across the table. "After the men are out from underfoot, I thought I'd show you the books I've got tucked away for the girls' schoolin'. I've taught 'em their A-B-C's myself but not much more. What with me bein' sick, their learnin's sorta been put aside. I don't want that for my girls."

"I'd like to see the books," Rachel answered, her eyes staring down at the eggs and fried potatoes on her plate.

"We'll wait a day or two to actually start lessons. After the herd's gone out'll be soon enough, I figure. In the meantime, the girls and Gavin can show you around the place."

Conversation died around the table as the family and ranch hands settled into the business of eating. With surreptitious glances from beneath a heavy fringe of golden-brown lashes, Rachel studied each individual.

Jess Chamberlain was young, younger even than she was. He looked hardly old enough to worry about using a razor on his smooth cheeks. He was long and lanky, much like the proverbial bean pole. When they'd been introduced the night before, he'd blushed scarlet and stammered a greeting. This morning, he had yet to even look her way, his complete attention centered on the food on his plate.

Stubs Martin, on the other hand, had already winked at her twice, as if he sought to share some special secret with her. Though not a tall man, he appeared solid as a rock. She supposed he was close to fifty but knew his grizzled jaw and balding pate might make him look older than he really was.

Her glance fell on Gavin, and she felt that

strange but now familiar flutter in her stomach. There was something about him—was it an aura of indisputable power?—that set her heart racing. It was more than his dark good looks. Much more. Sometimes she was almost afraid when he was near, although she knew without question he was not a dangerous man.

Gavin was making short shrift of his breakfast. He was leaning forward over the table, his raven-black hair falling across his forehead and his brows drawn together in a minute frown, as if he was thinking about something that troubled him. Rachel had a strong inclination to ask him what it was, but was thankfully able to curb that desire.

As her gaze moved to Drucilla Blake, she found herself wondering once again what had caused a man like Gavin to marry her, a widow with two daughters to raise. Dru had said Stubs and Gavin and Charlie built this cabin more than two years before. Had Gavin been in love with Dru even before her husband died?

Rachel dropped her eyes to her plate and took a few bites of her cooling food, mentally scolding herself for such thoughts. What concern was the Blakes' marriage to her? She was there to teach the children and help Dru in whatever way she could. That was *all* she was there to do.

Gavin's chair scraped noisily against the wood floor as he pushed away from the table and stood. A split second later, Stubs and Jess rose in unison.

"Pa?" Sabrina said softly.

Gavin had already taken a couple of steps

toward the door before he stopped, then turned to look at the girl.

"Did you see my calf? I helped Jess rope him."

"Is that true?" Gavin asked with a raised brow as he looked at his young ranch hand. "Brina roped a calf?"

"She done all right," Jess answered.

"He's in the barn. Will you come see him?"

Gavin reached out with one long arm and grabbed his wide-brimmed hat from a peg near the door. "I guess I can take the time for that."

Sabrina and her little sister jumped up from the table. They were halfway to the door when Petula stopped and whirled around. "Are you comin', Ma?"

"Not right now, Pet, but why don't you take Miss Harris? I'm sure she'd love to see Brina's calf."

The girl's gap-toothed smile widened, then she scurried over to Rachel's place at the table and held out her small, pudgy hand. "There's kittens in the barn, too," she whispered, "but we don't want Duke and Duchess to know."

Rachel's response was automatic. "No, I should think not." She took hold of Petula's hand and rose from her chair, then allowed herself to be led from the house.

The barn was warm and filled with earthy scents—hay and straw, dung and sweat. The barn's roof had a steep pitch, leaving room for only a narrow loft. Sunlight streamed in through the open hay door above, spilling through the cracks in the loft floor to create a swirl of bright light below.

"Over here," Sabrina called to Rachel as she and Petula entered the barn.

Rachel moved toward the stall where Gavin and Sabrina were standing. Inside was a reddish-brown calf with a white-blazed face and enormous brown eyes. It was lying down, its legs curled underneath its body.

"It's an orphan, and I've been takin' care of it." Sabrina's gaze shifted to Gavin. "It won't have to be sold yet, will it?"

He shook his head. "He's a bit young."

"May I . . . may I keep him?"

Rachel's eyes moved from the anxious child to the man's face above her. Unknowingly, she held her breath along with Sabrina, awaiting his decision.

Gavin knelt in the straw, one hand on Sabrina's shoulder. He stared at the calf as it struggled to its feet, curiosity getting the best of it. "Cows aren't pets, Brina. We raise them to sell."

Rachel heard the tenderness in his words, sensed the care with which he weighed his decision.

"But if you'll promise to take good care of it through the winter, see that it's fed and kept clean and stays healthy, whatever money it brings when it does go to market will be yours."

Sabrina screwed up her mouth and squinched her eyes as she gave Gavin's offer some thought. Rachel half-expected her to burst into tears over not being able to keep the calf, but finally she nodded. "I'll take real good care of it. I promise.

And I'll share the money with Petula."

Gavin patted her shoulder as he straightened, his gaze meeting Rachel's. She felt like she wanted to say something, tell him that he'd handled the request very well. She didn't know why she felt the urge to reassure him, but she did.

In that moment of indecision, the chance to speak was snatched from her by an impatient tug on her hand. "Now come see what I got," Petula insisted.

She was pulled across the barn to a tall ladder leading to the loft. Rachel looked at the contraption with some misgivings. It was a long way to the top, and it had been years since she'd climbed anything that tall. To tell the truth, she'd been afraid of heights ever since Tucker fell down the side of the Snake River Canyon on their way west along the Oregon Trail. She'd been only six at the time, but she'd always believed his accident was somehow her fault. If she hadn't been playing so near the rim. . . .

"You don't have to go, Miss Harris," the deep voice said from behind her. "Your dress will probably get dirty."

Since concern for her dress was the farthest thing from her mind, his comment made her instantly angry. With an indignant glance over her shoulder, she snapped, "My dress will wash, Mr. Blake. It certainly won't keep me from seeing whatever it is Pet wants to show me." She gave a haughty toss of her head before turning to grasp the rungs of the ladder.

Petula scampered up the ladder, leading the

way to the dusty loft overhead. As soon as Rachel's feet touched the board flooring—which wasn't quite as soon as she would have liked—her hand was clasped once again and she was guided toward a far corner. There, nearly hidden in a nest of hay, a gray-striped cat was calmly bathing one of her progeny while the other three mewling kittens happily gorged themselves on their mother's milk.

"That's Countess," Pet said, pointing to the tabby cat. "Ma thought up her name. Says it's next best to Duchess."

Rachel leaned forward for a better look at the kittens. "Duke, Duchess, Countess. Such regal names for all your pets."

"Dru's always wanted to go to England," Gavin explained as he stepped up beside Rachel. "She's got this fascination for royalty."

She turned her head and found herself looking into his gray eyes, his face bathed in the morning light spilling through the hay door. Her irritation with him seemed to vanish, and she smiled.

"Would you like to hold one?" Sabrina asked, thrusting a golden kitten between her stepfather and her governess.

Rachel took the small ball of fur into one hand, cupping her other hand over it as she brought it close to her face. She closed her eyes as she brushed the kitten against her cheek. "Perhaps she'll get to go to England one day still." She opened her eyes to look at Gavin once again. "She's young enough."

She wasn't sure what it was. There wasn't

really any change in his expression. Still, she knew the moment the words were out of her mouth that she'd said something wrong.

"I've got work to do, Miss Harris," he said abruptly. He turned and headed toward the ladder. "Brina, you and your sister get inside and help your ma with those dishes." He didn't look her way again as he disappeared over the edge of the loft.

Chapter Six

Rachel had forgotten more than just how early ranchers rose in the morning. She'd forgotten how endless the work was and how long the day lasted.

Perhaps Gavin Blake was right, she thought as she sorted clothes that first washday she was in the basin. She *had* been spoiled and pampered. She couldn't recall ever having to face so large or difficult a task. But she was determined to do her share and not to complain, especially since Dru seemed to accept it as just another chore.

"You weren't employed to be a maid or a laundress, Miss Harris," Dru had told her when Rachel insisted she wanted to help.

"No," she'd agreed, "but I was employed to help take care of you until you're well and strong again. I know you're still tired from the trip up here. I can see it in your face. I'm perfectly able to help, if you'll just tell me what to do."

Following Dru's instructions, Rachel put the heavier and dirtier things to soak in lye before dropping them into the copper kettle to boil. She gave the lighter, more delicate articles to Dru to wash by hand in a tub of lukewarm water.

Steam filled the kitchen area, leaving Rachel's face flushed and beaded with moisture. Her blond hair, most of it hidden beneath a scarf, curled in tiny wisps across her forehead. Her skin felt uncomfortably damp between her breasts.

Bending over the wash tub, she scrubbed the clothes and linens on the fluted washboard. It wasn't long before the muscles across the back of her neck and shoulders were complaining of abuse, but she gritted her teeth and kept at it. As each article was completed, she dropped it into another barrel-shaped tub to await rinsing.

The children were kept busy hauling clean water in and dirty water out. They chattered and laughed and generally filled the small log cabin with a feeling of happiness. Somehow, it made Rachel's task seem lighter as she listened.

"Here, Miss Harris," Dru said as she came around the washtub. "Let me take over while you get those things rinsed and hung out to dry. It would be a shame to waste the sunshine and days are so short now that autumn is here."

Short? Rachel felt as if they'd already been at it for twenty-four hours, and it wasn't even noon yet. As far as she was concerned, this day couldn't be over soon enough.

Wringing the water from the clean, rinsed laundry was hard, tedious work. By the time she had her first basket of clothes filled, her hands ached and her skin felt raw and chapped.

Mr. Gavin Blake certainly couldn't say anything about her lily-white hands today, she thought as she lifted the clothes basket and braced it against her hip.

"We'll help you, Miss Harris," Sabrina offered.

She shook her head. "Thank you, Brina, but I think you and Pet should spell your mother for a while. She looks tired."

"We *all* look tired," Dru responded wryly.

Rachel offered a weary smile of agreement, then went outside.

The Stanley Basin was being blessed today with the warm breath of Indian summer. A gentle breeze stirred the trees and long grasses, bringing with it the sweet scent of pine.

Rachel found the clothesline stretched between two trees and supported in the middle with a wooden prop. She set the basket on the ground, then placed her hands on the small of her back and bent backward, trying to relieve just a little of the ache that persisted there.

When she straightened, she found Gavin leaning against the corner of the log cabin, watching her.

"Not as much fun as a fancy dress ball, is it?" he said, sounding amused. He pushed off from the house and walked toward her.

She turned her back toward him and grabbed

for the shirt on top of the pile of clothes in the basket. "I told you before I'm not afraid of hard work."

"I can see that, Miss Harris."

The serious tone of his voice caused her to look up at him. Was that an apology she saw in his eyes? She looked away quickly, flustered by the intentness of his gaze.

She held the shirt against the clothesline and slipped the split wood pin over one sleeve. As she reached to fasten the other sleeve in place, the pin dropped from her fingers and fell into the thick grass at her feet.

Did she let go of the shirt and hope it held while she retrieved the other pin, or did she free the one sleeve and hold the shirt until she had both pins in hand? It shouldn't have been such a dilemma, but she could feel him watching her. For some reason, doing it right became of paramount importance. Her stomach was all aflutter, and her breathing came hard. She wished he would go away.

"Here," he said. "Let me get that for you." He leaned over and picked up the troublesome clothespin, then held it out to her.

She didn't want to look up at him. She was too distressed and afraid he would see it in her eyes. "Thank you," she said softly. She closed her fingers around the small piece of wood and tinned steel, careful not to touch his hand.

"Well . . ." The amused tone was back. "I just came in for a bite to eat. Better get to it." He stepped away.

"Mr. Blake."

79

He stopped. "Yes?"

Now she looked at him, her heart thundering in her ears. "Thanks for your help."

There was a pregnant pause before he replied, "You're welcome, Miss Harris."

As she watched him stride toward the house, she chose not to analyze why she reacted to him this way all the time. It was far better to ignore it and hope it would go away.

"We're in for a bit of rain, I'd say." Gavin turned from the window, his gaze falling on the two girls. "You two better get your animals tended to now."

"Okay, Pa." Sabrina set aside the square of fabric she'd been trying to embroider. "Come on, Pet."

"It's gettin' cold out. Put on your jackets," Dru reminded the children as they headed for the door.

Gavin crossed to a chair near the fireplace and sat down. "Where's Miss Harris?"

"Lying down, I imagine. She insisted on doing just about all of that washin' by herself today, and then she helped me with supper." Dru leveled a reproachful gaze on him. "It's entirely your fault, you know. She's tryin' to prove she's up to doin' *everything* because you've made it clear you don't think she can do *anything*."

"Wait a minute, Dru. I never—"

"Don't argue with me, Gavin. You haven't been the least bit nice to Miss Harris and you know it. I didn't want her up here to clean house and wash clothes. I wanted her here to teach the children, to get them to trust and care for her so that when I . . . when I'm not here, they'll have a woman they can turn to."

Gavin's jaw tightened. What made Dru think Rachel Harris would stay once Dru was gone? Did she think that pampered hothouse flower would stick around?

"Gavin, it's not like you to be unfair."

Unfair? He considered the charge. Well, maybe. Maybe he should give her the benefit of the doubt. She *might* prove him wrong. She did dig in to help with the wash today. It could be there was more to her than he'd thought at first.

A lopsided smile curved his mouth as he recalled how she'd looked when he'd come in for lunch. She didn't seem to have any clothes suitable for this life. She'd been wearing a dress of sunshine yellow, the skirt narrow, flounced, and bustled, the bodice fitted, conforming nicely to her pleasantly feminine shape. What she needed, of course, was a simple, loose-fitting blouse and an equally simple skirt without lots of petticoats or bustles or other such nonsense.

But there she'd stood in that yellow dress out behind the cabin, her hair hidden beneath a matching yellow scarf. Come to think of it, she'd looked like a wilting sunflower. Her face had been flushed. Her hair had clung to her face in damp wisps. Her hands . . .

Her hands. They'd looked like the hands of a rancher's wife—red and rough and careworn.

"You're right, Dru," he admitted. "I haven't been fair." But then he remembered her as he'd first seen her. Beautiful and rich. She didn't belong here. He would never believe she belonged here. "But that doesn't mean I've changed my mind about her."

He turned his eyes on the fire. He never should have let Dru talk him into going to Boise to hire a teacher for the children. What was so all-fired important for them to learn that Dru couldn't teach them?

The Blakes sure didn't have a lot of extra money to be throwing away. The last year had been good to them, but if they wanted the Lucky Strike to be a success, they needed to put everything they made back into it. He was hoping to have his neighbor, Patrick O'Donnell, pick up a new bull for him next summer up in Montana, and a prize bull wouldn't come cheap.

No, it would have been better if they'd never gone to Boise. Rachel Harris didn't belong with the Blakes. Yet strangely, he couldn't remember what it had been like before she'd come to stay.

Chapter Seven

Gavin felt the stillness first. He opened his eyes, his body alert. The bedroom he shared with Dru was dark, but he knew instantly that his wife's bed was empty.

His feet touched the cool wood floor as he sat up. He reached for his trousers and slipped into them, then pulled on his boots. Listening for any sound out of the ordinary, he rose and quickly strode across the bedroom. There was a faint glimmer of red coals lingering on the sitting room hearth, shedding just enough light for him to see the open front door.

As he stepped outside, the first flash of lightning lit up the sky. Seconds later, the resultant crack of thunder split the silent air. Before the sound had faded, the heavens sparked again and then again.

She was standing in the middle of the yard, halfway between the house and the barn. She was wearing a brown shawl over her white nightgown. Her graying brown hair hung free down the middle of her back. She looked as if a breeze could blow her over. As if in response to his observation, the wind rose, stirring the white fabric around her ankles and revealing bare feet.

Gavin walked slowly forward. "Dru?"

She didn't turn to look at him. Her voice was soft, barely audible above the peals of thunder. "I could feel it coming. The air was so still. Thick, like you could cut it with a knife. I wanted to see the storm."

Silently, he stood beside her. He thought to put his arm around her shoulders, but something told him she didn't wish to be held.

"I'll miss these storms." She turned to look at him, her face spotlighted by another flash of lightning. "Do you know how many things I'm gonna miss about bein' here?"

He had no reply. He tried to pretend she was talking about leaving the basin, but he knew she wasn't.

"But I'll be with Charlie, so I guess I won't mind so much." Her fingers lightly touched Gavin's shoulder. "It makes the goin' not so hard when you love somebody the way I love Charlie. Can you understand that?"

He couldn't. He'd tried, but he couldn't.

The wind increased. Dru's hair billowed out behind her. Black clouds, turned silver by the lightning, rolled overhead.

"It wasn't right of me to ask you t'marry me, Gavin. You should've had a chance to find what Charlie and I shared. If it weren't for my girls . . ."

"I wanted to do it," he replied gruffly. "I'll do my best by Brina and Pet. They'll never want for anything."

Her face was turned up toward the sky. "Lovin's the only thing that makes sense in this old world, Gav. Only thing worth livin' or dyin' for." She turned suddenly, piercing him with a shrewd gaze. "What happened that made you so determined never to love a woman?"

His gut tightened. "I care about you, Dru."

She stepped toward him, placing her hand on his forearm. Her voice was softer now, her look somehow pleading. "I know you care. You care 'cause I was Charlie's wife and we were all family. You care for me as you would a sister if you'd had one. But that's not the kind of lovin' I'm talkin' about, Gavin. Just carin's not enough for a man like you."

"I like things just fine the way they are."

Dru leaned her head against his chest, whispering, "No you don't, Gav. No you don't."

She'd been awakened by Joker's scratching at her door. The moment she opened it, the big wolfhound had leapt onto her bed and burrowed under the covers. Suddenly, a loud crack of thunder shook the house. Rachel squealed and was about to close the door and jump into bed with Joker when she noticed the front door was wide open. She rushed across the room, prepared to close it quickly.

She saw them standing in the middle of the yard, Dru's head resting against Gavin's bare chest, his arms around her back as he stared up at the sky. There was something poignant, something overwhelmingly powerful about the scene that caught at Rachel's throat and made tears burn her eyes.

She took a quick step backward, then spun around and returned to her room, where she crawled beneath the blankets. She didn't bother to push Joker off the bed. She felt a sudden need not to be alone. Even that mangy hound was better than nothing—or no one.

In her mind, she kept seeing that strange expression on Gavin's face. Pain. It was filled with pain. She couldn't imagine a man like Gavin Blake feeling pain of any kind. She wished she could . . .

What? What did she wish she could do?

And in her mind's eye, she envisioned them— her and Gavin—standing together in the wind, beneath the crashing heavens, the earth shaking beneath their feet. She could feel the muscles of his chest beneath her cheek, hear the rapid beating of her heart, knew the moment she would look up at him and he would bend slowly forward and their lips . . .

Heat turned her cheeks scarlet. She pressed her cool fingers against her flesh and willed the image to go away. She couldn't be thinking such things about her employer, about another woman's husband. She wouldn't *allow* herself to think such things.

But she couldn't stop herself. She still imagined his arms around her, pressing her tightly against him.

"Stop!" she whispered, squeezing her eyes closed.

Joker whined and inched his way up until his muzzle was near her face. Rachel pressed her forehead behind his ear.

"Please go away," she whispered, but she didn't mean the dog.

Dru listened to Gavin's steady breathing and knew he was asleep at last. She let a tired sigh slip past her lips. She supposed she should try to sleep, too, but she felt the wasting away of time. She would have eternity to rest. She wanted to live now, while she still could. There was so much she still had to get done.

She heard Gavin shift on his cot. She turned her head toward the sound, gazing in his direction even though she couldn't see across the dark bedroom.

Strange. She'd known him for over five years now. He'd been a part of the Porter family, much more than just a friend. Charlie and Gavin had been like brothers. When things had been at their blackest for Dru, he'd been there. He'd been there to help comfort her when Charlie's son was stillborn. He'd eased her pain when Charlie died not long after. He'd been her rock when they first learned she was dying. Finally, he'd even married her to make sure her daughters had a home when she was gone, given them all his name and the security that went with it.

All this, and still she knew so little about him. If it weren't for what information she'd pried out of Stubs over the years, she wouldn't know anything about his past at all. It was Stubs who'd told her that Gavin's parents had divorced when he was a boy and that he never spoke about his mother. A woman's instinct had filled in the rest.

She knew there was a world of hurt inside the man Gavin had become. She knew he'd chosen to remain detached from women, sworn never to marry. If she hadn't become ill, he would have kept that promise too. And it was a shame. He had so darned much love to give, but he held it in, never let anyone get too close.

Except for Sabrina and Petula. Dru smiled into the darkness. Gavin couldn't hold his love for the girls in check. He was scared about raising them alone, afraid he didn't know how to be a father. He didn't talk about it, but she knew he was scared. She wasn't worried. She'd seen him acting like a father long before Charlie died. It was the one time he was truly happy, when he was playing with the girls.

What he needed now was a woman to share the rest of his love and to love him in return.

Her thoughts strayed across the silent house to the other bedroom—Gavin's room before they'd gone to Boise to hire a governess. She hoped and prayed her instincts had been right about Miss Harris. She wouldn't have another chance.

Dru rolled onto her side and hugged the

pillow to her breast as she pictured Rachel. She was incredibly beautiful. Anyone—man or woman—would have to be blind and half dead not to think so. Of course, if looks were all she had, Dru never would have brought her back with them. Rachel Harris had gumption, too, and she was bright and witty. As they'd sat in that room at the Overland Hotel, talking about Rachel's sister and her husband and their children, Rachel had revealed more about herself than she'd realized. She was a young woman with a lot of love to give to those around her, but she wasn't out to just marry any man that came along. When she married, it would be for love and forever.

Just like her and Charlie.

I don't have much left to do, Charlie, she thought as she closed her eyes. *You always said Gavin deserved the best. Well, I think maybe I've found her for him. She's gonna be good with our girls, too. She'll love 'em and make sure they don't forget us. Just a little more time so I can get 'em pointed in the right direction, and then I can come to you. Just a little more time, Charlie.*

She drifted off to sleep.

Rachel scarcely slept all night—and when she did, she was troubled by strange dreams of Gavin Blake. He seemed to be scowling at her, his expression dark and censuring. An unknown danger seemed to lurk in the steel gray of his eyes. And yet she wasn't afraid. Rather, she was drawn toward him. When she awakened for the third time, the dream always the same, her heart hammering madly in her chest, she decided it was better not to sleep.

She pushed aside the blankets and rose from the bed. The previous night's thunderstorm had been followed by a drenching rain. The air in her room felt chill and damp, and she shivered as she hurried toward the makeshift dresser. She didn't waste any time selecting what clothes she would wear. She just wanted to get dressed and get out of this room. She needed a deep breath of fresh air to clear her head.

Tying her flowing blond hair at the nape of her neck with a narrow scarf, Rachel slipped from her bedroom and through the sitting room. She lifted the latch with care, trying not to make any sound in the still house, then pulled open the door.

Dawn had painted the lingering storm clouds the color of grapes and poppies and dandelions. Moisture, crystallized by the crisp morning air, sparkled from every tree limb and fence pole and eave. The horses in the corral huddled together, their heads drooping toward the ground, their breath forming small white clouds beneath their muzzles.

Rachel wrapped her arms across her chest and hurried forward, not taking the time to return to her room for a wrap. By the time she stepped inside the barn, her teeth were chattering with cold.

She paused as the door closed behind her, drawing a deep breath. There. That was better. The quick walk across the yard had cleared her head. It was silly of her to be so disturbed by her dreams. They meant nothing. Just an over-active imagination and probably something she ate.

"Good morning, Miss Harris."

She gasped as she turned toward the deep voice.

Gavin was standing inside the stall beside the orphaned calf. "You're up mighty early," he said as he opened the gate and stepped out.

"I . . . I wanted to see Sabrina's calf."

One brow arched, his face held a clearly dubious expression. "I had no idea you were so fond of it."

She felt the blush rising from her neck and fought to control it. "I'm not," she replied in an indignant tone. "But Sabrina is, and anything that interests the children interests me." She moved forward, her head held erect, her eyes avoiding his.

As she stepped up beside him, his hand fell upon her shoulder, stopping her. Unable to help herself, she lifted her head to look up at him. His gray eyes stared down at her, seemingly merciless in their perusal. The change was minute, but she would have sworn she saw a softening within the steely depths.

"I believe you mean that, Miss Harris," he said softly.

"I do mean it, Mr. Blake, or I never would have taken this job." She glanced at his hand on her shoulder. It was warm. The fabric of her bodice seemed almost nonexistent, as if her flesh and his . . .She looked up at him quickly, her eyes wide and uncertain. She didn't understand why he made her feel this way.

Gavin withdrew his hand, the slight scowl returning to his face. "You'd better get back to the house before you catch cold."

"It's not cold in the barn," she softly replied, her voice quivering.

Did he draw closer? It felt as if he did, yet she knew he hadn't moved. Although she never took her eyes from his face, she was intensely aware of the breadth of his shoulders, the strength of his arms. There was a strange roaring in her ears.

"Go back to the house, Miss Harris," he said in a low voice. "It's colder out here than you think."

Her throat felt tight. She swallowed and turned away from him. "Yes," she whispered. "I'm afraid you're right." She forced her feet to walk slowly, but with her heart, she fled.

Chapter Eight

Rachel looked up from the book she'd been reading. The room was wrapped in silence while the usually boisterous girls concentrated on their studies.

Petula was scrunched over her slate, a piece of chalk pinched tightly between chubby fingers. Her mouth was screwed up in concentration as she tried to copy her teacher's letters.

Rachel smiled to herself. The little girl would have the alphabet conquered in no time. Petula was determined and bright and very eager to learn.

Her gaze shifted to the opposite end of the table, where Sabrina sat. The tip of the girl's tongue could be seen in the corner of her mouth as she frowned down at the math figures. She wrinkled her nose, and her freckles seemed to darken as they drew closer together.

Rachel was filled with a wonderful feeling of satisfaction. She had never dreamed she would enjoy teaching so much. If she had, she would have made it her vocation long ago. She didn't know why so many people regarded teaching as something suitable only for young, as yet unmarried women or aging spinsters who would never marry. It was so exciting to see the children's eyes light with understanding, to answer their questions, to expand their horizons. There were so many things to share with them. So many wonderful things to share.

This must have been why she came here. To discover how she felt about teaching. This must be her destiny. When she returned home in the spring, she thought, she would apply for a teaching position.

Her gaze focused once again on her two students. The idea of leaving these girls was not a pleasant one. She'd grown immensely attached to them in the short time she'd been here. And spring would come all too quickly. It wasn't nearly enough time to teach them all they would need to learn. Not nearly enough time.

A door closed softly and Rachel turned her head toward the sound. Dru smiled as their eyes met, but she didn't speak as she made her way across the sitting room to a chair near the fireplace. She pulled a lap rug over her knees, then leaned back against the chair and closed her eyes.

Rachel continued to watch the woman. In the four days since Gavin and the other men had left with the cattle, she had come to realize just how ill Dru was. The moment her husband had ridden away, the strength had seemed to ebb from her. Her face looked older, more tired. Her shoulders were stooped. She smiled less often; only her daughters brought a look of joy into her eyes.

Rachel had wanted to ask Dru exactly what was wrong but hadn't had the courage. Perhaps it wasn't as serious as it appeared. Dru was probably merely missing her husband. It was sadness Rachel saw on her face, not stress and pain. Surely that was all there was to it.

"Miss Harris . . ." An index finger poked her arm.

Rachel turned her head to meet Petula's sparkling brown eyes.

"I did 'em." She held out the slate. "I did 'em all. Just like yours."

"Why, Pet, these are very good. I had no idea you would learn so fast. Your mother wasn't exaggerating when she said you were bright."

Petula's head cocked to one side. "What's exag . . . exagger . . ."

"Exaggeration. It means to make things seem bigger or better than they really are."

"You mean *lie*?" The girl's eyes widened. She shook her head, her expression serious. "Ma wouldn't never tell a lie."

Rachel laughed as she smoothed Petula's hair back from her face. "Oh, I know that. She certainly didn't lie about you and Brina. You're both so pretty and smart. And it's wouldn't *ever* tell a lie."

"Girls?"

They all turned at the sound of Dru's voice.

"I think you could take a break from your lessons and get some fresh air. Why don't you take Miss Harris for a ride up to the ridge? You might not have another chance, as cold as the weather's turnin'."

The frown of concentration instantly disappeared from Sabrina's face as she jumped up from the table. "Will you come too, Ma?" she asked. "We could take a picnic lunch."

"No, darling. I think I'll stay here and rest. I'm a mite tired today. But I think a picnic's a good idea for you."

"Maybe we shouldn't go, Mrs. Blake." Rachel rose from her chair and stepped toward the fireplace.

"Nonsense. I could use some peace and quiet." Dru smiled faintly. "Go on and have some fun. It's good for the children to get to know you better. I don't want them thinkin' that bein' with you always means work. Not when you've got so much fun in you to share."

She supposed it made sense, yet she still didn't feel quite right about it. But the wheels— in the persons of Sabrina and Petula—had been set into motion, and there didn't seem to be any stopping them. The two girls had already scampered up the ladder to their loft bedroom, moments later returning with britches on beneath their skirts.

"We'll get the horses into the barn and brush 'em down," Sabrina told her. "Pet and me can do most of it, but you'll have to help with the saddles. I'm not very good with the cinch." A shadow of doubt darkened her eyes. "Can you *do* that?"

"I'm an excellent horsewoman, Sabrina Blake. I can certainly help you with the saddles. Let me change into riding attire, and I'll be right with you." The moment the front door closed, Rachel cast a glance toward Dru once again. "Is there anything I can get you before we go?"

Dru shook her head, not bothering to reopen her eyes. "Just take care of my girls," she answered softly. "When I'm not around, just take care of my girls."

"Mrs. Blake?" Rachel took another step forward. "Are you certain . . ."

Dru looked at her then. "Go on," she said, her voice stronger, more forceful than Rachel had heard in days. "I'm just going to enjoy my few minutes of peace, all to myself. You get on up to the ridge. It's our favorite spot 'round here. Take some of them dried apples and some cheese and bread. You'll likely all have an appetite by the time you get there." She smiled warmly at Rachel. "Go have some fun. Winter will keep us cooped up in the same room soon enough."

Suddenly a ride in the crisp mountain air sounded just like what she needed. She returned Dru's smile, then hurried to change.

Gavin slowed his horse as he approached the log cabin. He'd left Stubs and Jess with the herd along the Salmon River yesterday. They'd be able to get the cows up to the Lucky Strike without his help. Duke and Duchess knew how to work the cantankerous beasts as well as any cow dogs he'd ever seen. They were as good as a half dozen more cowboys. Maybe better.

It hadn't taken much encouragement from Stubs for Gavin to turn around and head back to the basin. He'd been anxious to return. Things had been quiet on the summer range this year, but he still didn't like leaving the women and children alone for long. The Bannock Indians had caused trouble before, and there were always a few strangers—miners mostly— wandering through. With the men gone with the cattle, there wasn't anyone there to protect them if trouble came.

Rachel stepped out of the cabin, instantly bringing his other thoughts to an abrupt halt. She was wearing a powder-blue wool riding habit with a matching bonnet swathed in a darker blue netting. She looked for all the world like some society debutante about to go riding in a city park. She looked like a woman who always got what she wanted, simply because she was beautiful.

He pulled his gelding to an abrupt halt, an old anger welling in his chest.

To be honest, it wasn't because she made him remember things he'd rather forget that bothered him as much as it was the way she'd begun to haunt his thoughts. When he should have been anxious to return to Dru and the girls, it had been Rachel's face that had continually come to mind.

As he watched, she checked the cinch on the rotund mare, then gave it a tug. With a wave of her hand, she motioned the children closer, lifting first Sabrina and then Petula onto the back of the docile steed. He saw her smile up at them, heard her laughter over something Sabrina said. He could imagine the merry twinkle in her eye. He'd seen it often in the few days she'd been with the children.

She turned away, moving aside the train of her riding habit with a tiny kick. It was an easy, graceful movement, as he'd come to expect from Rachel Harris. She mounted Dru's palomino mare with practiced ease, hooking her right knee over the pommel and ignoring the extra stirrup.

Fool woman. That was no way to ride a horse out here. If she had any sense, she'd know that.

He nudged his gelding forward.

Dru came outside just as he was riding into the yard. "Gavin!" She hurried up to his horse. "We didn't expect you back until tomorrow." She laid her hand on his knee. "You're just in time to go with Miss Harris and the girls up to the ridge."

His gaze flicked to Rachel, then back to Dru. "You coming too?"

"No."

"Maybe I'd better stay here."

"Please come, Pa," Sabrina urged.

"Yes, please," Petula chimed in.

"Perhaps your father is too tired," Rachel interrupted with a soft but firm voice. "You should let him rest, girls. I'm sure we'll do fine on our own, and Joker will be with us."

It irritated him that she'd used all his own

excuses before he could. And for the same purpose. So he could stay behind.

Dru's voice lowered. "Go with them, Gav. It'll be good for the girls to have some time with you."

He heard the slight pleading in her words and knew she was right. "We won't be long."

"Take all the time you want." Dru smiled.

"Bye, Ma," Petula shouted as the mare moved forward, guided by Sabrina.

"Have fun," Dru responded, lifting a hand to wave.

He didn't imagine that spending a few hours in Rachel Harris's company would be fun. Just looking at her fancy blue dress made him mad. Flashing her finery around Dru and the girls, as if making sure they knew she was different. The less he was around her, the better he'd like it.

"Gavin?"

He turned to look back at Dru.

"Give Rachel a chance. Whatever's stuck in your craw isn't her fault. There's a lot about that young woman to like."

He nodded but made no reply as he tightened his heels against the gelding's ribs and started after the other three.

She could feel his gaze on her back, as tangible as a touch of his fingers would be. For some strange reason, she found it hard to breathe, harder still to concentrate on the children's prattle. Why did he have to come back when he did? She didn't want him along. Being in his company was always the same—disturbing.

"Look, Miss Harris."

"What is it, Brina?" She focused her gaze on the girl.

Sabrina was pointing toward the tree line, where emerald-green forest turned suddenly to the gray, jutting crags of the Sawtooth peaks. "The sheep. Up there. See him?"

"Sheep?" Rachel squinted, trying to find what the girl was looking at high above them.

At last, she did find it, but the heavy-bodied animal didn't look like any sheep she'd ever seen. It reminded her more of a short, squat deer with its brown coat and white rump. It *could* have been a deer except for its head. Even from this distance, she could see the crown of massive, spiraling horns.

"It's a bighorn, Miss Harris," Gavin said as he rode up beside her. "The Sheepeater Indians were named for them 'cause they make such good eating. I agree with the Indians. The bighorn's better than mutton. We eat them more often around here than our own cattle. Pretty easy to hunt except when they climb up this high."

She was only partially aware of what he was telling her.

He has a very handsome mouth.

Rachel felt her breathing quicken once again as she looked away. Whatever was wrong with her to be thinking such things? She didn't even like the man. How could she, when he'd made it so clear he didn't like or approve of her? He'd been rude and abrupt with her since the day they first met.

But the rapid beat of her heart didn't slow nor the terrible awareness of how near he was to her. Should her horse take a slight step to the left, their boots might even chance to touch.

Stop it, she scolded herself, lifting her chin in determination.

She drew a deep breath of air into her lungs as she nudged her horse to the right. She concentrated on the terrain around her as the horses picked their way up a heavily treed trail, giant pines towering around them, blocking out the sunlight. The mountain silence was broken only by their passing. She could hear the breathing of the horses and the crunch of their hooves on the deep carpet of dried needles and Joker's occasional bark as he raced ahead, then returned to circle the horses. The scent of pine was sharp, pungent, delightful. The cool breeze made her cheeks tingle.

Slowly, she became aware of the children once again. She listened as they chattered easily, moving from one story to another so quickly she was often confused but definitely entertained. She almost succeeded in forgetting Gavin Blake was even with them.

Almost.

Gavin thought the expression on Rachel's face when she looked down at the basin from the ridge made the long trip up the mountainside worth it all. Her blue eyes widened, her mouth opened to release an amazed sigh before curling into an enchanting smile.

"It's spectacular," she whispered. "I never imagined it could be so beautiful. No wonder Dru loves it so."

From the ridge, they had a clear view of the rocky mountain sentinels that surrounded the basin. Through the dense forests, they caught glimpses of the crystal-clear lakes that dotted the area, the icy waters fed by melting glaciers. They could see the winding ribbon of the Salmon River, weaving its way through the tall grasses of the valley floor.

The bright colors of autumn were especially apparent from this vantage point. Reds and oranges and yellows were splashed among the forest greens, aspen and birch clapping their leafy hands in the breeze, as if applauding the new season.

"It's so . . . so untouched," Rachel said, her tone almost reverent.

Gavin stepped down from the saddle and walked over to her horse. He lifted his hands. "Let me help you down. There's a spot over there where you can see even better."

Their eyes met momentarily, then she leaned forward, her hands on his shoulders, allowing him to lower her to the ground. She was light, yet there was something real and solid about her. Not like Dru, who was wasting away so quickly. The light breeze ruffled the net of her bonnet and teased him with whiffs of her honeysuckle cologne. Her eyes looked bright, excited.

"Thank you, Mr. Blake."

It wasn't until she pulled away that he realized he'd still been holding onto her waist. His hands felt suddenly empty. He rubbed his palms on his trouser legs and turned toward the children's voices, hoping they could distract him from the odd feeling of loss that suddenly filled him.

Chapter Nine

It wasn't easy being the oldest. When you're older, you know things your little sister doesn't know. Sometimes you hear the adults talking when they think you're asleep. Or sometimes they think you're not smart enough to understand. And sometimes you just know things without anybody telling you anything at all, on purpose or by accident.

Like when Sabrina was seven and her pa was gored by the bull. Not Gavin, her new pa, but her real pa, Charlie Porter. She'd heard her ma's weeping after Mr. Stubs and Mr. Chamberlain brought him in on the back of the wagon, and she'd known he was dying. She hadn't had to be told. She'd just known.

She'd been just as sure of his dying as she was of her ma's. Nobody ever talked about her ma being sick, of course, but she was. Ma tried to hide it, tried real hard, but Sabrina still knew. Ma wasn't going to live much longer.

That's what made today so special. Sabrina didn't have to think of those things. She didn't have to see her ma getting thinner and weaker. She could pretend for a little while that nobody got sick and died, not Pa or Ma or anybody else. She could pretend that her ma was as healthy and pretty as Miss Harris and that she could run and play games and laugh a lot—just like Miss Harris.

"She'd be plenty scared," Petula whispered into Sabrina's ear.

"Think so?"

"Ah-ha."

"She'd probably scream for Pa."

There was a mischievous gleam in Petula's eyes. "Let's see."

Stifling her giggles, Sabrina agreed.

The two girls squatted behind the large tree, trying to stay quiet so Rachel wouldn't know where they were. They waited for what seemed an eternity before they heard her voice calling through the trees.

"Brina! Pet! It's time to go."

Sabrina squeezed Petula's hand, excitement racing between them, hazel eyes sparkling, brown eyes twinkling in return.

"Come on, girls. Your mother will be worried." Her voice was closer this time.

Sabrina nodded at her little sister. In unison, they jumped up and raced around the tree and down the path toward Rachel. "A bear!" Sabrina cried. "There's a bear after us!"

"It's gonna eat us!" Petula shouted.

They had expected Rachel to turn and run away with them, calling for their pa's help. Instead, she grabbed each of them by their hands, drawing them to a sudden halt and forcing them to stand beside her.

"Really?" she said, peering up the trail. "I've never seen a bear before. Let's wait and have a look at him. Is he very big? What color is he?"

Sabrina felt a flash of panic, suddenly believing she *would* see a bear any moment. Why were they just standing there?

"You know, girls," Rachel whispered without looking at them, her tone ominous, "when you're planning to scare someone, always make sure they're not listening on the other side of the tree. It spoils the surprise." She dropped their hands and tapped Sabrina and Petula on top of their heads. "Tag! You're both it."

Lifting the hem of her riding habit, her laughter trailing behind her, Rachel raced off down the trail. The two girls turned startled expressions on each other, then took out after their governess with shouts and laughter of their own.

Gavin turned from the horses just in time to see Rachel come running out of the trees. She had removed her hat earlier and now her hair had tumbled free of its pinnings. It flew out behind her like pale gold wings. Her laughter rang like clear bells in a mountain cathedral.

Sabrina appeared just as suddenly, her arm outstretched, obviously intent on tagging her governess. Petula's shouts were heard long before her short legs carried her into the clearing. But Rachel was far too quick for either of them. There was no hope of Sabrina catching her, let alone Petula.

Except Joker entered the picture at that exact moment, his excited barks added to the shouts and laughter. The big hound bounded between Rachel and Sabrina, then turned to run a circle around Rachel. She tried to stop, but it was too late. She tripped over the dog just as Sabrina, in hot pursuit, hurled herself through the air. They fell to the ground in a jumble of skirts, then the two of them were tumbling head over heels down the grassy incline, Petula scurrying after them.

Gavin sprinted forward, but by the time he reached them, their giggles told him no one was hurt.

"You're it, Miss Harris," Sabrina managed to say as she gasped for air.

"Yeah, you're it, Miss Harris," Petula parroted.

Rachel touched their cheeks with her fingertips, first Petula, then Sabrina. "I guess so," she responded breathlessly, smiling all the while.

Her face was flushed with color. Her tousled hair was filled with dried grass. There was a smudge of dirt on the tip of her chin, and her grosgrain cravat was all askew.

"Where is he?" she asked, her smile suddenly fading.

She glanced up at Gavin, and he thought for a moment she was angry with him.

Then she swung her head around. "Ah! So there you are."

Joker lay on the ground a few feet away. His chin was buried in the grass, and his dark eyes watched her apologetically as his tail slapped the ground in a slow rhythm.

"Benedict Arnold."

Joker whined and inched his way forward.

"Don't think you'll win my forgiveness so easily." Rachel turned her head away, her pert nose pointed into the air.

Joker slinked across the remaining distance, then laid his chin on Rachel's thigh, his ears flat against his head, his eyes pleading for absolution.

Gavin found himself waiting with the same rapt attention as the girls.

Rachel glanced down at the young wolf-hound, one eyebrow cocked, her head tilted to one side. "This time, you mangy hound," she said softly as her hand smoothed the wiry hair on top of his head. "But don't you turn traitor on me again."

Joker's tail smacked the ground in double time.

Children's laughter filled the air again as Petula fell on Joker, joined quickly by Sabrina. The oversized pup was on his feet in a flash, jumping away before flinging himself back into their midst. Then he was up and running, the two girls hard on his heels.

Rachel clapped her hands together, laughing gaily, her sky-blue eyes sparkling with mischief and pleasure.

It hit Gavin then. Perhaps she wasn't at all what he'd suspected. Perhaps she wasn't spoiled or vain or selfish. She was definitely lovely and vibrant and fun. Maybe Dru was right. There was plenty about this young woman to like.

Possibly too much.

He held out his hand to her. "Let me help you, Miss Harris."

She glanced up at him, laughter still lighting her eyes. "Thank you." She took hold of his hand, and he pulled her effortlessly to her feet.

"I promise to have a long talk with Joker when we get back to the house." He leaned closer, his voice falling to a confidential whisper. "I thought that boy had better manners than to trip a lady."

Rachel's eyes widened a fraction, her smile faded slightly. "Yes," she replied, sounding breathless once again. "You should do that, Mr. Blake."

"Gavin. Call me Gavin."

Whatever she might have said was interrupted by the return of barking dog and laughing children.

Rachel felt as if she might suddenly explode. Her nerve endings were screaming. It was hard to breathe, and her pulse was racing madly.

Her eyes fell on Gavin's back as he led the way down the mountainside. He rode his horse with an easy grace, his body moving in time with the animal. She could sense his strength even from this distance, felt his alertness as his head turned occasionally from side to side.

110

Call me Gavin. Her heartbeat did a little somersault as she recalled the warm resonance of his voice.

It couldn't be, of course. She couldn't be feeling this way about Gavin Blake.

He turned in the saddle. Their eyes met over the top of the children's heads. Her heart did another little hiccup.

Lord help her! It couldn't be this. It couldn't be now.

But it was. As clearly as she'd always known she was waiting for something special to happen to her, she knew that this was it. She'd been waiting for this fantastically wretched feeling. She'd been waiting to fall in love. But she was feeling it for the wrong man.

She glanced away from him, afraid of what he might see if she continued looking into those steely gray depths. She stared at the slick carpet of pine needles beneath the palomino's hooves, but her thoughts couldn't be controlled so easily. She kept remembering the sound of Gavin's voice, the warmth of his breath on her face as he'd leaned closer, the jaunty look of his black hair as it brushed his shirt collar, the shadow of a beard beneath his tanned skin.

What was she to do?

Suddenly, the magnificent mountains surrounding the valley had become menacing barriers, allowing no escape from the emotions that threatened to consume her.

Maggie, what do I do?

She closed her eyes, imagining herself back in the safety of her room at the Branigan ranch.

Her sister would know what to tell her. She'd always been able to count on Maggie. Her sister had raised her, shielded her from their abusive uncle, brought her West across the Oregon Trail and into the safe, loving arms of the Branigan clan. Maggie would be able to tell her what to do, if only she could get to her.

Why hadn't she listened to Maggie when she advised Rachel against coming? Why had she been so blasted stubborn, so determined to come to this wilderness with these strangers?

Her fingers tightened around the reins. Love might be that special something she'd been expecting, but her destiny couldn't be with another woman's husband. She wouldn't allow herself to feel this way. She would simply have to take control of the emotion.

Call me Gavin.

It was like the ground dropping out from under her, this feeling he caused within her. She was suddenly afraid she couldn't control the way she felt.

She wasn't prepared for this. She wasn't supposed to fall in love with a man who could never be hers. It was wrong. She had no right to feel this way.

She would have to leave. Despite her promise to Dru that she would stay through spring, she would have to return to Boise. Because if she didn't, something terrible was going to happen.

Already she could feel her heart breaking.

Chapter Ten

The temperature dropped sharply before the sun reached the horizon. By nightfall, the sky was hidden behind thick black clouds. A stillness blanketed the basin, making every sound inside the log house seem out of place, an intrusion upon nature.

Rachel pulled the warm quilt up from the foot of the bed. "Snuggle close. It's going to be cold tonight," she told the two girls, then leaned forward to kiss their foreheads beneath their white nightcaps.

She felt a sting in the region of her heart. She was going to miss them. She'd grown to love them in the short time they'd been together. Was it really just over a week since she'd arrived in the basin? Not even ten days, yet she felt as if

113

they'd been together ever so much longer than that.

"Good night," she whispered as she straightened.

"Miss Harris?"

"What is it, Pet?"

"I'm glad you wasn't scared about the bear. You're sure lots of fun."

She swallowed the lump in her throat. "Thanks, Pet. Good night, Brina. See you in the morning."

"Night, Miss Harris," came the two voices in unison.

Holding her skirt out of the way, she turned and eased herself onto the ladder leading down from the loft. When her feet touched the wood floor, she breathed a quiet sigh of relief and turned around just as the front door blew open, allowing Gavin entry. His hat and shoulders were dusted with crystals of snow.

Gavin closed the door quickly, then removed his hat and slapped it against his leg. "Good thing we got the herd out when we did. That's quite the storm blowing in."

His nose and cheeks were red with cold. His shaggy black hair, damp from snow and tousled from his hat, curled against the back of his neck and fell across his forehead. He desperately needed a shave.

And he was the most devastatingly handsome man she'd ever seen.

Rachel looked toward the fire. "It was so beautiful today. I never dreamed it could snow."

"Weather's sudden in these parts." He

shucked off his heavy coat and hung it on the peg near the door. "Where's Dru?"

"She was tired and went to bed."

Their eyes met briefly.

"I'll check in on her," Gavin said, walking swiftly toward his bedroom.

Rachel's heart continued to race as she crossed the room and moved aside the curtain to peer outside. Tiny snowflakes, blown before an icy wind, had already covered the ground with a light frosting. She couldn't see the barn or the corral through the blowing snow. She felt isolated from the world, as if all that existed were within these walls.

She heard the bedroom door close behind her. Her heart was doing those funny flip-flops in her chest again. "How's Mrs. Blake?" she asked without turning around.

"Asleep."

The lid of the wood box creaked as it was opened. She heard the crackle of fire and pitch as new logs were added to the flames. A chair scraped against the floor as it was dragged closer to the hearth.

Rachel turned around. He was seated on the edge of the spindle-backed chair, leaning forward, his forearms braced on his thighs. He was staring into the fire, the light dancing across his face, eerie shadows darkening his craggy features.

What would it be like to have the right to love this man?

She moved away from the window, feeling suddenly chilled so far from the fire. "It doesn't snow this early in Boise," she said softly, a slight quiver in her voice.

"It won't last long. A few days, week maybe." He glanced up at her as she settled onto the rocker opposite him.

"A week?" She'd planned to leave. She'd planned to tell them in the morning that she was going home.

Gavin raked his fingers through his hair, then nodded. "Could be longer, but I imagine we'll be up to the Lucky Strike before the end of October." He rubbed his hands together as a frown settled across his brow. "Never should've let Dru talk me into staying. No way to get a doctor to her if she'd need one."

"Gavin . . ." She leaned forward and lightly touched her fingertips to the back of his hand. "What's wrong with Dru?"

She was taken aback by the pain she read in his eyes as he looked at her. Despite the strange sensations swirling through her as a result of their touch, she didn't pull away. Instead, she closed her hand over his.

"Please tell me," she whispered.

"She's got a cancer. The doctors we've seen . . . none of 'em think she'll live 'til spring."

If Dru dies, he'll be free.

Rachel pulled her hand away from him as if she'd been burned. She was horrified that such a thought had ever entered her mind. How could she be so selfish when a woman was dying?

"Don't worry, Miss Harris," Gavin said sharply. "It's not contagious." He was glaring at her with scorn-filled eyes.

"I never meant . . . I'm sorry. I was just shocked. I never dreamed she . . . I . . . I'm so sorry."

His expression softened a little. "It's all right. I guess I thought you knew how sick she was."

There was so much she didn't know. Most of all she didn't know what to do with her feelings for him. Even now, she had to fight the urge to throw her arms around him, to kiss his forehead and hold his head against her breast, to comfort him from the pain he was feeling, to love him tonight and forever.

"I have to go," she said softly.

"Good night," he responded, looking once more into the fire.

That's not what I meant, Gavin. I meant I have to go. I have to leave this place.

"Good night, Gavin." She rose and hurried to the safety of her room.

Gavin heard the closing of the bedroom door even as he closed his eyes and rubbed his fingers in tiny circles over his temples. Why did he react to Rachel that way? Always expecting the worst from her.

But then, with the exception of Dru, Gavin always expected the worst from women. Always had. Well, maybe not always. Just since he was ten.

It started to snow early in the morning, and it was soon clear there was a real blizzard in the

making. The teacher sent her students home before the storm could get any worse.

Gavin was surprised to see the fancy black
buggy hitched up in front of the house. Mr. Hannah knew his pa was in Cincinnati and wouldn't
be back until the end of the week. Besides, they
always did business at Mr. Hannah's fancy house
in the middle of town.

When he went in the house, the parlor was
empty. Then he heard strange noises coming from
the bedroom. It sounded like his ma was trying to
scream but couldn't. Alarmed, he made his way to
the back of the house and pushed open the door.
There they were, Mr. Hannah and his ma, in bed
together, both naked as jaybirds. When she saw
him, his ma cursed at him and ordered him out.

He stood and watched, confused and scared,
when Christina Blake and Mr. Hannah came out
of the bedroom minutes later. His ma was holding
a worn carpet bag in her hand. She glared at him
for a moment, then walked on by.

Gavin jumped up from his chair and strode
toward the window. He swept the curtains aside.
Already there was close to an inch of snow on
the ground with no signs of its stopping.

It had been a lot like that the day his mother
left to live with Mr. Hannah.

His pa'd said Christina Blake always did hate
living on the farm. She'd always wanted to be
rich, and when Mr. Hannah had come along,
there'd been little she wouldn't have done to
become his wife. Gavin's father hadn't even
tried to stop the divorce, but he'd never gotten
over it either. He'd turned to drink and wal-

lowed in self-pity until the day he died.

Come to think of it, it had snowed that day too.

His pa was buried. The farm was lost. There wasn't anything for Gavin to do but move on. He had no family . . . except for his ma. And he hadn't talked to her in four years, not since the day she walked out of the house.

With old newspaper, he wrapped up the photo of his ma and pa and him that had always hung on the wall of his parents' bedroom. With a canvas bag containing all his worldly goods, he set off for the Hannah mansion in the midst of town.

He wouldn't ever forget what she looked like that day. She was wearing a shiny blue-and-white striped gown. Jewels sparkled at her throat and on her ears. Her pale blond hair was swept up from her neck. She looked absolutely regal. The most beautiful thing he'd ever seen.

Her cool blue eyes had perused him as they stood in the entry hall. "You look like your father. He was a handsome man too."

Gavin handed her the photo wrapped in newspaper.

She lifted an imperious brow, then opened the package. She stared at the picture for a moment. "Too bad he wasn't as rich as he was handsome," she said. With an outstretched arm, she held the photo up, then dropped it unceremoniously into a wastebasket.

His mother's gesture had been burned forever into his memory. Even now, nearly twenty years later, it brought the same bitterness to his chest. He'd never forgotten, would never forgive.

Rachel resembled Christina Blake a little.

Both of them beautifully blonde and blue-eyed. Both of them classically lovely.

There. He'd acknowledged it. Stubs had started to point it out that first day they arrived, but Gavin hadn't let him say it. He didn't want to admit he was predisposed to dislike her. She was beautiful and privileged and should have been spoiled and self-centered—just like Christina Blake. Only she kept surprising him, doing and saying things he never would have expected from her.

He turned from the window, his eyes moving toward Rachel's bedroom. A thin spray of light fanned out beneath the door. She .was still awake.

He remembered the concern in her eyes as they'd sat beside the fire, recalled too sharply the rising desire that had flooded through him. Lord, how he'd wanted her. He'd wanted to kiss that moist, rose-colored mouth. He'd wanted to remove the pins from her hair and see it tumbling around her shoulders as it had up on the ridge. He'd wanted . . .

Gavin made a sound of disgust as he returned to his chair by the fire.

Who was he kidding? It wasn't Rachel who was like his mother. It was him. He was married to Dru and lusting after Rachel. He'd known when he married Dru that they wouldn't be sharing the intimacies of marriage. They couldn't risk a pregnancy. It would kill her for sure . . . and the child too. Besides, Dru was still in love with Charlie.

Gavin had agreed with the conditions of this marriage, had even welcomed them. But how could he have known he would meet a woman who would create such a wanting in him?

God help me, he thought as he rested his head in his hands. *God help me*.

Chapter Eleven

By morning there was nearly a foot of snow on the ground, and the white flakes were still drifting to earth, this time without the wind to blow them.

As she stood at the window, watching the falling snow, Rachel decided there was no point in telling the Blakes about her decision to return to Boise until it was possible for her to do so. She would just continue instructing the children and helping Dru with the household chores. In fact, she decided, she would take on the lion's portion of duties so Dru could rest.

She hated to think she might be doing so out of guilt, but the thought did occur to her. She was still ashamed of that moment of unbridled hope when she realized Gavin would one day be a widower, a man free to love another woman. Perhaps if she worked hard and took extra special care of Dru, the woman's health would improve. Perhaps she could make amends for her selfishness.

"You're up early."

Rachel turned to find Dru standing near the fireplace, her white nightgown hidden beneath a plain brown robe. Her graying hair hung in a single braid over her shoulder, and there were dark circles beneath her hazel eyes.

"So are you," Rachel responded. "Did you rest well?"

Dru sighed. "Well enough." She walked toward Rachel. "How bad was the storm?"

Rachel stepped aside to reveal the snow-blanketed yard.

Unexpectedly, Dru smiled. "That means we can stay even longer."

"You really don't want to go, do you?"

"No. I love it here better than anywhere in the world. It's home."

"Gavin's worried."

Dru smiled softly. "You two talked late last night."

Rachel nodded and headed toward the stove, guilt returning in massive proportions. "I'll start breakfast. Why don't you sit next to the fire and keep warm. Would you like some coffee?"

"Tea, I think. Coffee doesn't sit well with me anymore."

Rachel busied herself with heating water for tea, then gathered the ingredients for flapjacks

and mixed them in a large bowl. As she poured
the batter into a hot skillet, the bedroom door
opened once again.

Gavin's eyes met hers the moment he stepped
through the doorway. She felt a dull thudding in
her ears as he nodded at her. She glanced back
at the skillet, and when she looked up again, he
was pulling on his coat.

"I'll check on the livestock," he said to Dru.
He opened the door, letting in a gust of wind
and a flurry of snow. "Looks like we're in for
another blow. I won't be long. Don't anyone
venture out. This looks like it could get nasty."

Be careful, Rachel thought, and felt the heat
rush to her cheeks. She had no right to those
thoughts. They belonged to Dru.

She fought back the threat of tears and forced
herself to think of the task at hand. She had
breakfast to cook and lessons to give and a
house to clean. She hadn't time for feeling sorry
for herself.

No sooner was she scooping the first flapjacks
from the frying pan than excited voices sounded
from the loft.

"Did you see the snow?" Sabrina cried as she
fairly skimmed down the ladder. "I'm hungry!"

"Me too," echoed her sister, following closely
behind.

Rachel laughed, her smile returning at the
sight of the two girls in white nightcaps and
heavy robes. "Good, because there's plenty of
food here for you."

The children hurried first to their mother,
giving her tight hugs and kisses on the cheek.

"Morning, Ma," they said in unison.

"Good morning, my angels."

Rachel paused to watch, her heart tightening in her breast as she realized how much Dru was losing. Every day, she had to be preparing herself to say good-bye to all the things, all the people she loved most.

Feeling the threat of tears, she returned her attention to the skillet, placing two pancakes each onto two plates and setting them on the table. When she felt she had control of her emotions again, she turned toward Dru. "Are you ready to eat, Mrs. Blake?"

Dru shook her head. "I'm not hungry this morning." A wry smile tweaked one corner of her mouth. "And don't you think it's time you called me Dru?"

No. If I call you Dru, that makes us closer, and I don't want to get closer to any of you. It's already too complicated. "All right," she answered softly. "But I do think you should try to eat something, Dru."

Again the woman shook her head.

"Please?"

There was something about the way Dru looked at her, searching with her eyes, that left her feeling unsettled. Did she know what Rachel was thinking, what she was feeling?

"I suppose I could eat one flapjack." Dru pushed herself out of the rocker and moved slowly toward the table.

"Can we go outside to play, Ma?" Sabrina asked before stuffing a large bite of hotcakes into her mouth.

"Not until the storm is over. When it's stopped snowing, you can go out."

At that moment, a gust of wind slammed against the house, rattling the windows and whistling beneath the door. Rachel's head snapped up as a sudden chill spread through her. She set the skillet on the stove and walked over to the window, apprehension growing with each step.

There was no earth or sky to be discerned. All was white. The barn was obscured by the billowing snow, driven almost sideways by the wind. She hugged her arms against her chest.

"How will he find his way back?" she said aloud. "He can't possibly see."

"He'll wait it out," Dru answered. "Come have your breakfast, Rachel." Her words sounded comforting, but there was an odd tightness in her voice.

"Are you sure?" Rachel turned to gaze across the room.

Dru nodded. "I'm sure." Her glance took in the children, then returned pointedly to Rachel. "Come and eat," she said softly.

Dru's silent message was clear. *Don't worry the children.*

Rachel knew she was right, but it was all she could do to return to the stove and scoop up the flapjacks from the skillet. She kept listening for the latch to lift and the door to open. All she heard was the howling wind.

"What if he *did* leave the barn for some reason before the wind came up?" Rachel stood once again at the window, watching the snow piling up against the house. "He might have been checking something in the corral. Or maybe he's hurt. It's been over an hour."

Dru saw the concern written on the young woman's face, a concern that mirrored her own. Common sense told her Gavin was waiting out the storm in the safety of the barn, but she knew all too well how things could go wrong when you least expected it.

"I could go check on him," Rachel said softly.

"You'd be blown clear away. We'll just have to wait."

Joker got up from his place by the fire and padded across the room, plopping down beside Rachel. He lifted his face up toward her, whined, then scratched the door with his paw before looking up at her again.

"No, fella," Rachel responded, her hand stroking his head. "You can't go out. Not yet."

"Ma?" Petula came to stand beside Dru's chair. "Is Pa okay?"

Her arm went around her younger daughter. "Of course he is, Pet. He's just tending the animals."

Rachel turned away from the window. Her chin lifted and her shoulders straightened as she headed across the room. "Whatever's wrong with me?" She laughed aloud, then said in a firm voice, "Girls, it's time for your studies. If we get our work done now, we can play in the snow when the storm blows over. Get your books and slates."

Dru gave Petula another quick hug, then patted the child's behind as she shooed her toward the table. In a matter of minutes, Rachel had the children laboring over their school work, their anxiety fading as they concentrated on other matters.

Dru closed her eyes as she set her chair rocking. The children's voices were comforting as they asked their teacher questions. She listened to Rachel's replies. The young woman was intelligent and patient. She'd put aside her own concerns about Gavin and made sure the children weren't worried. She would be good for them. Always.

I was right about her, Charlie. She'll make a good mother for them when I'm gone. And I think she's already falling in love with our Gavin. She frowned. *But he might be a problem. Wish I knew what was troublin' him so. Did I do wrong in askin' him to raise our girls once I'm gone?*

She opened her eyes and gazed out the window at the blizzard raging beyond the glass, worry returning to gnaw at her insides.

Gavin groaned as consciousness returned, bringing with it a terrible throbbing in his head. For a moment he was disoriented, but when he turned his head, he felt the straw scratching his face and smelled the pungent odors of the barn.

He groaned again and rolled onto his back, his fingers gingerly touching the back of his skull. He opened his eyes, then sat up.

"Damn," he whispered as the pain increased.

He heard a snort behind him.

"If I didn't need you to pull the wagon, I'd plug you between the eyes right here and now."

The big work horse snorted once again.

Gavin twisted toward the animal, which was calmly munching her hay on the other side of the stall. The movement caused hot darts to shoot up the back of his neck.

"Damn," he swore again.

As he pushed himself to his feet, he tried to piece together exactly what had happened. At first, it was hard to concentrate beyond the throbbing in his head, but slowly the memories fell into place.

He'd finished tending the horses and Sabrina's orphaned calf, then checked on Petula's kittens up in the loft. By the time he'd climbed down the ladder, the snowfall had become a raging blizzard. He'd known he would have to wait it out and had decided to work on some harness to pass the time. As he was passing old Patch's stall, the big piebald had kicked at him through the wooden slats, catching her hoof in the broken board. Gavin had entered the stall and worked the animal's leg free, only to have the horse wheel on him and strike again.

"You'd make great buzzard feed."

The piebald looked at him with bored eyes.

A wave of dizziness washed over Gavin, and he stepped backward, leaning his back against the wall as he waited for it to pass. He wondered how long he'd been unconscious. Seconds? Minutes? Hours?

Taking a deep breath to steady himself, he started toward the stall gate. His steps were uncertain and wobbly, and there seemed to be a curtain of darkness just beyond his vision, waiting to drop over him at any moment.

Just outside the stall, he stopped to rest again. He felt weak and foolish. It should take more than a wallop from Patch to knock the stuffing out of him. Lord knew, it wasn't the first time he'd been kicked by the cantankerous beast. Yet weak and foolish was exactly how he felt. He wondered if he could make it back to the house. He felt an overwhelming need to lie down until the weakness passed once and for all.

Cautiously, he moved forward again, using his hand to balance himself as he grabbed whatever was in reach. The floor seemed to swell and drop beneath his feet, like the rise and fall of the ocean beneath a ship. Unexpectedly, it rose up in a giant wave to meet his face.

Rachel tightened the rope around her waist.

"Do you understand the signal then?" she asked as she turned to meet Dru's anxious gaze. "Two tugs means to pull me back. That's only if I can't find the barn or if I get into some sort of trouble. Four tugs means I'm in the barn. If you get four tugs, just tie off the rope. We'll use it to find our way back if Gavin thinks we should. Otherwise, we'll just wait in the barn until the storm's over."

Dru touched Rachel's coat sleeve. "He isn't going to like it that I let you do this. I'm sure he's just working in the barn until the weather clears."

"Probably." She offered the woman a reassuring smile. "I'm sure he'll scold me soundly, and then I'll be stuck with a man in ill-temper until the sun comes out. And it'll serve me right for being so silly."

Rachel wished she believed what she was saying. It made perfectly good sense, and both she and Dru had used the same logical excuse for Gavin's tardy return to the house a number of times over the past couple of hours. If she had been the only anxious one, she would have dismissed the nagging feeling that something was wrong. But she wasn't the only one. Dru felt it too, although she'd tried to hide it for a long time.

With a deep breath for courage, Rachel tightened the scarf around her head and pulled open the door. The wind blasted against her. Shards of snow stung her cheeks. She leaned forward and stepped outside.

"I'll be all right," she hollered over the wind as she headed in the general direction of the barn.

In seconds, the house had disappeared from sight. She was surrounded by nothing but white. She touched the rope around her waist, reassuring herself that she wasn't alone and lost, then struggled forward, her feet sinking into drifts of snow, not knowing where she was headed. She could have been moving in tiny circles for all she knew. She had no sense of direction left to guide her. There was no up or down, right or left, forward or back, night or day. There was only snow. Snow, snow, and more snow.

It was a terrifying feeling.

She was cold. The blowing snow stung her face, and she bent her head forward to avoid the tiny missiles. Already she felt as if she'd been walking for ages. She paused and looked down at the rope. Two tugs and they would pull her back to the house. Just two tugs and she could be warm again, safe within the walls of the sturdy log house.

But I still wouldn't know about Gavin.

She pressed forward into the storm.

Was it really so far from the house to the barn? It hadn't seemed so before. Perhaps she should turn and try another direction. Perhaps she was headed the wrong way. Perhaps . . .

And then, it was there before her. She reached out and touched the board siding of the barn, working her way along until she found the door. With a hammering heart, she lifted the latch and tugged at the door. Drifting snow had piled up against it, making it impossible to open. She kicked at the snowdrift, then leaned down to dig with her hands. For every inch she swept away, two more seemed to land in its place.

Finally, her fingers numb with cold, she was able to clear enough snow to pry open the door and wedge her way through. As she stepped inside the barn, she gave the rope four distinct tugs, then let the door blow closed behind her.

She saw him almost immediately, lying face down in the straw.

"Gavin!"

With fumbling hands, she loosened the knot on the rope at her waist. Breaking free, she hurried toward the quiet form on the barn floor.

"Gavin? Gavin, what's wrong?"

Rachel knelt in the straw and grasped his shoulders, rolling him onto his back and pulling his head into her lap.

"Gavin?" she said again, whispering this time. "Gavin?"

Chapter Twelve

"**I**'m gonna kill that horse," he mumbled.

Rachel leaned forward. "What, Gavin? What did you say?"

His eyes opened slowly. He looked up at her with a glazed, unfocused expression. But when he spoke, his voice was clear this time. "I said I'm gonna kill that horse." And then he grinned, followed by a wince and a groan.

"What happened, Gavin? How are you hurt?"

"Patch tried to knock some sense into me. Caught me in the back of the head with a swift kick."

"Let me see." Rachel pulled him into an upright position, then leaned to one side and carefully probed the back of his head.

Gavin grunted but didn't flinch. He reached

up behind him to follow her hand over the lump on the back of his head. "Never been knocked stone cold before."

Their fingers met, his sliding over the top of hers. Both hands stilled. Neither tried to pull away.

Rachel felt the touch throughout her body. It spread through her veins, hot and churning, warming away the chill of the snowstorm and leaving her feeling as if a new kind of storm was battering her from the inside. Gavin turned his head. His gray eyes met hers, the force of his gaze strong enough to chase the wind from her lungs.

He moved his hand away and rose to his feet. "I guess the storm's over. How long was I out here?" he asked as he steadied himself by holding onto the top railing of a stall.

Rachel dragged in a breath of air and fought down the tide of emotions that raged within. "You were gone over two hours," she was finally able to respond. "We were afraid something must be wrong, so I came looking for you. The storm hasn't let up at all." She stood and brushed the straw from her skirt, not daring to look at him again.

"You came out here through that blizzard?" He scolded her as if she was a child.

"Someone had to. We were afraid something was wrong." Now she looked at him, her chin thrust up in indignation. "And we were right."

Gavin grunted his displeasure as he turned to walk across the barn to the door. Reaching it, he picked up the length of rope hanging through it, then looked back at Rachel.

"I had it tied around my waist so I wouldn't get lost. I told Dru to tie it off to the house once I signaled that I'd found the barn. That way we could follow the rope back to the house from here."

He tipped his head to one side. It seemed to be a silent acknowledgement that she'd done something right. But it didn't last long. He looked away almost immediately.

Placing his shoulder against the door and still holding onto the rope, he lifted the latch and tried to open the door. It barely budged, opening only far enough to let in a gust of icy wind and a flurry of snowflakes.

Rachel moved forward. "I cleared a pathway so I could open the door. It couldn't be covered over already." She stopped as he turned around.

"We'll just have to wait it out. If we can't get the door open when the storm stops, we can always get out through the loft window."

"Through the loft?" Her voice came out in a small squeak. "The snow won't get that deep, will it?"

Gavin gave a short laugh. "Not this time of year, no. I'll just lower you down with a rope and then follow after you. Nothing to it."

Rachel sat down on a nearby storage bin, her frantic heart causing the blood to pound in her ears. She turned her head so she could see the long ladder leading up to the loft and imagined an even longer drop down to the ground afterward. She swallowed hard as her hands clenched tightly in her lap.

Outside, the storm raged on.

Gavin closed the loft window. He'd never seen a snowstorm like this one, at least not so early in the year. You could expect them in January, but never in October.

He headed toward the ladder, stopping on the edge to look down. Rachel was still seated on the storage bin, her arms hugging her body. Even from up here he could see her shivering. He knew she had to be plenty cold. Her dress had gotten soaked with snow as she'd fought her way through the drifts to get to the barn, and there was no fire to help dry her out once she got here. But she hadn't complained once.

He turned and lowered himself down the ladder. As his feet touched the floor, he looked toward her. "No sign of it stopping yet."

She nodded, misery written on every inch of her pretty face.

"Come here," Gavin said, motioning with his hand.

She gave him a puzzled look.

"We need to warm you up. Come on."

She rose from the bin and moved toward him, her arms still folded tightly across her chest. When she reached him, he placed an arm around her shoulders and guided her toward the stall holding Sabrina's calf. He opened the gate, allowing them entry.

"Wait here," he told her, then walked away.

From the small tack room at the back of the barn, he grabbed several saddle blankets. On his

137

return trip, he took the lantern from its usual high hook and carried it with him to the stall.

"Hold this," he said, handing her the lantern.

With his boot, he kicked straw into a pile in the corner, then leaned forward to make a nest in the center of it. He placed one of the blankets on the bottom, smoothing out the wrinkles as best he could before turning toward Rachel.

"Take off that wet skirt and toss it over the gate to dry," he said. "Your drawers will just have to dry on you."

Her eyes rounded, and her golden eyebrows rose on her forehead.

"Come on. We need to get you warmed up before you take sick. I promise not to look until you're under the blankets here."

"Mr. Blake, I can't . . ."

He took a step toward her. His voice was low when he spoke. "Don't argue with me, Rachel. I know what's best. Look at you. You're shivering so hard your teeth are about to rattle." His hand closed over hers on the lantern handle. "I'll take this while you get out of those wet things."

When she tipped her head back to look up at him, he felt a sudden jolt in his belly. Everything tightened inside him. The desire to hold her, to kiss her, returned with a fury. His blood raced hot through his veins, stirring up a wanting that would take a will of iron to deny. The pounding in his head became a throbbing in his loins.

"Do as I say," he said harshly, jerking the lantern free of her hand as he turned around.

He filled his lungs with air, then let it out slowly as he fought for control. Most men would probably laugh at him. He had a wife who couldn't satisfy his sexual needs and desires. He should be free to take release with another woman. But his word meant more to him than that. He'd promised to be Dru's husband—and in Gavin's book, that meant he'd promised to be faithful too.

He heard the rustle of straw. "Are you covered up?"

"Yes."

He turned toward her. Her legs were drawn up toward her chest and hidden beneath the two remaining saddle blankets. Her eyes seemed wider and bluer than ever, her face pale even in the yellow glow of the lantern light.

"That's better," he mumbled as he hung the lantern on a hook just inches above her head. He turned up the flame as high as it would go, then sat down beside her, his left arm around her back. "Come here." He pulled her close against his side.

The blustering wind whistled around the corner of the barn. A horse blew dust from its nostrils. Another stomped its hoof. The calf rose, turned in a tight circle, and lay down again, his soft brown eyes staring at the pair in the corner of his stall.

Gavin felt the isolation creeping into his marrow. It was as if they were the only two people alive in the world. One man. One woman. Alone together.

He felt the rise and fall of her chest. Was her breathing too rapid? He lifted his right hand and began rubbing the length of her arm, ostensibly

139

to warm away the chill she'd taken. But he knew the truth was he just wanted to touch her, to go on touching her, to touch far more than he was able to through her heavy coat.

He closed his eyes and leaned his head against the stall wall and prayed for a little more self-control.

She hurt. She ached everywhere. But it was a different kind of pain from anything she'd ever felt before. It couldn't be described. It was an emptiness, but more than that. It burned, like a fire in her veins, but was more than that too. She yearned to move closer to him, longed to pull away from him. She felt torn in a thousand different directions all at the same time.

Rachel lost track of time. It could have been minutes that passed; it could have been hours. His hand continued to stroke her arm. She could feel his warm breath on her hair, could hear his heartbeat through his coat and shirt.

He knows what I'm feeling.

Her pulse quickened with fear and anticipation. If she should look up into his eyes, she knew with a woman's instinct that she would see her own confusion and desire mirrored in eyes of gray. She longed to do just that. She longed to see what was written there, to speak aloud the things she was feeling.

But she couldn't. To do so would give them life. To do so would make them stronger, and she couldn't allow that to happen. Not ever.

Heaven help her, she had to get away from him soon. But still she didn't move. She stayed within the circle of his arms, waiting out the storms—the one outside and the one within her heart.

Silence.

Rachel lifted her head from Gavin's shoulder. She stared toward the door as she whispered, "It's over."

He felt it too. Not just the cessation of wind, but an end to the right to hold her. He wasn't ready for it yet. He didn't want to release her. He wanted to hold her, to kiss her, to . . .

His arm slid from her back. "I'll have a look," he said as he got to his feet. "Stay here."

He knew there was no point in trying to open the barn door. The drifts would be too high against it. He climbed the ladder to the loft and opened the loft door.

The sky was a silver-gray. A few snowflakes fell in lazy circles toward the earth, the fury of the storm spent. In the west, strips of blue showed between breaks in the clouds. Tall pines lifted emerald arms above a world of ivory-white. Smaller trees and brush bent low beneath the heavy weight of snow.

As he gazed toward the house, the door opened. Dru, wrapped in a fur-lined coat and a thick scarf, appeared in the opening.

"We're all right," he called to her. "Stay there."

She looked up at him, and he could see the relief on her face even from that distance.

"We can't get the barn door open yet."

"I'll get the girls. We'll dig out a path for you."

141

"No," he called back. "Stay inside. We'll come down from here. I'll dig it out later."

Dru lifted an arm to acknowledge that she'd heard him. "All right."

Gavin returned the wave and watched as the door closed. Guilt, like a thick cloak, weighted his shoulders. She was a good woman. She was the first and only woman he'd known since boyhood that he'd felt he could trust. She didn't deserve the flash of resentment he'd felt when he knew the storm was over.

He ran his fingers through his hair as he turned from the door, his thoughts jumbled and confused. All his points of reference, all his firm beliefs, had been shaken and many of them discarded. He didn't seem to know right from wrong anymore. Worse yet, he didn't seem to care.

With quick strides, he moved to the edge of the loft and glanced down at Rachel. She stood in the middle of the stall, her skirt primly back in place. She was staring up at him with a strange look on her face, a look that made his heart twist in his chest.

"Put out the lantern and come on up. We'll have to go out from up here."

She didn't move, only continued to look up at him with wide eyes of blue.

"Hurry up," he growled as he turned away, unable to bear the look any longer.

Her reply was nearly inaudible. "I'm coming, Gavin."

Chapter Thirteen

No matter what she had to do, she had to stop this insanity before it went any further. She couldn't allow herself to go on feeling this way about Gavin.

And if she was right, if he knew what she was feeling, if there was any chance he might respond to her attraction to him, she had to make sure it ended now. If that meant making him hate her, then that was what she must do.

"It never snows this early in Boise." Rachel emitted a long sigh as she stared out the window for the third time in the last half hour. Darkness and silence had fallen early over the snow-coated basin. "I missed the Horace Clive ball again this year. The weather's almost always warm for the ball." She turned away from the window, casting a wistful gaze at the two girls seated at the table. "Do you know what a ball is? It's a dance, and all the women are dressed in beautiful gowns and the men in fine suits." She sighed dramatically.

Sabrina and Petula gazed over the top of their school books, waiting expectantly for her to continue.

"Tell us more," Sabrina encouraged.

"Mr. Clive is a very respected man in the Boise Valley. He was there when we first arrived in Idaho, and my sister, Maggie, got to go to the ball that year. In fact, it's where Tucker, my brother-in-law, proposed to her and she said yes. I was only six, but I remember just how she looked that night. Her gown was silvery-blue and there were little puffed sleeves on her arms right here." She pointed to the spot on her upper arms. "The dress had a big skirt, held out by lots of stiff petticoats. Well, maybe they weren't petticoats. Maybe she had a hooped skirt. Dresses were so different back then."

Rachel crossed the room and sat down across from the children. She closed her eyes, resting her chin in the palms of her hands, elbows on the table. "My first ball gown was very different from Maggie's. It was apple green and embroidered with red poppies, and it had a square neck, edged with white lace. I wore long white gloves that had gold bands at the wrists. The vogue was for long trains then, and my first ball gown had a very long one, indeed. I felt so grown up in it, especially when I was dancing. A lady held those long trains in one hand as she danced. It looked very elegant. I danced and danced and danced that night. Mr. Clive had an orchestra up in a loft above the ballroom, and they hardly ever stopped playing. You can't imagine how wonderful that first ball was for me. It was magic."

She'd gotten so caught up in the telling of the story she nearly forgot why she'd told it. She opened her eyes and glanced around the room, her gaze briefly meeting both Dru's and Gavin's. Then she looked back at the two girls across from her.

"Every year is wonderful. The men are so gallant, so debonair. And there are so many of them, all wanting to dance with you." She sighed again. "All those years I was back East, attending school and living with the Fieldings, I looked forward to going to Mr. Clive's ball again. I wish I could have been there this year."

Sabrina leaned forward. "Do you suppose, when I'm old enough, if I was to be in Boise City, I could go to the ball? Do you think anybody'd want to dance with me?"

Rachel wasn't prepared for Sabrina's question. Her purpose had been to let Gavin think she was terribly homesick, not to make his daughter long for things she couldn't have.

She looked at Sabrina's long, narrow face. The girl would never be truly pretty. But she had a generous, loving heart—like her mother— that carried a beauty of its own. She reached a hand across the table and clasped Sabrina's. "If you lived in Boise, you would most assuredly be invited. And you would be the belle of the ball, too."

"I don't know how to dance," Sabrina confessed in a whisper, her hazel eyes wide with worry.

"Oh my," Rachel responded with a frown. "That *is* a problem. We must fix it immediately. Put your book down and stand up."

Moving briskly around the room, Rachel shoved chairs back against the walls, clearing a wide space in the middle of the room.

Satisfied with her accomplishments, she turned toward Sabrina. "Come here."

In moments, she'd instructed the child how to stand, how to hold her partner's hand, how to follow the man's lead. "You must always smile while you're dancing, as if you know a secret that your partner doesn't know," she ended, then began to move to the imaginary music, drawing Sabrina along with her. "Just relax and enjoy. That's the most important part."

Sabrina gripped Rachel's hand as if it was a lifeline. She kept stumbling over her own feet.

Rachel laughed. "Relax, Brina. Dancing is supposed to be fun."

"I'll never get it," the girl answered, barely controlling tears.

"No one gets it right the first time. It's easier when you see others dancing."

"Will you show me with Pa?"

Rachel stopped abruptly. "Well, I—"

"That's a wonderful idea," Dru said, drawing Rachel's gaze.

Rachel hesitated. "Maybe it would be better if you just danced with your pa," she told Sabrina.

"He'll know how to lead a dance much better than I."

"Please show me," Sabrina pleaded.

She heard his steps on the wooden floor. Her heart was yammering in her chest. Oh Lord! This wasn't supposed to be happening.

"May I, Miss Harris?"

Her mouth was so dry she could scarcely speak. "Perhaps you shouldn't." She turned and looked up into Gavin's darkly handsome face. "Your head—"

"It quit aching hours ago." He held out his arms for her.

She stepped into them. They fit her like a fine kid glove. They seemed to be made for holding her.

He began to sway slowly from side to side, then, as he hummed a soft melody, they began to twirl around the room. Rachel stared up into his eyes. She felt mesmerized by the look in the steely gray depths. She knew she should look away but was helpless to do so.

They spun to a halt in the middle of the sitting room. Her skirts swished around her ankles, then stilled. Rachel drew her hand from his as she stepped backward.

"Thank you for the dance, Miss Harris." Gavin bowed his head.

"Thank you, sir," she whispered.

Suddenly, Dru and the girls were applauding.

"That was wonderful. Beautiful," Dru cried.

Gavin was still staring at her with dark, enigmatic eyes, causing her breath to catch in her throat. She was frightened by the swirling emotions that threatened to engulf her. Frightened by the wanting that heated her to the core of her soul.

Rachel turned quickly away from him, breaking the spell. "Your turn, Brina. Dance with your father."

Still shaken by his touch, Rachel walked stiffly to the table and sat down. She fought for composure, praying that there was no trace left on her face of her confused emotions.

Hearing the laughter, she looked up to find father and daughter whirling at a mad pace around the room. Dru and Petula were trying to sing but kept breaking into giggles. Dru's face was flushed with color and her eyes sparkled merrily.

I don't belong here.

But, God help her, it was where she wanted to be.

As suddenly as the temperatures dropped and the blizzard arrived, warming winds came to melt the snowfall. Water dripped from the eaves of the house and barn. Brown, muddy spots of earth appeared in the yard. In a few days, all traces of the snow would be gone, and they would be able to leave the basin.

Gavin tossed another flake of hay over the side of the stall, then leaned on the top rail as the black gelding buried his nose in the feed, searching for the most delectable shoots.

"We'll be on our way out in a couple of days, fella," he said aloud.

Scamp's ears twitched.

"Yeah. Guess it makes no difference to you."

He shoved off from the rail, turning toward the barn door. He'd be busy the next day or two, closing things up, getting the place ready for winter. Then they would load up and leave, head back to the Lucky Strike. It was time. Past time.

They needed to get out of this valley. They needed to get out, see some other people, say howdy to their neighbors. Things were too close here, too secluded. He needed to keep busy, get his mind back to the business of ranching instead of thinking so much on . . .

He didn't allow himself to finish that train of thought. It could only cause trouble.

Gavin walked across the yard, opened the cabin door, and stepped inside. He took off his coat and hung it on the nearest peg. "It's warming up out there," he said as he turned around.

Dru was seated in her rocking chair near the fireplace, a bundle of mending on the rug near her feet, needle and thread in her hands.

"We'll be out of here in a couple of days or so."

She nodded, but it was easy to see the thought didn't make her happy.

As he walked toward her, he said, "Spring will be here before you know it."

She smiled sadly up at him, her hands falling idle in her lap. "I always loved to see spring come. It's so beautiful here when the wildflowers are in bloom."

He rested his hand on her shoulder, squeezing his fingers in wordless acknowledgment.

149

Rachel's bedroom door opened, drawing their attention. She stepped into the sitting room wearing a gray cashmere walking outfit that displayed her delicate figure to perfection. It was amply bustled and flounced and totally preposterous for the rough log cabin.

Preposterous but positively beautiful.

"Where are the girls?" she asked.

Dru set aside her mending. "Outside playing."

"May I speak with the two of you a moment?" Rachel moved across the room, the hem of her dress swishing against the floor as she walked.

"Of course," Dru replied.

Rachel's hands were folded in front of her. Gavin could see that her fingernails were biting into her flesh. Her expression was strained, and she was obviously avoiding looking at him.

"I did a lot of thinking last night after I went to bed," she began. "I just don't think I can be happy up here. I'm very fond of Brina and Pet. Please understand that. They're wonderful children and bright and easy to teach." She was talking very fast, her words beginning to run together. "But you see, I miss my family, and I began thinking about the ball and the other winter activities that I'll be missing in Boise. With Tucker being a judge, we get invited to so many wonderful parties. And the theater season is always grand and . . ."

She glanced up at him at last, her words dying away. Color flared in her cheeks before she dropped her gaze back to her folded hands.

He'd been right about her after all. She couldn't cut it up here. Things were too tough for her. She wanted her fancy dresses and her balls and parties and all the wonderful things money could buy.

"I think I should return to Boise as soon as we're able to leave the basin," she ended softly.

Gavin stepped away from Dru, turning toward the door as he did so. "You'll have to wait for the stage in Challis." He slipped his arm back into his coat sleeve. "I'll check on the girls."

He slammed the door behind him.

Rachel felt the door slamming in her heart as well as hearing it with her ears. She wished she could retreat to her room and have a good cry, but she couldn't. Not quite yet.

"I'm sorry, Dru. I thought I could do this, but I was wrong."

"Sit down, and let's talk a while."

"I can't help it."

"Sit down, Rachel," Dru insisted gently.

She sat on the edge of the chair nearest Dru. She unconsciously continued to twist and wring her hands in her lap.

Dru emitted a short sigh. "When you took this job, you promised to stay through spring. I'm afraid I must hold you to that."

"But I . . ."

"I'm very ill, Rachel, and I'm going to get worse. My daughters love you. They're going to need you more than you know. You can't leave them now. They've suffered too much already. Please . . . keep your promise to me and to them."

It was so unfair. Dru didn't know what she was asking, and yet, Rachel couldn't find the words to deny her the heartfelt request. She had promised she would stay through spring. She knew that Dru was very ill. Dying even. How could she go away and leave Sabrina and Petula to face that alone?

Gavin will need me too.

Guilt stabbed at her heart.

"Dru, you don't understand. I really think . . ."

"I understand much more than you think, my dear. Please. You must stay. For everyone's sake."

"All right, Dru. I'll stay."

The journey to the main ranch, located twenty miles out of Challis, was a long and tiring one. There was no wagon road to follow, just an invisible path along a series of creeks and rivers, cutting through the mountains and valleys.

Gavin led the way on his black gelding, picking his way among the trees, climbing hillsides, crossing creek beds, and selecting campsites. Sabrina and Petula followed on Princess. The docile mare seemed oblivious to the closed basket, holding an unhappy Countess and her mewing kittens, that was strapped to her saddle.

Dru followed behind her children, riding her own palomino mare. She said little during the day. It seemed to Rachel that the woman grew weaker by the hour, and she knew the trip was taking longer than normal to accommodate plenty of rest stops.

The journey seemed all the longer for Rachel because of her plodding steed. Patch, the cantankerous old work horse, was her only choice of transportation, short of walking all the way out. Her sidesaddle wouldn't fit the animal's broad back, and she felt precarious riding astride the draft horse.

But the big mare's teammate, Checker, had an even broader back and more wretched gait, although she did have a somewhat more pleasant disposition; she followed behind on a lead rope, tethered to Patch's saddle horn, oblivious to the wooden cage holding several squawking chickens that was strapped across her back.

The two milk cows and Sabrina's orphaned calf trotted along beside them, kept in line by a rambunctious Joker. The young wolfhound seemed to have learned a few things from his parents, but his enthusiasm got him into trouble a time or two with Patch. More than once, as Joker chased the calf between the two work horses, Patch sent a swift kick in his direction, nearly unseating Rachel. Luckily for Joker, he was faster than the horse, but his antics didn't go far toward endearing the mutt to Rachel.

Twilight was already spreading a gray mantle over the serene countryside as Gavin led his tired band of travelers into the yard of the Lucky Strike, six days after departing the Stanley Basin. Rachel was too weary to take more than a cursory glance about her before sliding from Patch's broad back with a sigh of relief. She leaned momentarily against the horse, waiting for strength to return to her legs. She ached from head to toe and wanted nothing more than a hot bath to sooth her sore muscles.

Stubs and Jess Chamberlain appeared out of the bunkhouse. Stubs exchanged a few words with Gavin about the trail drive out of the basin as he lifted the girls down from Princess's back.

Gavin nodded absently. "We'll talk about it tomorrow. Take care of the livestock, will you, Stubs?"

"Sure thing."

Gavin's voice softened. "Just hold onto my neck," he said as he held his arms out toward Dru.

Rachel watched as Dru slipped from the saddle into Gavin's strong embrace. The woman's head nestled into the curve of his shoulder and neck, her fingers laced behind him. She looked terribly small and fragile.

Gavin turned and his gaze collided with Rachel's. The gentle tone disappeared. "I'll need your help," he said abruptly, then strode up the porch steps and into the ranch house.

Rachel didn't know which she wanted more —to be furious at him for his tone of voice or to burst into tears of frustration. But she hadn't the strength for either.

Besides, she thought as she pushed herself away from Patch and started after Gavin, it was what she'd wanted. She'd purposefully set out to make him see her as shallow and selfish. And it appeared she had succeeded.

Perhaps too well.

Chapter Fourteen

Rachel sat up in her bed, her blankets tucked snugly around her. She stared at the cold black iron stove across the room from her. Perhaps it wasn't going to be so wonderful having a cabin all to herself if it meant having the fire go out every night.

Well, it wasn't going to get any warmer in here unless she did something about it.

With a swift motion, she threw back the covers and hurried over to the stove. She filled its darkened belly with wood and kindling, thankful for the tiny bit of warmth she felt emanating from the coals in the bottom. By the time she'd struck her fourth match, her teeth were chattering so hard her face hurt. But, at last, the fire took hold. She waited just long enough to make sure it was going to keep burning, then hustled back to her bed and leapt beneath the quilts.

Impatient though she was, it wasn't long before the fire began to take the chill from the room, and she was able to relax and survey her surroundings.

She'd been too tired last night to care what the small cabin looked like. As long as it had a bed, she was satisfied. In the pale light of morning, she was pleasantly surprised by her new lodgings.

The cabin had only a single room, but it was a comfortable size. In addition to the stove and the bed, there was room for a table and chairs, as well as a sideboard for dishes and a cupboard for storing food supplies. There were curtains over the lone window, no doubt hung there by Dru, and a rag rug covering the board floor.

It had been Gavin's home before he married Dru.

Her pulse quickened.

It had been Gavin's bed before he married Dru.

A strange heat spread through her loins. An aching heat.

She snuggled down beneath the covers and closed her eyes. She forced herself to take several slow, deep breaths as she silently lectured herself.

She couldn't allow herself to think such things. Besides, she was mistaken about her feelings for Gavin Blake. He was an attractive man—there was no denying that—but her feelings for him were no different than what she felt for Dru and her daughters. They were a nice family who'd had their share of heartache and hard times. She liked them all and wanted to do her job well for them. That was all there was to it. All there would ever be.

And once spring came, and Gavin was ready to take his family and his cattle back into the basin, Rachel would return to Boise. She would most likely marry one of Boise's up-and-coming men of business. They would have a fine home on Main Street or Grove and she would entertain the good women of the city and she would raise a family and she would be happy.

That had no doubt been her destiny all along. Look what had come of her silliness, thinking that something special, something unique was in store for her. Look what had come of her leaving home, of her trying to make something extraordinary happen. What had ever made her think that she deserved more than the next person?

"Silliness and bother," she said aloud, her voice echoing in the silence of the cabin. "That's all this is. I'm homesick. Nothing more."

With a sweep of her hand, she tossed her tousled blond locks behind her shoulder and once more lowered her feet over the side of the bed. She hadn't time for lollygagging in bed. Dru shouldn't have to worry about preparing the family's breakfast. Rachel had been hired to do a job, and it was time she got to it.

She dressed with haste. She intentionally didn't fuss with her hair in front of the mirror, being satisfied to simply tie it back from her face with a ribbon. She slipped into her coat, then

157

opened the door to the chilled mountain air.

Ribbons of smoke curled skyward from the chimneys of both the main house and the bunkhouse, and there was the delicious odor of frying bacon lingering in the air. Tardy again. Feeling chagrined, she hurried toward the ranch house.

She knocked on the front door and waited for the command to enter. It was Gavin's voice that called to her.

As she came through the door, he looked up from his place by the stove. Pork sizzled and spat from a frying pan as he flipped it with a fork. "No need to knock, Miss Harris." He waved the fork in the air. "Grab a plate off the shelf there 'fore this turns to charcoal."

Rachel shrugged out of her coat and tossed it over a nearby chair before crossing the room. She grabbed a blue-and-white platter from the shelf and held it out to him.

As he scooped the bacon out of the frying pan, he said, "Dru tells me you've changed your mind again. You're going to stay."

"Yes, I . . . I gave my word."

"Wouldn't want to put you out any."

Rachel met his hard gaze. She'd spent her waking moments convincing herself that she felt nothing more for Gavin Blake than she did for the rest of the Blake family. But with one look into his steel-gray eyes, she knew it was all a lie. She felt much more.

She tried to remember how hard she had worked to make him think the worst of her, but she was unable to stop her honest reply. "I *want* to stay." She read the doubt in his eyes before he turned his attention back to the frying pan.

"Why don't you check on Dru, see if she's ready to have a bite to eat?" Gavin suggested. "She's still in the bedroom." He jerked his head toward the far end of the house.

She continued to gaze at him for a moment, fighting the irrational tears that tried to well up in her eyes. Finally, she whispered, "All right."

She set the platter on the sideboard and crossed the large main room. She rapped lightly on the door before pushing it open.

"Dru?" she called softly. "Are you awake?"

"Come in, Rachel."

"Gavin's prepared breakfast. Are you hungry?"

Dru rolled her head from side to side on the pillow, her eyes still closed. "Not right now." She drew a deep breath, then looked at Rachel. "Are the girls up yet?"

"I haven't seen them." Rachel crossed the room to stand beside the bed.

"We're all a bit tired, I suppose," Dru said with a sigh. She smiled weakly up at Rachel as she took hold of the younger woman's hand. "It's a great comfort to me to have you here, Rachel."

Pangs of guilt and shame shot through her. Dru wouldn't be so comforted if she knew the truth about her, Rachel thought as she forced a tremulous smile onto her lips. *Thou shalt not covet thy neighbor's wife.* The commandment surely covered thy neighbor's husband as well.

She quickly squeezed Dru's hand, then pulled

159

free. "I'll tell Gavin you want to wait a while to eat." She turned toward the bedroom door.

"Have Gavin take you to town. There's plenty of things we should stock up on before winter sets in."

She glanced back, a protest on her lips. "I don't . . ." she began.

But Dru's eyes were closed, and she appeared to be asleep. Quietly, Rachel left the room, closing the door behind her.

With the completion in 1880 of the toll road from Challis into the mining district, people had poured into the area by the hundreds. Bonanza City and Custer became bustling towns complete with general merchandise stores, meat markets, livery and feed stables, restaurants, Chinese laundries, and hotels. Challis, located in a more bucolic section of the Idaho mountain country, thrived with them.

Gavin, Stubs, and Charlie had first seen the land that would become the Lucky Strike Ranch nearly six years before. Tired of chasing color from one gold camp to another, Charlie and Gavin pooled their resources, bought themselves a herd of cattle, and settled in as permanent residents of the Salmon River country. They hadn't become rich, by any means, but they hadn't done too badly either. Although it was not an easy life, Gavin had always found it a satisfying one.

As he drove the wagon toward town, Gavin ruminated on the early years. He and Stubs had finished the long cattle drive up from Texas that had reunited them. They'd collected their pay in Miles City, Montana, then headed west to find wealth in the gold-laden hills of Idaho Territory. Except they'd found, as did many others, that riches were more apt to come to those selling goods to the miners than to the miners themselves.

It was in Idaho City they'd met the Porter family. Gavin wasn't ever quite sure how it happened that Charlie and Dru and little Sabrina became such a part of his life. It just seemed to happen. Charlie felt like a long-lost brother, and their friendship became an unbreakable bond. But it was Dru who truly made them all into a family, Dru with her warm laughter and her enjoyment of life. When Petula was born in Bonanza City, Dru had asked Gavin to be the baby's godfather. Even now, remembering, it created a warm spot in his heart.

Gavin would have a hard time ever putting into words how he felt about Charlie and Dru and their children. He owed them more than he could ever repay.

"Oh!"

As the wagon jerked out of the rut, the startled sound brought him abruptly back to the present. He glanced to the right and found Rachel gripping the wagon seat as the rear wheel fell into the same deep cut in the earth, then pulled out of it again.

"Sorry," he mumbled.

Her left hand rose to her black velvet hat with its fur-lined brim and cluster of ostrich tips. She pushed on its crown, as if to make sure it was still secure after the jostling it had been through.

It didn't seem to matter where she was or what she was doing or what she was wearing. Rachel Harris always managed to look beautiful. Even now, with wisps of hair spilling free from beneath that preposterous hat, he couldn't remember when he'd seen anyone more beautiful. Wouldn't she be even more beautiful without the hat, with her hair tumbling freely about her shoulders, with her face slightly flushed from . . .

"Are we nearly there?"

He nodded as he looked away, damning himself for his wayward thoughts. Did it take no more than a pretty face to make him forget the difference between right and wrong?

Silently, he cursed himself for ever allowing Dru to talk him into that trip to Boise City. Shoot! He could've tutored the girls himself. He wouldn't have been as good at it as Rachel was, but he could have managed. It would have been better for all of them without an outsider like Rachel Harris around.

A small grunt escaped his companion as the wagon wheel dropped into another rut. He hid a grin, finding some perverse satisfaction in her discomfiture. It was easier to blame his inner turmoil on her than to face the truth of his feelings.

Rachel let out a silent sigh of relief as the wagon rolled down the main street of Challis. The trip into town had seemed hours long.

Gavin hadn't spoken more than a half dozen words the entire time, and the few he'd spoken had sounded distinctly churlish.

She straightened on the wagon seat and allowed herself a look around. In comparison with Washington or Philadelphia, the town would hardly have been considered civilized. Even compared to Boise City—scarcely two decades old itself—it was small and rustic. Yet she felt strangely at ease as her gaze swept from a mercantile store, past a saloon, over a dry goods store, beyond the livery stable, and finally rested on a Chinese laundry. It was a little like coming home after a long trip abroad.

What a silly thought!

Rachel shook her head as the wagon drew to a halt in front of the Challis Mercantile. Gavin wrapped the reins around the brake handle, then hopped to the ground and walked around to the opposite side. Wordlessly, he held out his right hand to her.

She paused a moment before slipping her gloved fingers into his. Her insides seemed to jump at the moment of contact, but she managed to hide her inner pandemonium by averting her eyes, staring hard at the planks of wood that made up the sidewalk outside the mercantile. It wasn't until he released her hand that she was able to draw another breath.

"Gavin! Sure and I'm glad to see you're back."

Rachel turned with Gavin toward the deep male voice with the soft Irish burr.

The man who stepped up onto the narrow boardwalk was well over six feet tall, with a massive chest and shoulders. He was wearing a stylish suit coat and trousers and shiny leather boots. Rachel hadn't seen anything finer since she was back East. He looked strangely out of place in this remote mountain town. As he doffed his felt derby, revealing a shock of carrot-red hair, he flashed a grin in her direction.

"And I see you've brought a bit o' beauty out o' the basin with you." His laughing green eyes never left her face. "Sure if I'm not thinkin' I should be summerin' my cattle there too."

"Hello, Patrick."

"Faith and begorra!" He paused a few moments. "Have you lost your manners? Introduce me to the young lady 'fore I have to do it myself."

Rachel glanced quickly from the man called Patrick to Gavin and then back again. In comparison with the stranger's friendly smile, Gavin's look was dark and decidedly inhospitable.

"I can see I'll get nowhere waitin' for my friend here to do me the honor of an introduction." A large hand clad in a fine kid glove reached out and took hold of her fingers. "Patrick O'Donnell, at your service. 'Tis proud I am to make your acquaintance." His smile broadened. "Now if you'd be so kind as to tell me your name, I'd be forever in your debt, lass."

She couldn't help herself. His smile was as irresistible as the open appreciation written across his pleasant, if not handsome, features. She tilted her head slightly to the side as she looked up at him. "Rachel Harris," she replied, returning his smile.

"Sure and I should have known. A name that would make the angels in heaven rejoice." He bowed low and kissed the back of her hand.

Gavin made a disgusted noise in the back of his throat.

"Ignore the blighter," Patrick said as he slipped her hand into the crook of his arm and drew her toward the door of the mercantile. "Now tell me. What has brought you to our fair community, Miss Harris?"

"I'm working for the Blakes at the Lucky Strike."

"Then you're here for a stay?" Patrick asked, pulling open the door and ushering her through. As she moved passed him, he offered an exaggerated wink. "'Tis the luck of the Irish that made me a neighbor to Mr. Blake. Tell me, Miss Harris, what is it you do for the likes of this disagreeable mate o' mine?"

"I'm teaching the Blake children."

"A teacher? What a fine and noble trade. I'd wager my mother's own jewels that you're a fine one, too."

Gavin stepped up beside her and claimed her other arm. "You'll excuse us, Patrick," he said gruffly. "Miss Harris and I have some business to see to."

Patrick lifted an eyebrow, but the twinkle in his eyes never faltered. "Sure and I can see he has want of you to himself," he said to Rachel in a stage whisper, "but I know now where to find you. Good day, Miss Harris." He nodded to Gavin. "Good day, mate."

As the door swung closed behind him, Rachel

let out a deep breath, feeling just a little wind-blown by the brief encounter.

"If you've got the list, Miss Harris, we'll get done what we came to town for." If anything, he sounded even more surly than before.

Killjoy, she thought angrily as she pulled the list of shopping items from her reticule.

Yet, for some strange reason, she felt elated by his sour mood, knowing instinctively that it had something to do with the way Mr. O'Donnell had looked at her.

Chapter Fifteen

"**D**on't be silly. I'm feeling as strong as an ox today. We've been home several weeks now and I've not gotten to go visiting once. I have no intention of missing Pearl Johansen's wedding, and it's time you met some of our friends and neighbors, Rachel."

Rachel watched helplessly as Dru pulled her best dress over her head. Three weeks of rest had done wonders for the woman, but she was far from being as strong as an ox. Perhaps as feisty as one of Countess's kittens would be a more accurate comparison.

"Now we'd better hurry or we'll miss the wedding. Stubs and Jess have already left." Dru fastened the last button up the front of her autumn-plaid bodice, then glanced toward Rachel once again. "Will you help me with my hair?"

Rachel shook her head even as a smile curved the corners of her mouth. "Gavin isn't going to like this. I was supposed to convince you to stay home."

"I know." Dru grinned in return, then settled onto a stool in front of the dresser mirror. "But it doesn't do any of us any good to just sit around waiting for me to die."

Rachel sucked in a startled breath.

Dru's hazel eyes met Rachel's in the reflection of the mirror. "There's no point in dancin' around the truth any longer. We all know what's coming. And my stayin' in bed all the time isn't going to change a thing." She twisted to look directly at Rachel. "I'd rather live right up to the end, Rachel. I don't want my girls' last memories of me to be lyin' in bed, lookin' old and tired and sick. Can you understand that?"

"Sure," she whispered, her throat tight as she fought hot tears. She made a big production out of picking up the brush and selecting a ribbon from a box on the dresser while she gained control of her emotions. "Now," she said as she straightened, "how would you like your hair, Mrs. Blake?"

"Anything you can do to make it look halfway pretty will do."

Rachel ran the brush through the fine gray-brown hair, wishing there was something special she could do. "I know!" she exclaimed suddenly as she dropped the brush onto the dresser. "Wait here. I'll be right back."

She rushed out of the bedroom and across the sitting room, not even pausing long enough to pull on her coat before rushing outside and toward her own cabin. She scarcely noticed the cold. She was too excited.

She pushed things aside in the wardrobe, then rummaged through her trunk, tossing things out onto her bed until she found it.

"There it is."

She pulled the hair ornament from its box.

"Perfect," she whispered.

She felt surprisingly light-hearted as she hurried back to the main house. Dru was still sitting at her dressing table, wearing the same surprised expression that had appeared when Rachel rushed out of the bedroom.

"Look. Isn't it wonderful? It goes perfectly with your dress." Rachel held up the spray of satin tiger lilies, the orange flowers interspersed with burnt-sienna leaves of the same shiny fabric. Rich brown ostrich feathers completed the ornament.

Dru held out her hands, cradling the satin and feathers as if they were fragile glassware. "This is much too fine for me to wear, Rachel. I'm not the right sort for it. It's meant for someone young and pretty like you. And what if I lost or damaged it? I couldn't ever repay you."

"What nonsense," Rachel said as she picked up the brush once again and quickly swept Dru's hair into a smooth twist at the back of her head. "Anyway, I'm not lending it to you. It's yours to keep. Then I don't have to worry about it being lost or damaged, do I?"

Dru tried to shake her head, but Rachel stopped her with a light tug on her hair.

"Besides," Rachel continued, "I look dreadful in brown and orange. I don't know whatever possessed me to buy such a thing. You'll be doing me a favor to take it and wear it. Otherwise, it's just a waste." As she talked, she took the object from Dru's hand and slipped the comb into the knot of hair. Smiling, she leaned down and met Dru's gaze in the mirror. "There. It's perfect with your hazel eyes. See? You make it look beautiful."

"Yes," Gavin's deep, male voice said from the doorway. "You do make it look beautiful."

Rachel straightened and turned around, half expecting to find him scowling at her as usual. But he wasn't. He wasn't even looking at her. There was a tender smile on his mouth, a soft look in the gray of his eyes as he gazed at his wife. Rachel felt like an intruder and slowly moved back from Dru's side.

But she stopped when Gavin's gaze shifted to her. When the tenderness didn't alter or disappear, she felt a strange warmth rushing through her veins, ending in a tight ball in her midsection. Her mouth felt as dry as dust.

"It's a gift from Rachel," Dru said softly, breaking the growing silence.

Gavin glanced back at his wife. "I heard." He crossed the bedroom in several easy strides. "I guess this means you won't stay home."

"I haven't seen my friends and neighbors since last May. This may be my last chance before . . . before the snow falls. Please don't argue with me, Gavin."

A wry grin lifted one corner of his mouth. "Since when did it ever do anyone any good to argue with you, Drucilla?" He rested his hand on her shoulder.

Her fingers came up to cover his. "Never," Dru answered as she leaned her head back to look up at him.

Once again, Rachel felt her presence was intrusive and sought to quietly leave the room. And once again, she was stopped by a pair of compelling gray eyes.

A maelstrom of feelings stormed through her in response to his look. Pleasure, confusion, bewilderment, satisfaction. She felt warm and cold at the same time. Joy and sorrow mingled within her. She felt hope for what could be, despair for what could never be.

"I'd better get ready too," she whispered, then retreated to her own cabin as quickly as possible.

"Good heavens," Rachel said in a hushed voice as the wagon pulled to a stop on the crest of a hill. "What *is* that place?"

The two-story stone house, U-shaped and sprawling, resembled a medieval castle. It was set against a tree-covered mountain and surrounded by a sloping lawn. Threads of smoke drifted above numerous chimneys jutting up from the steep-pitched roof. Green shutters bordered the many windows that looked over the panoramic countryside.

"That's the O'Donnell ranch. They call it Killarney Hall. Pretty impressive, isn't it?" Gavin responded. "The Johansen girl didn't do too bad for herself."

Dru jabbed him in the ribs, and he had the decency to be ashamed of himself. From all reports, Pearl was head over heels in love with her intended, and nothing he'd ever seen of the girl indicated that she would marry for any other reason.

"Is *this* where the wedding's to be?" Rachel asked. "I thought we were going into town."

"There'll be too many people at this wedding for the little Episcopal church to hold," Dru answered. "It's not every day one of the O'Donnell boys gets married. Folks from miles around are going to want to see this."

"Mr. O'Donnell is the groom," Sabrina piped up from the back of the wagon, pleased to be supplying some information.

"Patrick O'Donnell?" Rachel asked as she turned to look at Gavin.

Was that disappointment he heard in her voice? "No. His brother, Shane."

"Oh."

Sabrina stood and leaned her head forward between her mother and Rachel. "Patrick O'Donnell is the oldest one. He must be as old as Pa. Shane O'Donnell, the one who's gettin' married, is next. Then comes Jamie and then Trevor. Trevor's about sixteen."

It would be hard not to be impressed with the O'Donnell ranch, Gavin thought as he slapped the reins against the horses' backsides. The house was enormous and the many outbuildings looked nearly new. Success and wealth were written on every nook and cranny.

He glanced quickly to the side. Rachel would fit right in with these people, he thought as he looked at her profile, her blond hair tucked up beneath a pretty indigo bonnet.

As soon as they pulled into the yard, the front door of the house opened and three of the O'Donnell brothers—strapping, tall men with matching thatches of red hair—came out onto the porch.

"Gavin!" Patrick called to him, his usual friendly grin in place. "Sure and I told Shane you wouldn't miss seein' him trussed up and married."

The big man jumped down from the porch, ignoring the five steps that led to the ground below. Even as the horses drew to a stop, he was lifting a giggling Petula from the back of the wagon, swinging her high in the air before setting her on her feet.

"This can't be the wee lass, can it?"

"I'm Pet!" she squealed in delight.

"And can this be Sabrina? Faith but she's become a young lady while up in the basin." He lifted the older girl to the ground as he spoke.

Sabrina blushed even as she turned her eyes toward the two younger men still standing on the porch. "Hello, Trevor," she said in a soft voice.

There was something about her tone that brought Gavin up short. He'd been so caught up in looking at the O'Donnell ranch and wondering what Rachel must think of it in comparison with the Lucky Strike that he'd scarcely noticed what Sabrina had been telling her governess about the O'Donnells.

Trevor's about sixteen. He heard it again in his head and felt a sudden alarm. Sabrina was hardly more than a baby!

Dru seemed to read his mind. "Puppy love," she whispered as her hand touched his knee. "It won't hurt anything."

Patrick stepped over to the side of the wagon just then, his arms outstretched toward Rachel. "'Tis pleased I am to see you again, Miss Harris. I've been meanin' to come callin' on you like I promised, but my brother has had the whole place in a turmoil. Such a fuss over takin' a bride." And with that, he lifted her to the ground as easily as he had the children.

Gavin stepped over Dru and jumped down from the wagon seat, then turned back and helped Dru descend.

Patrick let out a low whistle. "Faith and begorra. This can't be Sabrina's mother. You're lookin' no more than a girl yourself, Drucilla Blake."

Dru's laughter filled the air. "Leave off your Irish blarney, Patrick O'Donnell. It'll get you nowhere with me. I've known you for too many years to have my head turned by your flattery."

"A shame you feel that way, lass, for I meant it from the heart." He turned toward Gavin. "'Tis not fair you should have so many beautiful women at the Lucky Strike, mate, while I've got nothin' but brothers to look at." He motioned with his hand for Gavin to follow, then hooked Rachel's hand through his arm. "Come in out of the cold. You've a house full of friends who're eager to see you again."

Gavin hung back for a moment while Patrick squired the ladies inside. There wasn't any reason for him to be feeling so much antagonism toward Patrick; in fact, he'd always considered him a friend in years past. What had changed? Ever since he'd seen the man in Challis several weeks ago, there'd been something stuck in his craw that wouldn't go away. Was he jealous of what the O'Donnells had here? He'd never thought so. He'd always felt great contentment with his ranch, his home, his way of life since settling down.

Still, he hadn't wanted to come to the wedding, and he sure as heck didn't want to go inside and listen to Patrick lavishing compliments on the womenfolk.

Womenfolk? Or just Rachel?

Pressing his lips together in a grim line, he climbed the steps and entered the house.

Dru hadn't been exaggerating when she said folks would come from miles around to see an O'Donnell get married. The house seemed to be bursting at the seams with people, young and old alike, all of them in good spirits as they gathered close to hear the tiny, dark-haired bride promise to love, honor, and obey the strapping, red-headed groom.

After the brief ceremony, servants carried vast platters of food to the long tables set up at the back of the great room that made up the center of the house. People milled about, chatting with neighbors, sharing gossip, eating and laughing and, in general, enjoying themselves immensely.

Rachel's head was swimming with names. It seemed that in the past two hours Patrick, who'd been at her side throughout most of the afternoon, had introduced her to nearly every person who lived within a hundred square miles of Challis. There were even some dignitaries from the state capital.

Patrick had just introduced her to Senator Brewer when his brother Jamie called to him from across the room. "Excuse me a moment, Miss Harris. Senator."

Senator Brewer rubbed the whiskers on his chin as he grinned at Rachel. "Of course, Mr. O'Donnell. You can be sure I'll take good care of Miss Harris in your absence."

"I won't be long," Patrick promised as he moved away.

"Don't believe I've seen you in these parts before, Miss Harris. And I'm sure I'd have remembered a pretty little thing like you. You look like you just got off a train from the East."

Rachel tried to quell her instant dislike for the rotund man with the sagging jowls and prying eyes. "Actually, sir, I grew up in Boise City."

"You don't say. You've got family there?"

"My sister and her husband. Maggie and Tucker Branigan."

"You're Judge Branigan's sister-in-law? Well, well. I had no idea he knew the O'Donnells. But then, I shouldn't be surprised." He lowered his voice. "It never hurts to have wealthy friends if you're the least politically motivated, I always say. I'll have to have a talk with that brother-in-law of yours. He carries a lot of weight in this territory. Very influential man. Well-respected. If he were to have the money of the O'Donnells behind him as well as his own, there'd be no stopping him in the politics of the territory. I can see why he sent you here to represent him."

She didn't much care for the man's insinuations. "Tucker doesn't know the O'Donnells, Senator Brewer," Rachel replied, trying to keep the irritation out of her voice. "I'm working as a governess for the Blake family. They own the Lucky Strike Ranch south of here."

"A governess? Out here?" Bushy gray eyebrows jumped up on his wrinkled forehead. "Well, I . . . that is . . ."

She could almost read his thoughts. Was Judge Branigan in financial trouble? Was Rachel in some sort of disgrace, sent away where few people would see her? Was there a scandal brewing? Something which might even be politically convenient to know? It made her blood boil. And if she didn't want to say anything that would embarrass Tucker later, she knew she'd better withdraw before her temper got the better of her.

177

"Excuse me, Senator. I'd better make sure my young charges aren't up to any mischief. You know how children can be."

"Of course. Of course."

"Pompous ass," she muttered beneath her breath as she turned away from the older man, not even caring particularly if he overheard her.

She moved off through the throng of people crowded into the great room. She wasn't really concerned about Sabrina and Petula. Dru had told her earlier that the little ones were being entertained by the older children in a far corner of the house. What she wanted most of all at this moment was just a few minutes of peace and quiet while she tried to cool her anger.

It took her a while, but finally she reached the hallway leading to the east wing and escaped into its blessed quiet. Seeing an open door near the end of the hall, she walked in that direction.

As she stepped into what turned out to be a sunny solarium, she stopped abruptly. Gavin was standing near the window. His expression was pensive as he stared outside. Feeling like an intruder, she started to back out of the room.

As if he'd heard some infinitesimal sound, his head turned and their eyes met.

"I'm sorry. I didn't mean to . . ." She swallowed. "I was looking for the children."

"They're upstairs. Except for Sabrina." He jerked his head toward the window.

Curious, Rachel moved forward and glanced outside. Seated on the veranda steps was Sabrina, her face a portrait of abject misery. Rachel followed the girl's woeful gaze toward the opposite end of the wide porch where Trevor O'Donnell leaned against the banister, his boot heel hooked over the bottom rail. He was smiling down at a pretty girl in a frilly pink dress. As they watched, Trevor removed his suit coat and draped it around the girl's shoulders.

"I'd like to break his jaw," Gavin murmured.

Rachel's eyes returned to Gavin. It was clear from the look on his face that he was suffering nearly as much as Sabrina. "Brina would never forgive you if you did," she said softly.

He sighed as he turned his back toward the window, his gaze meeting hers. "I don't know much about being a father, I guess."

"I think you're feeling what any father would feel." She smiled up at him.

"Think so?"

She nodded. Her throat felt tight. "The girls are very lucky to have you." She tried to swallow but couldn't. "So is Dru."

His gray eyes seemed to darken. "Are you having a good time?"

She nodded again.

"You must be used to this sort of shindig."

"Weddings are always fun."

"I won't ever be able to give Sabrina a wedding this fancy." He sounded angry again.

"It won't matter as long as she's in love with the groom," she whispered.

As he glared down at her, standing so close she could smell the faint odor of whiskey on his breath, she had the strange feeling they were locked in some sort of battle and that every word she said was important. She wanted desperately

179

to say the right things but wasn't even sure she knew what they were discussing any longer.

She might have discovered what it was if Patrick hadn't appeared in the solarium doorway at just that moment. "Ah, so here it is you're hiding. I thought I'd lost you, Miss Harris."

Gavin held her gaze a heartbeat longer before turning toward their host. "I was just keeping Rachel company until you were free again, Patrick. Now I'd better go find my wife."

A moment later, he had disappeared into the dim hallway.

Chapter Sixteen

"**I**'ll be payin' you a visit soon," Patrick said as he leaned against Patch's hip and looked up at Gavin and the two women on the wagon seat.

Gavin knew good and well it wouldn't be *him* Patrick O'Donnell was coming to visit. He mumbled something as he picked up the reins and slapped them against the teams' broad rumps, causing Patrick to jump quickly backward.

"See you soon, mate," the Irishman called after him, laughter filling his voice.

"Gavin, what's wrong with you?" Dru asked gently.

"Nothing."

"Gavin?"

He looked at her. Her face was drawn with weariness. Despite protests to the contrary, the day had drained what little energy she possessed. He should be ashamed of himself for causing her any extra worry. But then his eyes shifted to Rachel, and he felt his mood grow even more foul.

Damn the woman! She even had him snapping at Dru.

He swore silently once again as he returned his attention to the road ahead. But he couldn't stop the flood of anger that washed through him. He'd give almost anything to be able to go back in time, to be able to refuse to go to Boise in search of a woman to teach Dru's daughters. Nothing had gone right for him from the first moment he'd met Rachel.

She was a selfish, spoiled, rich girl with nothing bigger to worry about than what to wear to the next party. She wasn't even the proper sort to have around, influencing the children.

Yet, even as he worked so hard to convince himself he still believed those things about Miss Rachel Harris, he couldn't rid himself of the memory of her blue eyes looking up at him, bathed in the sunlight pouring through the solarium window, her pale golden hair capturing the warming rays and reflecting back the light. He remembered the rapid rise and fall of her breasts, so clearly outlined beneath the bodice of her indigo gown. He thought of the soft curve of her mouth, her lips moist and rosy. Her honeysuckle cologne lingered yet in his nostrils, stirring something basic in his vitals. He remembered her laughter, her gentle encouragement of Sabrina and Petula, the thoughtfulness she continually showed toward Dru. Even now, her voice seemed to echo in his ears, soft, melodic, soothing.

Soothing? Hellfire and damnation! There was nothing soothing about Rachel Harris.

He raked his fingers through his hair as he leaned forward, resting his forearms on his thighs, trying hard to ignore his keen awareness of her.

Dear God, what a base creature he was! His wife was right there beside him, her head resting on Rachel's shoulder, and he was thinking . . .

It was like a fire raging in his belly. The wanting, once he acknowledged it, flared white-hot and undeniable. He wanted to hold Rachel, touch her, possess her as he'd never wanted another woman in his life. And the thought of any other man—Patrick O'Donnell in particular—having the right to do any of those things nearly drove him mad.

Is this what had happened to his mother? Was it lust rather than greed that had made her forget she had a husband and son, that made her turn her back on everything right and honorable?

With a slap of the reins, the team broke into a trot as twilight fell over the valley.

Rachel felt the tension drawing her as tight as a bow string. Gavin never said a word, never even took his eyes off the road before them throughout the long drive home. His mood was dark and strange, and somehow he transmitted it to her and she grew afraid.

The first stars were already visible by the time they arrived at the Lucky Strike. Dru stirred and lifted her head from Rachel's shoulder as the wagon rolled to a stop in front of the ranch house. Wordlessly, Gavin jumped from his perch, then lifted Dru down after him.

"Wake up, girls," Rachel said softly, turning to look at the two sleepyheads curled up in the back of the wagon. "Come on. Let's get you to bed." Neither of them stirred.

"Don't bother waking them, Miss Harris," Gavin said sharply. "I'll see they get to bed."

She turned toward his voice. "It's no bother. I—"

"I said I'll take care of them. Good-night."

She couldn't see his face, but there was no mistaking the finality of his voice.

"Gavin . . ." Dru began.

He cut her short. "I can take care of my family, Dru." He lifted his wife in his arms and turned toward the house. "We won't need you anymore tonight, Miss Harris."

Rachel drew in a breath of night air even as she felt heat rush to her cheeks and tears burn her eyes. Unseeing, she scrambled down from the wagon seat and raced to her own little cabin.

She found it nearly as cold inside as it was out, the fire having long since burned down to a few coals. It seemed somehow fitting after the icy words Gavin had flung her way. With her fingertips, she dashed away the tears that clung to her lashes, then hurried toward the wood box, all the while fighting back more tears that threatened to replace them.

She made several attempts before the fire took hold. As soon as it did, Rachel pulled a heavy blanket from the bed and wrapped it around her, coat and all. Then she sat in a chair beside the stove and gave herself over to a good cry.

She didn't understand anything anymore. She didn't know what she felt or believed or wanted. It was all a crazy mix-up inside her head, inside her heart. Every time she thought she knew what she should do, what she wanted, something happened to change it.

She sniffed and dried her eyes and forced her shoulders to stiffen, her back to straighten.

No. It wasn't true that she didn't know what she wanted. She knew she wanted him to dislike her. She'd tried her best to make him think she was just as useless and vacuous as he'd thought her when Dru first hired her. Therefore, his anger and rudeness shouldn't upset her. It simply meant she'd succeeded.

Only the victory was a bitter one. She couldn't rid herself of the memory of that afternoon, the two of them standing near the solarium window, so close she could almost hear his heart beat. He hadn't disliked her then. There had been a moment—a brief and fragile moment—when she had hoped . . .

"Gavin," she whispered as hot tears coursed her cheeks once again. She choked over a sob. "Oh, Gavin."

* * *

Dru rose from the bed and pulled her robe tightly about her shoulders as she walked toward the bedroom door. Had she been mistaken? she wondered wearily.

She'd been so sure in Boise when Rachel entered that hotel room. She would have sworn something special had passed between Gavin and the girl the moment their eyes first met, just as it had been for her and Charlie.

But could she have been wrong?

She made her way to the table and sat down, leaning her forearms on the smooth surface while she stared toward the children's bedroom door. She could hear Petula mumbling sleepily. She could hear Gavin's gentle response.

She *wasn't* wrong. She couldn't be. There was no time for error.

She heard his footsteps and watched as he stepped through the doorway. Looking at the unhappiness, the tension that pulled at the handsome features of his face, she knew she had to keep trying. She wasn't wrong about those two.

He frowned when he saw her. "What are you doing up?"

"I don't know what's wrong with you, Gavin. I've never known you to be cruel to anyone."

His lips pressed together in a firm line as he walked toward her.

"You hurt Rachel's feelings. I think you should go over and apologize. See that she's all right."

"She's fine." He sat down across the table from her.

Dru reached forward and took hold of his hand. "Please, Gavin. I want you to go to her. Apologize. Please."

His gray eyes were as troubled as storm clouds. His voice, when he spoke, was tight and low. "Leave it be, Dru. You don't know what you're asking of me."

"Yes, I do," she whispered, tightening her grip on his hand. "Please, Gav. It means so much to me. Don't let her go to bed in tears."

"Dru . . ."

"I know I've asked too much of you already, takin' on a sick wife and two girls to raise. I haven't any right to ask anything more. Not a thing. But I *am* askin'. Go to her, Gavin. For me."

Moonlight bathed the yard in a white light, casting an eerie glow across the barn, the grasslands, the mountains, everything. But especially across the small cabin that stood apart from the other buildings. It seemed especially bright there.

Gavin walked slowly across the expanse of ground that separated the main house from the one-room cabin. He tried to repress the resurgence of anger that increased with each step he took.

He stopped. He was here because Dru wanted him to be here. He would do as she'd asked and then leave. Taking a deep breath, he raised his hand and knocked firmly.

It seemed a long time before he heard the latch lifting, saw the door opening. And then she was there, standing in the doorway, her hair cascading over her shoulders, her eyes swollen from crying, her mouth parted in surprise. She was wearing a pretty robe over her long night-gown, and she clutched the front of it near her throat.

His anger began to evaporate the moment he saw her, replaced by a tender yearning, some-thing he'd never felt before—a feeling far more dangerous than his anger had ever been.

"Gavin," she whispered as she stepped sud-denly back from the doorway, disappearing into the dark shadows of the cabin.

"I came to apologize," he said, his voice loud in the silence of night. He stepped inside, hesi-tated, then closed the door.

"Apologize?"

"I was rude. And tired. I didn't mean to hurt you."

A pale sliver of moonlight fell through the curtains over the window. Just enough light, added to the red glow from the fire in the stove, to help him see her face, to help him see the sparkle of tears in her eyes.

"It's all right," she answered softly.

"No. It's not all right."

The darkness seemed to close in around them even while her face became more clear. She was beautiful. So damn beautiful.

"Nothing's been right since I met you." He stepped closer. "What have you done to me, Rachel?"

Her words were breathless. "I . . . I don't know what you mean."

"Don't you?" He reached out, his fingers closing over her arms. "It's not right what I feel for you. It's not right how I think about you."

He wasn't sure how it happened, but suddenly, she was pressed against him, her face turned up to his, her eyes filled with wonder instead of tears.

"Not right," he whispered again.

Then his mouth descended toward hers.

Rachel had been kissed before, but nothing had prepared her for the explosion of feelings that erupted within her the moment their lips touched. Her knees became as wobbly as a newborn colt's. She lifted her arms and clung to his neck, afraid she would fall to the floor and splinter into a thousand pieces if she didn't hold on. The skin on her face tingled, and her breath caught stubbornly in her chest.

His lips were warm and moist, gently moving against hers. She responded, parting her mouth ever so slightly and touching her tongue against the flesh of his lower lip, as if tasting some strange and exotic delicacy.

His hands—pressed against her lower back, holding her close but not close enough to assuage the strange ache that was growing inside her—began to move. His touch seemed to sear her skin right through the fabric of her robe as his fingers traced the length of her back, then moved down her arms and back again. Finally, his hands came up to cradle her head. His thumbs lightly caressed her cheeks as his fingers plunged into her unbound hair.

Her thoughts were like chaff in the wind, scattered in all directions. She couldn't think straight. Who was this man? Who was she? What wondrous place had he brought her to? What miracle was he working in her body?

But even as her mind toyed with illusion, reality tried to reassert itself. Time became her enemy. She wanted it to stand still. She wanted them to remain forever as they now were.

Gavin's mouth released hers, yet hovered close, so very close. "It's not right." His voice was low, hoarse. His breath was warm upon her face.

He'd said the same thing moments before— or was it hours before?—but only now did she truly understand what he meant.

"I've never wanted any woman the way I want you." There was something almost frightening in the resonance of his whispered confession, a depth of emotion she felt incapable of accepting and unwilling to deal with.

From what well of strength did she summon the courage to free herself from his embrace? Perhaps she would never know.

She dragged in a quick gasp of air as she stepped away from him, her hands pushing against the wall of his chest. "You must go."

"Rachel . . ."

"Go now!" she cried, knowing that soon there would be no stopping the tide that carried them into perilous waters.

For a breathless moment, she thought he would refuse. Then she saw him take his own step backward.

She forced the quiver from her voice, speaking louder than was necessary in hope that it would give her words conviction and strength. "We'll forget this ever happened."

But she knew, even as did he, that they could not forget.

Chapter Seventeen

Rachel's fingers fumbled nervously with the buttons of her bodice. Her stomach was tied in knots, and a sleepless night had left her without energy. Yet she knew she couldn't delay going to the main house any longer. She couldn't expect Dru to prepare the family's breakfast. The woman had been exhausted by yesterday's outing.

She glanced quickly at her reflection in the small mirror atop the bureau. There were gray shadows beneath her blue eyes, and her face looked as white as a sheet. She pinched her cheeks several times between her forefingers and thumbs, trying to revive a hint of color. She couldn't risk Dru thinking she was ill—or worse, suspecting that something had happened the night before.

Her stomach tightened with a jolt as the

memory of Gavin's kisses flooded over her, around her, through her. It had been like this throughout the night, his specter invading the cabin time and again. Relentless. Persistent.

"No more," she pleaded softly. "No more."

Before she could turn coward and return to her bed, she pulled her fur-lined cloak from the peg by the door and threw it over her shoulders.

It never happened. It never happened.

Oh, Maggie, I wish you were here. You could tell me what to do.

It never happened. It never happened.

Gavin . . . Oh, Gavin.

She jerked open the cabin door, and with head bent forward beneath the warm hood of her cloak, she hurried toward the main house.

Just as her hand touched the doorknob, she heard the clatter of hooves and turned to see Gavin riding his black gelding out of the barn. He never looked toward the house, never saw her standing there, would never know how she longed for just one glimpse of his steel-gray eyes.

It was just as well. It would have been her undoing.

She twisted the knob and entered the house.

"Look what you did!"

Sabrina's shrill cry brought Rachel up short. With a quick glance, she assessed that the disaster wasn't as dire the girl's voice had indicated. But by the time Rachel closed the door and rid herself of her cloak, Petula was already in tears as she stood in the middle of the egg-splattered floor, broken eggshells surrounding her feet.

"Don't cry, Pet. It's not so terrible," Rachel

said as she hurried forward.

"But it is, Miss Harris," Sabrina insisted. "Those were all the eggs. We've been out and collected them and there won't be any more until tomorrow. And Ma said she'd like an egg for breakfast. She hardly ever eats any more, but she wanted something this morning, and now Pet's *ruined* Ma's breakfast."

The younger girl's sobs increased. "I . . . I did . . . didn't mean . . . mean to."

Rachel pushed tangled brown hair away from the child's face as she knelt beside her, unmindful of the hem of her dress mixing with the gooey mess on the floor. She kissed Petula's cheek. "Hush, now. Shhh. Your mother will understand. We'll make her a grand breakfast, something she'll like much better than eggs."

"Wh . . . wha . . . what?" Petula sniffed, then rubbed her sleeve beneath her nose.

"Well . . . why don't I go ask her?"

"But then she'll know what Pet did," Sabrina interrupted in the same high-handed tone.

Rachel turned her head, casting a meaningful glance toward the older girl. "Do you think your mother wouldn't understand about a little accident?"

Sabrina bowed her head. "No," she mumbled.

"No," Rachel repeated. "Of course not. Now, help Pet clean this up, and I'll go see what we can tempt your mother's appetite with."

The set of Sabrina's shoulders was still slightly mutinous, but she nodded her head as Rachel rose from the floor.

"Miss . . . Miss Harris?" Petula stuttered, still

trying to control her tears. "I . . . I ruined your dress too. Look." She pointed at the egg stains on Rachel's skirt.

It was one of her favorite day dresses, a pale blue wool, and it did, indeed, look ruined. But Rachel managed to conceal her dismay as she calmly reached for a cloth lying on the dry sink and wiped away what she could. "It'll wash," she told Petula, her voice light. "It's not important." And she knew as she spoke the words that they were true. Petula's feelings were far more important than any dress.

For the few minutes it had taken to deal with Petula's crisis, Rachel had forgotten her own problems, but as soon as she reached the door to Dru's bedroom, they came rushing back. Dru was more than an employer. She was Rachel's friend. She was sick and dying, and Rachel had come so close to betraying her. How could she face her?

She leveled her shoulders, drew a deep breath, and pushed open the door. "Dru?" The room was shrouded in shadows.

"Is everything all right out there?" Dru's voice was barely more than a whisper.

"Yes." Rachel crossed the room with measured steps. "Just a little tiff between sisters. I've seen it before with my nieces and nephews." She stopped beside the bed. "I'm afraid there won't be any eggs for breakfast."

"It's not important," Dru replied with a shallow sigh. "I doubt I could have eaten it anyway."

Rachel's eyes had adjusted to the dim light of the room by this time, and she stared down at the woman in the bed. It seemed to Rachel that Dru had withered away overnight.

"Dru, please. You must try to eat something." She leaned forward, touching the papery skin of Dru's arm.

"Perhaps later. What I'd like is for you to sit with me a while. Would you do that for me, Rachel?"

A shiver of fear raced down her back. "If you'd like." She reached for the chair against the wall.

"Wait." Dru's voice seemed even weaker. "Help the girls with their breakfast first. Then come back. I'll just close my eyes and rest for a while. I'm so terribly tired today."

He was a coward and he knew it.

Gavin reminded himself of that fact numerous times as he rode Scamp across the acres of grassland that made up the Lucky Strike. There was little a cattleman could do in the winter except pray and hope that the blizzards and freezing temperatures didn't last too long, that the calves didn't drop too soon, that the wolves and coyotes didn't strike too often. There wasn't anything he could accomplish by spending the day in the saddle, chilled to the bone by the icy November winds.

But he *was* a coward and he knew it.

He couldn't face Dru this morning, not while Rachel's image was still burned into his brain, not while he longed to taste her lips, feel her soft flesh beneath his hands; not while desire to possess her raged in his body.

He jerked back on the reins, bringing the

gelding to a sliding stop. He pushed his hat back on his head and rubbed his fingers across his forehead.

What sort of spell had that blonde witch cast over him? Never once in his thirty-three years had he been so obsessed with a woman. He'd known his share and found out he could get along well enough without them in his life, at least any particular one for any particular length of time. When he'd felt the need of a woman, he'd found the saloon girls in any town were sufficient. He could spend a few hours with them, finding release within the soft warmth of their bodies, then forget them.

Perhaps that was what he needed now. Perhaps he needed to head up to Bonanza City or Custer, somewhere far enough away that Dru— and Rachel—would never hear of it. For a few dollars and a little time, he could rid himself of this obsession. He'd been abstinent too long.

But even as he thought it, he knew it was useless. He knew he would return still wanting Rachel Harris. And not just her body. He wanted to sit with her while she read to the children. He wanted to watch her brushing her hair by candlelight. He wanted to race with her through another mountain meadow, hear her laughter as she tripped over Joker's clumsy feet.

He wanted her completely, totally, absolutely, unconditionally.

And with all he was, all he'd ever believed, he knew it was wrong to want her. As long as he had a wife, it was wrong.

He dug his spurs into Scamp's black sides and

sent the horse hurtling forward at a mad pace, afraid to think any longer, afraid of where his thoughts were leading him.

After preparing the children's breakfast, Rachel went to her cabin and quickly changed out of her soiled gown. Upon her return to the main house, she found Dru fast asleep. Knowing that Dru always read to the children from the Bible on Sunday mornings, Rachel sat down with them near the fireplace and read several parables from the Gospel of John. More than once she paused in her reading, feeling a terrible hypocrisy.

Thou shalt not covet.

Could God ever forgive her the rebellion of her heart?

Rachel returned to Dru's bedroom throughout the morning, but every time, she found the woman sleeping. She couldn't bring herself to wake her, not when she could see so clearly the fatigue written on her face.

Several times, she stepped outside, her gaze sweeping over the valleys and mountains, never admitting to herself what she was watching for. Once, she saw Stubs come out of the bunkhouse, his coat collar pulled up against the cold. He raised a hand and waved to her before entering the barn. She shivered as a lonely wind whistled through the trees, then turned and went back inside.

It was shortly after noon that a knock sounded on the door. The girls were in their bedroom, involved in cutting out scraps of cloth for doll dresses, so Rachel went to answer the door herself, certain that it was Stubs. When she pulled the door open, she was surprised to find Patrick O'Donnell's giant frame filling up the opening.

"Good day, Miss Harris," he said as he pulled his hat from his head. "I hope I've not come at a bad time?"

"Not at all, Mr. O'Donnell. Please. Do come in." She opened the door wide to admit him.

There seemed to be something almost awkward about the big man today. Rachel sensed his nervousness even as she reached to take his hat.

"Won't you have a seat?" She motioned toward the chair near the fireplace. "I'm afraid Gavin isn't here at the moment."

"It's not Gavin I've come to see."

Rachel's eyes widened as she looked at him. He'd flirted with her the day they met, and at the wedding he'd monopolized much of her time. But it wasn't until now that she took his interest seriously. Perhaps it was that schoolboy look on his face or the way he was pressing his fingers together, turning them white at the tips.

"I see," she replied softly, sinking into another chair.

She liked Patrick O'Donnell. Despite his size, she sensed a gentleness about him. He had a fine face, not truly handsome, but pleasant. She imagined his broad nose had been generously freckled when he was a boy, though there was no trace of them now. His mouth was full, the hint of a grin lingering in the corners, even now when he was serious. His green eyes promised mischief.

She'd enjoyed his company yesterday. He'd always been the gentleman. And he'd made her laugh often.

She wasn't quite sure why she was silently cataloging Patrick O'Donnell's assets. At least, not consciously. But somewhere deep inside, in a secret corner of her heart, she realized that here might be an answer to her quandary. This man could be her shield. This man could protect her from herself, from her own sinful desires. If she were to turn her affections upon him, she needn't fear being around Gavin any longer.

"I'm glad you came, Mr. O'Donnell. Would you care for some coffee? There's plenty and it's fresh."

"I'd like it very much." He grinned, all traces of nervousness disappearing. "I'd find even more pleasure, Miss Harris, if you could bring yourself to call me Patrick."

As she rose from her chair, she returned his smile. "I should like that, Patrick. And you must call me Rachel."

She could see Charlie. He was waiting for her, smiling, his arms open wide. He was surrounded by light—warm, comforting light. When she reached him, there wouldn't be any more pain. She wouldn't be tired any longer. She could laugh again. She could run through the woods and fall down with Charlie in the grass. She could be happy.

He beckoned for her to hurry.

I'm coming, Charlie.

But something held her back. Something was unfinished.

Soon, Charlie. Soon.

She made her way back through the darkness she'd come part-way through. It was an arduous, tiring journey, but at last she made it.

Dru awakened to find Rachel at her bedside.

"I was worried about you," Rachel said softly. "You've been asleep all day."

Dru lifted her hand from the bedclothes, reaching toward Rachel. Sensing the woman didn't have the strength to keep it there long, Rachel grasped hold of the cool fingers, wrapping both of her hands around Dru's frail one.

"Mr. O'Donnell was here to see you. He said he'll come again soon." She paused, then added softly, "Let me get you some broth. You need to eat."

"No." Dru shook her head. "Just sit with me."

Rachel couldn't seem to let go of Dru's hand. She lowered herself onto the edge of the bed.

"I haven't much time, Rachel."

She opened her mouth to protest but was stopped by the look in Dru's eyes.

"There's so much I wanted to do before I joined Charlie."

Rachel swallowed the lump in her throat and tightened her grip on the feeble hand within hers.

"Gavin's a good man, Rachel. He wasn't to me

what my Charlie was, but we loved each other in our own way." Her eyes seemed glazed as she stared into space beyond Rachel's shoulder. "He wasn't meant to marry me. There's so much of love he doesn't know about. So much he needs to learn."

Dru closed her eyes. Her breathing was shallow, almost nonexistent. Rachel leaned forward, her heart aching in her chest. She, too, was afraid to breathe.

"Rachel . . ." Dru opened her eyes once more, this time her gaze focused and meaningful. "Gavin's going to need you. Don't forget your promise. You'll stay through spring. Time. Give him time."

"Don't talk this way, Dru. You're going to be well by spring. You'll see."

"Promise me."

"I promise. I won't leave. I give you my word, but—"

"Ask Stubs about Gavin. Make him . . . make him tell you everything. There's so much I never knew. Make him tell you . . . everything."

Panic raged in Rachel's breast. She wasn't acquainted with death, yet she could see its shadow slipping over Dru's face and knew it for what it was.

"Brina . . . Pet . . ." Dru whispered. "I'd like to see them now. Will you help me sit up? Comb my hair?"

"Yes, Dru. Of course. I'll help you." She was blinded by tears and fought to keep them from falling. "Please, won't you eat something? You'll feel stronger if you do." She rose from the bed and grabbed another pillow to place behind Dru's back.

"No. I just need to see my girls."

Gavin tossed a flake of hay into Scamp's stall, then made his way toward the house. His mood was as dark and heavy as when he'd taken off that morning, but he'd been gone too long already. Dru would be wondering what was wrong. He didn't know yet what he would tell her. He only knew he couldn't tell her the truth.

The moment he pushed open the door, he sensed something was wrong. The house was quiet. Too quiet.

Rachel appeared suddenly in the bedroom doorway. Her face looked pale and drawn.

"Gavin," she whispered.

His heart skipped a beat, cold tentacles of dread spreading through his veins.

She took a step forward. "Dru . . ."

Quick strides carried him across the parlor. He brushed past her and into the dimly lit bedroom, stopping just inside the doorway.

Dru's arms were around Petula's shoulders. She kissed the child's forehead, then lay back against the pillows. Her eyes met Gavin's and she offered a tiny smile. "Here's your pa. It's time I talked to him. And then I must rest. Good night, children. I . . ." Her voice broke. "I love you."

"Ma . . ." Sabrina was having a hard time controlling her tears.

"I know, Brina. I know." She sighed as she closed her eyes. "Now go with Miss Harris."

Gavin watched as Sabrina took hold of Petula's hand and led her little sister across the room. Hazel eyes, identical to her mother's, glanced up at him as they walked by. He felt immobilized by the pain he saw written in them, helpless to remove or heal the hurt.

"Come along, girls," he heard Rachel say behind him.

A moment later, the door closed with a soft click.

Dru opened her eyes once more. "I was waiting for you."

He moved forward on stiff legs.

"Hold my hand, Gavin."

He knelt on the hard floor and did as she'd asked.

"You've been a good friend. To me and to Charlie."

"Dru . . ."

"No, don't say anything. There isn't time." Her gaze, although weary, was tender. "From the moment I first laid eyes on Charlie, I knew there was somethin' special between us. There wasn't anything in this world that would've kept me from bein' his bride. Not anything."

He nodded, his throat too tight to try to speak again, even if she hadn't told him to keep still.

"I'm not afraid to die, Gavin. The girls have got you and Rachel. They'll be fine. Just fine. And I'll be with Charlie."

Her eyes closed again, and she was silent for a long time. Her chest scarcely moved. Gavin tightened his grip on her hand.

"Don't be afraid to love someone . . . like I

204

did Charlie. It makes . . . everything in life . . .
worthwhile." She looked at him then, and it
seemed to Gavin that she was already far away.
"What happened in the past . . . can't be
changed . . . but the future . . . can." Again the
lengthy silence. "I . . . wish you . . . love."

She pulled her hand from his, lifting her
fingertips to touch his cheek. Then her hand fell
listlessly to her side as her eyes fluttered closed.

"Charlie . . ."

The name was whispered with an exhaled
breath. There was no matching intake of air to
replace it.

Gavin had no idea how long he knelt there,
unmoving, unthinking, scarcely even feeling.
There was a great hollowness inside him, devouring everything, leaving only emptiness. He
didn't hear the door open, wasn't aware of the
rustle of petticoats as Rachel entered the room,
coming to stand beside him. He didn't feel her
hand upon his shoulder.

"Gavin?"

He lifted his head, raising his eyes toward the
woman at his side. He wondered why she was
there.

"Gavin, she's gone."

He looked once more toward the bed. He
knew that what he saw was only an empty shell.
The essence that had been Drucilla Porter Blake
was gone, escaping the bonds of earth, leaving
behind the pain.

"She's with Charlie," he said hoarsely.

A sob caught in Rachel's throat. "I know."

He picked up Dru's hand and tenderly laid it

across her chest. Her voice seemed to echo softly through the room.

I wish you love.

And as he heard the silent words repeated, a chink appeared in the carefully constructed wall around Gavin's heart.

Chapter Eighteen

Rachel stood on the grassy knoll, her right hand on Sabrina's shoulder, her left on Petula's. Patrick stood beside her, likewise offering what comfort he could with an arm around Rachel's back. Gavin stood on the other side of the grave, his face a controlled mask.

The minister's voice droned on, dispensing words of consolation and hope. Overhead, gray clouds rolled across the heavens, driven by a frigid wind. The weather seemed in keeping with the sorrow that blanketed the friends and neighbors who had gathered to bid Drucilla Blake farewell. As Reverend Keating's final prayer was carried to the mourners on the wind, the snow began to fall.

People departed somewhat quickly after that.

Rachel gazed across the grave site at Gavin, but he made no move to leave, even after the last person had offered his condolences and gone. Her heart ached for Gavin. She wished desperately for a means to console him. But even as she wished it, she knew she couldn't. She was an outsider to his grief. He'd made everyone an outsider in the two days since Dru's death.

"Come along, girls," she said. "We must get inside."

When Petula, blinded by tears and sobbing, stumbled over a ground squirrel hole, Patrick caught her up and cradled her against him. Rachel held tightly to Sabrina's hand as the foursome made their way down the gentle slope and back to the house.

As the others entered the front door, Rachel turned around and looked back toward the knoll. The snow was falling in large gentle flakes, but she could still see Gavin's silhouette against the mountain.

"Rachel?"

She turned toward the sound of Patrick's voice.

"You'll take cold, lass. Come in. Sure and I've got a fire goin' on the hearth."

She nodded, then cast one final glance over her shoulder before entering the house and closing the door.

Patrick seemed to understand her concern. "Give him time, Rachel."

That's what Dru had said. Give him time. But, Lord help her, she wanted to give him much more than time. She wanted to offer real comfort. Not just words and platitudes. She wanted to share his grief, help him carry the burden of sorrow.

"Come here, lass," Patrick said gently as he took hold of her hand and drew her toward him. He pushed the hood from her hair, then loosened the clasp of her cloak and removed it from her shoulders. Finally, he pulled her into his embrace. "There now. You'll not have to worry. Patrick O'Donnell is here for you."

She was grateful for a strong shoulder to lean on. Even now, with so much else on her mind and in her heart, she knew that by doing so she was indicating the direction her relationship with Patrick was headed. But that was what she'd wanted, she reminded herself. Nothing had changed since she'd made that decision. Not really. Gavin seemed as forbidden to her now as ever before, though why that should be she wasn't quite sure.

That was a lie, she thought as she pressed her face against Patrick's shirt. She had envied another woman her husband. She had succumbed to his kisses. She had been tempted to do much more than that. She was guilty of a cardinal sin, lusting after a married man. Her punishment now was to be forever denied what she wanted most.

She felt as if she were shattering into pieces. How was she to keep her promise to Dru to help Gavin and the children through this time of sorrow? How was she to survive Gavin's nearness, knowing that their time together was fleeting at best?

Patrick's arms tightened around her. "I'm here for you, lass," he repeated, as if in answer to her silent question.

"I don't know how I'd get through this without you," she whispered.

The door slammed shut, and she lifted her head from Patrick's chest to meet Gavin's remote gaze. His black hair was dotted with white flakes of snow, wet tendrils curling at his nape. His face was red from the cold. Without a word, he moved on toward his bedroom, his door closing firmly behind him.

Rachel pulled away from Patrick, taking a step toward Gavin's room, but she stopped herself. Her shoulders slumped. There was nothing she could do for him. Not now. Not ever.

Instead, she turned toward the children's bedroom. At least there she could openly pour out her love and caring.

She found them curled up together on Sabrina's bed. Sabrina was stroking her little sister's hair and whispering, "Don't cry, Pet," while large teardrops streaked her own cheeks.

Looking at them, she was reminded of her childhood back in Philadelphia, of the many times Maggie had talked to her in just that tone of voice. After so many years, the memories were fuzzy, but she knew they'd been very lonely in those early years and so terribly unhappy. Just the two of them against the world.

Maggie had often played the "Good Things"

game with her whenever Rachel was too unhappy or too frightened. They would hide up in the attic, where Uncle Seth never thought to look for them, thinking of all that was good and happy and bright. No matter how grim things seemed, they'd always managed to think of something.

She remembered how very badly she'd wanted a family, a family to love her. And she'd been lucky. She'd been given a wonderful one. Not just Maggie, who had always been a comforting presence, but Tucker and Fiona and Neal and Mr. and Mrs. Foster. She'd been granted so many things good and happy and bright.

She wondered how long it would be before Sabrina and Petula could think of something good about their lives. She wondered what she could do to help them find the happiness their mother wanted for them.

Rachel slowly crossed the room. Wordlessly, she pulled back the covers and guided the children beneath them. Then she sat beside them and waited until they fell asleep.

She was surprised to find Patrick still there when she came out of the children's room more than an hour later. He rose from his chair the moment she appeared in the doorway.

"I thought you'd gone, Patrick." She walked toward him.

"I couldn't leave until I made sure you were all right."

She sighed deeply. "I'm all right. Just tired."

"You shouldn't have to carry this burden alone, lass. Sure but there must be something more I can do."

"Yes, Patrick. There is." She sank onto the chair nearest the fire. "Just sit with me."

"If you wish."

She looked into the orange and gold flames. "I was remembering how Maggie used to make me feel better when something bad had happened. We used to try to think about good things, pretty things. Like a fine black horse pulling a shiny black carriage. Or a lady's hat with a purple ostrich feather. Or maybe a winter snowfall. Sometimes we'd play the game for hours."

"Did bad things happen often to you, Rachel?" He leaned forward in his chair.

"Yes . . ." she whispered. "I guess they did. But you know, it's strange. I can't really remember what they were. After we came to Idaho, I have only good memories."

"I'm glad, lass. I'd not ever have you sad if I had my way about it, and that's the truth."

She turned her head to look at him. "How do I keep them from being sad, Patrick? I don't know what to do for them."

"There's not much you can do but have patience. Be there to listen when they want to talk. Be there t'hold them when they want to cry. Mournin' takes time, lass, and each goes about it in their own way. What of you? How will you go about it, Rachel? Will you allow someone to listen and hold you when you're needin' it?"

He truly was a good friend. A gentleman. Dependable. The sort she could count on in good times and bad. Would it be so harmful to encourage his interest, knowing her heart yearned for another? Surely, with time, she could grow to feel more for him than simple friendship, and the guilt for what she'd done, what she'd wanted, could be forgotten.

"Yes, Patrick," she replied. "I will."

Chapter Nineteen

The days and weeks drifted by little noticed by Gavin. He was weighed down by shame and remorse. Illogically, he blamed himself for Dru's death. If he hadn't gone to Rachel's cabin the night before, if he hadn't kissed her and burned with desire for her, if he hadn't left Dru alone the next day—if he hadn't done these things, Dru might still be alive.

He mentally flailed himself for his neglect, for his disloyal thoughts and behavior. He could have been a better husband to her. True, their marriage had been one of convenience, never consummated and never meant to be. True, their mutual affection had been based upon friendship and no more. But wasn't there something he could have done to change the course of things? It seemed so, now that it was too late to try.

While Gavin wrestled with the demon of guilt, winter arrived in earnest in the high country. It blanketed the Salmon River Range with thick layers of snow, sometimes with lazy crystals drifting to earth, sometimes with vengeful blizzards, winds howling across the mountains and valleys. Temperatures fell well below zero at night and lingered there until noon. The skies seemed eternally gray, days scarcely discernible from nights.

Gavin went about the business of running the ranch by rote. Although Stubs and Jess could have managed well enough without him, he needed something, *anything*, to distract him from his troubled thoughts. Rachel took care of the house and the girls, preparing meals, washing and mending their clothes, caring for every detail of their day-to-day existence. Patrick O'Donnell came often, but Gavin rarely spoke to him. He rarely spoke to anyone.

Christmas would have been a dismal affair in the Blake house, if not for Rachel and Patrick. If it weren't for them, there would have been no tree strung with popcorn and paper garlands. There would have been no stockings filled with fruit and nuts, no special gifts awaiting the children on Christmas morning. Without Rachel and Patrick, there would have been no sleigh ride, no singing of Christmas carols. Although it was impossible for the day to be a joyous one, there was at least an effort to make it a normal one.

But Gavin didn't notice. For him, Christmas was merely another day to get through as best he could.

Gavin awakened suddenly in the middle of the night. Silence enveloped the house. No wind whistled beneath the eaves, no snow blew against the window panes. There was only silence.

And as he lay there, he began to hear Dru's words to him once again. But this time, more than five weeks after she'd whispered them to him, he wasn't just hearing them in his head. He was hearing them with his heart.

Don't be afraid to love, she'd said.

Don't be afraid to risk it all. Don't be afraid to trust and give. Don't be afraid to take in return. Don't be so embittered by what some did in the past that you can't look for the good in others in the future. Don't believe that every woman is like Christina Blake, selfish and spoiled. Believe, instead, in the best in people.

Don't be afraid to love. Really love. Love with everything, heart and body and mind and soul. Don't be afraid to love.

I wish you love.

He stared up at the ceiling as a strange peace descended. She'd known. That's what she'd been telling him. She'd known what he felt for Rachel and she'd wanted it for him. Not just the physical passion, although he didn't doubt she'd wanted that for him too. She'd wanted him to experience that tender yearning, that desire to

216

be a part of the whole that was made from two people.

He wondered, now that he understood, if it was too late for him to learn how to love.

Patrick proposed to Rachel on Christmas day, just before he left the Lucky Strike for home, and she accepted. But she insisted the wedding couldn't take place until mid-June. She'd given her promise that she would stay on at the Lucky Strike until then. She would keep her word.

She wasn't surprised by the proposal, nor even by her acceptance, although she didn't lie to herself about her reasons. As fond as she was of Patrick, she knew she didn't love him. She'd turned down numerous proposals from men every bit as wealthy and many of them more handsome for that exact same reason. She might have liked them tremendously, but she hadn't loved them. And she hadn't wanted to marry for any reason except love. She'd wanted to be just like Maggie in that respect.

But this time, she couldn't turn the man away. She accepted this as her destiny. Perhaps even her punishment. To be so close to happiness but never quite able to grasp it.

Rachel awakened in the wee hours of morning the day after Christmas. It was still as black as ink outside, and she knew the girls wouldn't be awake for some time. She jumped out of bed and scurried across the room, quickly plucking some wood from the wood box and stuffing it into the black iron belly of the stove. Then she raced back to the warmth of her bed and waited for the fire to do its work in the small room.

She hadn't slept a great deal through the night, and when she had, it had been fitful. She knew she should write to Maggie and tell her of Patrick's proposal. Maggie would want to meet the man intended to be her brother-in-law. Of course, no one could find fault with the big Irishman. He would be a kind, adoring husband, and she knew he would always be good to her.

But there was an ache inside Rachel for more than kindness, more than goodness.

She could see him in her mind. Hair as black as raven's wings. Eyes like gun metal. The features of his face boldly handsome. Tall and broad of shoulder, his arms whipcord-strong, his legs long and powerful. A man capable of joyous laughter and explosive anger. A man who could drive her to tears and carry her to passion.

Gavin.

With a moan deep in her throat, Rachel tossed aside the heavy blankets and rose once again from her bed. She drew on a warm robe as she walked across the room to the window, pushing aside the curtains to stare across the snow-covered yard.

Everything was so still. For the first time in weeks, the sky was clear. Stars twinkled against the black backdrop of night, their light reflected in the crusty blanket of snow that covered the earth.

As beautiful and peaceful as nature appeared at the moment, Rachel felt a terrible longing for the relative mildness of the Boise Valley. It never snowed there for days on end, let alone weeks on end. And there were all sorts of winter activities to take part in.

Not like here. Here she was alone, separated by distance and weather from everyone else in the world. If it weren't for Patrick's stubborn interest in her, which brought him several times each week across the miles that separated the two ranches—even in near-blizzard conditions—she doubted she would have seen another soul until the spring thaw.

But if she was honest, it wasn't being snowbound that caused this feeling of loneliness. It wasn't mere isolation from the town or even her family that troubled her.

She glanced toward the house, understanding now that the distance between her cabin and Gavin's home was much farther than the mere yards it was measured in. More than heavy snows stood between them. She was more isolated from Gavin than from anyone in Challis or her family in Boise.

Rachel leaned her head against the window casing as her throat tightened and her eyes misted. What would Gavin think of her engagement? Would he even care?

Of course not. He'd never expected her to stay longer than spring. Once he left to take the cattle back into the Stanley Basin, he wouldn't give her another thought.

She saw a light flicker inside the children's bedroom. It was so early. She couldn't imagine them being awake yet, not after the activities of Christmas day. Was Petula ill perhaps? The girl had partaken rather liberally of the candy Patrick had brought with him.

Rachel turned from the window and quickly pulled on her boots over warm stockings. She didn't take time to change, merely pulling her cloak over her robe.

The serenity of the outdoor scene through the window of her cabin had been misleading. When she opened the door, she was blasted by a wall of frigid air. Crystals formed immediately on the tiny hairs inside her nostrils. Her lungs complained as she dragged in a frosty breath.

Pulling her cloak more tightly about her, she hurried across the yard, the snow crunching beneath her footsteps. In her hurry, she strayed once from the hard-packed trail between the buildings. She broke through the crusty surface, her leg sinking in snow almost to her knee. She caught herself just in time to prevent a nasty wrenching.

By the time she reached the house, the light had disappeared from the children's room, but she had no intention of returning to her cabin without making sure everything was all right. Quietly, she opened the door and let herself in.

She was midway across the spacious room when his voice stopped her.

"The girls are fine. I just looked in on them."

A sharp intake of air produced a tiny protest of

surprise as she whirled around. He was standing near the fireplace, the banked coals glowing softly behind him.

"You're up early," he said.

Her heart was pounding madly in her chest, and she pressed her hand against it, as if to keep it from breaking free. "I saw the light in the children's room. I thought perhaps Pet . . ."

Gavin stepped toward her. His voice was low. "You couldn't sleep?"

She shook her head, her breathing slowed by his nearness. She could make out the outline of his face now, the bold cut of his jaw, the sharp line of his nose, the deep set of his eyes.

"Neither could I."

She realized then that there was something changed about him. It was his voice. It sounded different. Stronger. Like Gavin again.

"I was thinking about Dru."

Her knees felt weak. She turned away from him and sat quickly in the nearest chair.

Silently, Gavin returned to the fireplace, hunkering down as he stoked the fire with new fuel, coaxing it back to life. Hungry flames licked at the wood, curled around it in a hot caress, then reached toward the chimney, as if in joyous celebration.

The glow of the fire played over his ebony hair, still tousled by sleep. It was reflected in the steel gray of his eyes as he turned his head to meet her gaze. Unnerved by the look, she lowered her eyes to the hearth.

He swiveled on the balls of his bare feet, still

crouching. She realized then that he was clad only in his long johns. Her gaze jumped quickly over his knees and the lower part of his body, afraid of what she might accidently see—and even more frightened by her desire to see. The warm flannel stretched smoothly across his shoulders. The sleeves were pushed up to his elbows, revealing muscular forearms. Finally, her gaze returned to his face. She found him still watching her, his expression enigmatic.

Enigmatic, yes, but different from any look she'd seen before. There was life in the gray depths of his eyes. Perhaps even hope. There was something about the way he was looking at her. Something . . . A name for it eluded her even while she yearned to understand.

When he rose and came toward her, she closed her eyes, concentrating on the thundering of her heart. She heard the chair creak as he settled onto the seat. She opened her eyes but kept her gaze on the floor near his feet.

"I've been thinking about Dru," he repeated after a lengthy silence. "About what she was hoping for. For everyone."

The wanting increased. That terrible, irresistible urge to be a part of him. She was aware of her own near-nakedness beneath her robe.

She had to get away. He was too close. Far too close. She could scarcely breathe, let alone think. "I gave my word I wouldn't leave until you'd taken the cattle back to the basin in June," she said. "I'll keep my promise."

"Maybe you could come with us." He paused.

"The girls would miss you. Besides, they could use the schooling, even in summer, and I—"

"No." The word came out more like a croak. "No," she said again, stronger this time. "I couldn't come. I . . . I'll be getting married in June." She hadn't meant to blurt it out that way, but she desperately needed her shield against the overpowering desires that flowed like hot lava through her body.

She looked up at him then. His face was set like granite, unyielding and harsh.

"Who?" he demanded in a voice as hard as the look on his face.

She whispered her response. "Patrick."

"I should have known."

"He's been so kind to us these past weeks. To me, especially." Was she justifying it to Gavin or to herself? "He's a good man and he'll make me happy."

It happened so quickly that she wasn't aware of his rising, of his hands on her arms, of the way he pulled her up from the chair and against his chest. Just as suddenly his mouth was devouring hers, and she was helpless to prevent it. Unwilling to prevent it.

She savored the taste of him the way a starving woman savors a succulent meal. His hands roamed over her back, then stroked up the length of her sides until his thumbs came to rest beneath the swell of her breasts. She gasped into his mouth but didn't pull away, waiting eagerly for him to continue. She wanted more. Much more.

"Gavin," she whispered, the sound pleading.

And then he set her away from him. His tone was angry, almost hateful. "He might make you happy, but I wonder if he'll ever be able to make you feel like this."

Her eyes flew open in time to see him turn and stalk away.

Chapter Twenty

Patrick pulled the fur blanket over Rachel's lap.

"Ready?" he asked.

She nodded.

He glanced behind them at the two girls snuggled beneath another lap robe in the back of the sleigh. "Are the wee lasses ready?"

"Yes," they cried in unison, both of them wreathed in excited grins.

"Good. Let's go!" He picked up the reins and smacked them smartly against the rump of the dappled gray mare.

As the sleigh slipped across the yard between house and barn, Patrick lifted his arm to wave at Gavin, who was standing near the barn door.

"He should have come with us," he said loudly to Rachel.

But he was mightily glad that Gavin had refused the invitation. Patrick didn't much care for the changes that had come over his friend since his wife died. Mourning was to be expected. Grief was a personal thing that had to be worked through. He hadn't been particularly surprised by Gavin's withdrawal from those around him, and he'd been willing to wait things out, give the man the time he needed to heal.

But he'd seen something different this past week. Gavin was an angry man, his eyes cold and heartless, his words sharp, biting. And he seemed especially so with Rachel. It made Patrick want to knock some sense back into him.

He glanced to his right, a warm happiness replacing his displeasure as he looked at Rachel. Her pale blond hair was hidden beneath a fur bonnet. The cold air had left splashes of pink on her cheekbones and the tip of her pert nose. Her blue eyes glittered as she squinted into the sun and wind.

He couldn't yet believe the lovely lass had consented to be his wife. He'd been in a dither ever since he'd left the Blake ranch on Christmas Day. He'd been over to see her every day this past week, and miracle of miracles, she hadn't changed her mind on him yet.

Today, New Year's Day 1884, they were going to announce the news to his family. It had been hard to keep from telling his brothers this week, but he'd managed to keep that promise to Rachel, just as he hoped to keep all his promises to her for the rest of his life. And today he was going to show her the wedding ring—the prettiest damned ring she'd ever see. It had been in Patrick's family for six generations and had come over from Ireland on his mother's hand. As the oldest O'Donnell son, it was his honor to give it to his bride. He couldn't wait for the day he'd be able to put it on Rachel's finger.

Patrick turned his attention back to the glistening white landscape before him. He didn't want the horse leaving the beaten path and sinking into a drift. This was no day for accidents.

He'd never thought he would find a girl like Rachel Harris who would consent to marry him. Not that he'd given much thought to matrimony until he'd met her. Faith and begorra! He'd thought Shane a blathering fool when he started spoonin' over Pearl Johansen. But Rachel had changed his way of thinking fast enough. He'd seen how just a little slip of a thing could turn a man into a first-rate buffoon.

Not that Patrick O'Donnell was running with blinders on. He didn't have the fair maid's heart—at least not completely. She'd never said she loved him. But he knew she was well enough fond of him. Most married folks were lucky to share that much between them, let alone be asking for the moon and the stars and love in the bargain. With time, she might grow to love him. He'd have to be satisfied with things as they were until then.

Only he kept having this nagging feeling that all wasn't as right as he'd want it to be. The months leading to June stretched impossibly long in his mind. They couldn't be over too soon for his liking. Sure and if that wasn't the truth.

Rachel stared at the O'Donnell house as the sleigh sped toward it. This was the first time she'd been there since the day of Shane's wedding, and it seemed even more impressive to her today. It sprawled against the backdrop of a tall mountain, its stone exterior a solemn gray against the pristine whiteness of winter. It resembled a castle more than the home of a cattle rancher, seeming very out of place here in the high country of Idaho.

As if she'd voiced her thoughts aloud, Patrick said, "Killarney Hall. 'Tis fashioned after the O'Donnell estates in Ireland. I was born there, but my parents left while I was still a lad. My father never forgot his homeland, never stopped missing the emerald-green valleys or the cool, misty mornings—though in truth it was his own decision that brought us to America. When we settled here, he built this house, according to his memories of our old family home."

"Where are your parents now, Patrick?"

"Buried, both of them, beneath the aspens." He pointed up the slope of the hill. "Three years ago now."

"I'm sorry," she said faintly.

She cast a surreptitious glance to her left. She realized with a jolt that she knew surprisingly little about Patrick. They'd spent hours together —entire days together—but he had never talked much about himself.

It's because I've never asked, she thought, and was instantly ashamed.

How could she have been so selfish, so callous toward a man who'd treated her with such kindness? She truly wasn't any better than Gavin thought her.

Gavin.

She closed her eyes as the onslaught of feelings slammed into her. It was always the same. Ever since that morning when he'd branded her with his touch, tasted her with his lips. She couldn't rid herself of the memories or the sensations he'd stirred.

It was bad enough that those feelings raged within her when she was engaged to another man—worse still because Gavin had made it so clear what he thought of her. It was clear in his eyes when he chanced to look at her, clear in his voice when he was forced to speak to her. He detested her, despised her, hated her.

And yet, to her shame, she knew she would find it impossible to resist him should he take her once again into his arms.

"Rachel? Have you heard a word I've said, lass?"

"What?" She looked at Patrick, startled. "Oh, I'm sorry. I . . . I was daydreaming. I didn't hear what you said."

"I said 'tis time we broke the news to the O'Donnells. Are you ready?"

She swallowed the rising dread. "Yes, Patrick. I'm ready." There was no going back now. She had to be certain there was never *any* going back.

It didn't take Patrick long to hustle Rachel and the two girls into the warmth of the cavernous entry hall. A servant, dressed in a black suit, white shirt and collar, appeared instantly to take their wraps.

"The family is waiting for you in the salon, sir."

"Thank you, Crandal. Do you think Cook might be able to find a piece of cake or two for the wee lasses?"

Sabrina's and Petula's eyes immediately sparked with enthusiasm.

"I think so, sir," Crandal replied in the same obsequious tone. "Come along, young ladies. The kitchen is this way."

"May we, Miss Harris?" Sabrina asked.

Rachel was relieved that the girls would be elsewhere when Patrick made the announcement of their marriage plans. She knew she would have to tell Sabrina and Petula eventually, but she wasn't ready to do so yet. She didn't know why she wanted to wait, just that she wanted to.

She tenderly smoothed back Sabrina's unruly hair. "It will spoil your lunch, Brina."

"It won't hurt them this once," Patrick chided.

Sabrina's gaze was hopeful. "Please, Miss Harris."

She felt rather helpless against such powers of persuasion. And there'd been little enough happiness for the children lately. She supposed Patrick was right. It wouldn't hurt them this once. "Well, if you promise to mind your manners. You too, Pet."

"We will," they promised in unison.

Patrick offered her the crook of his arm. "'Tis time we went inside, Rachel."

She forced a smile onto her lips. "I'm ready," she said, her voice tremulous.

There wasn't a one of the O'Donnell brothers that could have tipped the scales at less than two hundred pounds, or measured under six-foot-two. They all had the O'Donnell red hair, although the shades varied slightly, from Patrick's carrot red to Trevor's rich auburn. They had the same open, friendly faces and the same laughing eyes, Shane's and Jamie's the same green as their elder brother, Trevor's a golden-flecked hazel.

It was a bit daunting, walking into the brothers' midst. They greeted her with grand enthusiasm, their voices booming and boisterous. They crowded close, paying Rachel outrageous compliments and saying it was about time Patrick brought her back to Killarney Hall.

It was Pearl, Shane's bride of a little more than six weeks, who relieved some of her apprehension.

"Get back, you big ox," she said sternly, pushing on both Shane's and Jamie's shoulders at the same time. "Can't you see she's about to suffocate?" She took Rachel's arm and pulled her away from Patrick and the others. "You can't imagine how wonderful it will be to have an afternoon of conversation with another woman.

And don't mind the lot of them. They can be overwhelming at times, but they're basically harmless."

Rachel glanced over her shoulder. The brothers were all wearing satisfied grins, and she thought they'd probably already guessed at the reason for her visit.

"You must come to see us more often, Miss Harris," Pearl continued. "Patrick can come for you in the sleigh whenever you'd like."

"Thank you. I . . ."

Patrick interrupted her. "Come summer, you'll be able to see Rachel whenever you want. She's going to be living at Killarney Hall . . . as my wife."

"I knew it!" Jamie shouted.

"Sure if I didn't see it coming!" Shane slapped his older brother on the back. "Congratulations, Paddy."

Trevor gripped Patrick by the upper arms and gave him a shake. "We'd given up hope you'd find the courage before you were too old, brother."

Pearl gave Rachel an impetuous hug. "I'm so glad. Patrick's a lucky man, Miss Harris."

"Please. It's Rachel." She laughed nervously.

And then the brothers surrounded her. She received a bear-like hug from each of them, followed by a kiss on each cheek, as she was profusely welcomed into the O'Donnell clan.

Finally, she was claimed once again by Patrick. He led her to a sofa, then sat beside her, his arm around her shoulders. As the brothers and

Pearl quickly took nearby seats, he regaled them with stories of his courtship of the lovely Rachel Harris, much of it dramatically embellished. The room was filled with laughter as the minutes ticked away on the mantel clock.

Rachel felt like a terrible fraud. If Patrick loved her, the whole clan would love her. That was apparently the way it was in the O'Donnell family. But she didn't deserve it. They believed she was in love with their brother, that she was marrying him for all the right and proper reasons, that she would make him happy. She wished she did love him. It would make things so much easier. Could it happen? Could she grow to love him? Could she make him happy?

She turned her head to look up at him and prayed she would be able to do so. If not, it would be one more sin, one more lump of burning coal upon her head that she would have to live with.

Crandal's imperious voice interrupted her musings. "Cook reports that dinner is ready, sir. Shall I inform her you are adjourning to the dining hall?"

"Yes, Crandal. Do so at once." Patrick turned a solemn look toward Rachel. "'Tis the devil to pay if the O'Donnells aren't ready when the food is. Cook is a ferocious, unforgiving woman who rules that corner of the house with a vengeance. You'll meet her later."

She met his sober gaze with one of her own. "I'm not sure I want to," she answered, half-serious, half-jesting.

The brothers burst into laughter.

"Sure you've got yourself a fine woman, Paddy," Shane said, once again slapping his brother on the back.

"A regular O'Donnell," Jamie added.

Patrick beamed down at Rachel with pleasure as they all rose and left the salon.

Chapter Twenty-One

And this will be our bedroom, once you're Mrs. Patrick O'Donnell."

Patrick shoved open the door, revealing the massive chamber with its large four-poster bed, gleaming wood floors, and cherrywood bureaus. Exotic Persian rugs were scattered around the room. Upholstered chairs sat in a cozy semi-circle before the fireplace. Heavy draperies framed the large windows.

Rachel felt a cold lump growing in her belly as she stepped into the room. "It's beautiful, Patrick," she said softly.

"Not nearly as beautiful as you." He closed the door behind him.

She knew she would feel his hands on her arms any moment, that he would turn her toward him, that he intended to kiss her. There was no avoiding it this time. Except for a quick kiss on the mouth the night she'd accepted his proposal, she'd managed to forestall anything more than a few pecks on the cheek, always having the excuse that the children were nearby. And she'd managed to keep them nearby throughout his courtship.

But they weren't there now.

"Rachel . . ."

His hands did touch her arms. He did turn her toward him. And he did intend to kiss her. She closed her eyes and waited. Patrick pulled her closer into his embrace, drawing her up as his mouth lowered. He held her tenderly, lovingly. His lips were warm upon hers.

She wasn't revolted by his kisses. That was her first thought. The second was that she didn't feel much of anything else either. She knew then that she'd hoped to feel all those wonderful, terrible things that she'd felt when Gavin kissed her.

A sudden heat spread through her at the thought of him. She longed for his kisses, craved his hands upon her body. These weren't the right lips, weren't the right hands. She broke away from Patrick, feeling a flush rise to her face.

Patrick's gaze changed from restrained passion to amusement. "There's no need for embarrassment. We're to be wed."

"I . . . I'm just not ready for . . . for this," she stammered.

"Aye, I can see I'll have to go slowly. I forget

what an innocent you are. You needn't fear me, Rachel."

"I'm not afraid of you, Patrick. Truly I'm not. It's just that . . ." *It's just that you're the wrong man.* "It's just . . ."

"You've no need to explain to me. You'll get over your shyness with time. I'm a patient man. I'll wait."

Rachel nodded as he put his arm around her shoulders and drew her toward the bedroom door. Someday, she knew, he would expect far more than kisses from her in this room. What was she going to do then?

Joker rose from the rug by the fireplace and trotted toward the door. He whined, then returned to sit by Gavin's chair, flopping his big head into his master's lap.

"I know, boy," Gavin said as he stroked the wolfhound's head. "They've been gone a long time. It's almost dark."

The house was too quiet when the children were gone, he thought. And it was empty without Rachel.

He squelched that thought quickly. It was the children he missed.

He rose from the chair and paced across the room to the window, much as the dog had done only moments before. He rubbed a small circle on the frosty glass and peered out.

He'd done a lot of thinking that day and had made some unpleasant discoveries about himself. He'd married Dru to provide her children with a home and a father once she was gone. But look at him. First he'd withdrawn from everyone, including Sabrina and Petula, so overwhelmed with guilt that he'd given no thought to anyone else. And then, when he'd realized what Dru had been trying to tell him, he'd again thought only of himself, about how wonderful it was to be rid of the guilt. Finally, when he'd been rejected by Rachel, he'd taken his anger and hurt out on the children.

It was time for it all to stop.

He'd known all along that Rachel Harris wasn't cut out for the hard life of the Blakes. They weren't rich and probably never would be. This would go on being a working ranch, with all family members needing to pitch in and help. There would be too few new gowns, too many long winters.

Joker whined again, jumping up on his hind legs and resting his paws on the window sill. Gavin laid his hand on the dog's head.

He should have known the minute they met Patrick in Challis that Rachel would set her cap for him. The Irishman was as rich as King Midas. His father had made a fortune in the gold fields of Idaho, and Patrick O'Donnell had repeated the feat in Bonanza City. Now he'd settled into that castle like some kind of medieval lord, waiting to rule his kingdom.

Damn! That wasn't fair and he knew it. Patrick was a generous, good-hearted man. That he was rich and able to offer a wife a life of ease shouldn't be held against him.

But he could hold it against Rachel, for it was clear it was for money she was marrying him. It had to be or she wouldn't come so willingly into Gavin's arms.

He cursed aloud and turned abruptly from the window, his angry voice sending Joker scurrying back to the rug by the fireplace.

The worst of it was that he still wanted her. He burned with the want of her. And it infuriated him. He'd always kept a firm control over his life. Hunger, fatigue, passion. They could all be overcome with a strong will and mind.

"Hell!"

He grabbed his coat from the peg by the door and shoved his arms down the sleeves. He'd started out knowing he needed to be a better father to Sabrina and Petula and here he was thinking about Rachel again. If he had two licks of sense, he'd take her to Challis and put her on the next stage to Boise. If it weren't for Dru wanting her to stay for the sake of the girls, he would have done it, too.

Damn it, he would have!

"Oh look, Miss Harris!" Petula cried from the back of the sleigh, her voice filled with excitement. "Look at the deer!"

As Rachel began to twist around, she caught a glimpse of Petula jumping up on the seat, her arm pointing off behind them. Just then, the sleigh jerked abruptly to the side, then back again. With a scream, the child bounced over the back of the sleigh.

"Patrick, stop!"

He pulled back on the reins, but it seemed an eternity before the horse was brought to a full halt. Rachel shoved the lap robe to the floor of the sleigh and jumped to the ground. She stumbled in the snow, falling to her knees.

"Pet!" she cried. She scrambled to her feet and raced back along the sleigh tracks toward the whimpering child.

"My arm. Oh, my arm."

Before Rachel could reach for the child and lift her up from the snow, Patrick's hand on her shoulder stopped her.

"Don't move her yet. Let me have a look."

Sabrina arrived, her face ashen. She grabbed Rachel's hand. "Is she gonna be all right?" she whispered. "She's not gonna die, is she?"

"Oh, heavens no," Rachel replied, giving her hand a squeeze. She dropped to her knees and hugged Sabrina. "It's all right, Brina. Pet's going to be fine, you'll see." She understood the child's fear. Her father was dead, and now her mother too. It wasn't surprising that she might think an accident would take Petula from her as well.

Patrick's voice was concerned as he turned toward Rachel. "It looks as if her arm is broken. It doesn't look right to me." He was frowning. "We're almost to the ranch. I'll take you there, then head for town to get the doctor."

Petula's crying increased as Patrick lifted her gingerly from the ground and carried her toward the sleigh, Rachel and Sabrina close on his heels. As soon as Rachel was seated, he passed the child into her waiting arms, then hurried around to the opposite side and got in. Moments later, they were hurtling across the frosty countryside again.

"It hurts, Miss Harris," Petula said amidst sobs.

"I know, kitten. But it won't for long. We're almost home, and then we'll get you taken care of. Hang on, sweetheart."

Despite her assurances to the child, it seemed to take forever before they dashed into the yard and stopped in front of the house.

Gavin stepped through the doorway at that very moment. Perhaps it was something on their faces or the hectic way they'd arrived, but he seemed to know that something was amiss even before his gaze fell on the whimpering little girl in Rachel's arms.

"What happened?" he demanded as he came forward.

"She fell. We think her arm is broken."

"Pa, it hurts," Petula cried, giant tears streaming down her cheeks.

Gavin lifted her into his own embrace. "I'll be careful," he promised her.

Rachel jumped out right behind him, hurrying to open the door. "I'll be back with the doctor as quick as I can," Patrick shouted after her.

Rachel heard him, but it didn't mean much to her at the time. She wanted only to take care of Petula. She followed Gavin into the children's bedroom and watched as he laid Petula on the bed.

He frowned as he straightened. "We're going

to have to take your coat off, Pet. It's going to hurt, but there's no way around it."

"No. It hurts too much already. No. Don't take it off."

Gavin's gaze met Rachel's. She felt the same helplessness she could see in his eyes. She knew he was right, but she hated the thought of causing the child more pain.

She went around to the opposite side of the bed and sat down. "You're going to have to help us, Pet. We must get your coat off before the doctor comes."

"Let me wait. No, let me wait."

Rachel felt like crying too. This was her fault. If she hadn't let the children go with her to Killarney Hall to have dinner with the O'Donnells, this wouldn't have happened.

"Get a hold of yourself, Miss Harris," Gavin said sternly, his voice low.

She drew a quick breath, startled by his sharpness. But he was right. She couldn't fall apart now. She had to be strong for Petula. She swallowed the lump in her throat.

"We can't wait, Pet," Gavin told the little girl. "It has to be done now."

Rachel clenched her jaw and leaned forward to help him.

"Children mend mighty quick from a thing like this, Mr. Blake" Dr. Forester said as he led the way out of the bedroom. "She's going to be in some pain, but I think her arm will heal up fine, long as you can keep her from doing too much until it's good and mended. You'll have to keep her quiet until then."

"For how long?"

"Oh, 'bout five, six weeks, I'd say. It was a good, clean break. Should heal up quick."

"Keep a five-year-old quiet for six weeks?" Gavin asked incredulously. He might not have much experience as a father, but he'd learned enough to know that was nearly an impossible request.

Dr. Forester chuckled as he pulled on his coat. "Do the best you can, sir." He turned toward Rachel, standing just outside Petula's bedroom. "The laudanum should help her sleep for several more hours. Watch the clock and don't give her more until I said."

"I'll be careful, doctor. Thank you."

The doctor turned toward Patrick. "Well, Mr. O'Donnell, since you insisted on bringing me here, I'm afraid you'll have to drive me back to Challis as well. But if you don't mind, could we try a more sedate speed? I'm an old man."

Patrick nodded. "I'll be happy to do that for you." He glanced past Gavin toward Rachel. "I'll be back in a day or two to look in on the wee lass. You . . . you take care o' yourself, Rachel."

Gavin thought the man would have liked to say more, if the moment and place had been more private. As it was, he simply nodded again and pushed his hat over his red hair as he followed the doctor out the door. Gavin went with them and waited until they'd pulled out of the yard before going back inside. He found Rachel and Sabrina sitting in the bedroom beside Petula's bed, Sabrina in her governess's lap.

"Please stay in here tonight, Miss Harris," Sabrina said as he stepped into the room. "You can sleep in my bed and I'll sleep on the floor." When Rachel didn't answer immediately, she added, "Please, Miss Harris. I don't wanna be alone. Please."

"You won't have to sleep on the floor, Brina," Gavin interrupted. "I'll set up a cot for you."

Light blue eyes widened as they met his gaze, eyes clouded with worry.

"I'll move your things over from the cabin. I imagine you'll want to stay in here for a while."

Rachel nodded, then turned her eyes back toward the bed while her fingers tenderly stroked Sabrina's hair.

Wordlessly, Gavin headed for the cabin.

"Rachel, may I have a few words with you before you retire?"

She lay the damp cloth across Petula's forehead, then glanced toward the doorway where Gavin stood.

"Of course," she responded softly.

As she straightened, she looked toward the cot near the window. Sabrina, too, was fast asleep, her mouth open and one arm thrown above her head. It had taken some doing before the older girl relaxed enough to fall asleep. Her fears that something worse would happen to Petula had increased as the night grew later, and Rachel had nearly despaired of reassuring her that everything would turn out all right.

Taking a steadying breath, she returned her attention to the matter at hand. Gavin wanted to speak with her. She wasn't sure if that was good or bad.

He was standing beside the fireplace, hands shoved into the pockets of his trousers. "Sit down, Rachel."

She was inclined to believe it was more than likely bad news that had dictated this meeting.

"I've been thinking about my behavior lately," he began, "and I owe you an apology. Whatever . . . whatever's been wrong between us, I'd like us to call a truce. For the sake of the children if nothing else."

She remained silent, but her heart was pounding furiously in her chest.

His eyes were the color of granite, his face set like stone. "We'll forget what happened."

Forget? It would be impossible for her to forget, especially when she was so close to him.

"It's already forgotten," she said with more conviction than she felt. "I'd like very much for us to get along while I'm here. The children need us both to help them get over the loss of their mother. It would be nice if we could get along in a civilized manner."

She should have been an actress, she thought, the way she spoke those lines. She almost believed them herself.

Gavin stepped toward her, stopping within arm's reach. His eyes searched her face. Rachel lifted her chin and met his gaze with cool control. Finally, he extended his hand toward her.

"Truce?" he asked.

"Truce."

Chapter Twenty-Two

A blizzard blew in from the northwest during the night. Rachel wouldn't have thought it possible for more snow to fall, but fall it did. The wind howled through the canyons and valleys, bending trees before its relentless fury. The temperature plummeted. Roads became impassable.

Rachel awakened to Petula's small voice calling for her mother as she tossed restlessly in her bed. She pulled on a robe and went to sit beside the child.

"Hush, Pet. It's all right."

Petula opened her laudanum-glazed eyes. "Where's Ma?"

Not knowing how to answer, Rachel gathered the girl into her arms and rocked her to and fro. "You've been dreaming," she whispered.

Gavin appeared suddenly in the doorway. "What's wrong?"

He was wearing trousers over his long johns, the top of his undergarment open at the throat to reveal a light furring of dark chest hair. His hair was rumpled, his chin covered with black stubble. His feet were bare.

Rachel felt slightly winded by the sight of him. "Just a dream," she managed to reply.

Petula raised her head from Rachel's chest. "Pa, I hurt."

"I bet you do." He crossed the room to stand on the opposite side of the bed. "That must have been some fall you took. Almost as good as the time I fell out of the barn loft and broke my nose." He sat on the bed, and Petula slipped from Rachel's arms into his.

"You broke your nose?" Petula asked.

"Right here." He touched the slight bump on the bridge of his nose. "My father held my head and shoved it back into place or else I'd have looked mighty funny now."

"Did it hurt?"

"Something awful."

"Mine too." The child laid her head on his shoulder and closed her eyes. "Mine too."

They have their father back. Rachel's heart felt lighter than it had in weeks.

They sat in silence for a long time, listening to the wind wailing around the corners of the house. Rachel continued to stare at the man and child, drawing immense enjoyment from the simple scene. Perhaps what made it so special was that she felt a part of it too.

Realizing that Petula had fallen asleep, Gavin kissed the top of her head, then raised his eyes toward Rachel.

There was nothing cool or remote about his gray eyes this morning, she thought. They seemed warm and intimate and friendly. She smiled in response and self-consciously smoothed back the disheveled mass of hair from her face.

"You look mighty pretty when you first wake up, Miss Harris," Gavin said softly.

Her heart started a mad thumping in her chest. *Is this part of the truce*? she wondered. And then, *You look mighty handsome yourself, Mr. Blake*.

"Well . . ." He laid Petula back on her pillow. "Guess I'd best check on the animals."

"You can't go outside. There's a blizzard raging." She could hear the thudding of her heart in her ears now. "You might not make it to the barn this time."

The look in his eyes told her he was remembering the last blizzard—those hours he'd held her in his arms—just as she was. "Guess you're right. I'd better stay inside."

Surely he could hear the crazy pounding too. "I'll get dressed and fix you some breakfast."

His gaze slid down over her loose hair to the opening at the front of her robe, then back again. His voice sounded husky. "Yes. You get dressed." He rose and was gone in an instant, closing the door behind him.

* * *

She was a good cook, Gavin thought as he stretched back in a chair after supper that night. His belly was full after two helpings of the beef and vegetable stew. And cooking wasn't her only skill. He'd watched her throughout the day, realizing how much she'd done for them in recent weeks.

She was constantly there for the children, caring for them, teaching them, playing with them. She'd even made them each a new dress out of fabric she'd found in Dru's old chest. And she hadn't done too badly for a city girl used to store-bought clothes.

He glanced her way. There she was, wearing another of those ridiculously fashionable outfits of hers, looking like she was ready to go calling on a society neighbor or for a walk in the park, and yet her lap was covered with socks to be darned. At the moment, she was squinting as she tried to thread a needle.

Begrudgingly, he admitted that, while she might be ambitious when it came to choosing a husband, she wasn't averse to hard work. It was a strange mixture.

And she was so beautiful too. At the moment, the firelight had turned her wheat-colored hair to a dark gold. A fringe of bangs kissed her forehead, and loose tendrils curled near her ears. She'd left her hair down today, held back from her face by tiny combs just behind her temples. He liked it that way, falling down her back in gentle waves, simple and unadorned.

He felt the beginnings of desire stirring and

knew he should look away, should turn his
attentions elsewhere. But he didn't do so. He
wanted to look. He wanted to know the lady. He
wanted to understand what it was about her that
held him so spellbound. What made her different from other women? Why wasn't he able to
keep his feelings for her in perspective the way
he'd always done in the past?

He frowned. Perhaps it was because he
thought her different.

He remembered the way she'd looked into his
eyes, the way she'd fallen into his arms, the way
she'd returned his kisses with a passion to
match his own. He'd thought her an innocent
young woman, but perhaps . . .

Gavin's eyes narrowed.

Would an innocent respond as she had?
Would a naive young lady accept the kisses of a
married man? Would a virtuous woman melt in
his arms while she was engaged to another
man?

Maybe Rachel Harris wasn't what she appeared. Why *had* she come looking for a job at a
"remote mountain ranch"? She couldn't have
been looking for a husband. So what *was* the
reason? Could she be hiding from discovery of
some scandalous behavior?

Like a dog worrying a bone, Gavin mentally
chewed on all the unsavory possibilities.

And then she glanced up at him, meeting his
gaze, and he knew what he was doing. He was
trying to justify his own lust. He was trying to
find an excuse that would allow him to cross to
her chair, lift her into his arms, and carry her

into his bedroom—some way to make himself blameless for his actions.

She smiled. It was a sweet smile, completely unsuspecting of the carnal storm raging in Gavin.

He rose quickly from his chair. "Think I'll go talk with Stubs. Night, Rachel."

She felt the blast of cold air through the open door as he left the house. The sewing lay idle in her lap for a long while afterward. She continued to stare at the closed door, trying to understand the strange mood that had permeated the room just before he left.

A truce he had called it, but what did that mean? Were they friends or merely respected adversaries?

It had felt so good, so right, having him in the house today, helping with Petula, talking with Sabrina. He hadn't snapped at Rachel once or looked as if he despised her. He'd even complimented her on the stew and taken a second helping. She'd thought they might truly become, if not friends, then at least friendly.

But she'd felt something else pass between them moments ago. There'd been something in his eyes, something dangerous, something exciting. She might be inexperienced, but she recognized the sensual brooding of his glance, knew what would happen if she allowed it to.

She could deny it as much as she wanted, but it wouldn't change things. She was in love with Gavin Blake. She was engaged to Patrick but in love with Gavin. Gavin wanted her in his bed.

Patrick wanted her for his wife.

She knew what was the right thing for her to want, the right thing for her to do. But she didn't know if she was strong enough to make the proper choice. She didn't know if she was strong enough to walk away from her heart's desire.

Gavin tipped his chair back until it leaned against the bunkhouse wall. He sipped at the whiskey in the tin cup, his thoughts still back in the main house.

Stubs finished pouring his own whiskey and sat in a chair opposite Gavin. "Jess oughta be in tomorrow. Hope he made it to the line shack 'fore the storm hit."

"No reason he shouldn't have. He knows how to read the sky as good as any cowboy I've ever seen."

"I reckon you're right." Stubs took a quick swallow of the golden liquid. "How's Pet?"

"She's going to hurt for a while, but she's okay."

"How 'bout Brina? She was pretty shook up over the little one's fall."

Gavin finished off the whiskey. "Fine. She's fine."

"Good." Stubs cocked an eyebrow, as if waiting for Gavin to say more.

Instead, Gavin leaned forward, grabbed the whiskey bottle, and poured himself another drink.

Stubs rubbed his grizzled chin, his expression pensive. "You know," he said, his voice low, "I been doin' me a lot of thinkin'. Helps pass the time when the winters get long." He stared at a spot on the floor and sipped his whiskey. "Been thinkin' that a man don't often meet just the right girl for him. Most settle for somethin' less. Sorta like you and Dru. Don't get me wrong, Gav. Nicer woman I ain't never known, but if she hadn't been ailin' and needin' a pa for them young'ns, you two wouldn't never tied the knot the way you did."

Gavin stared hard at his foreman and friend, not sure he cared for where Stubs' thoughts were taking them.

"You gave that woman all the carin' she could've asked for. She was lucky to have you. Yes, sir. Lucky, she was. And Dru knew it too, don't think she didn't."

Gavin remained silent.

Stubs shook his head thoughtfully. "All kinds of love in this world. You ever thought about it? All kinds. Kind you got for them girls in there. Kind you had for Dru. Shoot. Guess there's even the kind you might have for an old coot of a friend like me. Yes, sir. All kinds."

Stubs got up from his chair and walked over to the window. He pushed aside the curtains Dru had made in an effort to make the bunk-house more homey and stared outside for a long time before speaking again.

"No man oughta feel guilty for lovin' people in different ways. Dru knew that. She never quit lovin' Charlie. Loved him right to the last." He turned and this time his gaze met Gavin's. "She loved you too, an' she never expected or wanted nothin' from you that you didn't give to her. Except one thing, Gav."

He was reluctant to ask. "What was that?"

"She wanted you to find what she and Charlie had. She wanted that real bad like."

Gavin let out a long sigh. "I know." He thought of Rachel, sitting near the fire back at the house. "But sometimes the things a person wants don't happen."

"Sometimes," Stubs agreed softly, then added, "and sometimes they do."

Rachel was listening for his return. She tried to tell herself she wasn't, that it was merely the sound of the storm that claimed her attention, but she knew better. Was Gavin going to spend the night in the bunkhouse with Stubs?

Perhaps some warm milk would help her fall asleep, she thought as she rose silently from her bed. She slipped into her robe and tightened the belt around her waist.

A flicker of light from the sitting room fireplace faintly illuminated her path to the bedroom door. She paused long enough beside Petula's bed to see that the child was sleeping peacefully. Satisfied, she left the room, closing the door behind her.

She didn't bother to light a lamp. The firelight was ample to find her way to the icebox. She filled a small kettle with the white liquid, then carried it to the fireplace where she hung the kettle on the chimney crane and swung it over the low-burning flames. She grabbed some wood from the wood box and added it to the fire before sitting in the nearest chair and staring into the flames, her thoughts drifting and disjointed.

For some reason, she thought of Tucker. She was six years old when she first saw him. Six and very shy. She wasn't used to being around people. Her early life with Uncle Seth had been a nightmare of shadows and shouting in that old Philadelphia house. But it had at least been familiar. Suddenly she'd been thrust out into a frightening and very unfamiliar world full of strangers.

But it wasn't so frightening when she was with Tucker. She remembered the way he had made her feel, almost from the very beginning. He'd made her laugh. She remembered the night, there on the Oregon Trail, when he'd brought back that rabbit for supper and she'd cried because she'd had a pet rabbit once. He'd told her a story about his old hound dog back in Georgia while he helped her peel the potatoes for the stew, and soon the rabbit was forgotten.

If Maggie had been as much mother as sister to Rachel, then Tucker had been the father she'd never known. From the moment they met the Branigans outside Independence, Missouri, Rachel had been surrounded by love. She'd been a witness to what a grand passion meant in a marriage, for no two people had ever loved more than Maggie and Tucker. And she'd been the recipient, along with her nieces and nephews, of parental love. What would her life have been like without Tucker and the rest of the

Branigans? She couldn't imagine. Didn't want to imagine.

Rachel felt a sting of homesickness. She wished she was with Tucker and Maggie right now. She wished she could crawl up into Tucker's lap and nestle against his chest and have him stroke her hair and tell her stories about that old hound. She wished she was a child, with no more worries than what kind of grades she would get from Miss Creswell on her schoolwork.

She heard the moaning of the wind through the chimney and felt the isolation of this place more than she'd ever felt it before. She was a city girl, used to having lots of people around. Now she couldn't even get to a small town like Challis to buy a hair ribbon or go to church. She was trapped by the winter weather, held captive by the snow. She was alone, with only Gavin and the children for company.

Gavin.

If she truly had Gavin, she wouldn't even notice the seclusion.

Gavin.

What twist of fate had brought him into her life? If she hadn't been feeling restless . . . if she hadn't read that ad in the newspaper . . . if she hadn't been so certain that life held something special for her if she'd only go out looking for it . . .

Gavin.

Was he even what he seemed? Was he the wonderful husband and father she'd thought him? After all, he'd come to her cabin and . . .

and kissed her while his wife lay dying in the house. She should hate and despise him for it, not long for him to do it again.

And she did long for him to do it again.

Her hands clenched in her lap. Was she so different from him? She'd accepted Patrick's proposal, yet burned for Gavin's touch. Should he hate and despise her any less?

"Oh, Gavin," she whispered.

The door flew open, allowing entry to a flurry of snowflakes before Gavin shut it quickly, but not before the temperature of the room plummeted dramatically. Rachel shivered as she hopped to her feet, feeling exposed by her secret thoughts.

Gavin looked up and found her watching him from beside the fireplace. He felt a warmth surge through him that had nothing to do with the fire on the hearth or the whiskey he'd consumed in the bunkhouse.

"I thought you'd be in bed by now," he said as he shucked off his coat.

"I was just fixing some warm milk. To . . . to help me sleep."

Warm milk. How like her.

Or was it? Just who was Rachel Harris? Was she the apparent innocent who stood before him now, clothed in a prim, high-collared nightgown and warm robe? Or was she the scheming temptress who came willingly to his embrace but promised herself to another man for the wealth he possessed?

Perhaps without the whiskey dulling his

thoughts, he could have figured it out.

Gavin stepped toward the fireplace as he ran his fingers through his wet hair. "Looks like we're in for a long winter. Lots more snow falling tonight." He sniffed the air and wrinkled his nose. "Your milk's scorched. Can't you smell it?"

"Oh!" She reached quickly for the chimney crane, swinging the kettle out from the fireplace. Another cry—this one of pain—quickly followed, and she pulled her fingers to her mouth.

He stepped toward her. "Did you burn yourself?" he asked, instantly concerned.

"It's nothing."

"Here. Let me see." He took hold of her wrist and drew her hand from her face.

"Really. It's nothing." She sounded breathless.

In the glow of the fire, he could see the red marks across the pads of her three middle fingers. "I'll get some snow to help cool it. It'll take out the sting."

"Really, it's—"

"Sit down, Rachel, while I get the snow."

Her eyes were wide as she looked up at him, and he thought she looked terribly fragile at the moment. He felt the pain as if it were his own.

He left her, grabbing a pan from a hook in the kitchen and taking it outside to fill with snow. It wasn't long before he was back, kneeling by her side, instructing her to bury her hand in the icy white crystals.

"It was silly of me," Rachel said softly.

He looked into her eyes and felt the warmth returning to his veins. "You should be more careful."

"I will be."

He reached for her free hand and turned it palm up. Where once her hands had been smooth and white, now they were calloused and red. "You weren't meant to work this way. You were meant to have servants caring for you." Patrick had servants who would care for her, he thought as he met her gaze once more.

What would happen if he took her in his arms and kissed her? What would happen if he loosened the belt of her robe and ran his hands over the thin fabric of her nightgown? What would happen if he were to cup her breasts in the palms of his hands and feel her heart beat against his fingertips?

"Do you love him, Rachel?" he asked hoarsely. "Do you love Patrick O'Donnell?"

Her eyes rounded as she met his gaze. She pulled her hand from the snow, bringing the fingers once more to her lips.

"Do you?"

She stared at him for the longest time. Her face seemed pale, even in the golden glow of firelight.

"Tell me," he demanded, his voice stronger this time.

"I . . . I'm going to marry him. How do you think I feel?"

"Tell me you love him, then."

She made no reply.

Strange. He wasn't sure if her silence made

him feel better or worse. But he did know that if he didn't move away from her soon, it wouldn't matter to him if she loved Patrick or not. He would take the kisses—and more—that were promised to someone else.

He rose from her side. "Good night, Rachel."

Only the silence followed him into the solitude of his room.

Rachel remained by the fire until it had burned down to mere embers. A numbness settled over her, stopping all thoughts, all feelings. It wasn't until the wee hours of morning, when the cold began to creep into her joints, that she realized what her silence had cost her.

"It's you I love, Gavin," she whispered.

It became so terribly clear to her in the cold darkness of the sitting room. She'd been right when she'd decided not to sit back and wait for that something special to happen to her. She'd been right to get out and find it. And now that she'd found it, she had to make it her own.

Somehow, she had to make it her own.

Chapter Twenty-Three

"**I**'ll be gone for a few days," Gavin announced as he pulled on his coat the next morning.

"Gone?" Rachel felt an alarmed chill spreading out from her heart.

"Jess was riding line when the storm hit. He might need some help. In weather like this, the cows can just bunch up and wait to freeze or starve to death. Stubs will stay and take care of things here. If you need anything, see him."

Gavin, wait. I want to tell you it isn't Patrick I love. It's you. "We'll be fine."

"I'm taking Duke and Duchess." His hand rested on the doorknob. "I'll leave Joker with you. He might not seem like he's very smart, but he'd let you know if something was amiss."

She nodded.

"My guess is the worst of the storm is past, but

stay close to the house anyway. It can change in a minute. Stubs'll take care of milking the cows in the barn and feeding the stock."

"We'll be fine," she repeated, feeling just the opposite.

"I should be back by Sunday, but don't worry about me if I'm not."

I'll worry every moment you're away. "I won't."

He wrapped a wool scarf around his neck and ears, pulled his hat down low on his forehead, and opened the door. For a fleeting moment, he glanced back at her and their eyes met and held. Then he was gone, the door closed behind him.

Rachel felt the emptiness closing in all around her. Sunday seemed a decade away.

She glanced around the sitting room. Perhaps this would be a good day to scrub the floors. Anything to keep herself busy. Anything.

Sunshine poured in through the sitting room window, belying the frigid temperatures that reigned through the high country. Petula, feeling restless after several days abed, was seated in a chair beside the fireplace. Sabrina sat cross-legged on the rag rug near her little sister's feet. A book was open in her lap, and she was reading aloud.

It was Saturday, and Rachel was busy with the butter churn. Every so often, she glanced through the small glass window in the over-and-over to see how the cream was doing.

This time when she looked, she found the little grains of butter she'd been watching for. ("Look for 'em to be about as big as Number Six shot," Dru had told her. "Then you'll know it's time to add the water.") She opened the end of the churn, flung in some cold water, and continued churning.

"Miss Harris?"

Rachel looked across the room. "Yes, Brina."

"Are there really places in the world where it never snows? Where it's like summer all the time?"

"Yes."

"Have you ever been some place like that?"

"No. I've only read about them in books, like you. But I've talked to people who've been to such places."

"Can you imagine, Pet?" Sabrina glanced up at her little sister, her voice filled with wonder. "A place where it never snows." With a shake of her head, she lifted the book and continued reading.

Rachel listened to the story with half an ear as she carefully poured the buttermilk from the churn into a large pitcher.

Sabrina stopped reading again. "Can we have some, Miss Harris?" she asked, eyeing their favorite drink.

"Help yourself," Rachel answered, her hands busy as she dumped a large quantity of clean, cold water in with the butter to wash it, then turned the churn and tipped the water out.

While Sabrina got down the cups and poured some buttermilk into them, Rachel found herself musing over the things she'd learned since leaving Boise City. She'd certainly never known anything about churning butter, although she was vaguely aware of seeing the cook hard at it a time or two when she was growing up. She supposed Maggie knew how, for the Branigans hadn't been wealthy when they'd arrived in the territory. But she doubted Maggie would believe her eyes if she could see her little sister now.

Rachel smiled to herself as she emptied the contents of the churn onto the butter worker. It was a shallow wooden trough with a wooden fluted roller that moved up and down the trough when the handle was turned. She poured generous amounts of water over the butter as she worked it, squeezing it off with the roller, making sure the butter was washed absolutely clean. ("If it's not," Dru had said, "the butter will never keep.")

When she was certain there was no buttermilk left in it, she salted the butter and worked it some more, then flung it in handfuls into an earthenware crock for storage. She pounded the salted mixture again, then rammed it hard with a wooden tool to drive out all the water and air so the butter wouldn't go rancid.

She let out a satisfied sigh as she surveyed her accomplishment. She'd done it. Without anyone's help or instructions, she'd done it. She'd remembered everything Dru had told her. Perhaps it was silly to feel so proud of herself. Women had been churning cream into butter for centuries. But this was *her* achievement, and she *was* proud.

As she finished cleaning up, there was a knock on the door.

"See who it is, Brina," she said, but she

already knew it would be Patrick. Bad weather had kept him away for four days. The sunshine had guaranteed he would soon arrive.

"Ah, lass, 'tis good to see you," he said to Sabrina as she opened the door. His big frame filled the doorway. He pulled off his hat with one hand, his other held suspiciously behind his back. His gaze flicked to Rachel, then to Petula as he stepped inside and closed the door. "And how's the wee lass? Are you feelin' better, Pet?"

"Miss Harris let me get out of bed today."

"Then you've been mindin' the doctor an' stayin' out o' mischief?"

Petula frowned. "There's nothin' to do."

"Well, then, you might take a likin' to a new friend to play with." As he spoke, he brought his arm around from behind his back, producing two porcelain-faced dolls. "Sure and I thought your sister might like one too."

"Thank you, Mr. O'Donnell," Sabrina said, wide-eyed, as she took the dolls reverently from his hand and carried them over to Petula's chair.

Patrick's eyes now returned to Rachel. "Faith and begorra," he said softly. "'Tis good to see you, my lovely."

"Hello, Patrick." She swept her hair away from her face with the back of her hand.

"You've been hard at work, I see."

"Just putting up some butter. We were nearly out."

He walked across the room. "Best time is in summer when the grass is lush and green. 'Tis hard to get much milk from a cow this time of year."

"We weren't here then." She was surprised by how defensive she felt.

"But look at you, lass." His green eyes moved slowly down the length of her rose-colored cashmere gown, then up again. "You look like you should be sittin' in a garden filled with spring flowers, rather than churnin' butter." He took hold of her hand and raised it to his lips. "Once we're married, you'll not have to do such things again."

"Married?"

Rachel spun toward the startled sound of Sabrina's voice. How had she let this happen? The day Patrick had announced their engagement to his family, she had asked that they not speak of it in front of the children. She'd wanted to tell them herself, in private. A sixth sense had warned her that they wouldn't welcome the news. It would mean another departure from their lives.

If it hadn't been for Petula's accident, she would have told them by this time. At least, she believed she would have. But it hadn't seemed so important after the child was hurt, and she hadn't seen Patrick since then, and . . .

She stepped away from Patrick, moving slowly toward the children. She pulled a chair over next to Petula and sat down, her hands folded in her lap.

"I'm sorry I didn't say anything sooner. I . . . I wanted to keep it a secret a little longer. We're not going to get married for quite some time. I'm going to be staying right here with you."

Sabrina's tone had changed to anger. "Does Pa know?"

"Yes, Brina. He knows."

"And he's going to *let* you? He's going to *let* you leave us?" With a betrayed cry, she ran into the bedroom and slammed the door.

Rachel's breath caught in her throat. She stared at her hands as she fought the tears that welled up.

"Miss Harris?"

"What is it, Pet?"

"You won't really go away. You're gonna stay with us, aren't you?"

"Pet, I . . ."

"Don't you love us?"

"Oh, Pet . . ." She slipped from the chair, kneeling on the floor as she placed her arms around the child and hugged her. "I love you very much. You'll never know how much. And I won't be far away at all. You know how quickly we can get to Mr. O'Donnell's house in the sleigh."

Petula sniffed. "Will you . . . will you go with us to the basin when we go? Ma always . . . always liked it there best."

She just couldn't say she wouldn't be going with them, not when that was what she wanted more than anything else. "Spring's so far away," she whispered so only the child could hear. "We'll just have to wait and see."

Petula sniffed again.

"Now, why don't you go see if Brina's okay. Tell her I didn't mean to hurt her by keeping it a secret. I just . . . I just didn't think."

Petula slid from her chair and started to walk away, then turned suddenly back and gave Rachel a hug with her good arm. "I don't want you to go either, Miss Harris." Then she ran for the bedroom as her sister had done moments before.

Rachel drew a deep breath as she rose to her feet. "Seems I made a mess of things," she said as she turned toward Patrick.

There was a perplexed expression on his face. His eyes watched her intently. "You should have told them."

"I know." She sighed, feeling drained of energy.

He came toward her. "Why didn't you, lass?"

She shrugged. "After Pet was hurt . . ."

"But you did tell Gavin?"

Something about his tone of voice surprised her. There was a hard edge to it. She'd never heard Patrick sound that way before, especially not with her. He always seemed so bright and jovial. Even with his immense size, he'd never seemed threatening. Yet, there was something about him now that sent a thrill of alarm up the length of her spine.

His hands closed around her arms and he drew her toward him. "I love you, Rachel Harris, and there's no mistakin' that I do. It's proud I am that you've consented to be my wife. I'd have everyone in the territory knowin' it too."

With quiet resignation, she accepted his kiss, while inside a storm of despair began to brew.

Chapter Twenty-Four

Gavin hadn't seen Jess, but he'd seen signs of him. Enough to let him know the young cowboy was okay. By the looks of the tracks he'd found south of here three days ago, Jess had rounded up a good portion of the herd and was heading them toward the hillsides where the wind had blown snow off the grass.

Gavin knew he should probably be headed back to the house—he'd already been gone a couple more days than he said he would be—but he just wasn't ready yet. He needed this time alone to mull things over, sort things out. He kept feeling that he was right on the verge of some important discovery, but it always seemed to slip away before he could grab hold and see what it was.

He turned Scamp's head and rode toward the

line shack. He and Charlie and the men had put up four such shelters after settling in this river valley. In comparison with the mammoth ranches he'd seen in Wyoming and Montana, the Lucky Strike wasn't large, but it still covered more acres than could be effectively managed from the ranch compound. The cowboys used the line shacks for temporary shelter while trying to keep the cattle from starving and freezing to death in the winter or from wandering away during the rest of the year.

This line shack was at the north end of the Lucky Strike range, far from the main ranch house, far from just about anything but the wind and the snow and the trees. He supposed he'd chosen it for its remoteness.

He heard the barking of the wolfhounds from some distance away. He knew the animals well enough to recognize that they were at play rather than sounding an alarm. If they'd found the carcass of a cow or sniffed out a predator, it would have been a different cry he heard. He let out a sharp whistle. Before long, he saw the two dogs barreling across the white terrain.

"You two hungry?" he shouted at them as they bounded through the snowdrifts and yipped in delight.

He dismounted in front of the shack and, after unsaddling Scamp, turned the horse into the corral. Then he entered the building, the two dogs dashing inside before him.

This particular line shack was built up against a mountain, the backside of it dug into the south slope. The back wall and part of each of the two side walls were formed by earth. The remainder was made of logs chinked with mud. Inside there was a cot, a table, and one chair, plus a small stove for cooking and heating.

Gavin didn't bother to remove his coat right away. It would be a while before the fire took the chill off the room. It never would be warm, no matter how hot the fire, but it was better than outdoors and for that he could be thankful.

He was stirring up his supper in a pan when she popped into his thoughts. He wasn't surprised by it. It happened all the time. It seemed there wasn't any escape from Rachel. Where she couldn't be, her memory was.

He sat down in the chair. "Wish I could figure her out."

Duke's tail thumped against the dirt floor.

Gavin raked the fingers of his left hand through the hound's shaggy hair. "I couldn't ever give her what she wants."

Duchess whimpered and lifted her head to look at him.

"Hell, it doesn't matter anyway. She's made her choice."

Patrick was at the Lucky Strike when Stubs announced that he thought he'd better check on Gavin and Jess. They'd seen neither hide nor hair of the two, and Gavin was several days later returning than he'd said he would be.

"Nothin' to worry 'bout," Stubs told Rachel. "Just like to keep track of where everybody is this time of year. I'll be back by nightfall, so you needn't worry about that."

"Sure but I think I'll go with you, Stubs, if you wouldn't mind the company."

"Glad t'have you. I'll saddle you up a horse."

It was Patrick's voluntary offer that caused Rachel the most alarm. Gavin had told her not to worry if he didn't return by Sunday. It hadn't been easy, but for the most part, she'd been able to follow his directive. She'd kept herself occupied with baking and cleaning when not busy teaching the children or entertaining Patrick, who came over daily in his sleigh.

"Patrick," she said softly so the children wouldn't hear, "do *you* think something's wrong?"

"No, lass. I feel more a need to get out from under your feet while you teach the wee ones here. You've been patient with me. It will do me good to sit a horse for an afternoon. I'm gettin' soft in that sleigh."

Rachel wasn't convinced. Stubs wouldn't go out looking for Gavin if he didn't think something could be wrong. And Patrick wouldn't volunteer to accompany Stubs if he didn't think so too.

She absently turned her cheek for Patrick's kiss, then followed him to the door where she stood, shivering from the cold, and watched the two men ride away.

As she closed the door, she inhaled deeply, reminding herself she couldn't go falling to pieces in front of the girls. They would sense her anxiety and make themselves sick with worry. It had taken several days to smooth things over after they learned of her engagement to Patrick.

She didn't need them upset again.

"Well," she said as she turned around, "it's time for our math lessons. Brina, get the slates, please."

It made no sense at all, but she felt that Gavin's absence was her fault. He'd wanted to get away from her. That was why he'd left. Not because he wanted to check on Jess but because he wanted to avoid her.

So what did that mean? Did it mean he might care for her after all?

"Miss Harris?" Then louder. "Miss Harris?"

She shook her head, as if to clear it of confusion.

"What lesson, Miss Harris?" Sabrina asked.

She picked up the book. "Let me see. Where did we leave off yesterday?"

Later she would give it some more thought. Later . . .

It was around two in the afternoon when Jess Chamberlain rode into the yard. After several weeks out on the line, he looked ragged and weary. Confronted in the barn by an anxious Rachel, he was unable to offer any information regarding Gavin's whereabouts.

"Didn't see him when I come up from the south range. Come past all three of the line shacks that're down that way. Reckon he might be up at Lone Pine Gulch. Gotta line shack up there. Though why he'd take himself up that away, I can't say. Most of the cows winter south of here."

"Thank you, Mr. Chamberlain." She started

out of the barn, then stopped and glanced over her shoulder. "Just where is Lone Pine Gulch?"

Jess walked over to the barn door and pointed. "See that double hump of mountains there? The gulch runs right up between them."

"It looks a long way off."

"Not bad. You can get there in a little more'n a half hour with good weather and a fast horse."

"I see," she replied thoughtfully, then added, "When you're through here, come on up to the house. I need your help with something."

"I'll be there, Miss Harris."

Her mind was made up before she really knew what she was doing. She hurried into the bedroom she shared with the children and dug out a warm pair of woolen underdrawers. She shed her light day dress for a black cashmere and moire walking dress, pulling on the underdrawers beneath it. She grabbed her fur bonnet but left her muff. She would need gloves to drive the sleigh.

She was dressed and ready when Jess knocked on the door.

"Come in, Mr. Chamberlain. I'd like you to stay here in the house until I return."

"Return? Ma'am—"

She slipped into her fur-lined cloak. "You needn't worry. The children won't cause you any trouble. Just keep Pet from doing too much. There's a hot stew on the stove if they should get hungry. Help yourself. You must be starved." She pulled on her gloves.

"But, Miss Harris, where are you—"

"If Mr. O'Donnell comes for his sleigh before

I return, tell him not to worry. I'll bring it back without a scratch on it. I'm perfectly capable of handling a horse and buggy and shouldn't find a sleigh any more difficult."

"Miss Harris—"

She closed the door before he could argue with her. She didn't have time to waste. She had neither good weather nor a fast horse, and she didn't know how long it would take her to reach the line shack at Lone Pine Gulch.

He thought about his childhood as he lay back on the cot. There hadn't been much to that farm in Ohio—a few hardscrabble acres, a pigsty, a broken-down team of mules, and a three-room house complete with field mice. His father hadn't ever had much success at farming. Never had much success at anything, Gavin supposed.

But Timothy Blake had loved his wife. Gavin had grown up hearing stories of how he'd seen her when visiting cousins in Pittsburgh and how he'd wooed her and brought her to his farm in Ohio. Gavin was born nine months after the wedding day. His father had always said that his biggest heartache was that Christina was warned by the doctor not to ever have any more children. Gavin would be their only child.

Hell, Gavin knew the truth about his mother. She just hadn't wanted to have any more children by a poor dirt farmer. She'd set her sights elsewhere, and Gavin's father had been too blinded by love to see it.

Gavin sat up on the cot and leaned his head in his hands. Lord, he didn't want to think about this. It made his gut twist with anger. Anger at his father's blind foolishness. Anger at his mother's treachery.

As if to further torture him, Rachel's image reappeared. From almost the first moment he'd seen her, he'd thought she was like his mother. Both of them were blondes. But Rachel's hair was paler, like a field of wheat. Both of them had eyes of blue. But Rachel's were lighter, like the blue of a robin's egg. Both of them . . .

He stopped himself. Was Rachel really *anything* like his mother? Was she *really* out to snare a wealthy husband, no matter who it was?

He ran his hand over his hair, cursing beneath his breath. He didn't know. Damn it, he just didn't know what was what anymore.

Duke jumped suddenly to his feet and ambled toward the door. He cocked his square head to one side, then to the other. Finally, he growled low in his throat.

"What is it, boy?" Gavin reached automatically for his rifle as he rose from the cot.

Duchess joined her mate by the door, her head low, her ears alert.

"Get back," Gavin ordered as his hand closed around the latch.

The last thing in the world he expected to see when he pulled open the door was Rachel Harris driving up to the shack in O'Donnell's sleigh—alone.

Chapter Twenty-Five

Her heart was racing as he walked toward her, rifle hanging at his side.

"What are you doing here? Is something wrong with the girls?"

"No. I . . ." Rachel paused, unable to come up with a reply that made sense at the moment.

Gavin continued to watch her with dark, stormy eyes.

"We were concerned when you didn't return," she finally answered.

"Where's Stubs?" His gaze shifted to the stretch of land behind her.

She shivered inside her cloak. "I think he went down to check the south range."

"You came up this way alone?" Now there was real anger in his voice.

She nodded.

His eyes returned to her. His black brows were drawn together in a scowl, his mouth a thin line of disapproval. "Get down," he said at last. "We'd better get you inside and warm you up."

She tried to say thank you, but the words caught in her throat. She allowed him to take her arm and help her from the sleigh. He didn't release her immediately. Instead, he steered her forcefully toward the dismal little shack set against the hillside, its roof buried under a thick layer of snow.

If she'd thought the exterior dismal, the inside was even more so. There were no windows in the walls of the cabin. A lantern sat on the table, shedding what light it could. The room smelled damp and heavily of wood smoke.

"Here." Gavin pulled the spindly-looking chair from the table and set it right next to the stove. "Sit there."

She did as she was told, glad to be off her feet. She seemed to be shaking uncontrollably now. She set her jaw so her teeth wouldn't chatter and hugged her arms tightly around her chest.

Gavin leaned his rifle against the wall near the door before sitting on the cot. "Are you sure the girls are okay?"

"They're fine. Jess is with them."

"He let you come out here in that contraption? Damn it, I'll—"

She spoke in a rush. "It wasn't his fault. He couldn't have stopped me. I—I had to talk to you."

Gavin's frown eased a bit, although he didn't

look any more welcoming of her company. Now that she was here, she could see that it had been reckless for her to come alone. Perhaps it had been foolish for her to have come at all. At the moment, she was hard pressed to remember what she'd thought she would say if she found him.

That had been her worst fear, of course. That she wouldn't find him. Or that she would find him injured—or worse. Now that he was here before her, looking strong and handsome and angry, it was easy to guess what he would think of her escapade.

Rachel glanced toward the stove. "Is there any coffee in that pot?"

"Yes." He crossed the room and reached for a tin cup set on a shelf above the stove. With a towel, he picked up the coffeepot and poured the dark brew into the cup.

"Thank you," she whispered as he handed it to her.

He returned to the cot and sat down again, continuing to watch her as silence filled the room.

She looked down at the cup in her hands, then took several sips, choking down the bitter brew. It tasted as if it had been on the stove for several days, but it was hot. And she felt a strong need for something hot to fortify her.

She looked as pretty as he'd ever seen her. The black fur hat covered her hair and the tips of her tiny ears. Her cheeks, nose, and chin were as red as apples in autumn. Her blue eyes were positively dazzling, like a piece of clear winter sky.

As foolish as it was for her to have come alone, he couldn't deny that he was glad she had come. Just sitting there, she brightened the lonely little shack. As he watched her sipping her coffee, his anger began to fade.

She always did that to him, he realized. She had a way of making him unreasonably angry and then making him forget *why* he'd been angry as the desire to hold her replaced it. That's what was happening to him now. He wanted to take her in his arms and warm her with his embrace. He wanted to let his kisses change the bright glitter of her eyes to a sultry gaze. He wanted his breath against her cheeks to make her forget the icy weather outdoors. He wanted to pull that fetching fur bonnet from her head and let her hair cascade over her dark coat.

And then he wanted to remove that coat and everything beneath it and feast his eyes upon her.

Rachel's eyes widened a fraction as she looked at him. Her mouth parted, as if to release a sigh, although he heard none. It took almost more strength than he possessed to pull his thoughts back to safety.

"Now, tell me what you're doing here."

"We were concerned when you didn't return on Sunday."

"I told you not to worry if I didn't get back then."

"I know, but . . ." She set the cup on the table. "Well, I thought . . ." Her gaze dropped to her lap.

"What was it you thought, Rachel?"

"I was afraid . . . I was afraid I was the reason you were staying away. The girls need you. If I'm the reason you're staying away from them, I'll leave." Her words came faster as she spoke. "I know you never wanted Dru to hire me as the children's governess. I'd hoped . . . Well, I'll understand if you'd prefer that I go." Her voice faded.

Gavin rose slowly from the cot. Three strides was all it took to carry him to her. He reached down, taking her gloved hands into his, and pulled her to her feet.

He knew there was some reason he shouldn't take her in his arms, but at the moment, he was damned if he could remember what it was.

He kissed her, lightly at first. She tasted fresh and sweet—and just a little like coffee. He felt the captured-bird pulse beat in her throat as his hands cradled her face.

The kiss changed, deepened, set fire to his blood. He removed her hat, just as he'd imagined doing. He freed her hair from its twist and ran his fingers through it as it tumbled free, over her shoulders and down her back. His hands followed the hair, drifting over her coat until he found the small of her back. He drew her closer, but not close enough to satisfy the building fury.

She didn't protest. Her arms remained at her sides, neither pulling him closer nor pushing him away.

Encouraged, he moved his right hand to the clasps of her cloak. Slowly, carefully, he released each one, then pushed the heavy garment from her shoulders, allowing it to drop to the floor around her feet.

Once again, he drew her body close against his. How perfectly she fit in his arms. She seemed to belong there, seemed to have been made for him. But he wanted to feel her without all the trappings between them. He wanted to run his hands over her fair skin. He wanted to look at her breasts. He wanted . . .

He broke the kiss, resting his cheek against her head near her ear. *Rachel*, he mouthed, but no sound came out.

"When you kiss me," she whispered, "when you touch me . . . I can't think. I can't remember . . ." She ended with a sigh.

His lips brushed her hair. "Can't remember what?"

Her voice seemed small and far away. "When I'm near you, I can't remember why I must marry Patrick. Gavin, I . . ."

He could have put his hands around her throat and squeezed the life from her. He could have, but he didn't. Instead, he claimed her mouth in another kiss, punishing her the only way he knew how for her cruelty. That she should be here in his arms, returning his kisses, and still speak of Patrick. He should hate her.

Damn it! He *would* hate her.

If his mouth hadn't covered hers, she would have told him she loved him. She would have told him she couldn't marry Patrick after all. She would have told him she would die without him.

But he was kissing her again with renewed fury, and she couldn't break away. She would tell him later. For now, she would enjoy the feel of his lips against hers.

The sudden cry of the dogs broke them apart. Gavin shoved her aside and grabbed his rifle.

"Stay put," he ordered as he eased open the door.

Rachel could scarcely breathe. Whether from sudden fear or from his kisses, she wasn't sure.

Gavin let the door swing wide. "You'd better fix your hair and straighten your clothes, Rachel. Your *fiance* and Stubs are here." Then he stepped outside, closing the door behind him.

She stood riveted to the floor, feeling a coldness seeping through her. She'd thought . . .

She forced her hands to move, twisting her hair back in place. She leaned down and retrieved her hat, then pulled it over her hair. She could hear voices outside as she picked up her cloak and slipped into it.

He would know. Patrick would know just by looking at her. She felt feverish. Her lips were swollen. Her skin tingled. Her knees felt weak. Surely he would look at her and know what had been happening just before he arrived.

What *had* been happening? she wondered as she fastened the top clasp of her cloak. Would she have allowed more than his kisses?

She steadied herself with a hand on the table as the answer came to her.

Yes! Yes, she would have allowed more. She'd wanted more. She'd wanted him to teach her everything about the intimacies between a man and a woman. God forgive her, she'd wanted it all, and Gavin despised her because of it.

She drew a deep breath and stepped toward the cabin door, pulling it open with more courage than she felt. It wasn't just the loathing she'd heard in Gavin's voice that made her reluctant to go out. She knew she was in for a scolding from Stubs. And Patrick? She wasn't sure what Patrick would say or do.

The moment he saw her, Patrick skirted around Gavin and strode quickly toward the door. In an instant, he had her in his arms, lifting her feet off the ground.

"Sure but you scared the living daylights out o' me, lass. 'Tis a fool thing you did."

"I'm sorry. I didn't . . . I didn't think. I . . ."

"I'll not be havin' my wife doin' such things. You may as well make up your mind to it now, my lovely."

"Patrick . . ."

His kiss silenced her. It wasn't until he released her and she turned to meet Gavin's gaze that she knew what a devastating kiss it had been.

Chapter Twenty-Six

"**S**tubs? May I talk to you?"

He set the horse's hoof down and peered up at Rachel from beneath the wide brim of his hat. "What's on your mind, Miss Harris?"

She glanced over her shoulder toward the house, then closed the barn door. As she walked toward the grizzled cowhand, he leaned against the stall gate and pushed his battered hat back on his head. She stopped, made all the more nervous by the way he was watching her, as if he already knew why she was there.

"Stubs, I . . . I'm not quite sure how to start," she said when she reached the stall.

"Beginnin's always a good place."

"Yes." She inhaled deeply, then let the air out slowly. "I . . . I want to ask you about Gavin."

An eyebrow lifted. "What about him?"

This was harder than she'd thought it would be. "I . . . I'm not sure. Dru told me to ask you. She told me to have you tell me everything about Gavin, about the things she never knew."

Now he was frowning. "What for?"

"I don't know. It . . . just seemed important to her."

Stubs pulled open the gate and stepped out of the stall, then turned and slipped the rope noose over the corner post to fasten the gate closed. "What about you, Rachel?" he asked as he turned around. "Is it important to you?"

She wished she could say no. Her life would be so much simpler if it wasn't important, if *he* wasn't important. "Yes," she answered in a small voice, her gaze dropping to the straw-covered floor.

The silence seemed interminable. Rachel didn't dare look at the cowboy. She was afraid he'd guessed too much already.

"Let's go up to the bunkhouse. It's warmer there, an' we won't be bothered by anybody. Jess went into town. Probably won't be back 'til tomorrow some time." He took hold of her elbow and steered her out of the barn.

A cold wind whipped at her skirts as she walked beside Stubs across the yard, sending a chill up her spine and along her arms. She was afraid to glance toward the house, afraid she would see Gavin watching what she was doing. He would be furious if he knew she was asking his old friend about him, about his past.

While she took a seat on the bench near the table in the center of the bunkhouse, Stubs stoked the fire in the pot-bellied stove.

"Coffee?" he asked without turning around.

"No, thank you."

"Think I'll have me some."

Rachel twisted her hands in her lap as she waited. Her insides felt as tight as a bowstring. She'd been that way ever since Patrick released her from his embrace yesterday and she'd looked into Gavin's eyes. He despised her. Minutes before, he'd been making love to her, and then he'd despised her. Why did it always turn out that way?

Stubs turned from the stove, cup in hand. "I wasn't more'n fifteen when I went to work for the Blakes back in Ohio. My folks had died, and I didn't have a place of my own. Guess I wasn't much better at farmin' than Timothy Blake was, but I was mighty willin' to try. Gavin's pa, Timothy . . . well, he was one nice fella. Lousy farmer. Never did have two nickels to rub together, didn't seem like."

He walked across the room and sat down on a bench opposite Rachel. "Gavin was about three when I first started livin' there. Cutest little tyke you ever saw. And Mrs. Blake . . ." He shook his head slowly, his eyes looking back through time. "Lord, what a beauty she was. Her husband worshipped the ground she walked on, an' that ain't no exaggeration. Early on, I think she'd tried to make that place into a home, but I never seen it. She hated that farm. Hated bein' poor. Never did a lick of work around the place. Timothy waited on her hand an' foot. Treated her like she was a queen."

Stubs pierced her with a sharp gaze. "You look a bit like her. Don't suppose Gavin ever told you that. She had blond hair and blue eyes and a figure. . . . Course, you really don't look nothin' like her once a fella gets t'lookin'. Your hair's lighter and your eyes are different, but for just a moment, I could see. Maybe it's 'cause she could turn a man's head, just like you."

"But I don't . . ."

"There's the difference. You don't seem to know you're turnin' men's heads. Christina knew, and she used it. She wanted to be rich, and she wasn't ever gonna get there as a farmer's wife. 'Spect she knew all along just how she was gonna get rich. Didn't matter to her that she had a husband and a little boy."

Rachel felt a pain in her heart. She wished she could tell him to stop, not to tell her anything more. She had an awful feeling that she hadn't heard the worst of it.

"I don't know for sure. Gavin never talked about it later. But I think he found his ma and Mr. Hannah together while his pa was away. Guess there wasn't any reason for her to sneak around and pretend after that. She left the farm in Mr. Hannah's company, bold as you please. Just up and walked off and left her husband and son and went to live in that big house in town. I suppose Gavin was about ten, maybe twelve years old at the time. She never saw her boy agin 'til after his pa died. Why would she? She'd married herself the rich Mr. Hannah. She didn't have no use for the boy."

"Poor Gavin," she whispered.

"Gavin watched his pa drink himself t'death. Place 'bout fell down around their ears. I took me a job elsewhere 'cause there wasn't anythin' more I could do. I'd moved West by the time Timothy died."

The room was silent for a long time while Rachel imagined what it must have been like for Gavin and his father.

"Christina kinda soured Gavin on women, least as far as formin' any kind of lastin' attachment goes. I guess he always figured he'd come home one day an' find the woman in bed with another man."

She felt herself blushing. Was that what Stubs had meant about Gavin finding his mother together with another man? "But . . . but she was a married woman," she protested, not wanting to believe it.

"Promises didn't mean nothin' to Christina Blake. She was beautiful an' selfish an' was lookin' out for herself. She found herself a rich man an' she was gonna have him. Funny thing was, I doubt she ever loved old Mr. Hannah. I guess if she ever loved anybody besides herself, she loved Timothy. But not enough to stay poor an' keep livin' on that farm." Stubs shook his head. "Easy to understand why the boy would decide not ever t'marry after havin' such a ma."

"But he married Dru."

Stubs smiled. "That was different. Charlie'd been Gavin's friend. Closest thing he could ever have for a brother. After he died, it just fell to Gavin to look out for the family. 'Spect that would've been good enough if Dru hadn't got the cancer. When she knew she was dyin', she asked Gavin t'marry her so her girls would have a pa when she was gone. She didn't want 'em to be orphans.''

"But he *loved* her. I could see it."

"We all loved her. Couldn't help but love her. You know that. You loved her too.''

Rachel agreed with a nod and a wistful smile.

"But she an' Gavin didn't have the kind of marriage most folks think about. She was his friend more than his wife. She wanted Gavin t'learn t'trust his heart. She wanted him to find a woman an' fall in love an' have a family, just like her and Charlie. That's what Dru wanted."

Rachel swallowed a lump in her throat, then whispered, "She told me he wasn't meant to marry her, that he had a lot to learn about love."

"I might be a fool," Stubs said as he leaned forward, his voice low, "but I 'spect she was hopin' he'd learn about it from you."

"Dru wanted *us* . . ." She let her voice fade away. Of course. It seemed so clear now. While she and Gavin had been feeling guilty about their feelings, Dru had been trying to throw them together.

Suddenly the rest of the pieces began to fall into place as well. Despite her love for Gavin, Rachel had accepted the proposal of a wealthy man. Yesterday, she had gone into Gavin's arms, returning his kisses with as much fervor as his were given. She would have done even more if they hadn't been interrupted. Lord only knew how far she might have gone.

She put her hands up over her face as shame

washed over her. She would have allowed him to do anything, everything. She'd wanted it. And then, when Patrick came, she'd found herself in his arms instead.

No wonder Gavin despised her. He'd always feared she would be like his mother, and not just because of the physical resemblance. He was afraid she was spoiled and not cut out for the hard life he'd chosen here in the back country. He'd been afraid she would leave him for a wealthy man, even if she loved him.

Well, she'd done all those things, hadn't she? She'd proven him right.

Except he wasn't right. She wasn't spoiled or too pampered for the life he'd chosen. She was willing to work hard. As hard as it took to make the ranch grow and prosper. She didn't need money and a house in town.

And she wasn't going to marry Patrick O'Donnell. Whether or not she could ever convince Gavin that she loved him, she wasn't going to marry Patrick.

"Thank you for telling me everything." She rose from the bench and started toward the door.

"What're you gonna do now, Rachel?"

She didn't look back at him. "Try to fix things if I can, Stubs. Try to fix things."

"Gavin?"

He stopped, his hand already on the door. They hadn't spoken in three days, not since they'd returned from Lone Pine Gulch. Of course, he'd heard her voice whenever she

291

spoke to the children, but he hadn't heard her speak his name.

He turned. "What is it?"

He steeled himself against looking at her. Whenever he did, he felt the pain of loss. Not for things he'd once had, but for things he might have had if things were different.

"I want to ride over to Killarney Hall today. I need . . . I need to talk to Patrick."

His jaw tightened. "You don't need my permission to see him."

"Then I may take one of the horses?"

He turned back toward the door. "No, but I'll have Stubs hook up the team to the sled. It's not fancy, but it'll get you there."

Her soft "thank you" followed him out the door.

Gavin didn't like being confused, but it seemed that confusion had been his constant companion since he first met Rachel Harris. Before that, his life had been carefully arranged. He had his few friends. He had his ranch. With the exception of Dru's illness, he'd been able to control the events of his life. He'd even been able to control his emotions.

Until Rachel.

He didn't know what he felt anymore. He wanted her. He hated her. He needed her.

His hand closed around the latch on the barn door, and he jerked it open with fury.

Hell, no! He didn't need her. He *wouldn't* need her. Gavin Blake wasn't the sort of man to ever need a woman.

He'd been right about women and love and marriage all along. Shoot, if Charlie hadn't died and left a sick widow and two children, Gavin wouldn't have ever married. Not even Dru, no matter how much he liked and admired her.

"Stubs!" he shouted.

The barn was empty. He spun on his heel and marched toward the bunkhouse.

He never should have let Dru hire Rachel. The blasted female was driving him crazy. He didn't know what he wanted, what he felt anymore. Damn, maybe he should just tell Rachel to forget her promise to Dru to stay until spring. Maybe she should just marry Patrick now and get out.

"Stubs!" He rapped once and opened the door.

His grizzled friend was leaning back in a chair, whittling a piece of wood. He raised a curious eyebrow at Gavin but remained silent.

"Hook up Patch and Checker to the sled and take Rachel over to the O'Donnell place."

He stormed out, making a beeline for the barn, without giving Stubs a chance to respond. Before Stubs ever got to the barn, he'd saddled Scamp and was headed out for a quick look at the herd and more solitude.

But it was impossible to escape his troubled heart.

She felt Stubs' disapproving gaze but didn't offer any explanation. She had to talk to Patrick before she could try to set anything else right.

And if that meant she had to endure Stubs' unspoken condemnation, then that was what she would do.

The Blake sled was nothing more than a wagon box set on crude runners, and the two big workhorses didn't exactly glide over the snowy terrain. The journey was long, tense, and silent. Despite Rachel's anxiety over the anticipated confrontation with Patrick, she was relieved to crest the hill and see Killarney Hall come into view.

Once they'd stopped in front of the house, Rachel didn't wait for Stubs to help her from the wagon seat. She scrambled to the ground, then turned to look at him.

"You needn't wait, Stubs. I . . . I don't know how long I'll be. I'm sure Mr. O'Donnell will see that I get home."

Home. Home to the Lucky Strike. Home to Sabrina and Petula and Gavin. Home.

But it couldn't be her home until she talked to Patrick. Maybe it couldn't ever be her home, but she had to try.

She turned, squaring her shoulders, and climbed the steps to the veranda. Insides aquiver, she knocked on the door.

Patrick knew what was going to happen the next time he saw Rachel. He'd known it the day they'd found Rachel and Gavin at the line shack. That was why he hadn't hooked up the sleigh and driven over to the Lucky Strike today or yesterday or the day before that. He wanted to postpone the inevitable as long as possible.

Perhaps, with a little more time, he could change fate.

"Mr. O'Donnell?"

He looked up from the papers strewn across his desk. "What is it, Crandal?"

"Miss Harris is here, sir. I've shown her into the solarium."

So . . . He couldn't stop the chain of events simply by staying at home. She'd come to him.

"Thank you, Crandal."

"I'm getting some tea for the young lady, sir. Can I bring anything for you?"

"No." He had a feeling he would need something stronger than tea to brace him for this meeting. But he didn't pour himself a tumbler full of Irish whiskey, despite how much he wanted to.

Sure but you can take this like a man, O'Donnell, he thought as he left his office and walked down the hall toward the solarium.

She was standing at the window, gazing out across the range. She looked as sweet and lovely as he'd ever seen her, perhaps more so. She turned her head when she heard him enter, and he saw the trouble brewing in eyes of blue.

"This is a surprise, Rachel. Have you come alone?"

"Stubs drove me over."

Patrick glanced around the room.

"I sent him back to the ranch. I was counting on you for a ride home."

He wanted to take her in his arms and keep her there. Instead, he motioned toward the brocade sofa. "Crandal is bringing tea. It'll warm you. I'd not have you takin' cold after comin' all this way to see me."

"Patrick . . ."

"What did I tell you? Here he is."

She'd been like a dream. He'd known it wouldn't last. He would have to awaken one day and she would be gone. He guessed he'd known it from the first time he saw her in Challis. She was in love with Gavin. He wondered if she'd known it then. He knew Gavin well enough to know he hadn't guessed yet, and Patrick had hoped he could win Rachel for himself before Gavin saw it too.

Well, the dream was about to end, but he meant to prolong it a few more hours if possible. Just a few more hours was all he asked.

It seemed to Rachel that they'd talked about almost everything under the sun except the reason for her visit. Her insides were coiled as tight as a spring, and her head was throbbing painfully. It was getting late. She had to take care of this and get home.

She stood abruptly. "Patrick, I must speak with you about something important."

The smile left his face. "You don't have to, my lovely. 'Tis already clear why you've come." He rose from the sofa to stand before her, taking her hands into his as she looked up at him. "'Tis no surprise to me."

Could he truly know and understand?

"We've been foolin' ourselves. At least, I have. I've known your heart belonged to another, but I hoped I could change that. I thought myself a lucky man when you said you'd marry me. I knew you were weak with sorrow at the time, and I took advantage of it. You'll have to forgive a man for tryin'."

"Oh, Patrick . . . You've always known," she whispered, tears forming in her eyes. "I thought I could marry you and make you happy. I really did."

"I know, lass."

Tears traced her cheeks. "Take me home, Patrick. Please."

Chapter Twenty-Seven

Rachel prepared a roast and fried potatoes with onions for supper, but Gavin wasn't there to eat it. She scarcely touched the food either. Her stomach was balled into knots.

"He prob'ly decided to bed down in a line shack. Don't s'pose we'll see him for a day or two," Stubs said when she took some of the supper over to the bunkhouse.

At nine, she put the children to bed. She read to them for a short time, then turned out the lamp.

At ten, she changed out of her dress into her nightgown and crawled into bed, but sleep wouldn't come.

At eleven, she put on her robe and went to sit by the fireplace in the sitting room. She tried to read a novel, but she couldn't keep her mind on the plot. Finally, she put the book aside and simply stared into the fire, wondering where Gavin was and how long it would be before she could talk to him.

It was nearing midnight when the dogs lifted their heads toward the front door, ears cocked forward. Joker got up and wandered across the room. Rachel held her breath. She wasn't ready, she realized as the latch lifted and the door opened.

Gavin paused on the threshold, letting in a gust of cold air. He stared at her for what seemed a very long time, although later she would guess it had been only a matter of seconds. Finally, he closed the door and removed his warm coat and gloves. He hung his hat on one of the pegs next to his coat, then turned around.

Just how did she begin to tell him all she was feeling? Did a woman dare to speak of love first? Should she simply tell him she wasn't going to marry Patrick?

He crossed the room, his gaze locked once again with hers. He looked unhappy to see her sitting there. Perhaps it was already too late. Perhaps he would never want to hear what she wanted so desperately to say. Perhaps he wouldn't care one way or the other about whom she married.

She pushed herself up from the chair. "I didn't expect you to return tonight."

"Neither did I."

"Are you hungry?"

"No."

Her legs seemed to move of their own volition, carrying her to stand before him. Her heart began its erratic beating. Her head felt light.

"Gavin . . ." she whispered.

His voice, when he responded, was also low— and he sounded angry. "What do you want from me, Rachel?"

What did she want from him? To love him. To spend her life with him. To be a mother to his children. To be at his side through good times and bad. To grow old together.

But she couldn't say those things, and so she did the only thing she could. She stood on tiptoe, placed her arms around his neck, and kissed him.

What she'd meant to be only a tender gesture, a means of telling him how much she loved him, became a fire in her veins, spreading violently through her, leaving her skin tingling and her limbs weak. When he clutched her tightly to him, she could only moan in acquiescence. His mouth moved hungrily over hers and she responded with equal greed.

"No more, Rachel," he whispered huskily as he swept her feet up from the floor. "God help me, I can't resist you anymore."

She pressed her face against his shoulder as he carried her across to his bedroom door.

Just as he stepped into the darkened room, he paused. "Do you know what's happening? Do you want to be here?"

"I . . . Yes." Her voice quavered as she answered the second question. As for the first, she wasn't sure what was happening, only that she knew she couldn't bear to stop it now.

He closed the door with the heel of his boot, then carried her to the bed. She felt cold when he released her, moving away into the darkness. She felt like crying out, begging him to return. A moment later, a match flared, then the lantern came to life. He turned it low, leaving only an eerie golden glow to spill across the bed. The rest of the room remained in shadows.

Gavin sat on the edge of the bed and removed his boots, then turned and took her into his arms as he stretched out beside her on the bed. His mouth returned to claim hers, first with gentle nibbles and then with a renewed vigor.

The blood surged hot through her veins once again. She clung to him as his mouth pillaged hers, teasing her lips until they opened to the exploration of his tongue. Lightheaded, she responded in kind, delighting in the taste of him.

When his hand slid slowly from her back to cup her breast, she gasped lightly into his mouth. She'd never felt such an intimate touch. It frightened her. It intrigued her.

His mouth moved away once again, this time to trail kisses across her cheek to her ear, then to her throat, his lips pressing against the pulsing vein just below her jaw. She closed her eyes and arched her neck, offering herself willingly to the new sensations he stirred within.

"Don't move," he said softly in her ear.

Goose pimples rose on her arms and legs. She felt the gentle movement of the bed as he slipped away from her. A sixth sense told her he wouldn't be gone long, yet she opened her eyes to make sure he wasn't leaving her completely.

His shirt was already missing. Lamplight played across the muscles of his broad chest, shed golden highlights upon the dark chest hair, turned his skin to bronze. She'd never seen anything more beautiful, more magnificent in all her life.

She met his gaze, and her stomach seemed to drop, as if falling from a great height. She was vaguely aware of the movements of his hands and arms as he removed his trousers, knew that he stood naked before her if only she had the courage to look, but she couldn't move her eyes from his. She was locked in his power, helpless against it, caught in a maelstrom of new and wondrous emotions.

Kneeling on the bed, Gavin took hold of her shoulders and drew her up onto her knees to face him. He pushed her robe from her shoulders. She caught the sleeve with her fingertips, pulled the garment free and tossed it aside. His hands drifted down her sides, stopping near her hips. Slowly, he began to gather her nightgown into his hands. Cold air swirled around her ankles, her thighs, her waist as the flannel garment inched upward. And then he was pulling it up over her head, flinging it aside as she had the robe.

Only now did his eyes release their magnetic hold on hers. His gaze drifted down just as his hands came up to play lightly over her breasts. Again, she gasped, this time audibly. She swayed toward him, her knees feeling unsteady, a strange ache beginning in the apex of her thighs.

"Gavin . . ."

He drew her closer, their bodies brushing lightly against each other. She was aware first of the silky feel of his chest, and then of the unique physical differences between them as his hands cupped her buttocks and drew her to him.

Her eyes widened, and there was a moment of fear, of wondering what it was she was doing. And then he was kissing her again as he lowered her back onto the bed. Fear vanished, and she surrendered willingly to the inevitable.

He was like a starving man presented with a banquet. He wanted to feast on it all. He wanted to make it last in case he should never be presented with such glorious delicacies again.

She was more beautiful than he'd imagined. Her skin was porcelain-smooth. Her breasts were full and firm, the nipples hardening in response to his touch. Her waist was narrow, her stomach flat, her hips rounded, her legs long and shapely. When he kissed her throat, he could feel the rapid beating of her heart and her ragged breath against his hair.

Braced above her on his hands and knees, he trailed a path of kisses from the hollow of her throat down to her breast. He covered the areola with his mouth, laved it with his tongue, sucked it up between his teeth.

She writhed beneath him, and he groaned in response, feeling his own need for her increase until his whole body was pulsing with it.

He stretched out beside her again, this time leaving her on her back. With a careful touch, his hand slid from her breast to her belly, and then lower, lower. He heard her gasp, felt her startled flinch. He covered her mouth with his, stopping her protest with the fire of his kisses.

The rhythm of his touch sent a river of heat flooding through her. After the initial surprise, she gave herself over to a world of wondrous sensations, delighted in the flashes of color and bursts of light that danced inside her head. Her body felt at once languorous and tense.

His hand tutored her body, readying her for him. When he rose above her for the second time, she intuitively reached up to draw him closer. When he entered her, she scarcely felt the pain, an instinct as old as time lifting her toward the sinuous drive of his hips, fitting them together in perfect union.

She murmured something, though she knew not what.

He sighed near her ear.

She felt the cadence of his movements and found pleasure in learning the ancient dance, the beat growing in fevered tempo until, at the final crescendo, she cried out, her body arching against his. He spoke her name even as he shuddered against her. And then she seemed to spiral slowly back to earth.

They lay replete, bodies sapped of energy, each locked in the other's embrace. Gavin rolled onto his side, taking her with him, their bodies still joined. Rachel smiled as she nestled her face against the base of his throat, finding pleas-

ure in the sated intimacy that followed the
tumult of moments before.

I love you, Gavin, she thought.

And then she slept.

The waking was slow and blissful. She slept
against him, her hand upon his chest. His face
was buried in the abundance of her hair. He felt
a tightening as he remembered their love-mak-
ing.

And then he felt the guilt.

He was supposed to be Patrick's friend, but he
had taken Rachel to his bed, lay even now with
her in his arms. From nearly the first moment
they'd met, he'd felt his desire for her growing.
He had nearly betrayed Dru. He had betrayed
Patrick. All because of the woman lying in his
arms.

Worse yet, he knew he wouldn't be able to
control himself if she stayed until spring. He
would take her to his bed again and again. And
they would continue to betray Patrick. She'd
shown her willingness to share Gavin's bed,
even while choosing to marry another man.

She would have to leave the Lucky Strike. He
would have to make her leave at once. At first
light. Today.

His arms tightened around her. It was going
to hurt to make her go.

Chapter Twenty-Eight

She stretched languidly, reluctant to awaken. She knew it was still early, too early to be up when she would much prefer to linger in bed and remember the loving she'd found in Gavin's arms. It had been a thousand times more than anything she might have expected.

She would tell him she loved him. Of course, he would know that already after last night. He would have to understand. And he would tell her he loved her too. Nothing stood between them any longer. Not Dru. Not Patrick. They would wait an appropriate length of time before marrying, but then nothing would ever keep them apart again.

She opened her eyes to find him standing beside the bed. He was fully dressed. She felt herself flush as he stared down at her, remembering the way he'd gazed at her naked body during the night.

"Good morning," she said and smiled.

"You'd better get dressed. I don't want the girls finding you here."

Her eyes widened at the anger she heard in his voice.

"I want you to pack your things and leave. Stubs will take you to the O'Donnell place. At least, that's where I imagine you want to stay until your wedding."

"My wedding?"

"Don't tell me you've forgotten the unfortunate Mr. O'Donnell so quickly. You remember Patrick. Your wealthy fiance."

She sat up, holding the blankets against her breasts. "Gavin, you don't think . . . About last night . . ."

"I don't give a damn about last night, Miss Harris. I just want you off the Lucky Strike as fast as you can get your things packed." He spun on his heel and marched toward the door. He turned for one more glance in her direction, the set of his face hard and unrelenting. "After breakfast, I'll take the girls out with me. I don't want them to know you're leaving. I'll tell them something after you're gone. Stubs will take you to Killarney Hall."

"Please, Gavin," she whispered, her throat thick with tears. "You must let me explain."

"Nothing you could say would make any difference to me." With that, he left the bedroom, closing the door snugly behind him.

She was too stunned to move at first.

But I love you, Gavin.

Nothing she could say would make any difference to him.

I don't want to marry Patrick.

He just wanted her off the Lucky Strike.

But I love you . . .

Numbly, she found her nightclothes. She slipped the nightgown over her head, remembering with burning clarity the way it had felt as he'd removed it the night before. She pushed away the pain the memory stirred as she pulled on her robe and walked across the room. She listened at the door, then opened it, thankful to find the sitting room empty.

She pushed her tangled hair back from her face. Her fingers touched her lips where just hours before he had kissed her so lovingly. A tiny moan tore free of her throat. She gripped the door jamb as a dizzy weakness shook her to the core. She dragged in a breath of air to help steady herself.

Get dressed. You must get dressed.

If she concentrated on what she had to get done, if she didn't allow her thoughts to stray to Gavin or the night in his arms, she would be all right.

Get dressed.

She released her hold on the door jamb and forced one foot to move in front of another. Step by agonizing step, she crossed the main room. She eased open the door to the children's room.

Her gaze went first to Petula's bed. The child's covers were tangled into a heap. Except for a glimpse of brown curls, it would have been impossible to tell if she was in the bed.

She turned toward the cot against the wall. Sabrina was lying on her back, her mouth slightly parted, one arm thrown over her eyes. Her covers, in contrast with her sister's, were barely rumpled.

Rachel blinked back the tears that stung her eyes. She would miss them. She loved these girls more than she could have believed possible. For over three months, they had been her primary concern. She had played with them, laughed with them, cried with them. She had washed their clothes and cooked their meals. She had watched them struggle with their school work and beamed with pride at their accomplishments.

She couldn't have loved them more had they been her own.

And now they were lost to her forever.

She choked down the sob that threatened to escape her chest. With head hanging, she moved silently toward her corner of the room. She dressed hastily, trying not to make any sound to awaken them. The longer they slept, the longer she could remain.

It would make no difference, of course. A few minutes. A few hours. It would never be long enough. She would still have to leave today.

Oh, Gavin. You don't understand. I thought . . . I thought you wanted me because you loved me. I thought you would know I love you too.

Perhaps he did know, she thought as she pulled a brush through her hair. Perhaps he knew she loved him and just didn't care. She didn't want to believe it could be true, but perhaps it was.

With a heavy heart, she returned to the kitchen to make breakfast for the children. The last breakfast she would ever make for them. The next few hours would be filled with things she would be doing for the last time within these walls, with this beloved family.

She wondered if she had the strength to survive the hours to come.

Gavin didn't give Stubs a chance to ask any questions. He just told him to help Miss Harris load up her things as soon as Gavin left with the children and take her to the O'Donnell place.

They set out—Gavin, the girls, Duke and Duchess—well before noon, while the air still held its nighttime chill and their breath turned to frosty clouds in front of their faces. Gavin carried Petula with him on Scamp. Sabrina rode Princess, two pairs of ice skates tossed across the mare's rump behind the saddle. The horses plodded along, plowing through occasional snowdrifts, while the dogs raced ahead, then came back to see what was keeping horses and riders so long.

The skating pond was frozen solid, as Gavin had known it would be. The wind had swept most of the snow from the crystal-smooth surface, and it didn't take him long to finish the task, using a broken tree limb from a nearby pine tree.

Petula shivered inside her coat. "Why couldn't Miss Harris come with us?"

"She's busy," Gavin answered without looking at her.

"What am I gonna do while you skate? I'm cold."

"I told you. I'll carry you." Gavin leaned over to strap on the blades.

"What if you fall? It'll hurt my arm."

"For cryin' out loud, Pet! I'm not going to fall."

Great teardrops clung to her lower lashes as she stared at him with wide brown eyes. Her lips were pressed tightly together and her chin quivered.

Gavin sighed. "I'm sorry, Pet. I didn't mean to yell at you. I just thought it would be fun to get out of the house. We haven't done anything together for a long time. I thought you'd like to come skating. I promise to be real careful so you won't get hurt. I'm a good skater, remember?"

Petula sniffed and dashed away her tears as she nodded. "But I still don't see why Miss Harris couldn't've come," she added in a whisper.

Rachel turned slowly, her eyes moving over the airy main room of the ranch house. There wasn't anything fancy about it. The furnishings were plain and simple and sparse, but they were also solid and built to last. Dru had made the rag rugs that covered the wood floors and the pillows that rested against the backs of the chairs.

Gavin's own hands had fashioned the large table and the sideboards.

Rachel was leaving a few of her own touches. She'd made the curtains hanging in the children's bedroom, and the dried flower arrangement on the table was hers too. She wondered if Gavin wanted them out of his sight along with her. She decided to leave them. Perhaps, in time, he wouldn't think so badly of her and would be glad to have them. Or perhaps he didn't even know she'd made them.

Joker brushed his head beneath her hand. She looked down at the scruffy-looking animal. "Why didn't you go with the others?" she asked, kneeling beside the dog. "Mangy hound." She scratched his ears. "You've been a thorn in my side from the day we met." She buried her face in his wiry coat and fought back the tears.

The door opened behind her, and she heard Stubs' footsteps on the floor. "Got your trunk loaded on the sled."

She rose from the floor. "You take care of everybody for me, Joker," she whispered. She completed her circle, her eyes continuing to caress each nook and cranny of the log house. "All right, Stubs. I'm ready."

She walked past him and out to the waiting sled, climbing onto the wagon seat without waiting for the cowboy's assistance. She pulled the hood of her cloak up over her head and clutched it tightly beneath her chin. She refused to turn her head to look at Stubs when he joined her on the seat.

"Where to, Miss Harris?" Disapproval was

clear in his clipped question.

"Challis."

There was a pause. "But I thought . . ."

"I'm going to catch the stage for home."

"The wedding's to take place in Boise?"

"I broke off the engagement with Mr. O'Donnell yesterday. There isn't going to be any wedding."

"Does Gavin know that?"

Rachel turned her head and met the man's direct gaze. "It wouldn't make any difference if he did. May we please get started? I want to be gone before he returns with the children. There's no point in upsetting them more than necessary."

He opened his mouth as if to speak, then clamped it shut. With a shake of his head, he slapped the reins, and the team surged forward.

More than anything else, Rachel wanted to twist on the wagon seat and look back at the house and outbuildings. She wanted to memorize every board, every window. Very soon, memories would be all she would have. But she resisted. If she looked back, she would fall apart.

Joker's barking announced his arrival. He galloped beyond, then circled the trotting horses and wagon bed, returning to Rachel's side of the sled. His long tongue lolled out the corner of his mouth as he ran beside them.

"Go back, Joker," Rachel shouted at him.

"No point in tellin' him t'git. He's taken a particular likin' to you. Prob'ly senses you're goin'. I'll bring him back home with me. Won't do him no harm to follow us into town."

She remembered the first time she'd seen the unruly hound. She remembered the way he'd jumped up on her, soiling her blouse and pushing her to the ground. She remembered Gavin's laughter.

Your dog, no doubt, she'd said to him.

Lord, she was even going to miss that stupid dog.

Chapter Twenty-Nine

"**Y**es, ma'am. Sometimes the stage is gettin' through now, but it'll be Saturday 'fore the next one is due in. Might be here. Might not. Can't never tell this time o' year."

"Saturday?" Rachel stared at the man behind the counter. "But that's four days."

"Yes'm. Reckon it is at that."

"Rachel?" Stubs' hand touched her shoulder. "Why don't I just take you back to the Lucky Strike? I'll bring you into town on Saturday."

She swung around to look at him. "No," she said emphatically. "I can't go back with you."

"Well, I don't take too well to leavin' you alone in town. The man's right. Never can tell about the stage in the winter. It can get snowed in by one of the passes. You could be here for a couple weeks even."

"Weeks?" she repeated softly. She mentally calculated the amount of money in her reticule.

"Come on, then." Stubs took hold of her elbow. "Let me take you back."

"No. I am not going back to the ranch, and that's final. You may take me to the hotel. I will be perfectly all right until the stage arrives."

"Obstinate fools, the both of you," he muttered as he escorted her out of the stage line office.

Stubs couldn't understand how much she longed to return with him to the Lucky Strike, but she'd said her good-byes, however privately, and couldn't bear to go through it again. And Gavin? He would be furious if he should find her there. No, she would have to stay in Challis and wait.

There wasn't anything fancy about the hotel Stubs took her to, but it was clean and affordable and far enough away from the nearest saloon to remain reasonably quiet at night.

Stubs was still frowning as he stood in the door of her hotel room. "What're you gonna do about gettin' your trunk to the stage? It's too heavy for you to drag over there."

"I'm sure I can hire someone to take it over for me. Please don't worry about me anymore, Stubs. I'll be fine."

"I'm not so sure."

She felt her self-control slipping. In another moment, she would burst into tears in front of him, and she didn't want that. "I'm going to lie down now and rest. Thank you again."

He touched the brim of his hat. "It's been a pleasure, Rachel."

"Good-bye," she managed to whisper. "Take care of everyone for me."

The door closed behind him.

Rachel sank onto the bed. The sob she'd been holding in all day tore its way up from her chest, and she curled into a tight ball in the center of the bed and gave herself over to tears.

He'd done it for her own good as well as his. He'd had to be cruel. He hadn't had any choice. They weren't good for each other. Hadn't been from the start. They would only have made things worse if she'd stayed even one more day. This way, at least, she could have the rich husband she wanted. Perhaps Patrick would never know what had happened.

She'd been a virgin. Why had she thrown her virtue away on him? Wasn't she smart enough to know it could ruin everything for her? She could be pregnant with his child even now. What if she and Patrick still didn't plan to wed until summer? Everyone would know what she'd done.

Why had she come so willingly to his bed?

Rachel walked along the boardwalk toward the hotel as dusk fell over the town. She had to pass several saloons on her way back from the restaurant, and she'd already had to skirt two scrubby-looking men who were well into their cups despite the earliness of the hour.

She wondered if a drink of whiskey might be

the cure for what ailed her. Could alcohol heal a broken heart? And even if it couldn't, she wouldn't care as long as it brought her just a few hours of oblivion, a short respite from the pain.

But, of course, she didn't dare go into a saloon, nor did she really want to find solace in drink. She just wanted to get back to Maggie. Maggie would help her make sense of it all.

"Rachel!"

She stopped and turned at the familiar voice.

"Sure but I never thought to see you in town," Patrick said as he strode across the street and stepped up onto the sidewalk. "What are you . . .?" He stopped abruptly as he looked down at her face. "Rachel, my lovely, what's wrong?"

"I'm going home," she answered.

A sudden crash of glass and wood sounded from a nearby saloon.

"Here. Let's get you off the street. 'Tis not safe for you t'be out alone at night. What's Gavin thinkin'? Where is he?"

She felt too tired for explanations. "Gavin's not with me. I'm alone." The truth of those words cut her like a knife. "I'm all alone," she repeated.

"Rachel . . ." His big hands closed gently over her arms. "Tell me what's happened."

She lifted her chin in a show of mock strength. "I've left the Lucky Strike. I'm going home to Boise as soon as the stage comes. Until then, I'm staying at the Gumbel Hotel."

"Come on, then." He started walking, pulling her along with him. "I'll not have you stayin' alone. You'll come with me to Killarney Hall. Pearl will see you have a hot bath and a good night's sleep, and then you can tell me all about it."

"I'm going home."

"Fine. If it's to Boise you're determined to go, I'll see you get there myself."

"Oh, Patrick." She felt the threat of tears returning. "I can't let you . . ."

"There's no letting to it. I'll have my way in this, and there'll be no argument from you."

Petula's wan face was streaked with tears. "Can I lay down, Pa? I don't feel like doin' school work today."

"Sure. Go ahead," Gavin answered, feeling as miserable as the little girl looked.

"I think I'll go with her," Sabrina said as she closed the history book she'd been reading.

They'd been like this for three days now, ever since they'd returned from the skating pond and found that Rachel was gone. He'd made up some story about her needing to be at Killarney Hall to get ready for her wedding. It sounded like a lame excuse even to him, and he doubted if either of the girls believed him. Sabrina had said Miss Harris would never leave without saying good-bye to them unless something terrible happened. Petula had kept asking if they couldn't go to Mr. O'Donnell's to make sure she was all right. She hadn't taken his negative response well.

It seemed to Gavin that everywhere he looked, he could still see signs of Rachel. There were the curtains at the windows and the flowers on the table and the dresses that the children wore and even the buttons on his shirt. The reminders were relentless, and he knew he missed her as much as the children did.

He more than missed her. He needed her. He'd been a fool not to admit it to himself sooner. Maybe if he had, she would have been engaged to him instead of Patrick O'Donnell. After all, she'd seemed happy enough here with the children. He couldn't give her the things Patrick could, but he could promise she wouldn't ever be in want. And Sabrina and Petula would give her plenty of love.

Ah, hell! Who was he kidding? Why would she choose him when she could have a life of ease with Patrick? And why would he want her? She'd shown her true self when she'd come to his bed while intending to marry another. He'd been right about her all along.

So why didn't he feel right about her? Why did he feel like the one in the wrong? Why did this sense of foreboding persist?

Finding no answers, Gavin put on his coat and went outside. The air was crisp, the sun brilliant. Icicles dripped from the eaves, and the snow was mushy underfoot. He found Stubs in the barn, repairing Patch's stall railing.

"Look what that piece of buzzard meat did last night," Stubs said as Gavin approached him. "I swear I'd like t'take a two by four and put it right between her eyes."

"I've thought of it myself a time or two."

Stubs drove a nail through the board. "Got us

a bit of a thaw today. Stage oughta make it up from Boise after all.''

"You expecting something?"

"Not me." Stubs straightened. "Just be glad to know Miss Harris isn't stayin' in town alone anymore."

Gavin stiffened. "What are you talking about? Isn't she at Patrick's?"

"Nope. Had me take her to town to try to catch the stage, but she had to wait a few days." He sent a hard glare toward Gavin. "Seems she broke off her engagement with Mr. O'Donnell the day I took her callin' on him. Day before she left here."

"Broke off? But I thought . . ."

"Seems to me you ain't done enough of the right kind of thinkin', Gav. My guess is you sent that girl away when what everybody wanted most was for her to stay for good. You included." He scratched his head. "You most of all."

"Why didn't you tell me where you'd taken her?"

"I shouldn't've had to."

Please, Gavin. You must let me explain.

What had he done? She'd been going to tell him about Patrick, but he wouldn't let her. Oh, God. She'd looked at him with love in her eyes, and he'd been too blind, too stupid to see it for what it was. He'd been so sure she would prove him right about women, he hadn't noticed she'd been teaching him all along how wrong he was.

He spun toward his saddle, perched on a saddle tree near the barn door. In several quick strides, he'd picked it up, along with the blanket and bridle, and was walking toward Scamp's stall. Wordlessly, he entered and began saddling the black gelding.

"Goin' somewhere?" Stubs asked.

"Where's she staying?"

"The Gumbel."

Gavin led the gelding out of the stall and headed toward the door.

"Gav?"

"Yeah?" He opened the door, then swung up onto the saddle.

"You bring her back. She belongs here."

"I mean to do my best, Stubs."

Bundled beneath fur-lined lap robes, Rachel watched as the snowy landscape slipped away. Patrick had tried to convince her to stay at Killarney Hall just one more night, but she'd insisted that either they left at once or he took her back to Challis where she could meet the stage. Finally, he'd given in and they had departed.

Rachel was going home to Boise, but her heart had yet to leave the Lucky Strike.

Chapter Thirty

Despite his promise to Stubs, Gavin returned home without Rachel. In Challis, he'd found that Patrick had taken her to Killarney Hall. He rode quickly to the O'Donnell place, only to learn that Patrick and Rachel had left for Boise that morning.

"He's only seeing her home, Mr. Blake," Pearl had told him. "Rachel hasn't changed her mind about marrying him, although Patrick did his best to make her see the light."

As night fell over the Lucky Strike, Gavin sat staring into the fire. He would leave the next morning. He would go after her, and somehow he would convince her to return with him. He wasn't sure how he was going to do it, but he *was* going to do it.

Sabrina wandered out of her bedroom

around midnight, complaining of a sore throat. When he touched her forehead, he found her burning with fever. Petula too sickened during the night. Stubs left for the doctor before dawn.

"Influenza," Dr. Forester said in a low voice as he turned toward Gavin two hours later. "Both of them. I'd heard there was an outbreak up in the camps, but I was hoping we wouldn't see it here."

"Is it serious?"

"Influenza's always serious, Mr. Blake." The doctor led the way out of the children's bedroom. "We'll have to do what we can to break the fever. Get lots of fluids into them. They're both strong girls. With God's grace, we'll see them through this."

Dr. Forester's meaning was clear. They could die. Both of them. *Rachel, I need you.*

But Rachel wasn't there. She didn't know the children were sick. He would have to get through this without her. But so help him, when this was over, he was going after her. He was going to make sure they went through the rest of their lives together.

Patrick didn't like the look of her. Rachel seemed to grow more and more pale with each passing day. She slept much of the time. When not asleep, she stared blankly into space, the expression on her beautiful face heartbreaking to behold.

He'd traded his sleigh for a sturdy carriage once they left the snowy terrain behind, and he'd pushed the team of horses to the limits of their endurance, covering as much ground as possible between sunrise and sunset every day. But it still wasn't fast enough to suit him. He was anxious to get her home to her sister.

Patrick stopped the team on the crest of the ridge above the river valley. Boise City, their destination, sprawled between the snow-capped mountains and the tree-lined river. He turned in his seat and laid his hand on Rachel's shoulder.

"Rachel? Wake up, my lovely. 'Tis home you are."

Her eyes opened. "Home?" She straightened and looked down at the capital city. "I'm home," she whispered. But her expression seemed to grow even more sad as she gazed into the valley. "Home . . ."

"You'll have to guide me to your sister's."

Rachel pointed to the west of town. "That way."

Patrick jiggled the reins and the team started forward. "I've not been to Boise in some time. 'Tis grown and that's the truth. Seems like a fine place."

Rachel nodded.

"I look forward to meeting Judge Branigan. He's a fine and honest man, so I've heard. 'Tis not many that can be said of. And I'm eager to meet your sister too. If she's anything like you, she must be a lovely woman."

Again she nodded.

He wondered if she heard what he was saying or if he was just talking to hear himself think.

* * *

Maggie slowed the buggy as it swung into the drive leading to the house. A strange carriage was standing near the hitching post. She wondered who might be calling so late in the afternoon.

"Who's here, Mama?" Sheridan asked.

"I don't know." She felt an odd sense of apprehension. She stopped the horse and climbed out of the buggy. Sheridan hopped down from the other side and raced up the porch steps ahead of her.

"Sarah?" Maggie called as she opened the front door. The housekeeper was nowhere in sight.

"Who are you?" Sheridan demanded in the forthright manner of an almost-five-year-old as he stood in the archway leading to the parlor.

Her gaze was drawn instantly in that direction. The stranger rose from the sofa, his hat in his hands. The expression on his face brought another surge of foreboding.

"Mrs. Branigan?" he asked.

"Yes?"

"I'm Patrick O'Donnell."

She wasn't sure if she felt relief or not. She'd received Rachel's letter, telling of her engagement to the Irishman, but she'd been troubled by the tone of the missive. It hadn't read like a young woman in love.

"Sheridan," she said softly, her hand on the boy's shoulder, "why don't you go to the kitchen and see what Cook is fixing for supper?"

"But I want to—"

"Do as I say, Sheridan. I think she was baking cookies when we left."

"With icing?" The boy hurried off toward the back of the house, shucking off his coat as he went.

Maggie turned back toward her guest. "I'm pleased to meet you, Mr. O'Donnell. Rachel didn't tell me you'd be coming to Boise when she wrote to me. I'm pleased to have a chance to get to know you. Won't you have a seat? Can I get you something warm to drink?"

He glanced toward the stairway leading to the second floor. "I've brought Rachel back to Boise, Mrs. Branigan."

Maggie's face broke into a smile. "Rachel? She's here?" She turned in the direction of his gaze, hoping to see her sister coming down the stairs.

"Mrs. Branigan . . ." His voice had an ominous tone, drawing her eyes back to him. "She's not well."

"Where is she now?"

"I believe your housekeeper was seeing her to bed."

Maggie whirled away and raced up the stairs. She was met by Sarah outside Rachel's bedroom.

Sarah put her finger against her lips. "She's asleep, ma'am. I've sent for the doctor."

"The doctor? Sarah, what's wrong?"

The housekeeper shook her head slowly. "I'm not sure, Mrs. Branigan. She just seemed to collapse the minute she come through the door.

Perhaps the gentleman downstairs can tell you more.''

Maggie turned the knob and opened the door, then moved silently across the bedroom. Rachel's pale yellow hair spilled over the white pillowcase, and her fingers were curled around the edge of the blankets. She looked hardly more than a child to Maggie and frightfully frail.

She sat on the edge of the chair beside the bed. "I never should have let you go up there," she whispered as she stared at her sister's beloved face. "I knew something would go wrong. I just knew it."

"I won't give you false hope, Mrs. Branigan. Your sister is a very sick young woman." Dr. Weick rubbed his fingers across his furrowed forehead.

"What are you saying, doctor?" Maggie whispered. "Are you saying my sister could die?"

"I'm afraid so, ma'am." The doctor opened the door to Rachel's bedroom. "I'll be back to check on her in the morning. Be sure you keep the children away from this room. Influenza is highly contagious, and it's especially dangerous for the little ones."

Maggie turned around to stand at the foot of Rachel's bed. She couldn't believe that her sister's life could be in danger. She was too young. She had so much before her. Love. Marriage. Children.

Rachel moaned and turned her head on her pillow from side to side. "Please . . . Let me explain . . ."

Maggie moved around to the side of the bed. She leaned forward, taking hold of Rachel's hand. "Kitten, it's Maggie. You're home. Everything's going to be all right now."

"Gavin . . ." Rachel murmured. "Please, Gavin . . ."

Maggie straightened, a frown etching two vertical lines between her eyebrows. "Get well, Rachel," she whispered. "Then you can tell me about Gavin."

The door eased open, and Sarah's head poked through the opening. "Mr. Branigan is home, ma'am. He's in the parlor now with Mr. O'Donnell."

"Mr. O'Donnell? Oh, my! I completely forgot he was here."

The door finished opening to allow the housekeeper entry. "I'll sit with Rachel while you go down, ma'am. It'll take the two of us to see her through this. I already told Mr. Branigan that he's not to come in this room until the danger's passed."

"Thank you, Sarah. What would I ever do without you?"

"That's something you'll not have to know, God willing." Sarah's smile was subdued. "Now go on down to your husband. He's mighty worried."

Maggie glanced at Rachel, then left the bedroom. She could hear the men's muted voices as she walked toward the stairs, but she was stopped by the opening of Colleen's door.

"Mother? Will Aunt Rachel be all right? Can I see her?"

"No, darling, I'm afraid you can't see her. She has influenza. It's very serious, and any of us could take ill from it. You'll have to help keep everyone away from her room until she's well again."

Tara Maureen appeared at her older sister's side. "I heard Sarah telling Cook that Aunt Rachel could die."

She would have to ask Sarah to be more careful about what she said, Maggie thought as she looked into her middle child's wide green eyes. "We'll ask God in our prayers to spare her." She smoothed Tara Maureen's auburn hair back from her face, thinking how like Tucker's mother she looked. The girl had always been especially close to her Aunt Rachel. "We mustn't worry. We must keep our hopes up."

"Will you tell her we love her?" twelve-year-old Colleen asked.

"Of course, dear." She kissed her daughters on their cheeks. "Now I must go downstairs and see your father. I'm sure he's worried, too, and I haven't had a chance to speak with him yet."

She felt the tension mounting as she walked toward the stairs. It was just becoming real to her what the doctor had said. Not only could Rachel die, but the children were in danger too. How could this happen so suddenly? How could life be so easy and carefree one moment and so threatened with calamity the next?

As always in a time of crisis, Maggie hurried toward the shelter of Tucker's arms. She knew that within his embrace she would find the strength to face whatever lay ahead of them. It had always been so.

Chapter Thirty-One

It was hot. So hot. And her throat burned. It hurt whenever she swallowed. And the coughing. Sometimes, she thought she wouldn't be able to draw in another gasp of air for the coughing. There was a heavy weight on her chest, crushing the life from her.

Why didn't Gavin come? She'd called and called for him, and still he didn't come. Why was he leaving her alone with these strangers?

Gavin, let me explain.

But he wouldn't. He hated her. He didn't care if she lived or died.

I love you, Gavin.

Even she didn't care if she lived or died.

"Here. Drink this, Rachel."

She felt the fingers slip behind her head,

easing her up from the pillow even as a glass was pressed against her lips. The tea was warm and felt good as it glided down her sore throat.

She opened her eyes to see the kindly woman who was so tenderly administering to her. It took a moment for her eyes to focus.

"Maggie?" The word came out a hoarse croak.

"Yes, Kitten. It's me."

"Why are you here? Where's Gavin?"

"You're home, Rachel. Mr. O'Donnell brought you. Don't you remember?"

Her memory was fuzzy. It was difficult to recall anything. "Patrick's here?" She closed her eyes.

"He's in town at the Overland. He didn't want to leave until he knew you would recover. He's a nice man."

Rachel didn't reply. The cobwebs were beginning to clear, allowing the memories to return with sharp clarity. The night in Gavin's bed. His scorching rejection of her. The nights in the Gumbel Hotel while waiting for the stage. The ride to Killarney Hall in Patrick's sleigh. Her insistence on returning to Boise, and Patrick's insistence on bringing her.

But mostly she remembered Gavin—the way he'd looked, the way he'd sounded when he said he wanted her off the Lucky Strike. She'd given him her heart, her body, her soul, and he had despised her gift of love.

She groaned and turned her head toward the wall. Why hadn't she died? She should have died. This hurt too much. She couldn't bear it. She couldn't.

"You rest now, Kitten," Maggie said softly as her fingers brushed Rachel's forehead. "We'll talk more later."

Rachel nodded. She wanted Maggie to leave before the hot tears fell from beneath closed eyelids. She couldn't talk about it. Not to anyone. It was her private shame, her personal heartache. She couldn't share this, not even with Maggie.

"I'll be goin' back to the ranch tomorrow, now that I know the lass is out of danger."

"I'm afraid she isn't up to company as yet, Mr. O'Donnell. Don't you want to wait until she can see you? I know she'll want to thank you for everything you did."

"'Tis not me she wants to see," he replied in a solemn tone. "But I would like a few words with you, Mrs. Branigan, before I go."

Maggie motioned the big man into the parlor. "Of course, Mr. O'Donnell. You're always welcome."

Patrick twirled his hat in his hands as he sat across from her. He reminded her a little of Tucker's cousin, Keegan, the most Irish of the Branigan clan. Keegan had always had a big heart and usually a smile to match. She imagined that Patrick did too—most of the time.

"I told you Rachel had called off our engagement before I brought her back to Boise. I think you must know I love the lass and would do my best to make her happy. But I never could do it. She's lost her heart elsewhere."

"Gavin Blake," Maggie murmured.

"So she's told you."

"No. I—I just guessed."

"Mrs. Branigan—"

"Why don't you call me Maggie?"

He nodded and gave her an appreciative smile. "Maggie, I'm not sure what happened between Rachel and Gavin that sent her back here. Not sure I'd want to know. But 'tis easy to see the wrong of her bein' here when she belongs up north. And 'tis somethin' that shouldn't be. Gavin loves her and she loves him."

Maggie sat up a little straighter. "Are you sure of that?"

"As sure as I've ever been of anything. I knew all along that Rachel didn't love me, but I was hopin' she would with time. Then I saw the way it was between them, and I knew it wouldn't happen."

Maggie recalled Gavin Blake from their one and only meeting as tall and darkly handsome. Tucker had taken his measure and not found him wanting. Maggie had noted his gentleness with his wife.

His wife . . . That was the thing that troubled Maggie the most. Mrs. Blake had passed away only two months before. Did Gavin truly love Rachel or had he only turned to her in his grief? And just how *much* had he turned to her?

She thought of the way Rachel had called for

Gavin in her fevered sleep. It was more than influenza that had made her sister ill. It was a problem with her heart.

Patrick rose abruptly from the sofa, placing his hat over his bright shock of red hair. "I'll be on my way." He headed out of the room.

Maggie followed after him. When he turned at the door, she offered him her hand. "Thanks again for all you did. You're always welcome in our home, Mr. O'Donnell."

"Patrick. The name is Patrick." He grinned.

"Patrick," she repeated, mirroring his smile.

"Maggie . . ." His hand tightened around hers. "About Rachel and Gavin . . . You may think I'm filled with blarney, but I think they were fated to be together. Don't be hard on her for . . ." He seemed to search for the right words, then shrugged. "Tell the lass I'll be lookin' forward to seein' her again."

Maggie watched as he walked down the steps and climbed into his carriage. He waved as he picked up the reins, and she returned the motion before closing the door against the January chill.

She turned and gazed up the stairs. She wished she could be as sure as Patrick O'Donnell about what the fates had ordained.

As soon as Sabrina and Petula were out of danger, Gavin's thoughts returned to Rachel. He knew he had to go after her. He knew he had to tell her how wrong he'd been and how much he needed her. He might not be able to win her forgiveness, but he had to try.

He wasn't sure if he cared much for these feelings. It had started with Dru, teaching him to trust just a little bit. Then it had been the two girls, wriggling their way into his affections with laughter and smiles and tears. And finally, there was Rachel, penetrating what was left of his resolve to remain detached.

It had been a whole lot easier when he'd kept his feelings in check. He hadn't had anything at risk. People could come and go from his life without it bothering him one way or another. But no more. Rachel, the children—they were his life.

Such were Gavin's thoughts when the loud pounding sounded on the door. He left the bedroom doorway, where he'd been standing and watching the children sleep. He strode quickly toward the door, hoping to stop the racket before it woke the girls.

Almost immediately after he pulled open the door, Patrick's meaty fist grabbed him by the collar and jerked him outside.

"Sure but I think I should knock some sense into that fool head of yours, Gavin Blake! I thought you a better man than this. You think I can't guess what it is you've done? D'you think I wouldn't like to break your neck in two? Shame on you, man. If you weren't a friend o' mine—"

Gavin pried Patrick's fingers free from his shirt collar. "Did she come back with you, Patrick?"

"Come back with me?" the Irishman exclaimed. "Faith, she was lyin' at death's own door when I got her to Boise. I have only her sister's word that she's gettin' well again."

Gavin's stomach dropped, and it was his turn to grab the other man's shirt. "What are you talking about?"

"The doctor called it the influenza. But if you'd've bothered to come after her like you should have, you'd have known it for yourself."

Gavin released his hold on Patrick's shirt and turned toward the house. "Brina and Pet have been sick with it, too. We nearly lost Pet last week. I couldn't leave them."

"Sorry, mate, I didn't know."

"Come inside. I've got coffee on the stove."

Patrick followed him into the house, closing the door behind him. "The wee lass—is she—"

"Dr. Forester says she's going to be fine. Sabrina too. I've been waiting for him to say they're completely out of danger so I can leave." Gavin turned from the stove, coffeepot in hand. "I have some business in Boise City to see to."

"You have at that," Patrick agreed. He sat down at the table and accepted the cup of coffee from Gavin's hand. "Why not let them come stay at Killarney. It would bring Pearl a joy to have them there. And me too."

Gavin couldn't help frowning as he looked across the table.

"So, you're wonderin' why I would do such a thing for the worthless likes of you. 'Tis not because you're my friend, though you are. If I thought keepin' you away would win her for myself, I would do it. But it wouldn't. She would have you or no one."

"She told you that?" Gavin leaned forward,

forearms resting on the table.

"Faith and begorra! Do you think she would tell me such a thing? I've got eyes, man. I could see it for myself."

A faint glimmer of hope began to shine in Gavin's heart. "Do you think there's a chance she'll forgive me?"

"Not if she's got any sense in that pretty head o' hers."

Gavin feared Patrick was right.

Patrick grunted in disgust. "Would you give up with such little discouragement? You'll have to go through more than that, I fear. When she's over the hurt, there's going to be fury to replace it."

Gavin nodded. He might not know much about women, but he knew Patrick was right about that. And he deserved her anger. He deserved everything he could imagine she might think about him or say to him. But if there was any hope she might still love him after what he did, he would gladly face the furnaces of hell to win her back.

Chapter Thirty-Two

The large parlor windows gave Rachel a clear view of the tall cottonwoods and poplars that lined the river. Sunlight streamed through the bare winter branches, revealing deserted bird nests and the tree house Tucker and Kevin had built one long-ago summer. Rachel smiled as she remembered the way father and son had scrambled up the boards they had pounded into the tree at intervals, and the way Maggie had stood down below, telling them she would tan the hide of the first one who fell and broke something.

She twisted on the sofa and lowered her legs to the floor, allowing her gaze to move slowly about the room. It felt good to be downstairs again, good to be surrounded by so many familiar things. She'd been wrong to ever want to leave. She'd been wrong to think she should go out and make her own future. She belonged here. Not with . . .

She cut that thought short, as she always did. She refused to think of him. Refused to let him enter her mind for even a second. He'd been a mistake and nothing more. Nothing more.

What had ever made her think she could love such a man? He'd been rude to her from the very start. It meant nothing to her that he'd been tender with Dru, that he was so wonderful with the children. She didn't even remember those hours with him in the barn, while he held her and shared his warmth as the blizzard raged outside. She couldn't recall that afternoon up on the ridge when they ran and played with the children, laughter ringing through the trees. She'd already forgotten the blue-black of his hair, the steel-gray of his eyes, the broadness of his chest and the strength of his arms. She had no memory of the night she'd spent in his bed, feeling his hands run over her skin, tasting his lips upon hers, reveling in the power of his body as he swept her away on tides of passion.

No. She wouldn't allow his name to even cross her mind. She'd forgotten the man existed.

Rachel returned her gaze to the window. There wasn't a trace of snow on the ground. Only if she looked to the top of the mountains could she see any of the white stuff. It seemed strange when she'd been surrounded by so much of it up at . . .

Luckily, a diversion arrived at that moment, stopping that train of thought. A carriage came rolling down the drive and stopped directly in front of the window.

"Fiona!" She rose from the sofa and walked to the window. She raised a hand to wave at her friend even as the auburn-haired beauty stepped down from the vehicle. Fiona returned the wave, then reached back into the carriage, straightening a moment later with what appeared to be a bundle of blankets in her arms.

Sarah appeared in the parlor doorway. "What's the ruckus?" Then, with knuckles resting on her ample hips and her mouth pursed, she added, "And what are you doing off that couch? You sit down before I have to send you back to your room. You know what the doctor said about getting your rest so you wouldn't have a relapse."

"It's Fiona. She's come calling, and she's got the baby with her. Open the door, Sarah, and let them in."

Moments later, she was embracing Fiona while Sarah stood beside them, unwrapping the infant.

"I wanted to come sooner," Fiona said as they released each other, "but Dr. Weick forbade it."

"Of course you couldn't come. You had little Myrna to think of. Oh, let me see her."

Sarah stayed stubbornly in place. "Not until you sit down, miss."

Rachel sighed and rolled her eyes in Fiona's direction, but she did as she was told. Fiona unbuttoned her coat while Sarah handed the smiling child to Rachel.

"Oh, Fiona, she's beautiful. She's got your hair and eyes, too."

"She wouldn't dare not have them," Fiona replied with a laugh. "Her father demanded that any girls we had should have my coloring."

"How is James?"

"He's as wonderful as always."

Rachel smiled across at her friend. "And he makes you happy. I can tell just by looking at you."

Fiona fairly beamed in response.

Rachel didn't need her friend's glowing confirmation. They had known each other too long not to be able to sense each other's moods.

Perhaps that was why Fiona knew hers so quickly. The young mother's green eyes narrowed as she perused Rachel. "What happened to bring you back so soon?"

She shrugged. "I was homesick. I missed Maggie and Tucker and the children. And you and James, too." She kissed the baby's forehead. "And look what I missed while I was away. Myrna is half-grown already."

"Hardly," Fiona replied. "But she's not the little baby she was when you left. She'll be six months old tomorrow."

"Six months already?"

Fiona was silent for a while before saying gently, "Rachel . . . you can tell me whatever it is. I'll understand."

Rachel swallowed the lump in her throat. "How could you, Fiona? Even I don't understand." She drew a deep breath. "Things just didn't work out the way I thought they would. That's all."

It was a long, cold journey from the central mountain country to the capital of the territory. It gave Gavin many hours to relive in his mind the events of past few months. His mood became more and more grim. There were times he was tempted to turn around and go back to the Lucky Strike. Surely nothing he could say or do would ever convince Rachel Harris to forgive him, let alone to agree to marry and spend her life with him. He hadn't done one single solitary thing to deserve her love.

But he didn't turn back. He couldn't.

Maggie had waited long enough for Rachel to come to her. It was time she took matters into her own hands.

"If she's too stubborn to admit she loves him," Tucker had told Maggie during the night, "she comes by it naturally. Seems to me her sister was much the same way."

Maggie couldn't argue with him. She'd been only seventeen when she fell in love with Tucker —and he with her—and she'd nearly thrown their love away because of her stubborn pride. Seventeen years later, she was as much in love with her husband as ever, and she thanked the good Lord every day for bringing her to her senses in time. She couldn't imagine what life would have been like without Tucker and the children. She didn't want to imagine it.

Maggie knocked on Rachel's bedroom door,

PROMISE ME SPRING

then opened it. "Is it too late for a visitor?"

Rachel put down the book she was reading. "Of course not."

"We've had hardly a moment to ourselves since you've been feeling better, between Tucker and the children and all your friends calling to see how you're doing."

"It is rather nice to have a moment of quiet."

Maggie sat down on the chair beside Rachel's bed and took hold of her sister's hand. "You don't know how relieved I am to see you looking strong again."

"I'm just glad no one else got sick." Rachel shook her head slowly. "I never would have forgiven myself if I'd given it to the children."

Maggie squeezed the fingers within hers and leaned forward, her voice lowering. "I think it's time you told me what happened."

"You sound like Fiona." Rachel sighed as she looked away.

"But I'm *not* Fiona. I'm Maggie."

Rachel continued to avoid meeting her gaze.

"All right. Let me tell you what I *do* know." Maggie released Rachel's hand as she sat back in the chair, folding her arms in front of her. "You are in love with Mr. Blake. No, don't try to deny it. I already know it's true. What's more, I suspect that you've spent at least one night in Mr. Blake's bed."

Color flamed in Rachel's cheeks.

"I thought as much." Maggie wore her most determined mothering glare. "Now talk to me."

Such a melancholy look covered Rachel's face that it made Maggie want to cry. At the very

345

least, she wanted to hold and comfort her younger sister. But she kept her resolve to be firm and waited for Rachel to tell her what had happened in the months she'd been away.

"I didn't mean to fall in love with him. I can't think why it happened. He wasn't even very nice to me at first. He thought I was just some silly rich girl who wouldn't be able to handle the work. But I proved him wrong." A sad smile lifted the corners of her mouth, then disappeared as quickly as it had come. "I tried to leave when I realized what I was feeling. I knew it was wrong. He was Dru's husband, and she was my friend. But Dru wouldn't let me go. She held me to my promise to stay until they took the cows back to the basin in the spring."

Rachel's blue eyes took on a faraway look. "Maggie, you should see the basin. The mountains take your breath away. And it's so green with pine trees, and the aspen and birch trees and the wild flowers are all so beautiful. You can't imagine it. You just can't."

Rachel's hands, folded atop the quilt, were clenched so tightly her knuckles turned white. She lifted her gaze to meet Maggie's, and her eyes were glimmering with unshed tears.

"Oh, Maggie," she whispered. "I should have come home then. I knew I loved him, and I knew it was wrong. I should have come home."

Maggie's resolve nearly faltered. She wanted so badly to scoot onto the bed beside Rachel and offer comfort.

"He kissed me the night before Dru died. He came to tell me he was sorry for being short-tempered with me, and then I was suddenly in his arms. It was as much my fault as his." She sighed. "I think we both felt that if we hadn't done it, Dru might have lived. Of course, I know that wasn't true. Dru hadn't been well for so long. But I guess what you feel doesn't always make sense. It's just what you feel." She choked back a sob. "But, oh Maggie, I loved him so very much."

Rachel turned away from her older sister and slipped out of bed. On bare feet, she padded across to the window. She swept back the curtains with one hand to look outside.

"And you *don't* love him any longer?" Maggie gently prodded.

She didn't turn away from the window. "I don't know. No. No, I don't think I do anymore. I couldn't."

"If you loved Gavin so much, why did you agree to marry Mr. O'Donnell?" Maggie thought she already knew the answer, but she wanted to hear it from Rachel. She wanted to make sure she understood everything before she tried to help her sister.

"Because I thought he would protect me from doing anything else wrong. I felt so guilty for loving Gavin. And I felt guilty because I knew he wasn't married any longer. He was a widower. There wasn't anything wrong with my loving a widower, but it was almost like being glad Dru had died." Her voice fell to a whisper. "But I wasn't glad. God knows, I wasn't glad. I loved her, too."

Rachel let the curtain fall back into place.

"Patrick was so good to me after the funeral. Gavin pulled away from everyone, and I was left alone to care for the children. Patrick was just always there. He was good and kind and I knew he loved me and so I said yes when he proposed. And that wasn't fair to him either. I made such a mess of everything."

Maggie patted the quilt. "Get back in bed, Rachel, before you take cold." She wondered if she'd made a mistake to ask about Gavin so soon.

Rachel nodded absently but didn't move from the window. "I thought Gavin loved me, at least a little, even though he couldn't say it. When Stubs told me what had happened back in Ohio, I understood better why he acted the way he did. I realized then that I couldn't marry Patrick, no matter what happened with Gavin. And Patrick understood. I guess he knew I was in love with Gavin all along."

Finally, Rachel drifted back to the bed. She crawled beneath the covers and pulled them up close beneath her chin. Her face looked pale, and the shadows of illness beneath her eyes seemed more pronounced.

"It was my fault," she continued in a whisper. "I waited for him and when he kissed me and asked me . . . I wanted him, Maggie. I didn't try to stop him. I loved him, and I thought . . . I thought he must love me."

A lengthy silence stretched between them. Maggie watched as a series of emotions passed across Rachel's face, heartbreaking emotions, nothing held back to hide the pain.

"He told me to get out the next morning. He said he wanted me off the Lucky Strike. He wouldn't even let me say good-bye to the children."

This time, Maggie followed the urge to hold and comfort Rachel. She pressed her sister's face against her shoulder and let her cry out the hurt. In the meantime, she indulged herself in her own orgy of loathing.

How could that man have done this to her sister? How could he have been so cruel? She would take great pleasure in seeing him whipped within an inch of his life. Boiling in oil would be too good for him. She would gladly pluck the chickens to be used to tar and feather the no-good blackguard. He was undoubtedly the most despicable man she would ever have the misfortune to meet. She should have known it when she first laid eyes on him. She never should have allowed Rachel to go away with him. Thank heaven she wouldn't ever have to see him again.

But, of course, Maggie knew that he couldn't be as bad as all that, especially since Rachel still cared more than she would admit. Her sister could deny it all she wished, but she was definitely still in love with Gavin Blake. And Rachel wasn't some silly-headed nitwit who wore her emotions on her sleeve or whose head was turned by any handsome man to come down the pike. Rachel was not the sort of girl to fall in love without the man being worthy in some way. There was more than one side to this story, and Maggie knew it wouldn't be complete until she'd heard Gavin's side too.

As Maggie smoothed the silky blond hair back from Rachel's face, she had the feeling that she would have her chance to find out the other side of the story soon enough. Perhaps it was only wishful thinking, but something told her that she would be seeing Gavin Blake before long.

She prayed she was right.

Chapter Thirty-Three

It wasn't difficult to find out where the Branigan ranch was located. Everyone in Boise seemed to know the judge and his family and were more than happy to give him directions. Once on his way, it hadn't taken him long to get there.

Gavin pulled Scamp to a halt at the end of the winding drive that led to the Branigan home. It was a sprawling gray clapboard house, built for a large family, two stories tall with a veranda wrapped around three sides. Just the kind of place Gavin could imagine Rachel growing up. The log house at the Lucky Strike paled in comparison. He felt the familiar surge of doubt.

He nudged the black gelding with his heels, and they moved forward. He wasn't about to turn back now.

He dismounted near the front door and twirled the reins around the hitching post before taking the steps two at a time. He paused on the porch, removing his hat and smoothing back his hair. He'd taken the time to clean up in town, paying for a bath and a shave, but he feared that no matter what he did he wasn't going to be welcome.

Taking a deep breath, he knocked at the door and waited. There was a slight commotion from the other side of the door before it was yanked open. Two boys, approximately the same ages as Sabrina and Petula, looked up at him.

"Hello. I'm here to see Rachel Harris. Is she in?"

"Who're you?" the youngest asked.

Before he could reply, he heard another voice, this one feminine. "Colin. Sheridan. Ask whoever is there to come in. It's too cold to make them stand outside."

The door swung wide and he caught a glimpse of emerald skirts on the stairway. A moment later, the woman wearing those skirts materialized beside the door. He knew the moment she recognized him. The smile vanished from her mouth and her gray eyes narrowed.

"Mr. Blake."

He nodded. "Mrs. Branigan. I've come to see Rachel."

She stepped back into the foyer. "Come in." She motioned toward the parlor. "Have a seat. I'll have Cook prepare some tea."

"Don't go to any bother for me," Gavin answered, feeling uncomfortable.

He hadn't given any thought to facing her family. That had been stupid of him, but he'd been on his own for so many years, he didn't think about families and sisters and brothers. He should have known that she would come back to Boise and tell Maggie everything that had happened.

Everything? Had Rachel told her sister *everything*?

From the look he'd seen in Maggie's eyes, he guessed Rachel hadn't held anything back.

"Colin," Maggie said, still standing in the entry hall, "go up to Aunt Rachel's room and tell her she has a visitor. Ask her to come down. Sheridan, go with your brother." She turned and entered the parlor.

Maggie moved with a kind of natural grace and had an air of confidence about her. She was beautiful, like her sister, although their coloring was different. It was easy, looking at her, to imagine what Rachel would look like in another ten or fifteen years.

Of course, if Rachel married him, she wouldn't have the life of ease her older sister had. She wouldn't be free to sit in an elegant house and let the cook prepare supper.

Perhaps it wasn't fair to ask her to give up so much, even if she did love him. Perhaps Dru had been wrong about that being the most important thing. Perhaps . . .

"Please be seated, Mr. Blake. We may have a few moments to wait. Rachel hasn't been down today and isn't dressed." She sat on a rose-colored sofa across from him.

Not dressed?

He glanced toward the stairs. It was mid-afternoon. Was Patrick wrong about Rachel getting well? Could she have had a relapse?

"Rachel has been ill since she returned home," Maggie answered, as if he'd asked the question aloud.

"Patrick told me, but he thought she was over the worst. Is she—is she going to be all right?"

"You needn't worry, Mr. Blake. She's doing much better. Now. Why don't you tell me what's brought you to Boise?"

Gavin knew from the sound of her voice that Rachel was in no danger and his concern vanished. He met the woman's direct gaze with one of his own. "I wanted to see Rachel."

"All that way in the middle of winter for a visit?" The question was asked in an innocent voice, but he wasn't fooled.

"I want her to come back to the ranch with me. We need her."

For the first time, Maggie flashed a genuine smile. As she rose from the sofa, she said, "I doubt it will be easy to convince her to return with you, Mr. Blake."

"I'll do whatever it takes." He stood.

"You'll have to." She stepped away from him. "Excuse me while I see about the tea."

Rachel was tempted to tell Colin to send down her regrets. Ever since her talk with Maggie the previous night, she'd been overwhelmed with lethargy. She didn't want to see

354

or talk with anyone. She just wanted to be left alone.

Still, she supposed it wouldn't hurt her to at least make an appearance, since someone had been kind enough to come out to see her. Perhaps it was Fiona and Myrna. She would love to see the baby again.

She dressed in a simple day dress of yellow linen and tied back her hair at the nape with a ribbon. She pinched her cheeks, hoping to give them a little color. Then she left her room and descended the stairs.

As she stepped beneath the archway of the parlor, she came to an abrupt halt. She felt as if the wind had been knocked from her.

There he stood, so tall, so gloriously handsome, his black hair unruly as usual.

He needed a haircut weeks ago.

He was watching her with those intense gray eyes of his.

He looks tired.

"Hello, Rachel."

"Gavin." She hated the breathless sound of her voice. She didn't want him to know what seeing him again was doing to her. She didn't even want to acknowledge it to herself. "Where's Maggie?"

He took a step toward her. "She went to see about some tea."

"What are you doing in Boise?"

"I came to see you. We need to talk."

The anger came, sudden and unexpected, a fury so great she felt on fire with it. "I don't think we have anything to talk about, Mr. Blake."

"We do, Rachel. I made a mistake. If you'd just give me a chance to explain."

She gave a sharp laugh. "Explain what?" She stepped forward, her chin thrust high in the air as she glared up at him. "Nothing you could say would make any difference to me."

He winced as she flung his own words back at him.

The strength born of anger disappeared as quickly as it had come, and Rachel sank into the closest chair. "We haven't anything to talk about. Go back to the Lucky Strike."

Gavin moved toward her. He stopped only a foot away, towering over her, but she refused to look up. She was too tired to look up. She didn't want to fight with him. She just wanted him to go away.

He knelt down on one knee, bringing himself to her eye level. She inhaled, surprised by his action. Or perhaps it was the expression on his face. Almost afraid. Somehow vulnerable. Nothing like the Gavin she'd grown used to seeing.

"I was wrong, Rachel. I hurt you because I wanted you to leave. I—I didn't understand. I'm sorry."

"You're sorry," she repeated softly, feeling the hurt of his rejection all over again.

"The girls miss you. They need you." He paused. "*I* need you."

She shook her head, scarcely hearing him.

"I would have come sooner, but Pet and Brina were sick. They had the influenza, like you.

There's been an outbreak of it up in the mining camps."

Rachel covered her mouth as she gasped. "Oh no! Are they—"

"They're well now, but they want you to come back with me."

It wasn't fair of him. He was using her concern for the children against her. "It's better if they don't see me again," she replied bitterly. "They would only have to see me leave again later."

His voice deepened, hardened. "All right. What about your promise to Dru? She hired you to take care of her girls until we returned to the basin. You made a promise to her, even as she lay dying." He stood. "And if it's me you're worried about, I promise not to—not to make any more improper advances. You'll be safe while you're there. You don't need to be afraid of me."

"I'm not afraid of you or your *advances*, Mr. Blake." She rose from the sofa. "And you needn't remind me of my promise to Dru. *You're* the one who threw me out, if you'll recall." She spun away and hurried toward the doorway.

"Rachel—"

For some reason, she stopped, turning back to look at him.

"I've gone about this all wrong. I want to make it right with you. You don't understand. It's not easy for me to put it into words."

It was only guilt that had brought him here. Guilt and the need for a woman to watch his children. She wished she could hate him, but

357

she couldn't. She loved him. She loved him as much as she'd ever loved him, but she swore he would never hear those words falling from her lips. She might be a thousand kinds of a fool for loving him, but she wouldn't give him the satisfaction of knowing it.

Once again she turned her back on him. "It doesn't matter, Gavin. We both made a mistake. That's all. All right. I forgive you. Does that make you feel better? Now you can go back to the ranch with a clear conscience and quit bothering me." With shoulders erect and head held high, she walked toward the stairway and the sanctuary of her room.

"I'll be back, Rachel," Gavin called after her. "I promise you, I'll be back.

"Tucker, we've got to do something!"

"What is it exactly you think we *can* do, Maggie? Rachel isn't a child. She's got to make up her own mind."

Maggie stood at the window and stared up at the starry sky. "But she's so in love with him. He's been out here every day for the past week, and she refuses to see or talk to him. Then she cries herself to sleep. She's determined to make him pay for hurting her, and she's only hurting herself. He loves her, too. He loves her very much. I know. I can feel it. I can *see* it."

Tucker slipped his arms around her and pulled her back against his chest. "You should be an expert on knowing when a man is in love," he whispered. "You've lived with one long enough." His lips nuzzled her earlobe.

Maggie closed her eyes, a smile flitting across her mouth. She did know about how wonderful it was to be in love and loved. That's why it was so important to her that Rachel didn't throw it all away out of pride and stubbornness, and she said as much to Tucker.

"Okay. I understand that," he replied. "But that still doesn't tell me what we can do to help. If she won't see him, she won't see him. I think we should just let the two of them work it out."

Maggie's eyes widened and she twisted in his arms. "Tucker, what if she's pregnant?"

"Wait a minute." He stepped back from her, his hands gripping her arms. "You mean to tell me . . ." His face darkened with anger.

She hadn't meant to reveal all of Rachel's secrets. Some things were better kept just between sisters. But when the thought occurred to her, it had just slipped out.

"I'll see him in jail," Tucker muttered.

"No, Tuck, you mustn't." She moved back into his embrace. "Jail would keep them apart. I want them together. They should be married."

And that's when the ideal plan occurred to Maggie Branigan.

Chapter Thirty-Four

"**I** won't take no for an answer, Rachel. You're going with me. We'll have lunch with Tucker. He's expecting us."

"Oh, Maggie. I'm too tired to go into town."

Rachel wasn't about to admit the real reason she wanted to stay home. She was afraid she might run into Gavin. She didn't want to see him. With each passing day, it had become more and more difficult to refuse him when he came to call.

"Well, you're going," Maggie said firmly. "I'll not have you sitting and moping your life away. It's time you got out and socialized. After lunch, we'll stop and see Fiona. Now put on something pretty. I'll meet you downstairs in half an hour."

Rachel could tell from the tone of Maggie's voice that it wouldn't do any good to argue.

When her sister made her mind up, it was nearly impossible to change it.

Besides, she thought as the bedroom door closed behind Maggie, maybe it would do her good to get out. The weather had been unseasonably warm this week, and a buggy ride in the fresh air might be just what she needed to pick up her spirits. Yes, it might be just exactly what the doctor ordered.

"I'm Mr. Blake," Gavin told the clerk. "Judge Branigan sent for me."

"I'll tell him you're here, sir." The young man rose from his desk and disappeared into the adjoining office.

Gavin remained standing as his eyes perused the waiting area. The leather upholstered furniture was large and impressive. Dark wood paneling rose to a high, ornate ceiling. The room smelled faintly of cigar smoke.

He wasn't sure exactly why he'd been summoned here, but he had a few suspicions. There was a strong likelihood that the judge meant to order him to quit pestering Rachel. He had no intention of following such orders and could very well land in jail for his refusal. Of course, there was the remote possibility that Judge Branigan might be willing to help him. Gavin sensed that Maggie understood that he loved her sister. Perhaps the judge believed it too.

"You may go right in, sir," the clerk said as he reappeared. He stepped back, holding the door open for Gavin to pass through.

"Thank you."

The judge's chambers were even more vast and impressive than the outer office. The walls were lined with books from ceiling to floor. Burning wood crackled in a wide-mouthed fireplace, throwing dancing fingers of light across the ornate rug spread before the hearth. A massive oak desk stood before tall windows cloaked in heavy brocade draperies. Judge Tucker Branigan sat in a high-backed chair behind the desk.

"Come in, Mr. Blake. You may close the door, Sedgewick. See that we're not disturbed."

"Yes, sir."

The door closed behind Gavin.

Tucker motioned toward a chair opposite him. "Have a seat, Mr. Blake."

Gavin strode across the room and sat down in the indicated chair. He rested his hat on his knee as he leveled a curious gaze on the judge. He would guess that Tucker wasn't more than five or six years his senior, yet he had a great air of confidence and authority about him. What's more, he commanded a sense of trust. Gavin began to relax.

Tucker drew a cheroot from a redwood box on his desk. He motioned with his hand, offering the same to Gavin, but Gavin declined with a shake of his head. As Tucker ran his fingers over the cheroot, his gaze narrowed, never wavering from Gavin's face. Then he struck a match and lit the thin cigar.

Exhaling a cloud of bluish smoke, Tucker said, "I suppose you know my wife's taken an interest in you, Mr. Blake."

"She's been very kind to me, under the circumstances."

"Maggie loves her sister a great deal and wants to see her happy. She seems to think you could make her happy, given a chance."

"I'd like to think I could."

"My sister-in-law has the same stubborn streak as my Maggie, I'm afraid. Sometimes they don't see what's best for them, even when it's as clear as the nose on your face. Sometimes they have to be forced to see it. Do you understand what I'm saying, Mr. Blake?"

"I suppose so," Gavin answered, although he wasn't sure that he did.

A light rapping on the door interrupted them. The door eased open just enough for the clerk to show his head.

"I'm sorry, sir, but Mrs. Branigan insisted I let you know she was here."

Tucker stood. "Of course, Sedgewick. Show my wife in." He walked around the desk and headed for the door.

"Oh! I'm sorry, Tucker. Mr. Sedgewick didn't tell me you had someone with you. We'll just wait in . . ."

"It's all right, Maggie. Come in."

Gavin rose and turned in time to see Rachel entering the room. She was wearing something dark blue and shimmery and a bonnet with matching blue feathers over ringlets of blond curls. She stopped the moment their eyes met. The color drained from her cheeks.

He tried to speak, but his voice caught in his throat.

Rachel took a step or two backward, as if to retreat, but Tucker caught her arm and drew her into the office.

"I'm glad you're here," the judge said. "My talk with Mr. Blake concerns you. Sit down, Rachel." He guided her to one of the chairs near the fire.

Gavin remained standing, continuing to watch her, only vaguely aware of Maggie sitting in a chair near her sister.

"Sit down, Mr. Blake." Tucker's voice had changed. It had deepened, harshened. As soon as Gavin had retaken his seat, the judge continued, "I don't think there's any point in beating around the bush. It's come to my attention that you took liberties with my sister-in-law while she was living with you and your family up north."

Rachel gasped, but Gavin kept his gaze locked on Tucker's implacable face.

"Rachel is as dear to me as one of my own daughters. She's been with me since she was six years old. It's my duty to protect her from harm and scandal. I'm sure you understand my concern over such behavior. If word of this got out, her reputation would be in shreds. And I may as well be blunt . . ." He turned his eyes on Rachel, directing his next question at her. "Do we know that there won't be a child resulting from this—this indiscretion?"

Gavin twisted in his chair to look at Rachel. Her blue eyes were wide and rounded. Her mouth was parted, as if she wanted to speak but couldn't. The silence stretched without a denial.

"I was afraid of that," Tucker continued, his

gaze swinging back to Gavin. "But even if that isn't the case, I'm afraid we must demand that you do the honest thing by my sister-in-law, Mr. Blake. I believe we can arrange for the wedding to take place without much delay, just in case there is that added . . . complication."

This wasn't what he'd wanted. He didn't want Rachel to be forced into marriage. He wanted her to come willingly. Gavin jumped up. "Judge Branigan—"

"I think, under the circumstances, you should feel free to call me Tucker." He also rose from his chair. He rested his knuckles on the desk and leaned forward. "Let me make this clear to you, Gavin. You have no choice in this. If you refuse to marry Rachel, I will see that you're ruined. A judge's power stretches far, and I will use it if I'm forced to. Maggie and I insist that you do right by Rachel."

Was it something in Tucker's voice or a subtle expression in his eyes? Something caused Tucker's words of just minutes before to echo through Gavin's head.

Sometimes they don't see what's best for them, even when it's as clear as the nose on your face. Sometimes they have to be forced to see it. Do you understand what I'm saying, Mr. Blake?

Yes, he did understand. Now.

Gavin sat down. "All right. I'll marry her."

Rachel stared at her hands in her lap. *Could* she be pregnant with Gavin's child? When was her last monthly flow? Not since before she was ill. Not since before . . .

Gavin's baby. Gavin's son. He would have his father's black hair and gray eyes, of course. And he would be tall and strong like his father too. Wouldn't his sisters adore him! She could just imagine Sabrina and Petula leaning over the cradle, talking and fussing over him.

A baby . . . Good heavens! What was she thinking? It wasn't possible. They'd only shared that one time together. Surely . . .

"All right. I'll marry her."

Her head snapped up as Gavin's voice intruded on her thoughts and she realized what Tucker had been saying. He was forcing Gavin to marry her.

And Gavin was agreeing to it!

Her traitorous heart knew a moment of joy. She would be Gavin's wife. She would live with him and Sabrina and Petula. She would bear his children. She would . . .

She rose from her chair, her chin held high. "Do I have anything to say about this?"

The men turned to look at her.

"What if I don't *wish* to marry Mr. Blake? We don't"—she steeled herself against the warm flush moving up her neck—"we don't know that there's a child."

Maggie spoke for the first time. "Tucker is right, my dear. We can't take a chance. If there is to be a child, it would already be difficult to conceal its—*untimely* arrival, but it might be possible, with you living so far from Boise. Besides, even if you are not expecting, if word of this should ever get out, your chances of marrying well would vanish forever."

Rachel couldn't believe this was happening. Tucker was forcing Gavin to marry her. Maggie was in agreement, concerned that her sister wouldn't be able to find a suitable husband now that she was "ruined." And Gavin had acquiesced under only slightly veiled threats of losing his ranch, perhaps going to jail.

And no one cared a whit about what she felt or wanted.

"I won't do it," she said emphatically, her gaze moving from Maggie to Tucker to Gavin.

"If she won't have me—" Gavin began.

"You're not getting away with this so easily, Mr. Blake," Tucker said. "I warned you."

It all seemed so unreal. The gravity of Tucker's voice shook her to the core. He meant it. He would ruin Gavin. And it was as much her fault as his. Instinctively, she knew she could have stopped him from making love to her. He never would have forced himself on her. He'd given her ample opportunity to stop it from happening. And now he would be the one who was punished.

What would happen to the children if he went to jail or lost his ranch? It would be because of her. She couldn't let that happen to them.

Her eyes met Gavin's.

She couldn't let it happen. No matter how much she tried to tell herself he might deserve it, she couldn't let it happen.

"If there's no other choice," she whispered, "I'll marry him."

She wasn't aware of the pleased smiles exchanged between Tucker and Maggie.

The minister had arrived. The guests were gathered in the parlor. In a few minutes, Rachel would descend the stairs and become his bride.

He wished he'd had some time alone with her, just a moment to tell her that he was a willing participant in this marriage. It had seemed logical in the judge's chambers to make her think he was only doing it to protect himself. It didn't seem so logical any longer.

But there hadn't been a chance to talk with her. He'd spent the same amount of time with Rachel in the ten days since he'd agreed to this marriage as he had in the days between his first visit to the Branigan home and that fateful meeting in Tucker's office. Which amounted to exactly no time with her at all.

He glanced toward the stairs, wondering how much longer it would be before Rachel appeared on the second floor landing.

She should know how he felt. She should know that he wanted her for his wife.

Maybe you love her.

Love her? No. He'd decided long ago never to allow that emotion to surface for a woman. He wanted her. She was the most desirable creature he'd ever seen. He admired her. She was intelligent and had grit and stamina and wasn't afraid to face life head-on. He liked her. She could make him laugh with her delightful sense of humor, and she was warm and caring with the children.

But love? The word wasn't even part of Gavin Blake's vocabulary.

Except, of course, he loved the children. There was no avoiding loving those two. But that wasn't the same thing.

Maybe he'd loved Dru, but that had been different too. She'd been his friend. She'd been in need. There hadn't been any risk in loving Dru.

Loving Rachel would be a terrible risk, especially if she didn't love him in return. She had loved him once. He'd seen it in her eyes, if only he hadn't been too blind to recognize it. But what if she could never love him again? What if she was trapped into this marriage and grew to hate him for what he'd done?

No, he couldn't love her. But he could let her know he wanted her to be his wife. He wanted her with him, not just to take care of the children, not just because she could be carrying his child, not just to keep house and help him with the ranch and to make her brother-in-law happy. He wanted her with him just to be with him.

Rachel stared at her reflection in the mirror. Swirls of white satin floated over and around her. Delicate lace edged her throat and wrists. Pearls studded the cap of her veil and the train of her gown.

She could stop the wedding, of course. She could tell Maggie that she wasn't pregnant. Her monthly flow had come and gone during the past ten days. There was no reason to go through with this travesty. Outside of the four of them, who would ever know of Rachel's indiscretion? Perhaps, should she decide to marry in the future, her husband would guess. But if he loved her, he would forgive her.

Only she didn't want another man's forgiveness, and she didn't want to be another man's wife.

She sighed and moved away from the mirror, stopping beside the open window. Although March was still a week away, there was the fresh scent of spring in the air and a renewed strength in the sun. The trees beside the river were full of birds, and the first new colt had arrived in the Branigan barn only three days before.

She took a deep breath, hoping against hope that it would clear the confusion from her head and heart. She loved him and he'd hurt her. She was glad he'd come to Boise, yet furious with him for his reasons. She wanted to be his wife, but hated the way it was happening. She could stop it if she wanted.

So why didn't she?

She heard the door opening. "I'll be ready in a moment, Maggie," she said without looking behind her.

Gavin's deep voice surprised her. "It's not Maggie."

Rachel turned slowly.

He looked different in the fine dress suit and silk hat. He was as handsome as ever, but she realized that she much preferred him in his denim trousers and boots, his black hair tousled by the wind. He was like the country he'd chosen to live in, strong and enduring, bending beneath strong winds like a mighty tree, but refusing to break.

He was silent as his gaze caressed her, starting with the filmy veil covering her hair and moving leisurely to the train of her gown that formed a satin pool around her feet. Her breathing slowed as she tolerated—no, delighted in—his perusal.

Finally, his eyes returned to her face. "We have to talk, Rachel."

So, it would be Gavin who called an end to it after all. She should have known it wouldn't be up to her.

"There are things I should have said and didn't, and you've got a right to hear them before you come down those stairs and agree to be my wife."

Her reply was nearly inaudible. "What things?"

"I want you with me, Rachel. I don't know what kind of husband I'll be to you. I'll do my best not to hurt you, my best to provide for you. I can't promise you an easy life. You know what it's like up there. You've seen it for yourself." He fell silent.

Rachel looked into the depths of those familiar steel-gray eyes and felt her heart give. "Is that all you came to say?"

"No."

She waited, longing to hear the words, longing to say them herself.

"I came up here to ask you to be my wife. Not because you were forced into it, but because it's what you want."

I love you, Gavin. "Yes, I'll be your wife. Not because I was forced into it, but because it's what I want." *Tell me you love me, Gavin. Say the words.*

He placed his hand on the doorknob. "I hope I'll never make you sorry, Rachel. I'll do my best." He turned, his hand twisting the knob.

"Gavin . . ."

He glanced over his shoulder.

"There's no baby. I'm not pregnant."

Now was his chance to change his mind. Now he could make a run for the hills. She had given him his out. Would he take it?

His smile was gentle. "There'll be plenty of time for babies." And then he was gone.

"And by the power vested in me, I now pronounce you man and wife."

Her heart racing, Rachel turned toward Gavin. His hands lifted the veil, and their eyes met.

Her husband. It seemed unreal. Like a dream. She was afraid she would awaken and find it all gone.

He cupped her face in his hands as he leaned forward and kissed her gently on the lips. Time seemed to stop. The guests, the minister—all disappeared except for the two of them.

I was right, she thought as he kissed her. That day up on the ridge, that first moment she'd realized she loved Gavin. *This was what I've been waiting for all along.*

Chapter Thirty-Five

It had been in a hotel room much like this that she had first seen Gavin Blake.

As Rachel crossed the sitting room toward the window, she remembered the way she'd felt when she first looked into his eyes, that jolt of awareness of another human being such as she'd never felt before. If she had been aware that day of what the next few months would bring, would she still have taken the job as governess?

She turned and looked at Gavin as he carried her valise across the sitting room to the bed-room.

Yes! her heart replied to her silent question. *Yes!*

When he returned from the bedroom, their eyes met. Her stomach fluttered in response. For so long her love for Gavin had been forbidden. She wasn't sure what to do now that it was allowed.

"I've ordered some supper for us," Gavin said. "I noticed you didn't eat anything after the ceremony."

She wasn't sure she could eat anything now.

He came toward her, stopping within arm's reach. "You never looked more beautiful than you did today."

She flushed with pleasure.

"I'd better add some fuel to that fire. It's getting cold outside. You can feel it through the windows." He turned away from her. As he walked across the room, he removed his suit coat and tossed it across the nearest chair. His tie and collar were the next to go.

Watching him, she wondered if all brides were as nervous as she was on their wedding nights. It wasn't that she didn't know what was ahead of her. In fact, the knowing brought a rush of anticipation that warmed her throughout. Still, she felt awkward, not sure what to do or what to say. And so she remained standing beside the window, the town beyond the glass bathed in the darkness of night.

He sensed her nervousness and wondered if she had any idea that he was nervous too. It seemed a cowardly, unmanly thing to admit, even to himself. It wasn't the first time he'd been in a hotel room with a woman, and it definitely wasn't going to be the first time he'd bedded a woman either.

But this time it was different. This time he was with his bride.

They lingered over the supper that was brought up to them, neither of them eating much as their eyes met and parted dozens of times across the mahogany table. The mantel clock chimed the hour, the quarter hour, the half hour, and still they remained at the table.

She was beautiful. She looked so exquisite, sitting there in her rose-colored gown. Did he have the right to take something so fine and delicate to the high country, to a life of hard work and few pleasures? Was it possible that she had freely chosen that life over the one she'd known here, over the one she could have had with Patrick O'Donnell—or had she really had a choice?

She was young and innocent. She couldn't possibly know what she'd done in marrying him. She'd felt remorse over their night of passion, and that had colored her judgment. She'd told him she was marrying him of her own free will, but society and her family were pressuring her all the same. She would come to regret her decision. Eventually, she would choose to leave him.

And, God help him, he couldn't bear the thought of life without Rachel.

A calm overtook Rachel, and she was no longer afraid. That same sense of destiny that had washed over her at the wedding, a certainty that here was where she belonged, returned. This was right. She had no reason to be nervous.

She placed her napkin beside her plate as she rose from her chair. She walked around the table, coming to stand beside Gavin. She held out her hand to him. He took it and stood. Then, as naturally as if they'd been doing it for a lifetime, she moved into his arms, tipping her head to accept his mouth upon hers.

A sweet yearning began in the secretmost part of her, a longing to be a part of the man she loved. It seemed that the only way she could convey to him the depths of her feelings was to be joined with him in the most intimate of acts, to share herself—body, soul and spirit.

She leaned into him, her hands moving over the smooth fabric of his shirt, feeling the ridge of his spine with her fingertips. She parted her mouth and gently nibbled on his lower lip, then ran her tongue along it.

When she opened her eyes and leaned back from him, she found him watching her with a smoky gaze, a look that set her blood on fire. The yearning for him was no longer tender and sweet. It was demanding, unrelenting, a furious storm raging through her limbs and igniting her loins.

"Gavin." His name came out in a hoarse whisper, conveying the aching need.

His fingers began to play with the buttons on the front of her bodice, slipping them free one at a time. When the last one escaped its loop, he pushed the dress from her shoulders. His hands brushed the length of her arms, causing goose-flesh to rise and her breath to quicken.

She saw his gaze move to the swell of her bosom above her corset. She had a decadent urge to be free of the binding garment, to have him gazing upon her bare breasts, to feel his mouth playing with the sensitive flesh.

A surge of such terrible wanting hit her that she swayed forward into his arms. He held her, kissed her, pulled the pinnings from her hair and set it free to tumble down her back.

And, finally, when she was able to stand freely once again, he continued to disrobe her. Article by article, her clothing fell away, until she stood before him, naked beneath his adoring gaze.

For a long time, he didn't touch her, merely looked. She felt the warmth of the fire upon her skin, felt the heat of her blood in her veins.

She reached forward, laying her hand upon his chest, and then she was helping divest him of his shirt and trousers. She was both delighted and horrified by her boldness.

When he stood as naked as she—but so gloriously, obviously male—he pulled her once again into his embrace, his mouth claiming hers in renewed hunger. She let her head fall back as her fingers tangled themselves in his black locks. His hands explored her body until the wanting, the need, the desire became paramount to everything else in the world.

At that moment, he lifted her into his arms and carried her to their marriage bed.

She lay nestled in the curve of his shoulder, her long blond curls mingling with the black hair on his chest. Gavin stared down at it, oddly touched by the sight, as if it signified something deep and meaningful.

Rachel moaned in her sleep and snuggled closer to him. He supposed he should reach for the blanket and cover her, but he wasn't ready to quit looking at her just yet.

Rachel Blake. His wife.

It seemed impossible that she should have chosen to marry him. Moreover, it seemed impossible that it should mean so much to him, that he could want it so very much. Gavin Blake, the man who'd decided long ago to be a loner, a man with no attachments. And here he was with wife, children, ranch, friends, neighbors.

He smiled to himself. Perhaps it would make sense to him later. He had other things to think about now. Like the way she looked, lying on her side, her leg thrown over his, her hand lying on the flat of his belly. Like the smell of her honeysuckle cologne, faint, fresh, and wild. Like the paleness of her skin in comparison to his. Like the ripe fullness of her breast pressed against his ribs. Like the way she responded to his kiss, his touch—inexperienced yet eager, hesitant yet somehow brazen.

His wife.

Her head pulled back from him, her eyes open but glazed with sleep. She smiled languidly, sending a shock of desire shooting through him.

"I fell asleep." Her voice was husky, amused.

"Not for long," he responded, drawing her closer to him.

"There was something I meant to tell you."

He felt himself grow hard with passion. "Later," he mumbled as he cupped her breast and teased the nipple with his fingers. "Tell me later."

Exhausted, sated, replete, they lay in a tangle of sheets and blankets, a fine shimmer of sweat glowing on their skin, the night air quickly cooling them as the fire of their union faded.

Gavin reached for the mass of blankets and shook them, then yanked the covers over the two naked bodies. His feet were left out in the open, but he didn't care. He hadn't the energy or the inclination to get up and straighten the bedding.

"Gavin?"

"Hmmm?"

Her voice was filled with awe and wonder. "Is it like this for everyone?"

"No," he answered truthfully.

She tilted her head. Her eyes seemed to glow in the dim light of the bedroom. "Will it always be this way for us?"

His arms tightened around her. He kissed the crown of her head, overwhelmed by the possessiveness that gripped his heart. "Better, Rachel. I hope it will always get better."

Rachel couldn't believe it could get better. She'd never imagined the "woman's duty" she'd heard about in whispers could be anything so wonderful as this. She sighed and closed her eyes, sublime happiness filling her.

"Wasn't there something you meant to tell me?" he whispered in her ear. His voice was teasing. "Before I interrupted you."

"Oh, yes . . ." She nestled closer as another sigh escaped her lips. "I love you, Gavin."

She smiled and drifted off to sleep, leaving Gavin to ponder her words in the silence of night.

Chapter Thirty-Six

Rachel stood in the middle of her old bedroom, saying a silent farewell to her childhood. At twenty-two, it had been many years since she'd been considered a child, yet there was a part of her that had always known she could return to the safety within these walls.

But now everything was changed. She was a woman. In pledging herself to Gavin, promising to love, honor and obey, she had left childish things behind forever. There was no turning back.

"Feel a little strange?"

Rachel turned to face Maggie, standing in the door of her room. She nodded.

"For me too." Her sister took a few steps forward. She lifted her hand to cup Rachel's chin. "You're happy." It wasn't a question but a statement of fact, tinged with relief.

"Yes." Rachel smiled. "I'm happy."

They hugged one another, swaying slowly from side to side.

"It wasn't so hard seeing you go," Maggie whispered, "when I knew you were coming back."

"It's not far away. We'll come visit. You'll come up to the basin in the summer. And we'll write. We'll write often."

"Of course we will."

But each knew that it wouldn't be so easy. Months would go by, perhaps years, between visits. Life was fragile. Anything could happen.

Rachel blinked away the gathering moisture as she pulled back from Maggie's embrace. "I love him, Maggie. Thank you for . . . well, for making me see it."

"I was afraid you were going to make the same mistake I nearly made. You're every bit as stubborn as I ever was. You were so young, you couldn't possibly remember, but I refused Tucker's proposal many times, even though I loved him. I was determined not to give my life over to a man. I was so afraid of losing my independence. You know what I found, Rachel?"

She shook her head.

"Loving someone as I love Tucker is the greatest freedom of all." Maggie hugged Rachel again, then turned away, flicking at her eyes with her fingertips. "Be kind to each other. Be patient and giving. Don't hold grudges and don't expect the other one to be perfect. Everything else will work out if you just don't give up on each other."

Rachel blew her nose on her handkerchief. "What will you do with this room?" she asked to change the subject.

"Well . . ." Maggie turned once again, this time wearing a slightly sheepish grin. "I guess we'll make it Sheridan's room. He won't want to be in the nursery . . . when the new baby arrives."

"Maggie, you're not . . ." She grabbed her sister's hands. "Oh, Maggie! That's wonderful. When?"

"August."

Rachel kissed Maggie's cheek. "I'm so happy for you."

"Say in there," Tucker said as he entered the bedroom, followed by Gavin. "We've got to get a move on if you're going to catch the stage."

Rachel released Maggie's hands only to turn her exuberant attentions on her brother-in-law. "Maggie just told me about the new baby," she said as she threw her arms around his neck. "It's wonderful news."

"We had to do something to fill the hole you've left in the family. Of course, a new baby can't take your place, Kitten—just help ease the loneliness a bit."

She felt the sting of tears once again. Tucker was the closest thing she'd ever had to a father, and she loved him dearly. She was going to miss him. She was going to miss them all.

As if he sensed her growing melancholy,

Gavin stepped forward to place an arm around his wife. "We really do have to go."

"I know," she whispered. "I know." She took one more quick glance around the room.

"Don't worry about the rest of your things. We'll send them to you," Tucker promised.

Gavin eased her toward the door. "Come on, Rachel."

As painful as the parting was, when she turned to look at her husband, she felt a rush of expectation for the future. She was embarking on a new life. She would be making her own memories with her own family. It was good. It was right. It was time.

"I'm ready," she replied.

Together, they walked from the room.

Rachel's trunks were strapped to the top of the stagecoach. Gavin's horse was tied at the back. Another series of quick good-byes were said outside the stage depot, and then they were on their way.

The stage from Boise had two other passengers besides the Blakes. Joseph Cohen, a grocer, was traveling to Bonanza City to open a shop with his son. Margaret Freedman was on her way to Ketchum to stay with her daughter, who was expecting her first child.

Both Mr. Cohen and Mrs. Freedman exchanged those bits of information shortly after departure. Then Mr. Cohen pulled his hat forward and promptly fell asleep. Mrs. Freedman chattered amiably about her daughter and son-in-law, about her first grandchild, and about how dreadful it was for her only child to be living so far away. Eventually, she ran out of things to say and fell silent, her eyes falling closed and her double chin bobbing against her ample breasts.

Rachel smiled at Gavin, then laid her head on his shoulder, thankful for the silence at last. She wondered, if they were alone, what they would find to talk about. What was it going to be like, married to this man? Would he discuss the business of ranching with her? Would he consider her opinions important?

She decided she was grateful for the other occupants of the coach. There would be time enough later to feel their way into this new relationship. She would rather savor the memory of their two nights at the Overland Hotel. At least she knew what to expect from the physical side of marriage.

Her smile increased as she closed her eyes and, like her coachmates, drifted off to sleep.

They rented a horse and sleigh in Challis and headed for Killarney Hall to pick up the children. Rachel couldn't get over the change that had overtaken the area during her absence. She had come to think of the land only in terms of white layers of snow, but in the six weeks since she'd left, a harbinger of spring had arrived in the form of Chinook winds, slowly melting away the worst evidence of a harsh winter.

"We haven't seen the last of it yet," Gavin said, reading Rachel's mind. "We'll see snow in March and maybe in April too. But if it seems long here, it's worse in the Stanley Basin. I don't envy those miners in Sawtooth City and whatever other camps have popped up in the last year or two." He chuckled. "I have to admit, even I got spoiled by the warm weather down in Boise City."

"It was nice, wasn't it?"

The sleigh crested the ridge, and Killarney Hall came into view. Rachel's stomach did a sudden flip-flop.

"Do you suppose they'll forgive me for leaving the way I did?" she asked, her voice quavering.

"They love you. They'll forgive you."

"I want to be a good mother to them."

"You will be," he assured her.

"Oh, Gavin, I'm so nervous."

"Don't be. It'll be fine. You'll see."

It seemed so easy for him to be self-assured. He wasn't the one who had married the girls' pa so soon after their mother's death. He wasn't the one who had up and left without so much as a good-bye. Why hadn't it occurred to her sooner that they might not be as happy to see her as she was going to be to see them?

But it was too late now. She would have to make the best of it.

The sleigh sped down the gentle slope and hurried toward the large stone structure, Rachel's anxiety growing with each passing minute.

Gavin had just lifted her from the sleigh when the door opened and Patrick appeared on the veranda. Her mouth went dry as her eyes met his. He grinned and came down the steps to meet them.

"Sure and aren't you a sight for sore eyes, my lovely." He picked her up and hugged her. "I never would've thought you'd be so much improved so soon. You look in the pink of health."

"Careful how you manhandle my wife, O'Donnell," Gavin said gravely.

"Your wife, is she?" Patrick set Rachel back on her feet and backed away from her. "Then that's what the spot o' color is doin' in those lovely cheeks. 'Tis the blush of happiness." He thrust out his hand toward Gavin. "Then 'tis my congratulations you've got, Gavin Blake. I'm glad you had the sense to marry her. I'd not have given you another chance."

"How are Brina and Pet?" Rachel asked, her face flushed with embarrassment.

"They're fit and full of vinegar and anxious to have their father back. Wait 'til they see you, Rachel. There'll be no containin' their joy then."

She wished she was as confident of her reception.

"Come in from the cold. I'll send Crandal for the wee lasses. They'll be playin' in the schoolroom this time o' day."

Gavin's hand settled in the small of her back as they climbed the steps behind Patrick. A quick glance at Gavin's face increased her uneasiness. It was set in hard, remote lines, a look she hadn't seen in many days now.

* * *

Gavin's gaze took in the opulence of the entry hall as they made their way to the salon. Everywhere he looked there was evidence of wealth and grandeur.

What, he wondered, was Rachel thinking as she looked at her surroundings? Was she remembering that all this could have been hers? Was she sorry for her decision? Might she have married Patrick eventually if Gavin hadn't followed her to Boise?

He glanced at Patrick, who was grinning and still chattering as they waited for the children. Patrick's love for Rachel was written all over the big man's face. Would the day come when she wanted that love?

I love you, Gavin, she'd whispered on their wedding night. He tried to comfort himself with the memory, only he was too aware that she hadn't repeated those words in the days since. What if he wasn't able to keep that love alive?

He would kill the man who tried to steal Rachel from him.

The realization struck him like a blow to the solar plexus, and he knew it was true. Unlike his father, who had given himself over to drink, Gavin would hold onto what was his. He had only to glance at Rachel to know he couldn't face life without her.

"Pa!"

"Pa!"

He swung around and knelt in time to catch the girls, one in each arm, as they hurled themselves at him. "Look at the two of you. Lord almighty, I've missed you."

"We missed you, too, Pa," Sabrina said, hugging his neck.

"Look, Pa," Petula interrupted. "My arm's all better." She bent and straightened it several times just to prove it.

Then, in unison, the girls wriggled free of his embrace, turning their eyes on Rachel.

"Have you come back to stay, Miss Harris?" Sabrina asked in the blunt manner of a nine-year-old.

Gavin rose and went to stand beside Rachel, placing his arm around her back. "We have a surprise for you, girls, and we hope you'll be happy about it. Rachel and I were married last week."

There was a pregnant silence.

Finally, Petula asked, "Does that make you our ma now?"

He felt a slight tremor pass through Rachel before she knelt, facing the youngest girl at eye level.

"I would like very much to be your mother, Pet, but I don't mean to take your ma's place. I know I couldn't do that, even if I wanted to. We all loved her too much. Perhaps you could call me Mother instead of Ma."

Another lengthy silence followed.

"I don't know if I could ever explain why I left the way I did," Rachel continued, "but I want you to know it had nothing to do with you children. I love you very much, and leaving you was the hardest thing I ever did."

"Was it 'cause you couldn't marry Mr. O'Donnell?" Sabrina asked. "Is that why you left?"

Rachel inhaled. "Yes. That was part of it."

"Do you love our pa?"

She sighed as a tiny smile curved the corners of her mouth. "Yes, Brina. I love your pa. Very much."

Gavin wasn't sure what kind of reaction he'd expected from the children, but his chest swelled with pride as he heard Rachel telling them how much she loved him. Moments later, the two girls were giving Rachel a hug and kissing her cheek.

"We're glad to have you back . . . Mother," he heard Petula whisper.

Life seemed pretty good to Gavin Blake.

She was home. Truly home.

It surprised Rachel how right it felt, walking in the door of the ranch house at the Lucky Strike and knowing this was her home. It suddenly seemed to her that she'd only been visiting Maggie for a few weeks, and now she was back where she belonged.

She watched as the men carried her trunks through the main room and into Gavin's bedroom. *Their* bedroom. Again, it had a feeling of rightness.

On his way back out of the bedroom, Stubs winked at her. She smiled in return, grateful for his silent approval.

Stubs and Jess stayed in the house for a while, updating Gavin on things that had happened while he was away. The girls slipped off to their bedroom, unpacking their valises from their stay at Killarney Hall.

As Rachel listened to the sound of the men's deep voices, she wandered into Gavin's bedroom.

Our bedroom, she reminded herself again.

She looked at the large fourposter with its heavy patchwork quilt. Except for summers in the basin, this would be where she spent her nights for the rest of her life. She would conceive babies, God willing, in this bed, and she would give birth to them here as well. This would be where she would lie in her husband's arms and they would plan out their future.

She ran her fingers over the smooth wood of one of the posts, then leaned her forehead against it.

Everything would be complete if only he would tell her he loved her, she thought, hating the stab of sadness that marred the perfection of this moment.

"Rachel?"

She turned, still holding onto the post.

Gavin closed the door. "You all right?" He moved a step closer.

She nodded.

He must have read something in her expression. "You don't mind that this was Dru's room, do you?"

She hadn't even thought of it until he mentioned it.

"It was *her* bedroom. Not ours. We shared the room but not . . ." He paused. "Our marriage . . . well, it was just a technicality so I could adopt Brina and Pet.''

It was a moment before Rachel realized what he was saying. He was telling her she was his only true wife. She was glad for the knowledge. But it wasn't enough to take the thin edge of pain away. Only his love could do that.

Somehow, she had to break through the barrier to his heart. Somehow . . .

Chapter Thirty-Seven

Days flowed into weeks and weeks into first one month and then two. It was a magical time for Rachel.

Life on the Lucky Strike hadn't changed in her absence. The work was always there, waiting to be done, and much of it was hard and back-breaking. She'd done it all before, but now it was *her* home, and somehow that made it different. Gavin often caught her humming as she scrubbed floors or bent over the big tubs on washdays or cooked meals for a hungry family.

Nights were even more magical. They made love often, and she found that he hadn't lied to her. It *did* get better. She became more confident in her response to him. She slowly learned the unique power she wielded as a woman and secretly reveled in it.

Often they lay awake a long time after making love, talking about the children, about the ranch, about their hopes and dreams. Rachel told him what little she remembered of her troubled childhood in Philadelphia with her Uncle Seth. She detailed the journey West on the wagon train as recalled through the eyes of a child. She shared some of her experiences in the finishing school and told anecdotes about the people—politicians and society matrons and businessmen—she'd met during her years in Washington and Philadelphia.

Little by little, with her gentle encouragement, Gavin revealed bits and pieces of his life, too. But he never talked about his boyhood in Ohio, never mentioned either of his parents. She heard about the rough years as the fourteen-year-old boy left home and grew into a man while learning to be a cowboy in Texas. She heard stories of the hot and dusty trail drives and long nights in the saddle, of the lightning storms, the drenching rains, the droughts, the stampedes. He told her about the months he'd spent in the gold camps, surrounded by people possessed by gold fever, the ridiculous wealth of a few, the abject poverty of many.

During those hours in his arms, Gavin often told her she was beautiful. He frequently said he was glad she was his wife. She waited, always hopeful, to hear those three precious words, but they didn't come. Still, Rachel felt herself becoming more and more a part of his life and he of hers, and she was happy.

There was a subtle change in the way the children reacted to her. They had always been close. With Dru's tender guidance, Rachel had learned to love the girls even as Sabrina and Petula learned to love their governess. But now there was a bonding that went deeper than what they'd had before. Rachel felt it every time she heard one of them call her Mother.

And when the day came that she first suspected there was to be another child calling her Mother, she felt an indescribable joy. She kept the secret nestled deep in her heart and anxiously waited until she could be sure it was true.

Gavin pumped the bellows. Sweat poured down his face, back, and chest as the heat of the fire blasted him. He pulled the iron from the forge and pounded it against the anvil, carefully shaping it to fit Checker's big hoof. The barn doors were thrown wide, allowing the late April sunshine entrance, along with a delightfully fresh breeze.

Spring was always a busy time of year at the Lucky Strike as they prepared for round-up and the annual drive into the basin. This year was no different.

Except that, this year, Rachel was with them.

Gavin grinned as she entered the barn, carrying a tray with sandwiches and something cold to drink. He dropped the horseshoe into the bucket of water and wiped the sweat from his brow with his forearm as the hiss of steam filled the air.

"If you won't come in when you're told, you'll have to eat in the barn." Her tone was scolding, but her rebuke was diluted by her smile.

He took the tray from her and set it near the bellows. "Suits me, long as I've got such pretty company." With a boot braced against the bottom rail, he leaned his back against the stall and took a bite from the roast-beef sandwich. "Mmmm."

She gave a saucy little toss of her head and turned away. "Well, you'll have to get along without the pretty company, Mr. Blake. Mrs. Blake has far too much work to get done. There's bread in the oven, and you're the one who has to eat it if it burns to a crisp."

He considered letting the horse go unshod and the bread bake to a cinder while he carried the impertinent lady to their bedroom. It wouldn't be a bad way to spend an afternoon.

As Rachel reached the doorway, she lifted her hand to shade her eyes. "We've got company."

Gavin took another quick bite, then a gulp of milk before walking over to join her.

"It's Patrick!" She lifted an arm to wave toward the approaching buggy. "And Pearl!" She hurried out into the sunshine, waiting for her friends to arrive.

Gavin wasn't as eager to greet their visitors. They hadn't seen Patrick since their return from Boise, and that had suited Gavin just fine. Those same nagging suspicions, forgotten these past few weeks, returned as strong as ever. What if Rachel should realize she didn't love him? What if she regretted not having the life of ease Patrick could offer her?

He reached for his shirt and slipped into it, then walked out of the barn.

Patrick hopped out of the buggy and immediately grabbed Rachel's hands as he gazed down at her face. "Look at you, lass. Sure if your happiness hasn't made you prettier than ever."

"It's good to see you, Patrick. We've missed you."

Patrick released her and turned to help Pearl from the buggy.

The two women hugged each other as Patrick stepped toward Gavin. Gavin hid his irritation and shook Patrick's offered hand.

"Pearl's been after Shane or me to bring her callin' for weeks now. I decided we'd given you enough time alone, and here we are." He grinned and slapped Gavin lightly on the back.

"Come inside, Patrick," Rachel called. "I'll fix you something to eat. There's fresh bread in the oven about ready to come out."

Patrick patted his stomach and grinned. "That's temptin', lass. Do I look like a man who could refuse such an offer?"

"There's never a moment the O'Donnell men *aren't* hungry," Pearl said as she and Rachel led the way into the house.

Patrick started after them, then turned and looked back at Gavin. "Are you comin', mate?"

"No. I've got work to do." He spun on his heel and strode back to the barn, ignoring Patrick's questioning gaze.

He stripped off his shirt. *Damn*! Why did they have to come today? Why did *he* have to come at all?

He lifted the horseshoe from the water bucket, then picked up Checker's leg and held the iron against the large hoof. It was a good fit. He should be pleased.

But his mind wasn't on shoeing the old work horse. It was on Patrick and Rachel, together in the house.

Rachel couldn't understand why Gavin still hadn't returned from the barn. It shouldn't have taken him that long to finish with the shoeing. Checker had been the last horse he had to do. He'd told her so himself. So why was he ignoring Patrick and Pearl? Because of the weather and the distances to be traveled, they'd had few enough guests come calling since the wedding, and Rachel thought Gavin should be as tickled as she was to see their friends.

"Sure but I think I'd better stretch my legs after such a meal," Patrick said as he rose from the table. "Maybe I can give Gavin a hand."

A tiny frown furrowed Rachel's brow. She hoped Patrick would be able to figure out why Gavin was acting so strangely.

Pearl helped clear away the dishes, oblivious to Rachel's quandary. "That was a wonderful lunch, Rachel. It's been so long since I've cooked a meal, I'd probably poison the whole family if I tried. The cook won't let me poke my nose inside the kitchen. She thinks I'm too young to have a single notion of what must be done to care for the O'Donnell men."

"I bet you'd do just fine, given the chance," Rachel replied. "I didn't know much when I first went up to the basin. I used to help with the cooking now and then when I was little, but Dru was the one who really taught me how to get around in the kitchen."

Pearl stopped and turned to look at Rachel. "Dru was a special person. Is it hard? Fillin' her shoes?" She blushed. "I'm sorry. I shouldn't have said that."

"It's all right." Rachel laid a hand over Pearl's. "We all miss her. Gavin, the children, me. All of us. But Gavin and I . . . well, we have something different, something uniquely ours."

"You're real happy, aren't you?"

"Very."

Pearl returned to her chair beside the table and sat down. "I was sorry you didn't marry Patrick. I wanted you for my sister. That place needs more women in it. But I can see it wouldn't have been right. You belong here with Gavin."

"Patrick will find the right woman someday. You'll see."

"I sure hope you're right," Pearl replied with a little shake of her head.

"I'm surprised you're not gettin' fat, Gavin, with a wife who can cook like that."

Gavin threw another forkful of hay into Patch's stall, replying with a noncommittal grunt.

"Thought I'd come out and offer you a hand.

Give Rachel and Pearl time alone for some woman-talk. A man's not welcome when two females put their heads together. So what can I do out here for you, Gavin, until I'm welcome inside again?"

Gavin glanced toward Patrick. The Irishman was leaning his shoulder against the barn door, his stance jaunty, his face bright with a grin. His shirt was white and starched, his black trousers smoothly creased, his red hair slicked back in place. At the moment, Gavin couldn't think of any way Patrick could help him without getting his fancy duds mussed.

It shouldn't bother him so much. Patrick had always been wealthy, yet they'd become friends. He'd never been envious or jealous before. But it was different now. Patrick had been engaged to Rachel. Patrick had kissed Rachel and held her in his arms. Patrick could give Rachel things that Gavin never could.

His fingers tightened around the handle of the pitchfork, and he jabbed it into the stack of hay.

Patrick wandered in, blithely ignoring Gavin's sour mood. "Faith and begorra! Would you look at this fine lass."

He turned to see Patrick leaning over a stall gate. Unable to help himself, he set the pitchfork aside and walked over to join Patrick. The palomino mare stood in the center of her stall, gently bathing the newborn filly with her tongue.

"Just arrived yesterday," he told Patrick. "Dru would've been pleased. She always did want a colt out of this mare. This little gal is Sunshine's first foal. The spittin' image of her dam."

"That she is."

He glanced sideways at Patrick. "My wife's birthday's coming up. I thought Rachel might like to have the filly."

Patrick didn't look his way. "'Tis a fine gift from a husband. Fine gift."

Sure. A fine gift. But not what Patrick could have given her.

"Gavin, what's wrong with you?" Rachel demanded as she closed the bedroom door. "I've never seen you so churlish."

"Maybe I just don't like people coming and staying for so long when there's work to be done." Gavin removed his shirt and tossed it across a chair. "It's only a few more weeks before we'll be driving the cattle up to the basin. We don't have time for lounging like some folk. If I could afford a houseful of servants and a dozen cowboys, I could spend my day visiting too."

She listened to him in stunned silence, still not understanding why he was angry. Finally, she stepped away from the door. "But it's nice to have friends come calling."

He paused in his undressing and leveled a dark look at her across the bed. "Tired of my company, Mrs. Blake?" he asked. Then he turned, sat on the bed, and pulled off his dusty trousers.

She was shocked first, then her own temper

flared. "It wouldn't take long for anyone to be tired of your company when you're in such a sour mood. Did you notice Brina's and Pet's faces at supper? They thought they'd done something wrong."

He sighed but remained silent.

Rachel skirted the bed and came to stand beside him, her anger forgotten. She placed her hand on his bare shoulder. "Is this something I just have to expect in the spring? Are you always like this?" She leaned over and nuzzled the back of his neck. "If so, I'll have to find some way to sweeten you up."

Gavin shook his head as he stared at the floor, unaffected for once by her caress. "There's always so much damn work."

"It gets done."

"No matter how many good years we have, it'll never be enough so you don't have to work so hard."

It was Rachel's turn to sigh. "Haven't we talked about this before, Gavin? I don't mind the work."

"You should mind." He twisted his head, his gaze meeting hers. "I got to thinking, having Patrick here. If you'd married him instead of me, you'd be the one going visiting while somebody else did the work. Someday you might wish you *had* married him."

"Is that what this is about?" She threw up her hands in exasperation. "I married the man I wanted to marry. Can't you accept that?"

She wished she could tell him she wasn't like

his mother, that she had married him "until death do you part." But she wasn't supposed to know about Christina Blake, and so she kept silent.

"I'll check on the bath water," she said as she turned toward the bedroom door.

She felt a sadness settling over her. This was the closest they'd come to an argument in all these weeks. She'd gotten spoiled, she supposed. No married couple got along one hundred percent of the time. Everyone fought occasionally. She shouldn't be afraid to disagree with Gavin.

This thing with Patrick and being afraid she would leave him—it was all tied up with the way his mother left his father. That was why he couldn't admit to loving her. He was afraid to love. A man so strong, so brave in every other way, but when it came to his heart, he was a coward.

She dragged the washtub into the kitchen and began filling it with steaming hot water, all the while wishing she was smarter about men. There had to be some way she could help him see that her love was enduring, that it was forever. But how? How did she break down those barriers?

Patience, she thought as she heard the bedroom door opening. She had to have patience.

He was acting like a damn fool, and he knew it. Rachel was his wife. She'd broken off with Patrick of her own accord. She'd willingly accepted his proposal. He had no reason to doubt her sincerity. She loved him. She'd told him so in more ways than mere words.

Gavin stood in the bedroom doorway, a towel wrapped around his waist, watching as she dumped a kettle of boiling water into the tub. The steam was causing her hair to spring into curls around her face and ears. Her cheeks were delicately flushed, and a fine mist made her skin glow in the lamplight.

"I'm sorry for the way I've been acting," he said softly. "I guess I'm just tired."

Her smile was wistful. "Your bath is ready. Get in. It'll make you feel better."

She was right. A hot bath to soothe his tired muscles *would* make him feel better.

He crossed to the tub, dropped the towel on the floor, and stepped into the water, sinking down into the tin bath until all but his head was submerged. He closed his eyes and felt his muscles begin to relax.

He wasn't sure how long he lay there before he heard her moving about the kitchen. He opened his eyes in time to see her lifting another kettle of hot water from the stove.

"Move your feet," she instructed.

He pulled his knees toward his chest and watched as she poured the water into the bath. She set the kettle on the floor beside the tub and swirled the added hot water with her hand. Her fingers brushed against his leg, and he felt a prickle of awareness. Her touch always did that to him.

Turning away for a moment, she picked up a

bar of soap and came to kneel beside him. She glanced toward him, her expression uncertain, as if asking permission. When he made no response, she lifted his arm and began to move the soap over his skin, slowly working up a lather.

He'd never had anyone bathe him before. It was more intimate, more pleasurable than he might have imagined. Her touch was light, almost nonexistent, yet he would have sworn he could feel her heartbeat through her fingertips.

She moved slowly, causing him to shift and lift with only the gentle pressure of her hand or glance of her eyes. He was unaware of the cooling water. A new, more enjoyable tension replaced the old. He could get use to such treatment, especially when he could feast his eyes on Rachel, her dress damp and clinging to her breasts.

"You know what you need, Gavin?" Rachel whispered, breaking the silence with her husky voice.

"What?" He could think of one very particular thing he needed, thanks to her ministrations.

"You need a dunking." With that, her hands landed on top of his head and she pushed him beneath the water.

He came up sputtering. "What was that for?"

"Your hair must be wet before I can wash it," she answered in feigned innocence.

"And do you know what you need, Rachel Blake?" He raised an eyebrow but hid the wicked grin that would have hinted at his intent.

405

She shook her head.

"You need a dousing." He grabbed her before she had a chance to move away, pulling her into the tin bath with him.

Water splashed over the sides of the tub and spread across the kitchen floor, but neither Gavin nor Rachel were aware of the mess they had made. Nor would they have cared if they'd known.

Chapter Thirty-Eight

Gavin rode out with Stubs and Jess at the crack of dawn that May morning, as they had every morning for the past week. The round-up had started. The spring counting of the calf crop. The branding. It was hard work that didn't wait for birthdays or anything else.

Rachel wasn't sure if Gavin had remembered today was her birthday. She suspected he had, since he'd told her he would try to be back earlier than usual. But she really didn't care if he'd forgotten. She had the best gift of all already, and she was going to surprise him with it when he got back.

She smiled as her hand lingered over her flat stomach. She was certain now that she was pregnant. She'd missed two monthly flows. By her calculations, she would be holding Gavin's child by Christmas. Who would have thought she would be wishing for the season of snow when spring had only just begun?

She pulled the cake from the oven and set it aside to cool, then tasted the soup that had been simmering for an hour. She glanced at the clock on the mantel. Would she have time to change her clothes and fix her hair before he got back? She wanted to look her very best when she told him the joyous news.

Rachel wandered across the main room and opened the door, stepping outside. An azure canopy spread from horizon to horizon without a single cloud to mar its blue perfection. The cry of a falcon, circling overhead, was added to the buzz of a bumblebee hovering over the flowers that bordered the south side of the house. She could hear the children's laughter coming from the barn loft. She knew they were busy planning a birthday surprise of their own.

She hugged herself, as if to contain the happiness that was close to overflowing. It all seemed so perfect, too wonderful to be believed.

She saw the horse and rider from some distance away. She recognized Patrick and was ashamed for wishing he hadn't come. She knew Gavin's insecurities about Patrick hadn't been swept away simply by the two of them making love in a bathtub, and neither of them had mentioned the Irishman's last visit again.

She drew a deep breath and silently scolded herself. *You've got no reason to be unkind to Patrick. He's your friend and Gavin's too. Gavin's*

408

got to realize it. That's all.

She waved as the horse trotted into the yard. "Hello, Patrick."

"Hello, lass. It's a beautiful day for a birthday, and I've come to wish you a happy one."

"Thank you."

Patrick dismounted. "I've also come to speak with your husband about a matter of some importance."

"He's not here, but I expect him in the next hour or so."

"Would you mind my waitin'? 'Tis rather important that I speak to him."

Rachel wondered what could be so important but decided against asking. If he wanted her to know, he would tell her. She opened the door. "Of course I don't mind if you wait. Come inside. I've a cake to frost."

Patrick stood in the middle of the main room, his eyes moving slowly over the interior of the house before returning to Rachel. "You've made the place feel like a home again. 'Twas that way when Charlie and Dru and Gavin first lived here. Always a happy place."

She wished she could ask him to tell her more, but again she refrained. It didn't seem right to ask Patrick the things her husband should tell her. She would have to be satisfied with waiting. Perhaps it wasn't even important for her to know. After all, she and Gavin were building a new life, one entirely their own.

And when their child arrived . . .

Her gaze drifted off into space as her hands

slipped to her stomach in that centuries-old manner of pregnant women, a cradling, protective gesture.

This child was this product of the joy she shared in Gavin's arms. She couldn't help but believe it would at last convince her husband not only of her love for him but his love for her. Surely he would be able to put the pain of his past behind him, once and for all.

"Faith and begorra!"

Rachel was brought abruptly back to the present. She found Patrick watching her and wearing a smile as bright as the sun itself.

"There's to be a wee Blake come winter, or my name isn't Patrick O'Donnell. Gavin must be burstin' with pride."

She lowered her eyes, blushing profusely. "He doesn't know yet. I'm going to tell him today. How did you know?"

"'Tis written all over your face, lass." Patrick's long strides brought him across the room. "Sure but 'tis wonderful news."

She looked up. "Thank you, Patrick. I'm glad you're still my friend." Her voice lowered. "You know I never meant to hurt you."

"'Tis forgotten. 'Twas my fault in any case. Only a blind man couldn't've seen how you felt. Now, will you let a friend congratulate the new mother and wish her well?"

Rachel nodded and was quickly enveloped in his embrace. It was a little like being hugged by a bear, but it was warm and unthreatening. They remained silent for a long time, Rachel feeling a new sense of peace, glad that her foolishness hadn't cost her a dear friend.

It was Patrick who finally broke the silence. "You deserve all the happiness life can bring, lass. All the happiness and more. And you'll have it now. I promise you that."

"Thank you," she whispered again as she stepped back.

And then she realized that the door was open. She turned her head, her gaze clashing with Gavin's. Dread turned her blood to ice in her veins as she stared into gray eyes filled with contempt.

"Gavin . . ." She reached for the dry sink to steady herself.

"I'm back early." His voice was like granite.

"And glad I am," Patrick proclaimed, moving away from Rachel. "There's a matter I must discuss with you. I've been waitin' for your return."

Gavin continued to glare at his wife. "So I see."

Rachel didn't know that she'd ever felt such fear. She knew how Patrick's hug must have looked to Gavin. It must have confirmed everything he'd believed would happen. She wanted to say something to reassure him but couldn't do it in front of Patrick. And so she remained silent.

There was a faint buzz in his ears, a dull ache in his chest. As he looked at Patrick, he vacillated between wanting to kill the Irishman and wanting to die himself.

"'Tis the matter of the bull from Montana. I'll

not be goin' up that way after all. I'm leavin' for
Ireland in the mornin'."

"Ireland?"

"'Tis a family matter. It may be two years or
more 'fore I return to Idaho. I know that I
promised to take a look at O'Malley's bull when
I went up there this summer, but I'll not be goin'
now. 'Tis sorry I am not to help a friend, but
there's no way out of it for me."

Gavin thought he probably should say something appropriate, like sorry to see you go or
hope you have a safe journey, but at the moment, he just couldn't do it. "Don't worry about
it. I'll make the trip up there myself."

"Well . . ." Patrick shifted and cleared his
throat. "'Tis growing late, and I've a long ride
back to the hall. I'll be sayin' good-bye."

Rachel moved from her spot in the kitchen,
coming to stand not far from Gavin's side. Her
voice was soft and quavery. "We'll miss you,
Patrick."

"Sure and I'm hopin' 'tis true, lass. Be happy
. . . and take care of *all* the Blakes."

Gavin sensed that Patrick was saying more
than just what those simple words indicated. He
glanced from Patrick to Rachel and back again,
unable to decipher the secret meaning.

Patrick turned from Rachel and thrust out his
hand. "Gavin."

He stared at Patrick, the anger still rolling
through him. Only after a lengthy deliberation
did he extend his arm and clasp the proffered
hand. "Good-bye, Patrick."

The Irishman's grip was firm. Again, Gavin

sensed the man was trying to communicate something—to *him* this time, and this time with his eyes. But Gavin wasn't willing to try to understand. He pulled his hand free and stood waiting for the man to leave.

Patrick placed his wide-brimmed hat over his hair. He glanced quickly toward Rachel. "Don't be a stranger at Killarney. Pearl still feels overwhelmed by the O'Donnell men and is eager for female company." With that, he left, closing the door behind him.

An oppressive silence permeated the house. Rachel felt as if it would smother her. She willed her legs to move, to carry her toward the nearest chair. With great effort, they obeyed.

Gavin, however, didn't budge—except for his dark, stormy eyes. They followed her—unrelenting, unyielding, unforgiving.

Say something! her mind screamed.

"Suppose," he said, as if in answer to her silent bequest, "you tell me what was going on here."

"Going on?" Her words were nearly inaudible.

"Was it a lovers' farewell?"

Rachel gasped. "You know that isn't true."

"Do I? What would you have me think, walking in and finding you in his arms? What would have happened if I hadn't returned when I did?"

"Nothing." She rose slowly, her voice growing stronger. "I didn't even know he was leaving for Ireland."

His fists clenched at his sides. "You should

have married him, Rachel. You wouldn't have been forced to deceive me then."

"I haven't deceived you. I didn't *want* to marry him. It was you I wanted." Even as she protested, she knew he was beyond hearing.

"It's worse than I expected," he continued. "You couldn't even be faithful for a few months. What was Patrick doing here? Was he asking you to go with him? Was that what those secret glances were about?"

"Gavin, you must listen to me. Patrick came to see you, not me." Tears were streaming down her cheeks. Anger, fear, frustration, and defeat mingled in a confused mass in her chest.

"Why don't you go with him? It's not too late. You could probably still catch him."

Then anger submerged all her other emotions. Without even realizing what she was doing, she slapped him. The sound echoed in her ears. Her palm stung. She was breathing hard, as if she'd been running for a great distance. "Maybe I should leave. Maybe I should just go now and get it over with. You're always going to be waiting for it to happen, aren't you? If not with Patrick, with someone else. Maybe I *should* leave."

There wasn't even the slightest change in the expression on his face. "Maybe you should. You only promised to stay until spring."

He might as well have run a knife through her heart. The pain was the same. A hurt gasp escaped her lips as she whirled around and headed for the door.

"You can probably catch him," Gavin repeated in that same toneless voice.

She stopped dead still. Anger drained from her, leaving her tired and broken. She turned her head to look at him. "All I've wanted was to make you happy, Gavin Blake. Tell me. Won't you ever realize how much I love you?" As she turned away, she added, "I'm not the same sort of woman as your mother. I never was." She stepped outside and closed the door behind her.

She was surprised to find that the sun still shone, that flowers still bloomed, that birds still sang in the treetops. How did spring dare to reign in bright glory when all her world was dark?

She walked toward the barn. She supposed, if she hurried, there was still time to reach town before nightfall. In a few days she could be back in Boise. And then maybe she would return to Washington. She could work for the professor again. She could return to her studies.

She stopped and looked back at the house. Once again, her hands touched her stomach where even now a new life grew.

Washington wasn't where she belonged. This was. Running away wasn't the answer. Perhaps it was time for her to listen to Gavin's heart instead of his words.

How long was it after she'd gone before he heard what she'd said? Really heard.

I'm not the same sort of woman as your mother. I never was.

And then he began to see and hear it all. He began to understand what it was he had done.

415

He'd been so afraid she would one day leave him that he'd made it happen. He'd driven her away so he wouldn't be surprised later. He'd forced the fulfillment of his own expectations.

No, Rachel wasn't like his mother. She never had been. She never would be. And Gavin had known it too.

All I've wanted was to make you happy, Gavin Blake. Won't you ever realize how much I love you?

Yes. Yes, he realized it. He realized it now— when it was too late.

Gavin sank down onto a chair and lowered his forehead onto the palms of his hands, his elbows resting on the table.

The weeks and months with Rachel all came back to his mind. The joy and laughter, the tears and sorrow. He saw it all. And he saw so clearly her steadfastness, her love for a man who didn't trust it, didn't deserve it. He had the world in his hands and had thrown it away. All that remained was the emptiness.

"What a fool I've been," he said aloud. "I loved her too."

"It's not too late to tell her."

His breath caught. He raised his head, afraid to look, afraid his mind was playing tricks on him.

"It's not too late, Gavin, unless you let it be."

He rose from the chair and slowly turned.

And there she was, standing by the open door, her brilliant blue eyes watching him, her pale cheeks streaked with tears. Waiting. Waiting for him to say what was in his heart.

They came with ease, those words he'd never spoken. "I love you, Rachel Blake. Stay with me. I love you."

She had done it at last, this slip of a girl, this woman, his wife. As he crossed the expanse of room that separated them and gathered her into his arms, the protective wall around Gavin's heart finally crumbled in defeat, falling beneath the power of her love.

Epilogue

Gavin's son arrived on Christmas Day, 1884. As a blizzard raged outside the sturdy log walls, Nicholas Tucker Blake slipped from the protection of his mother's womb into the safety of his father's arms. Moments later, his lusty cries filled the Lucky Strike ranch house.

"It's a boy," Gavin proclaimed loudly, knowing the girls were waiting, along with Stubs and Jess, on the other side of the bedroom door. Then, more softly, "Hello, Nick."

With care, he tied string around the umbilical cord, then cut the cord with a sharp knife. He bathed the protesting child with warm water before wrapping him in a soft blanket. Finally, he lifted his gaze toward his wife.

"We have a son, Rachel."

She smiled. "I know." The long labor had left

her beautiful face marked with fatigue, yet there was an inner glow emanating from Rachel such as he'd never seen before. She held out her arms. "Let me see him."

Gavin carried the bathed and swaddled infant to the side of the bed. Carefully, he placed him into his mother's arms, then he leaned low and kissed her brow.

The sudden depth of emotion that welled within him made speech impossible. He wished he could thank her for all that she'd given him. Not just a son but a full heart, a heart made complete with love. He hoped she understood.

Rachel stared for a long time at the baby, smoothing the dark, fuzzy hair on his head, counting his fingers and toes, kissing the tip of his tiny nose. The pain of giving birth was already forgotten. There was no room for anything but joy.

"He looks like you," she whispered.

"Do you think so?" Gavin's voice was husky with emotion.

"I wouldn't have it any other way. Just like all our other sons will look."

She glanced up. As their eyes met, she imagined the future stretching out before them. There would be more children to fill the Blake house. From their mother, they would learn their numbers and letters and a thirst for knowledge. From their father, they would learn a love for the land and a respect for nature. From both of their parents, they would learn a joy for living, loving, and giving.

Gavin knelt beside the bed. "I love you, Rachel Blake."

She marveled at what power those words contained. She sighed happily, contentment spreading through her like warm honey.

"I love you, Gavin. Now and always."

He leaned forward and kissed her.

Perhaps, she thought as Gavin's lips lingered over hers, the difference she'd been destined to make in this world could be found right here in this room. Perhaps changing the heart of just one man was the greatest destiny of all.

AUTHOR'S NOTE

Dear Reader:

When I was asked to continue the saga begun in *PROMISED SUNRISE*, I was only too happy to oblige. It gave me another opportunity to bring my readers to Idaho, a place particularly close to my heart. In keeping with the Women West theme, I wanted to take Rachel from the "ease" of city life in the capital of the territory to the rugged high country, where the best friend and worst enemy are often the same—nature itself.

There are many kinds of heroes and heroines in this world. We tend to remember the people who do something extraordinary, something above and beyond. But I believe the true heroes and heroines of the Western movement were the everyday people—"plain folk"—who came and lived and loved and died without fanfare. And in doing so, they took the boundaries of America from one coast to another. That's the story I tried to tell in PROMISE ME SPRING.

The Stanley Basin and Sawtooth Valley in the Central Mountains of Idaho contain some of the most spectacular scenery in America. Walled in by four mountain ranges—the Salmon River Mountains, the Boulders, the White Clouds, and the Sawtooths—winter reigns there for seven to eight months a year, with temperatures often falling to 40 or 50 degrees below zero. Summers are short but delightful. The valleys are carpeted with luscious grasses, sage, and wildflowers. Crystal-clear lakes, gurgling streams, and steaming hot springs are abundant. The Sawtooth Wilderness is home to the Bighorn Sheep as well as a host of other wildlife. People who choose to live in this secluded corner of the world must be hardy souls—just as their predecessors were—but their reward is the beauty Mother Nature has bestowed on the mountains, lakes, and rivers that surround them.

Due to the timing of my story, I took some "poetic license" regarding the bringing of beef cattle into the basin. The lush grasses growing in the Stanley Basin attracted cattlemen several years before settlers came, but Gavin Blake was still about six or seven years ahead of what research shows as accurate. In the summers of 1881 and 1882, a herd of dairy cattle was brought into the basin, the owner packing milk and butter over the narrow trail into the Yankee Fork Mining District. But the dairy cows failed to thrive as he'd hoped. Beef cattle were a different story. They were brought into the valley in the late eighties, and they grew fat on the basin's grasses.

PROMISE ME SPRING

I've enjoyed hearing readers' responses to the Women West Series and *PROMISED SUNRISE* and hope you enjoyed *PROMISE ME SPRING*. Please feel free to write me in care of Leisure Books.

All my best,

Robin Lee Hatcher

SPECIAL PREVIEW FOLLOWS!

DEVLIN'S PROMISE
By Robin Lee Hatcher

**The magnificent continuation of the
WOMEN WEST series
A Leisure Book**

**Coming in Spring 1992
At bookstores and newsstands
everywhere**

Prologue

Colorado
March 1885

If the Kid had to die, Devlin Branigan would just as soon be the one to bring about his demise. The problem was how to do it. It wasn't like he could challenge him to a shootout at high noon on Main Street.

Devlin groaned as he rolled onto his back, pain shooting out from the bullet wound in his right shoulder.

Damn! It was bad enough when young punks wanted to make their reputations in fair fights. It was a different matter entirely when they started ambushing a fellow from behind.

If Jake Thompson hadn't found Devlin in that gully three days ago and brought him back to his place, Devlin would have bled to death before nightfall. He was lucky to be alive.

And something told him his luck had about

run out. Instinct warned that whoever had shot him wasn't going to give up so easily. He'd be back once he found out Devlin wasn't dead, and Devlin knew he'd better be ready to shoot it out or be long gone from here before he was discovered.

He opened his eyes and stared at the ceiling of Jake's shack, his thoughts dark and gloomy.

Look at him. Thirty-five years old with nothing to show for it except a broken-down horse, a Colt Peacemaker .45, a saddle, a change of clothes—and the dubious honor of being known as the man who shot and killed the outlaw Chiver McClaine. Hell, it wasn't even Devlin Branigan who had the reputation as a gunslinger. It was a man folks called the Devil Kid. A legend.

And, as far as Devlin was concerned, a myth.

Yeah, look at him. He was the guy who was going to run the Yankees and carpetbaggers out of his Georgia home back in sixty-seven. He was the hotheaded youth who'd bragged to his brother—as Tucker and the rest of his family were leaving for Idaho Territory—that the next time they saw each other he'd be holding the deed to Twin Willows Plantation. Oh, he was one tough kid back then.

And here he was, eighteen years later, a hole in his shoulder and eight bits in his pants pocket. Wouldn't his mother be proud if she could see him now?

Eighteen years. He hadn't seen his mother or any of the rest of the Branigans in all that time. He hadn't wanted them to see what he'd become. But suddenly, as he lay there feeling sorry for himself, shut up in this miserable little cabin in the middle of nowhere, needles of pain tormenting him, he wished he could see them. He wished there was some way he could change the last eighteen years and become something other than what he was.

But he couldn't change the past, so what was he supposed to do? Ride into Boise and say, "Here I am. I couldn't get Twin Willows back, but I've managed to traipse all over the west and get shot at by the best of 'em. I'm now known as the Devil Kid. Rumor says there's no man faster. Aren't you all proud of me?"

But if the Kid was dead, if the Devil Kid didn't exist anymore, that would change everything. He wouldn't have to go through the rest of his life looking over his shoulder, wondering when the next gun-happy youth would show up. He'd even be able to see his family again.

So now all he needed was a way to kill the Kid without getting himself killed in the bargain.

Chapter One

Devlin ignored the first knock. Jake wasn't home, and there wasn't anyone else who knew that he was here—unless his whereabouts had been discovered.

He reached for his gun, hanging in its holster on the end of the bed, and stared at the door, waiting. He wasn't as good a shot left-handed, but he could do some damage. Hopefully enough to save his hide.

His head thundered with the sound of a thousand drums, punishing him for his night-long affair with the whiskey bottle. After ten days of being holed up in this shack with only his pain, his own dismal thoughts, and Jake's company, getting drunk had seemed a good catharsis for what ailed him. Now he thought differently.

Another knock, hesitant, tentative.

He could be wrong, but he doubted the fellow who'd ambushed him would come meekly knocking at the door. If he knew Devlin was inside, he would have barged in without announcing his presence.

The sound came again, with more emphasis this time.

Damn! Whoever it was wasn't going to leave him in peace until he chased them off.

Still holding his Colt .45, he pushed himself up from the chair with the heel of his left hand and crossed the room. Holding his right arm close against his body to alleviate the spasms of pain in his shoulder, he moved silently toward the lone window and eased aside the ragged cloth that served as a curtain. A black buggy, pulled by a gangly sorrel gelding, stood directly outside the window. He edged closer to the glass, but he still couldn't see who was at the door.

Again the knock.

The throbbing in his head and the fiery tentacles of pain in his shoulder increased. He slipped his revolver into the waistband of his trousers and reached for the latch. "All right. All right. Hold your horses." He jerked open the door. "Jake isn't . . ." His voice died in his throat.

He noticed her eyes first. Dark green, like a lush carpet of lawn after the spring rains. They sloped up at the corners and were fringed with dark sable lashes.

He noticed her hair next. Burgundy, like a fine

claret. It was swept high on her head, thick curls framing her face, its deep color glowing in the afternoon sunlight.

Her skin was smooth and pale, with just the right hint of color over high cheekbones. Her mouth was sensuous, full and inviting. And, Lord help him, her dress did nothing to hide the generous curves that proclaimed her all woman, despite its high neckline and long sleeves.

"Are you the Kid?" Her voice had a husky, breathless quality. She watched him with a direct gaze. "The Devil Kid?"

His eyes narrowed, and his whole body went on alert. "Who wants to know?" He glanced beyond her, quickly scanning the stretch of land that surrounded Jake's tiny house on the prairie.

"Angelica Corrall. I'm a friend of Jake's." She tilted her head slightly to one side. "I'd like to speak with you."

"What about?"

"I . . . I have a proposition for you, Mr . . . Kid. Please. May I come in?"

A proposition? Curiosity got the better of him. He stepped back and opened the door wide. "Why not?" He waved her in with his hand.

She moved past him with a delightful rustle of skirts. He caught a whiff of her cologne. A warm scent. Sensuous, like her mouth.

His gaze swept the length of her again. If she wasn't dressed like a lady, he would think she was interested in the Kid to build a reputation of a different kind. It had happened before. There was some prestige in being the Devil Kid's woman. He'd found it true wherever he went.

A smile curved his mouth, his headache forgotten. At least in that arena he deserved his notoriety. He knew how to please a woman.

And this lady looked like she'd be able to set a man's soul on fire.

He mentally reined in the first stirrings of desire. He wasn't exactly in the right physical condition to follow through with them, even if the lady was willing. And he had more than enough problems at the moment without the added complication of a female.

Angelica turned, her unwavering gaze once more meeting his. "Well . . . I suppose the best way to go about this is to just speak my piece and be done with it."

That voice. It sent shivers of awareness up his spine.

"Usually is," he replied. "Have a seat."

She obeyed, sitting on the edge of a precarious-looking chair, not daring to recline against its back. Devlin leaned against the dry sink and crossed his arms over his chest.

"Well . . ." She drew a deep breath. "Mr. Kid, Jake told me what you said last night."

Devlin was instantly suspicious. Jake wasn't much of a talker, and for that matter, neither was he. Devlin couldn't remember last night except that he'd started drinking early and kept at it late into the night. He'd been feeling mighty sorry for himself; he remembered that much.

"Just what was it I'm supposed to have said?" he asked her.

"That you wished the Devil Kid didn't exist and you could be somebody else." Her eyebrows drew together. "Jake assured me you aren't wanted by the law. Is that the truth? You're not an outlaw?"

"That's the truth." He didn't know why he bothered to answer. He should just invite her to leave. He didn't see any purpose in answering her questions.

She sighed again. "All right then. Here's my plan. The Devil Kid has a reputation with a gun and with the ladies. Am I right?"

Devlin shrugged, neither confirming nor denying her statement.

"So nobody would think to look for him with a wife and child, would they?"

"A wife and—"

"If you were to travel by train with me and my son to Washington, no one would think you were the Devil Kid. You could shave off that beard of yours and put on a suit and no one would ever suspect you're a gunslinger. You'd be a family man, going to homestead in Washington."

Devlin fingered his beard for a moment, then pulled his hand away. What was he doing? Was he considering this crazy plan of hers?

Hell, there was no question about it. He *had* had too much to drink last night.

"Listen, Mrs. Corrall—"

"It's *Miss* Corrall." Her chin lifted. "Jake told me you'd like to see your family in Idaho but didn't want them to know about . . . well, that you're the Devil Kid. We could stop and see them on the way to Washington. I promise you they would never think I was . . ." Her cheeks flushed with color and her gaze dropped to the floor. Her voice was even huskier when she continued. "They would never think I was anything but a lady."

"Listen, Miss Corrall. What makes you think I want to go to Washington? And even if I did, what do you think you'd be getting out of this deal?" He was practically shouting at her now. "Besides, I don't have the money it would take to buy a new suit, let alone take me and two more to Washington on the train."

She rose from her chair. "I will pay the cost of the train passage." Her gaze flicked over him. "And for a new suit of clothes for you. As for what I would get out of this deal . . ." Again her chin lifted. There was a defiant glitter in her green eyes. "I would get a name for my son. He won't have to grow up being ashamed of his mother."

"Wait a minute!" He pushed off from the dry sink. "I'm not about to marry you or anyone el—"

"I don't want you to marry me, Mr. Kid. I just want your promise that you would *pose* as my husband for the next eighteen months. After we've built a house and harvested the first crop, you'd be free to leave. When you're gone, I'd tell people you died while visiting your family back east. I'd be a widow and my child wouldn't ever be called a bastard again." She drew another deep breath and met his gaze with an unflinching one of her own. "That's what I would get out of this deal."

He stared at her with eyes as black as midnight. Was he considering what she'd said or did he simply think her mad?

He wasn't what she'd expected. She'd heard he was devilishly handsome and always popular with the ladies. She'd thought there would be an aura of danger about him. She'd expected to see a gun belt slung across his hip, the holster strapped to his thigh and a blood-thirsty look in his eyes. But she didn't see anything she'd expected in the man standing before her. Instead of handsome or dangerous, he looked tired and haggard, with dark circles under his eyes and his beard unkempt. He moved stiffly, like he was still in pain, although she'd been led to believe he was nearly mended.

He certainly wasn't her idea of a gunslinger, especially not the Devil Kid.

But if he wanted to put his past behind him as badly as Jake said he did—or even half as badly as she wanted to escape hers—he just might take her up on the offer. One way or the other, she had to leave the little hole-in-the-wall town that had been her prison for too long now. She had to get Robert away before he was old enough to understand people's cruel looks and remarks. And she had to get away before Lamar returned.

She'd been thinking for a long time about starting over again, somewhere far away from here, somewhere away from the snide looks and ugly whispers. A little farm, a place to grow her own food, a place where she could be independent. She knew she couldn't do it all by herself, and her savings weren't enough to hire a man to build a house, till the land, and plant the first crop. But once that was done, she was certain she could manage on her own. Once that was done, she wouldn't ever need a man in her life again.

But she'd run out of time. She couldn't just dream about it any longer. She had to get away and get away now. Surely a man like the Devil Kid could help her. He was quick with a gun. Fearless, they said. Lamar wouldn't dare. . . .

Suddenly she was aware of the way his eyes were perusing her. She knew that look. It spelled trouble.

"There's one more thing you should know." She looked him straight in the eye, her head held high and proud. "There are no *marital* duties included in this arrangement. If you ever need a woman to . . . well . . . You will certainly be free to pursue those interests elsewhere, as long as you're discreet."

He didn't so much as blink an eye. "Fair enough." He leaned once more against the dry sink. "How old's your boy?"

"Two."

"Where's his father?"

"He has no father."

A wry smile lifted one corner of his mouth. "Every boy has a father somewhere."

"Not my Robert," she answered firmly. "He's a good boy. He'd cause you no trouble. And neither would I. I promise you that, Mr. Kid."

He shook his head slowly as he walked over to the open door. He stood there a moment, then stepped outside. She could only see his back, but she imagined his black gaze was scanning the lonesome prairie that made up Jake's front yard.

He was going to turn her down. She should have known. After all, what was she offering him in return? Very little for a year and a half of hard work. She'd hoped, after listening to Jake talk about the Devil Kid and how he wanted to change his life, that this might be a solution for them both, that he might be as desperate as she.

But, of course, that wasn't the case.

She shouldn't be surprised. Nothing much had worked out for her the past few years.

Perhaps it was just as well that he wouldn't accept. She didn't know anything about this man, except the little Jake had told her this morning, and Jake wasn't always the most reliable source, good intentions or not. With her past, it was probably better not to get mixed up with a man like the Devil Kid. She would just have to find some other way to get out of this place.

"Have you been to Denver before?" he asked without turning to look at her.

She hesitated, feeling a cold dread squeeze her heart. "Once. A few years ago."

It wasn't *really* a lie.

Devlin turned around and looked at the lady standing in the middle of Jake Thompson's ramshackle cabin. He must have drowned his brain in whiskey last night or else he wouldn't be thinking this plan made sense.

But it *did* make sense. She was right about it being the perfect cover. No one would look for the Devil Kid with a wife and child. He knew he wouldn't be able to handle a gun for a while, not with anything bordering on speed and accuracy, and he wouldn't be safe here at Jake's much longer. This plan of hers would give him time to lie low and heal up.

He let his gaze slide from her face to her gown. It was simple but fashionable and well made. She apparently had the money to get them out of here. Of course, he didn't have any intention of staying with her for a full year and a half. He might not want to be a gunfighter, but he didn't hanker to be a farmer either. When he was ready to move on, he'd find somebody else to help her with her place. He wouldn't just walk out on her.

Devlin wasn't fooling himself. He didn't really think he could change his life so easily. He couldn't escape the past eighteen years simply by changing his clothes and shaving off his beard. But it would give him some time and he could go to Idaho, see his family one last time.

Then . . . well, then he'd just have to see what happened.

"All right, Miss Corrall, you've got a deal."

She gasped, her hand fluttering to her throat in a gesture of disbelief.

"You send me the money for that new suit with Jake. I'll meet you in Denver at the end of next week."

"But I . . . That's so soon. I'm not sure—"

"Would you like to rethink your offer?"

"No," she answered quickly. "I'll be there. Where do we meet and what day?"

"Do you know the Windsor Hotel?" he asked as he reentered the house, coming to stand before her. "I'll meet you at noon on Friday in the lobby of the Windsor."

"No!" she cried as the color faded from her cheeks. "Not the Windsor."

Devlin recognized fear on a person's face when he saw it. He'd seen it often enough. Shoot, he'd felt it often enough. There was more to the lady's story than what she'd told him. She was running from something. She needed help, and she was looking for it from him. She'd made a poor choice. He wasn't the type to take on damsels in distress.

That should have been a good enough reason to change his mind. He had troubles of his own. He didn't need to add hers. But he didn't change his mind.

"We won't be staying there, if it's the cost you're worrying about," Devlin explained calmly. "We'll simply reunite in the lobby."

"No. Please. I'll meet you at the stage office." She drew in a breath as she straightened her shoulders and lifted her chin, the calm facade slipping back in place. "It makes much more sense. The wife and son being met as they arrive by stage. No one would suspect we're anything but what we appear to be."

She was watching him with those wide, green, still-frightened eyes of hers, and he had a sudden urge to comfort her. He squelched it.

"I suppose you're right." Devlin took her hand. "The Branigan family, seeing each other for the first time in months. Should be a touching scene."

"The Branigan family?"

Her hand was small and warm within his. He could smell her cologne once again. She was beautiful. Beautiful and sensuous, although he didn't think she was aware of it. He could think of worse places to hide out than with a woman like Angelica Corrall.

Looking into her eyes, he felt a renewed prickle of desire. Maybe helping a damsel in distress wouldn't be such a terrible undertaking.

He raised her hand to his lips. When he straightened, he revealed the grin that had always made the Devil Kid so irresistible to women. "Angelica, may I introduce your husband. The name is Branigan. Devlin Branigan."

ROBIN LEE HATCHER

DREAM TIDE

"Robin Lee Hatcher writes lively, tempestuous romance!"

He'd married her only to fulfill the terms of a bargain, but Brandon Fitzgerald found his wife-by-proxy to be the most enchantingly beautiful creature he had ever beheld. Yet Chelsea could only recall fleeting images from her past. And her future, embodied by the handsome stranger who was not her husband, seemed no less uncertain. In his powerful embrace she knew dizzying ecstasy, but would his arms provide a safe haven or drag her deeper into swirling danger?

__2887-5 $3.95

SPEND YOUR LEISURE MOMENTS WITH US.

Hundreds of exciting titles to choose from—something for everyone's taste in fine books: breathtaking historical romance, chilling horror, spine-tingling suspense, taut medical thrillers, involving mysteries, action-packed men's adventure and wild Westerns.

SEND FOR A FREE CATALOGUE TODAY!

Leisure Books
Attn: Customer Service Department
276 5th Avenue, New York, NY 10001